Fall Into You

MORALLY GRAY BOOK 2

J.T. GEISSINGER

Published by J.T. Geissinger, Inc.

ISBN-13: 979-8-9892505-2-3

Editing by Linda Ingmanson

Cover design by Lori Jackson

www.jtgeissinger.com

To all the girls I've been and the dark roads we traveled alone.

Mostly it is loss which teaches us about the worth of things.
~ Arthur Schopenhauer

CHAPTER 1
Shay

The dark-haired man in the booth is gorgeous, but I can tell with one glance that he's also trouble. A wolf dressed in sheep's clothing. In a conservative black suit and white dress shirt, he could be any other businessman enjoying a drink with friends after work.

Except he's alone.

And he's not enjoying himself.

He looks how I feel: miserable.

"Now listen, Shay. You have to promise me. No more moping, okay? It's my birthday. The least you can do is act as if you're having a good time."

Chelsea propels me through the entrance of the swanky hotel bar in Beverly Hills, her hand on my elbow, her head bent toward mine. Jen and Angel are ahead of us. The three of them are dressed to the nines in stilettos, colorful outfits, and hair out to there. They look fantastic. A flock of flamingos on the hunt for single men.

I'm the raven of the group, all in black with a mood to match.

I'm only here because we're celebrating Chelsea's birthday. If it were up to me, I'd be home in bed with the covers pulled over my head.

The things we do for our friends.

"I *am* having a good time," I lie brightly. "That dance club we just left was so fun."

She squeezes my elbow. "Maybe you should tell that to your face. That smile is tragic. Stop thinking about the twatwaffle."

Hearing her nickname for my ex, I wince. "Please don't call him that."

"He deserves to be called a lot worse. Stop defending him. And every time you miss him, just remember there are plenty of fish in the sea."

"You know what else there's plenty of in the sea? Trash."

"Listen, the only way to get over a man is to get under a new one. That'll fix things."

"I need a new man like I need a roach infestation."

She clucks in disapproval. "Don't let one bad apple turn you off to the whole apple tree. You'll find Mr. Right eventually. In the meantime, let's find you Mr. Well Endowed so you can let off some steam."

We follow Jen and Angel, making our way into the lounge. Outside, it's a typical summer evening in LA, the air balmy, the palm trees swaying, and the stars shining bright, but in here, it's cool and dim.

All the upscale hotel bars around the city have this same intimate, candle-lit ambiance. It's as perfect for a deal-making meeting between studio executives as it is for a pair of lovers who are married to other people to sneak in a cocktail before heading up to their room.

The difference with this place—and the reason Chelsea chose it—is that it has a reputation for being the spot frequented by the wealthiest men in town.

If I've heard it from her once, I've heard it a thousand times: "It's just as easy to fall in love with a rich man as a poor one."

She might be looking for love, but I'm looking for peace of mind. My ex was hell on my sanity.

I glance over at the dark-haired man in the booth against the wall again. He's still staring at me. The hunger in his gaze makes my heart skip a beat.

When he licks his full lips, a little shiver of desire courses through me. But I look away and toss my hair over my shoulder.

The last thing I need right now is the attention of a hot stranger who looks like he's the cause of many a woman's therapy bill.

I've already got my own demons to deal with.

I don't need another one.

CHAPTER 2
Cole

The brunette is interesting.

Not because she's pretty, though she is. But there are a million pretty girls in this city. Los Angeles is known for its beautiful women.

What makes her interesting is the way she carries herself. It's like watching a champion boxer walk into a room. She's confident, almost cocky, but there's also a wariness that suggests she's used to taking punches.

Beneath the tough exterior, she's got bruises all over her soul.

Riveted by the contradiction, I can't look away.

Dressed in a black skirt, black blouse, and black heels, she struts through the entrance of the bar with three other women. Her companions are in brightly colored dresses, laughing and chatting with each other as they make their way inside, but the brunette is silent. She scans the room, sizing up the place and the people in it.

Her smile is small and cool, as if she's bored already.

She catches me looking at her but quickly glances away. When she glances back again, I stare straight at her and lick my lips.

She raises her brows. Then she tosses her hair over her shoulder, lifts her chin, and looks away, dismissing me.

Smart girl. She knows a monster when she sees one.

CHAPTER 3
Shay

"Wouldn't it be amazing if that existed in real life? An eight-foot tall blue alien with two huge cocks who's totally obsessed with me? Yes, please!" Angel laughs and takes another sip of her margarita.

"Only if he's also a billionaire," says Chelsea, giggling into her martini.

Jen shakes her head in disbelief. "You guys and your monster smut books. I just don't get the appeal."

Angel snorts. "Excuse me, Judgy McJudgerson, but you're not in a position to be snobbish about other people's choices in literature. May I remind you that your favorite TV show is a cartoon?"

Jen rolls her eyes. "First of all, monster smut isn't literature. Secondly, *BoJack Horseman* is one of the most brilliant—"

"Dark comedies ever written, blah, blah, blah, yes you've told us a thousand times,"

Angel cuts in. "It's still a cartoon."

The argument continues, but I've already tuned out.

The four of us are sitting at a round table in the middle of the room. We're surrounded by beautiful people on every side. The couple at the table behind me bickers over Tahoe or Tulum for their next vacation spot. A pair of young female models prowl past, taking selfies as they walk. Patrons jostle for position at the bar, trying to get the attention of the handsome bartender who I recognize as an extra from the television series *Succession*.

And sitting in the lone booth beside the bar, the dark-haired stranger is still staring at me.

It's strange how such a good-looking man can give off such an unpleasant vibe. He's a black hole over there, extinguishing all the light around him. He looks like he'd refuse to smile even if someone put a loaded gun to his head and ordered him to.

He's probably thinking the same thing about me.

Chelsea sighs. "Shay, seriously! Stop scowling. It's scaring all the hot guys away."

"Not all of them," notes Angel, glancing in the direction of Mr. Dark and Stormy.

Chelsea turns around in her chair and squints. "Who, that guy in the booth?"

"Yeah. He's been eye fucking Shay since we got here."

I scold, "Chelsea, for God's sake, don't look at him."

"Why the hell not? He's fine." She sends him a broad smile.

The glare he sends her in return is so freezing, it could crack stone.

With a low whistle, she turns back to us. "Wow. Ten for the face, zero for the personality."

"Maybe his dog died," Angel says.

Chelsea looks at me and suggests playfully, "Maybe you should go over there and cheer him up."

"Very funny."

"It wasn't a joke."

"Give me one good reason why I'd want to talk to that man."

"Because it's my birthday, and I want you to." She smiles and takes another sip of her drink.

My heart sinks. She always smiles like that when she's about to dig in her heels. The last thing I want right now is to be on the wrong side of her stubborn streak.

"He doesn't want to talk to me."

"I bet his dick does."

"If his dick has the same personality as its owner, I'm not interested."

"Give me a break, girl. Nobody's asking you to marry him. Just go over there and chat him up!"

"So I can be publicly humiliated when he throws his drink in my face and tells me to fuck off? No thanks."

"I'll bet you a hundred bucks he doesn't throw his drink in your face."

"No."

"Please?"

"No."

"Pretty please?"

"No."

"C'mon. If you won't do it for yourself, do it for me."

"That's blackmail."

She widens her eyes innocently. "Remind me again whose birthday it is?"

When I make a sour face but don't reply, she goes in for the kill.

Leaning forward, she grins. "If you go talk to that guy, I promise I'll stop calling Chet the twatwaffle. In fact, I won't say a mean thing about him ever again."

I pause to examine her expression. She appears earnest, but Chelsea's a slippery one. She'll conveniently forget this conversation by morning if it suits her.

"Okay, you're on. But you have to record yourself saying that and send it to the group text."

"Why?"

"Permanent evidence. If you renege on the deal, you have to buy me, Jen, and Angel new iPhones."

Jen and Angel scream with laughter, but Chelsea's eyes bulge in horror. *"What?"*

My smile is ruthless. "Deal or no deal, birthday girl?"

"That's like three grand!"

Knowing she'll agree eventually, and sooner if I act like I don't care, I shrug and take a sip of my whiskey.

Disgruntled, she huffs. "Okay, fine. You're on. But you have to stay over there and talk to him for at least ten minutes."

I glance in his direction. He stares back at me, his gaze intense and unwavering. Thunderclouds churn over his head.

The thought of approaching all that negative energy and trying to start a conversation is daunting, but if it will get Chelsea to stop her smear campaign against my ex, it's worth it. I've been enduring it for three months now, and I'm tired.

"I'll try, but I can't guarantee anything. He looks like he bites."

Angel snickers. "If you're lucky, he does."

"Okay, you win. Here goes nothing."

I sigh heavily, then chug the rest of my whiskey. Rising from the chair, I smooth my skirt with damp palms, then cross the room with my chin lifted and my shoulders squared, pretending a confidence I don't feel.

Dark and Stormy watches me approach with the all the warmth of a contract killer.

By the time I stop at his tableside, I've decided to go with the truth rather than some cutesy opening line. In my present state of mind, I doubt I could come up with one, anyway.

"Hello. I don't want to be here."

He looks me up and down, his gaze traveling slowly over my figure. After a beat, he says in an unfriendly tone, "Yet here you are."

We stare at each other in an oddly tense silence, as if both of us are waiting for the other to say something next and think whatever it is, it will be awful.

Finally, I say, "It's my girlfriend's birthday."

A crease forms between his dark brows. "I don't understand the connection between that and you standing there."

"She promised me she'd stop trash-talking my ex if I came over and talked to you."

He thinks about that for a moment. "That's blackmail."

"When it comes to Chelsea getting what she wants, all means of coercion are on the table."

He glances past me. "Which one's Chelsea?"

"The blonde."

"She looks harmless."

"All the most dangerous creatures do."

He leans back against the booth and tilts his head, showcasing his beautiful jawline. His gaze grows assessing. "Were there any other terms of this blackmail of hers?"

"I have to stay for at least ten minutes."

"And it's important to you that she stop trash-talking your ex?"

"Yes."

I can tell something about that pleases him, but can't imagine why. He says, "All right. Sit down."

He gestures to the empty space beside him in the booth. Somehow it doesn't look like an invitation. Though his mouth is saying I should sit, his expression says he'd prefer I take a hike in a distant, snake-infested wilderness.

Apparently, he only likes to stare at women, not speak to them.

Too bad for him I'm not intimidated by cranky men with bad manners.

I sit beside him and smile politely. "I'd apologize for the inconvenience, but I think I'm going to enjoy annoying you for the next ten minutes."

"Why would you want to annoy me?"

"You look like a lot of women's biggest regret."

We stare at each other in another tense silence. Only this time, I can smell his cologne. Spice, musk, something woodsy. Sexy and expensive. I can also see the color of his eyes, a fathomless dark blue that could be beautiful if it wasn't for their hardness.

His tone low and his gaze piercing, he finally says, "And you look like a diamond some clown discarded so he could play with dirt. How long were you and this clown together?"

Startled, I blink. "Hang on. I'm trying to pick myself up off the floor."

"What do you mean?"

"Is it really so obvious I've been dumped? How awful."

"It's your whole vibe. You're like one of those shelter dogs."

"Pardon?"

"You know. Barks real loud and acts tough, but only because it's scared it's about to get kicked again. And your man didn't dump you. He freed you. He did you a favor. Take all that energy back that you're wasting mourning the relationship and focus it on yourself. A queen doesn't need the love of the village idiot."

A breathless laugh of disbelief escapes me. I can't decide if this guy is a mind reader, a genius, or just a jerk.

I also can't decide if he's complimenting me or not. In the same breath he called me a queen, he compared me to an abused animal. Also, his entire demeanor suggests he thinks I'm a hopeless case who shouldn't be allowed to vote.

"And here I thought Chelsea was the trash talker. We're not even two minutes into the conversation, and you've already called my ex a clown and an idiot."

"That's being generous. Because any man who'd let a woman like you go is nothing but a little bitch."

Captivated by this strange person and his even stranger manner of speech, I angle my body toward his and focus my attention on him more fully. "You don't know me. *I* could be the bitch. Maybe I drove him away by being too needy."

He shakes his head, a sharp motion that makes a lock of dark hair fall out of place. It settles onto his forehead, boyishly charming.

"There's no such thing as too needy. The wrong person will never be able to meet your needs. Stop giving people grace who make you feel like you're the problem. And stop holding on to who he pretended to be. He lied."

Our gazes clash but hold. A frisson of electricity passes between us, supercharging the air.

Despite his prickly personality, the man is undeniably attractive.

After a moment, he looks away. He takes a swig of his drink and sets the glass on the table. A muscle flexes in his angular jaw. When he speaks again, his voice is gruff.

"I recently went through a breakup too."

The pain fueling that statement is stunning. He put an entire saga of lost love into it. He sounds even more devastated than I am.

I find that—and him—fascinating.

"May I ask what happened?"

He closes his eyes and exhales. "I surrendered to the reality that I wasn't her hero. I was the villain. So our story could never have a happy ending."

My heart beats so fast. Too fast. I resist the urge to reach out and touch him.

Shockingly, this unhappy stranger with angry eyes and heartbreak running through his veins is someone who might be able to understand what I've been going through.

God knows my girlfriends haven't shown me any sympathy. If I hear, "Just move on already!" one more time, I'll scream.

I lower my voice. "And so you broke it off?"

"Yes."

"But you didn't want to."

"No."

"You were still in love with her when you ended it?"

He nods. Then he opens his eyes and looks at me with such naked longing, I'm momentarily speechless.

"What's your name?"

It takes me a second to remember. "Shayna. But call me Shay."

"I'm Coleton. Call me Cole."

"Hello, Cole."

"Hello, Shay. How much time do you think it's been since you sat down?"

His edginess makes me smile. "Maybe ninety seconds."

"Feels like longer. Another eight minutes of this will make me want to jump off the nearest cliff."

"Out of curiosity, are you this way all the time?"

"Which way?"

I take a moment to search for the right words. "Aggressively ambivalent."

He arches his brows. "What is it you think I'm ambivalent about?"

I don't respond, instead reaching across to pick up his glass. I take a sip, holding his gaze over the rim. *He drinks whiskey too. Interesting.*

I set the glass back down in front of him without saying anything, but he understands my meaning.

"You think I'm attracted to you?"

"I think you'll be relieved when I leave."

"Maybe that's because you're boring."

"Is it?"

His glare could melt steel. He doesn't like being challenged. I get the impression he so rarely is that it's an unwelcome novelty for him.

He says flatly, "No."

"Thank you for not lying."

"Don't thank me yet. It's because you're irritating."

That makes me laugh. It startles both of us. We sit with the echoes of the sound dying in the air until another uncomfortable silence falls.

Yet neither of us breaks eye contact.

Emboldened by the alcohol and his unexpected authenticity, I say, "So you do find me attractive."

His glare is deadly. "Out of curiosity, are you this way all the time?"

Enjoying how he's throwing my words back at me, I smile again. "Which way?"

"Aggressively aggravating."

"Depends on who you ask."

"What did your ex have to say on the matter?"

A pang of heartache tightens my chest. I moisten my lips and look away. "I never aggravated him. I was too busy accommodating all his needs."

He studies my profile. I know he wants to ask more, but he doesn't. But his silence is active. He's paying very close attention to me, to my expression and body language. After being with a self-obsessed narcissist for so long, this kind of engrossment feels decadent.

Chet always made me feel like a thirsty little house plant who'd been left to bake in the desert sun.

Looking out over the elegant room, I say quietly, "It's funny. I know I'm an intelligent person, but when it came to my ex, I threw my brain out the window. I saw all the red flags. There were so many, he might as well have been a circus."

"But he was just so charming."

I return my focus to Cole, who's nodding.

"Yes. How did you know?"

"Narcissists are always charming."

"Wow."

"What?"

"I was literally just thinking that he was a narcissist."

"The only kind of man who would leave a woman like you has a personality disorder."

When I look into his eyes, what I find is a reflection of myself, all ache and want and loneliness.

I'm not sure I like him. But I do trust him. Courtesy of my ex, I know all the ways a liar can hide. This man isn't hiding anything.

He doesn't seem capable of it.

Which is maybe why he sits alone in a crowded room, glaring at the rest of humanity, and looks at me as if he'd like to make me his supper but would rather let himself go hungry than eat.

I say, "I changed my mind."

"About what?"

"About wanting to be here. I'm glad I came over. Thank you for letting me stay."

"You're not welcome."

Another smile tugs at the corners of my mouth. I've probably smiled more since I sat down with him than I have in the past three months. "Has anyone ever told you that you're strange?"

He shrugs. "Only everybody."

"It doesn't bother you?"

"You ever watch one of those documentaries on serial killers? Ted Bundy, Jeffrey Dahmer, those kind of guys?"

"Yes. Why?"

"The first thing the neighbors always say when they find out they've been living next to a guy who chops people up and eats them is, 'He seemed so normal.'"

"So you're telling me you're not going to dismember me for your weekend barbeque?"

"I'm telling you that the more normal someone seems, the more skeletons they've got buried in their backyard. Which you already know."

"How so?"

"I'd bet my house your clown of an ex seemed like the most well-adjusted man you'd ever met...at first. Then eventually the mask fell off, and you saw the monster underneath."

It's like he read a script of my entire relationship with Chet. The accuracy of all his assumptions is unnerving. But only because it makes me feel so naked. So *seen*.

A feeling I haven't enjoyed in a very long time.

"Yes. But he never regarded himself like that. It takes a man with a good heart to recognize when he's the monster in someone else's story. The courage it takes to break his own heart to save another's proves he's not really a monster. He's a hero. He just wants to think of himself as the bad guy so he never gets hurt again."

The silence stretches until it's taut and thrumming. Now we're not even trying to pretend the eye contact is anything but sexually charged.

When the waiter arrives at our table and asks if we need something, we both say "Yes" at the same time without looking away from each other.

Many months later, after both our hearts are battered and bloodied, after all our tears have been shed and we're strangers once again, I'll look back on this moment and realize I was already lost.

CHAPTER 4
Cole

She's beautiful, this woman with green eyes, a razor wit, and a weakness for men who need therapy. Beautiful, smart, and observant, which makes her the kind of dangerous I should be walking away from right the fuck now.

My feet have other ideas. They refuse to move, though I keep insisting they take us as far away from her as we can get.

They're not my only body part she's mesmerized.

My dick, my heart, and every nerve under my skin all ache for her.

Into the awkward silence, the waiter clears his throat. "Another whiskey, sir?"

"Make it two."

I say it in a tone he understands correctly as a dismissal. He withdraws, leaving Shay and me alone in our tense little bubble.

I say, "Don't romanticize me."

"I'm not. It was simply an observation. The bad guys never think they're the bad guys. They're too busy pointing fingers and blaming everyone else for making them do what they did. Besides, I don't have any romance left in me. Chet cured me of that."

I curl my lip in disgust. "Chet? Even his name sounds clownish."

"Really? I think it's a nice name. Masculine."

"Not masculine. Boyish. I'm picturing a sporty blond with perfect teeth and too much product in his hair."

She smiles.

I wish I could take a picture of that smile. It could end wars.

"That description is so accurate, it's disturbing. Tell me more."

"He works out every day. Gets spray tans. Calls everyone 'bro.' Never shuts up about his Rolex. Watches himself in a mirror when he fucks. Has one of those smug, entitled faces you want to punch as soon as you see it."

Shay blinks rapidly, shaking her head. "This is uncanny. Do you *know* him?"

"I know the type. Prep school frat boy fuckwit."

Her laugh is so attractive and disarming, I have to clench my molars together to stop from kissing her.

I can't remember the last time I had this kind of physical response to someone. Maybe never. There must be magnets under our skin, drawing us closer together.

"You and Chelsea would really get along."

"Why's that?"

"She calls him the twatwaffle."

I pause to think. "Interesting visual. But how the fuck—and I mean this in the most respectful way possible—did a woman like you fall for a cunt like that?"

Her laughter dies. She sits there looking stunned, which makes me feel like an asshole.

"I'm sorry. That was out of line."

"No, not at all. It just struck me that I've never heard a man call another man a cunt before. It's strangely satisfying."

"It's a very versatile word."

We're staring at each other again. It's becoming a habit. I never want to stop.

What the fuck is she doing to me?

Because I'm so unsteady, my words come out more angrily than I intended. "So he cheated on you."

"Oh my God."

"What?"

"How do you *know* that?"

She's visibly upset. The pulse in the side of her neck is throbbing. I want to press my lips against it. I want to bury my face in her hair. Instead, I stare into her eyes and fight the desire heating my entire body.

"Just a hunch."

Her laugh is small and nervous. She smooths a trembling hand over her hair and looks down at her lap. "It was a good one."

We sit silently for a moment as I watch her struggle to regain her composure. She's fighting bad memories, something I know all about.

Then, because I find her fascinating and want to know all her secrets, I say, "How did you find out?"

"His phone. He left it out on the counter by accident one day, open to this dating app. He was messaging all these different women. Asking for nudes. Arranging times to hook up. I stupidly believed him when he said he was always on his cell because of work."

"What kind of work did he do?"

"He's a personal trainer."

"Of course he is."

"Don't sound so disgusted."

"It's not disgust. It's contempt. I'd like to find this shitty little loser and see how loud he can scream."

After a thoughtful silence, she says, "I can't decide if that's a red flag or just a genuinely nice thing to say."

"It's a red flag."

"I'd like to think it's partly both."

"It's not. I just threatened violence on a stranger and meant it."

19

"I know, but you did it from a protective instinct. It's almost chivalrous."

I realize I'm glaring at her, but I can't help it. She's being willfully naïve. Confusing antiheroes with good guys. She probably reads too many romance novels. "You need to get better at discerning which men you should stay away from."

"Hey, I'm only sitting here because I was blackmailed into it."

"Here's a serious question for you. Have you ever considered that maybe you didn't get what you wanted because you deserve better?"

Now she's glaring back at me. What I said irritated her, and she's about to use that sharp tongue of hers to tell me exactly what it is.

"What I wanted was love. What's better than that?"

"Men don't abandon women they love. They abandon women they were using."

That one hit her hard. A mixture of pain and anger flares in her eyes.

I say more gently, "There's something missing in him. You knew that. You just chose to ignore it. All I'm saying is don't make the same choice with the next man."

She snaps, "Maybe there won't be a next man. Maybe I'm done with all of you."

"There will be a next man."

"What makes you so sure?"

"Because even a complete stranger can see how you deserve to be worshipped."

Her lips part. Unblinking, she stares at me with her brows drawn together and her beautiful face pale. Then she demands, "Who *says* that?"

"Are you offended?"

"No, I'm confused!"

"Why?"

"Because you act like you think I'm contagious, but you talk like a hero from a romance novel!"

"I knew it."

"You knew what?"

"You read romance novels."

"So?"

"So that shit will rot your brain."

"Oh, please, it's fun, escapist fantasy. It's also feminist, because it encourages us to explore our own sexual pleasure. Are you afraid women will have too high of standards after reading about being loved by fictional men?"

"No, I'm afraid their standards will fall too *low*."

"What the hell are you talking about?"

"Christian Grey has multiple personality disorders caused by intense childhood trauma. Edward Cullen is a controlling stalker who wants to kill Bella by drinking her blood. Mr. Darcy is an arrogant prick with crippling social anxiety and prejudice against the lower class. Yet all these flawed characters have inspired millions of women to think that broken men are somehow ideal, or could be, if only the right woman loved them."

I'm glad there isn't any cutlery on the table. Judging by her expression, Shay would've already thrust a knife into my spleen.

"I think you're the most annoying man I've ever met."

"Only because you know I'm right."

She looks around, as if to ask the nearest person for a meat cleaver.

The waiter returns with our drinks. Sensing the tension, he carefully sets the glasses down, his gaze darting between us, then sends us a stiff smile and runs away without a word.

Shay picks up her glass and chugs the whiskey, making a face and shuddering when it's gone. "Blech."

"Why did you drink it all so fast?"

"It was either that or murder."

I shock both of us then by chuckling.

She turns to me with her brows raised and says drily, "I must already be drunk. That sounded suspiciously like a laugh."

I scowl at her. "It wasn't."

She studies me for a long time, her expression unreadable and her eyes intense. Then she slowly sets her empty glass back onto the table and levels me with a look of such frank sexual desire, I'm stunned.

I'm even more stunned by what comes out of her mouth next.

"I'm no angel either. I've got all kinds of faults."

"Really? Like what?"

"Like that I'm reckless."

"How so?"

She doesn't even hesitate when she pulls the rug out from under me.

"Well, we only just met, and until tonight, I was sure I'd be celibate forever, but I'm seriously considering asking you to get us a room in this hotel."

Everyone and everything else in the bar vanishes. A distant roar fills my ears and my heart starts to hammer.

Then I tell a lie so fucking outrageous, I barely manage to force it past my lips.

"Don't ask me. I'll say no."

CHAPTER 5
Shay

My smile is almost as incandescent as my humiliation. "Ah. In that case, you'll have to excuse me. I'm leaving now."

"Your ten minutes aren't up."

"I know, but I have to go to the ladies room so I can drown myself in the toilet."

When I make a move to rise, he grasps my wrist and pulls me closer. His tone low and urgent, he says, "Don't mistake that for a rejection."

"Funny, but I always thought the word 'no' is a pretty good indicator of rejection."

"It doesn't mean I don't want you."

My cheeks burn with embarrassment. My ears are scalding. It feels as if someone turned the temperature up by thirty degrees. I have no idea what possessed me to say that, but the cat's out of the bag now. I can't take it back.

I also can't meet his eyes when I say, "Okay. I understand."

"Shay. Look at me."

It takes a while for me to gather the courage. When I do, his intensity is so intimidating, I forget to keep breathing.

He says, "You don't understand. Not only is your ex an idiotic clown, he's a fucking child. He needs to have his face rearranged. I want to beat the living shit out of him."

While I process that, I hear Chelsea cackling in the background. Painfully aware that we're being observed, and that I'll have to recount this story later, my face grows even hotter.

"There's a lot to unpack in that statement. However, embarrassment has clogged my normal brain functions, so you're going to have to explain it to me like I'm a toddler."

Nostrils flaring, he inhales. He hasn't blinked in thirty seconds. He's trying hard to stop himself from doing something, but I'm not sure what it is.

By the looks of it, throwing his whiskey glass against the wall.

"First explain to me why you'd ask a total stranger to have sex with you."

Pride rears its head. Snooty as a schoolmarm, I sniff and lift my chin. "I didn't ask. I said I was *thinking* about asking. And I didn't say anything about sex either. Maybe I just wanted to cuddle."

"Give me a break. You don't want to cuddle."

God, this guy is impossible. "I know. You could've been a gentleman and let that one slide."

"I'm not a gentleman. Finish the explanation."

Exasperated, I sigh. "You're not going to let me leave until I do, are you?"

"Correct. Stop stalling."

My tone is irritated, but I can't help it. He's pushing all my buttons, and not the right ones. "You'll have to sit there while I think about it, because I honestly don't know."

His frustration is palpable. Not only is he unused to being challenged, he's not used to being made to wait, either.

What kind of work does he do? Probably something involving barking orders at terrified underlings.

"All right. Here it is. You're the first man I've been attracted to since Chet and I broke up, and the first person who seems to understand the hell I've been through. Chelsea might have had a good point when she said that the only way to get over a man is to get under a new one, and I'm tired of being the only person in the room when I have sex. I know it's not that simple, but I've tried everything else. Nothing's worked. So I suppose I was thinking that maybe we could make each other forget our pain for a while."

I clear my throat. The schoolmarm is back. "Also...I have condoms in my handbag."

Cole stares at me with fury blazing in his blue eyes. But then his gaze drops to my mouth, and I realize I'm mistaken. That's not anger.

It's passion.

Suddenly, I'm dizzy.

I think he's about to say yes.

CHAPTER 6
Cole

I f we were alone, I'd have already torn her clothes from her body with my hands and teeth and buried my face between her legs.

As it is, I'm having a hard time holding myself back from doing just that, even with a hundred onlookers.

I inhale slowly, savoring her scent and enjoying the feel of her pulse beating wildly under my thumb. My voice comes out gravelly. "You'd hate yourself tomorrow."

Her lips curve upward. Her eyes flash. "Maybe. Only one way to find out."

Fuck, those eyes. I have a bad feeling the exact gold-flecked shade of green is going to be permanently inked onto my memory.

We're sitting close. Too close. I've still got her wrist gripped in my hand. Our thighs are pressed together, hip to knee. All it would take is for me to dip my head and I could slide my tongue between the cleft in her breasts.

How fucking badly I want that.

But I'm too busy trying to talk her out of doing something foolish.

"Your girlfriends wouldn't approve."

She laughs. It's a happy sound, light and airy, but there's a darkness underscoring it that resonates inside me like a lone note played on a melancholy violin.

My broken pieces make music with hers.

"Chelsea would not only approve, she'd probably pay for the room herself if I asked her to. Will you have many of these objections?"

"Why?"

"I'm wondering if I should leave now or order another drink to give you time to wrestle with your conscience."

She looks at my mouth then. Looks at it and licks her lips, as if she's imagining tasting me.

Then she has the fucking audacity to say, "Or are you worried you won't be able to get an erection?"

I glower at her from under lowered brows. "Don't test me, Shay."

"Oh, you're much too scary to test. I wouldn't dare."

She says it exactly like a fucking dare.

Okay. Game on.

I take her hand and place it on my lap, curling her fingers around my dick, stiff and throbbing under my zipper.

Her eyes widen. This time, her laugh is breathless. "Oh. That answers that." Cheeks flushed, she glances around the bar. "Thank goodness for the tablecloth."

"Look at me."

When she sends me a wary, sideways glance, I lean closer and lower my voice.

"Yes, I want to fuck you. But you were right when you said I look like a lot of women's biggest regret. You already have enough of those."

Considering her cheeks are so red, it makes her composure even more impressive when she answers. "True enough. But the batteries in my vibrator died this morning, so the timing is actually quite good."

I don't know if I'm more pissed off or turned on.

27

What the fuck is she doing?

I growl, "You're right. You are reckless. You'll get yourself in trouble if you keep going around propositioning strangers."

"You're the first and last stranger I'll ever proposition, so there's nothing to worry about. May I please have my hand back now? Unless you're about to undo your zipper, this is really awkward."

"You can't actually believe jerking me off under the tablecloth could be less awkward."

"At least I'd be holding onto something other than my humiliation."

Aroused, frustrated, and helplessly charmed, I can't think of anything else to say but a gruff, "Fuck."

"Is that a yes?"

She stares at me with those big eyes, her cheeks blazing red. She's flustered and embarrassed but holding her head high, still not giving me an inch. She's completely unapologetic.

Many months later, I'll look back on this moment and realize I never had a chance.

I was a goner the second she sat down next to me and smiled.

CHAPTER 7
Shay

T his is so not my style, I might have unknowingly been taken over by one of those sex-obsessed aliens Angel was talking about.

Also, I know it's perverse, but there's a part of me that's really enjoying how uncomfortable this conversation is making Cole.

That he's used to being the one in control is obvious.

That he wants me is also obvious.

What's not obvious is why he's holding back. There's got to be more to it than he's trying to keep me from making a mistake.

No man is that unselfish. Not when no-strings sex is involved.

He says, "No, it wasn't a yes. And stop looking at me like I've got a hidden motive. It's very simple: I think you'd regret it."

"What makes you so sure?"

"You're emotionally vulnerable. You've had a few drinks. Those things never mix well."

Okay, maybe he is unselfish. Better test him to be sure. "What I'm hearing is that you just don't have the courage to tell me you've got an STD, and it's flaring."

He closes his eyes, grits his teeth, and draws a slow, aggravated breath.

Into his bristling silence, I say, "Cole. Please look at me. I want to say something, but I want you to be looking at me when I do."

When he turns his gaze on me, the air ripples from the heat of it.

My pulse flutters. My mouth goes dry. I have to swallow before I can speak. "Will you please get us a room in this hotel? I would very much like to take this girthy beast under your zipper out for a ride."

"Jesus fucking *Christ*, woman," he mutters, glaring at me in outrage.

"You're the one who put my hand on your dick. We're way past the polite chitchat stage."

He takes my hand off the bulge in his trousers and places it firmly onto my lap.

"Cole, will you—"

"Don't fucking ask again," he cuts in, his voice dark.

"Will you please get us a room in this hotel?"

"This is a game to you. Is that it? See how far you can push me before I lose my shit?"

He's starting to look really angry. I have no idea why, but that gets me even more excited. Chet was never this exciting. He was too busy preening in front of a mirror.

"No. I'm not playing games. I'm dead serious. Here, I'll prove it to you."

I lean in to kiss him, but he blocks me by grasping my jaw in his hand and holding my face inches from his.

His eyes blaze. His nostrils flare. Every inch of him bristles. He wants to kiss me so badly, his hands shake. But he won't let himself do it. He holds himself back with the kind of self-control that would be deeply impressive if it weren't interfering with me getting what I want.

I've never seen a more thrilling specimen of masculinity in my life.

It's probably all his red flags that are making me so hot. Maybe he's right about the romance novels.

I say, "It's not the drinks. It's not the breakup. It's not that the batteries in my vibrator died. It's that you're protective of me. You want to protect me, and you're trying to deny yourself something you want because of it. I find that extremely sexy."

When he only stares at me in that hot, angry, unblinking silence, I add, "I'd love to watch all this careful control of yours unravel."

"You don't even know my last name!"

"You don't know mine either."

"I could be abusive. I could be a psychopath!"

"We both know you're not."

"But I could be."

"Just kiss me already. People are staring."

"Let them fucking stare."

"Don't make me beg. This is embarrassing."

His eyes glitter dangerously. His laugh is low and hard. "You're not embarrassed in the least."

"I was earlier. Now I'm just horny."

His eyes soften, as does his voice. "Shay, seriously. What the hell are you doing?"

"Making myself happy. Putting my own needs first."

"This isn't about your needs. It's about your ego. That dipshit Chet bruised it, and you want to use me to patch it up."

"He didn't bruise my ego. He broke my heart. And you have five seconds, starting now, to decide before I get up and walk away. One night, Cole. That's all it is. One night and we'll never see each other again. Let's do this."

His look changes to one of genuine confusion. Somehow, his mercurial mood swings make him even more appealing.

"You're the most baffling woman I've ever met."

"You should see my tits. Then you'll really be impressed."

A sound rumbles through his chest. It's low and dangerous, like a wolf's growl.

When his gaze drops to my lips, I know I've almost got him. I whisper, "I have very sensitive nipples. I can't wait to feel your tongue on them."

There's a moment—a long, breathless moment—where I can almost hear the thread of his self-control fraying. Then the last of his restraint snaps.

He leans in and covers my mouth with his.

CHAPTER 8

Cole

She tastes like fine whiskey and bad dreams. The second our mouths fuse together, she moans. Low and soft, rising from deep in her throat, the sound fries the part of my brain that's responsible for restraint and good decision making.

I hold her jaw in my hand and drink greedily from her luscious mouth like a man who's been living without water for years.

She leans into me, flattening her hand over the center of my chest, arching closer to my body. Off in the distance, someone whistles a catcall and starts clapping. We both ignore it.

I slide my tongue against hers and wish we were already naked.

"Get us a room," she breathes, her lips moving against mine.

I capture her lips again because I'm not done kissing her.

She's delicious. Warm, soft, feminine, and completely fucking delicious.

I want to devour every inch of her body. I want to leave handprints on her skin. I want to bite her and lick her and fuck her in every way between tender and brutally hard.

I want to let this woman with pretty eyes and a sad soul ruin me.

At least for tonight.

Turning her head, I growl into her ear, "I'm going to the front desk. I'll meet you in ten minutes by the elevators. You shouldn't be there, Shay."

"I will be."

"You shouldn't."

Tearing myself away from her, I rise from the booth and nod at Matt behind the bar to put the drinks on my house tab. Then I walk away, weaving through the tables as I head out toward the lobby and front desk.

It takes every ounce of what willpower I have left not to turn around to see if she's watching me go.

CHAPTER 9
Shay

Unsteady, I make my way back to the table where Chelsea, Angel, and Jen await, gaping at me with matching expressions of shock.

I slide into my chair and look around the table. "Good news! I'm getting laid tonight. He just went to get us a room."

They erupt into ear-piercing shrieks so loud, they can probably be heard from outer space. Wincing, I wave a hand at them to stop. "Guys, please. You're making a scene."

Chelsea hoots. "This from the girl playing tonsil hockey with a stranger in the middle of a bar!"

"It wasn't tonsil hockey, you adolescent. And we weren't in the middle of the bar. We were all the way over there, up against the wall."

I grab Chelsea's water glass and suck down every drop of liquid in it. My mouth is a desert.

Must be nerves. Which is also probably what's making my knees knock, my heart thud, and my hands tremble.

Mr. Dark and Stormy has quite the interesting effect on my body.

Jen demands, "What the hell happened between you leaving this table like you were walking off to your own execution to you coming back ten minutes later drenched in sweat with a date for a dicking?"

I look down at myself. "Am I sweating? Oh God, I'm sweating. Fuck."

Chelsea cackles. "From the looks of him, you'll be a lot wetter in a few minutes. Good for you, girl! I'm so proud! You couldn't have given me a better birthday present."

Imagining what I'm about to do with Cole, I panic. My pulse surges into overdrive. I look at Chelsea beseechingly. "I haven't had sex in three months."

She makes a face at me. "You have sex with your vibrator every day."

"I meant with something breathing. What if I forgot how to do it? What if it's awkward and horrible? What if he's a premature ejaculator? Shit, did I remember to shave?"

"Shave?" repeats Chelsea, outraged. "How many times have I told you to wax your kitty? Shaving leaves stubble! Stubble is not sexy!"

Jen says, "I got all my pubes lasered off. Hurt like a bitch, but it was worth it."

Angel says, "I can't afford the laser, so I use that lotion that melts off all the hair at the root. Smells weird, but it works."

"Good grief, will you people stop yammering about pubic hair and give me some emotional support? I'm about to go have a one-night stand with a hot stranger! Give me some womanly words of advice. Angel, you go first."

"Why me?"

"You're the most experienced."

She frowns. "Did you just call me a slut?"

"Forget it." I turn to Chelsea. "You go."

She snorts. "So I'm Second-Slut-in-Command, huh?"

"For God's sake. Jen? Any help here?"

She regards me with a serious expression, then says, "Condoms. Multiple condoms."

"Obviously!"

Chelsea pats my handbag, lying next to her empty water glass. "I've been keeping her stocked for just such an opportunity."

Jen nods. "Okay. Lube?"

"Trust me, we won't need lube. When I tell you I'm soaked, I might as well have been hosed down by a fire truck. And I'm not looking for technical advice, I need emotional advice. I need support. How do I get through this?"

Angel says, "Just open your legs, honey. He'll do the rest."

I prop my elbows on the table, drop my head into my hands, and sigh. "You three have less nurturing instinct between you than the average quokka."

"What's a quokka?" asks Jen.

"A cute little furry marsupial that throws its baby at predators so it can escape."

Chelsea laughs. "Yeah, that does sound like us."

Jen leans over and rests her hand on my shoulder. "Listen, just relax. You must've felt a connection, right?"

I lift my head and look at her, then nod.

"So rely on the connection. You don't even have to talk." She pauses. "Unless he wants butt sex and you don't. You should probably talk about that."

"Discuss butt sex. Great. Thanks for the wonderful advice."

"Well, we don't want him ramming it into any hole you don't want him to ram it into, do we?"

"I cannot believe you said that with a straight face." I stand, pick up my handbag, and look at my friends, trying to think of some meaningful parting words in the event my strangled corpse is found naked in a hallway in the morning.

I don't believe Cole's dangerous, but in case I'm wrong, I want them to remember me fondly.

"If I die tonight—"

Chelsea sits bolt upright and interrupts me. "Ooh! If you die, I want your black leather jacket with the fringe."

Jen gasps, sitting forward. "And I want that cute green Fendi handbag! The white Prada one too."

I exhale heavily and turn to Angel. "Let me guess. The vintage Valentino dress I found at the thrift store?"

She grins. "Red is my best color. Makes my boobs look big."

"Thank heavens birth control was invented. If your DNA ever gets into the gene pool, humanity is doomed."

"Don't be such a sourpuss. You're about to get laid."

"Yet not one of you seems concerned for my physical or emotional well-being."

Chelsea scoffs. "Oh, for fuck's sake, girl, you're the baddest bitch out there. Chet just messed with your head and made you forget it."

After a beat, I say, "Thank you for not calling him the twatwaffle."

Her smile is blinding. "It's more fun hearing you say it. Now run along, princess, you've got some cock to gobble. Call me later if you want me to pick you up. Or bring ice for your chapped and swollen vagina." She laughs. "Kitty's gonna get hammered by a hound dog tonight!"

There's no appropriate response to that, so I simply turn and walk away, shaking my head.

CHAPTER 10
Cole

H er eyes bright and her color high, Shay rounds the corner to the elevator bank. She stops abruptly when she sees me standing in front of the mirrored wall at the end. We stare at each other while I mentally command her to turn around and run in the other direction.

She refuses.

Squaring her shoulders, she steps forward, holding out her hand as if we're about to shake on a real estate transaction.

I grab it instead, spin her around, and press her against the wall. Her surprised little gasp is so sexy, it makes my dick pulse in excitement.

Staring down into her wide eyes, I murmur, "Last chance to change your mind."

"I don't want to change my mind."

"You sure? You look nervous."

"I'm extremely fucking nervous, thank you very much. Press the button."

"Why didn't your girlfriends talk any sense into you?"

"Because they have the collective IQ of a twelve-year-old boy. Press the button."

"Why are they your friends if they don't look out for you?"

"They do look out for me. All three of them told me Chet was a jerk the first time they met him, and that I could do better."

"And you didn't listen."

"I was too busy being blinded by his shiny teeth and glittering narcissism. Are you going to press the goddamn button, or were you planning to stand here all night interrogating me?"

No one—ever—speaks to me like this. With this impatience. This defiance. This outright disrespect. She's even cursing. It's like she's purposely trying to provoke me. It's maddening.

It's also really hot.

When I lick my lips, her breath catches. A little shiver runs through her body. I know it's not from fear, and that's also really hot.

In fact, everything about this woman gets me so fucking hot, it's dangerous.

It's a good thing we're only spending one night together. She's exactly the kind of trouble a man could lose himself in.

Unless you're her stupid clown of an ex. I should get her to tell me his last name so I can call the chief of police and have that putz arrested for criminal negligence.

Stepping away, I jab my finger onto the Up button on the console on the wall, then fold my arms over my chest and stare at the closed elevator doors, ignoring her.

After several seconds of confused silence, she says, "What are you doing?"

"Following your directions."

I'm not looking at her, but from the corner of my eye, I see her scowl.

"Well, it's very unromantic."

My smirk is reflected in the mirrored doors. "Oh, it's romance you want, is it? And here I was under the impression you were after something else."

She comes to stand beside me and glare at my reflection. "I know what this is."

"I have no idea what you're talking about."

"You're trying to dissuade me from sleeping with you."

"Dissuade? My, we're using our big words tonight, aren't we?"

The poison in her stare could kill an elephant at fifty paces. It makes me smile. Then I remember I don't do that and scowl instead.

"Stop asking rhetorical questions. They're the sign of a weak intellect."

The doors slide open as I turn my head and stare down my nose at her. "Another sign of a weak intellect is going with a stranger to his hotel room."

I step inside, press the button for the floor the room is on, and hold her gaze as I once again fold my arms over my chest.

Lowering her chin, she narrows her eyes at me and marches into the elevator.

She likes a challenge, I'll give her that.

We stand side by side, glaring out into the lobby, until the doors slide closed. Then I turn, take her in my arms, and crush my mouth to hers.

Instantly, she melts against me. Pressing her chest against mine, she kisses me back with a small sound of contentment and molds herself against my body.

This woman is a goddess. She's absolute fucking perfection. Anyone who doesn't fall at her feet is a fool, and any man who'd make her feel like anything less than the queen she is deserves a bullet in his head.

I'm going to kill her ex.

Pushing the thought aside, I focus on the feel of her in my arms. The smell of her skin and hair. The warm curves of her body. By the time we reach our floor, both of us are panting.

When the doors open, I push the Hold button to give her one last chance to change her mind.

Breathing hard, she glances at the open doors, then rolls her eyes when she realizes what I'm doing.

"Not this again."

"It's not too late to turn back."

"Are you still going to be saying that when I've got your dick down my throat?"

The image of her on her knees with my hard cock in her mouth makes me draw a sharp breath.

Seeing my expression, the little smartass smiles at me and says sweetly, "Just checking."

She sashays out into the hallway, spins on her heel, and sends me a brilliant, victorious smile.

"Don't think you've won. You haven't won anything except another regret."

"For your information, all this reluctance is a huge turn-on, so if you're trying to get me to change my mind, you're doing it the wrong way."

Holding her gaze, I step off the elevator, moving closer until I'm looking down into her eyes. I can tell she's intimidated, but she refuses to step back or break eye contact. She stands her ground like a lioness defending her territory, all wild beauty and savage pride.

The tiny beads of sweat glistening on her hairline are so pretty, it's like art.

Jesus. Listen to yourself. Get a grip!

I growl, "Room 410. It's left down the hall. Walk."

She blinks, then frowns. "Walk?"

"Don't make me repeat myself."

Arching her brows, she says tartly, "I'm sorry, are you under the mistaken impression that you're in charge here?"

It's a good thing I don't have problems with my coronary arteries. If I did, she would have already given me a heart attack from stress.

My tone firm and dark, I say, "I want to watch you walk down the hall."

She thinks about that, then smiles. "Say please."

I seethe at her silently. Her response is to smile wider.

"All right, Shay. You leave me no choice." I pick her up and throw her over my shoulder, then stride down the hallway toward the room. She squawks and kicks her legs.

"Stop bleating. You sound like a sheep."

"Put me down!"

"I'm surprised you're not enjoying this, considering the kind of books you're into. Don't all those he-man romance heroes of yours toss their women around like sacks of flour?"

"I never said I was into romance novels!"

"Yet you knew all the culprits I mentioned."

"Those aren't *culprits*, they're characters!"

"Famous for their misdeeds, hence they're culprits."

She stops struggling and goes quiet. "Wait. You're trying a different tactic to get me to change my mind, aren't you?"

"Is it working?"

"No."

"What a gigantic surprise."

Hanging onto the back of my suit jacket, she mutters, "You don't have to be sarcastic, you big jerk."

I'm glad I'm carrying her, otherwise she might glimpse my huge smile.

CHAPTER 11
Shay

H e unlocks the room with an electronic card key, then strides inside, letting the door slam shut behind us.

I'm upside down, so I don't have the best view of the place, but I can tell it's a suite. A large main room opens onto a smaller dining space. A lighted nook displays a piece of contemporary art. There's a wet bar beside an enormous TV and an unlit fireplace in the living area across from a sofa and a pair of chairs.

Cole bypasses all that. He walks straight into the bedroom and flips me over onto my back on the bed.

I stare up at him standing at the edge of the mattress gazing down at me and try not to have a stroke.

Shucking off his suit jacket, he murmurs, "Those pretty eyes of yours are very wide, sweetheart. It's still not too late."

Ignoring the thrill hearing him call me "sweetheart" sent through my body, I pretend a calm I don't feel. "Say that one more time and lose your testicles."

He makes a clucking sound of disapproval. "Shame. I think they might come in handy soon."

He drops his jacket to the floor and starts to work on the buttons of his shirt.

I don't know what I was expecting. Actually, I wasn't

44

expecting anything at all. I've been too focused on my own anxiety to think about what he might look like under his clothes. But the moment Cole's shirt parts under his fingertips and he pulls it open to reveal his naked chest, I think I know the feeling the architects of St. Peter's Basilica in the Vatican were trying to inspire when they built the place.

Awe.

I sit upright, lay my handbag aside, and stare at him with my heart in my throat and my mouth hanging open.

"Now that's a new expression. If I didn't know better, I'd think you were at a loss for words."

I slide to the edge of the mattress and lightly place both my hands flat on his majestic abs. They contract under my touch, a ripple of hard muscle that's both masculine and intoxicating.

I whisper, "Wow."

It's insufficient, but it's all I've got.

Cole puts a knuckle under my chin and tilts my head up so I'm looking into his eyes. After examining my expression, he murmurs, "Thank you."

"No, thank *you*." I look back at his chiseled body, at his pecs and biceps and smooth, golden skin, and produce a small, semi-hysterical laugh. "God. No wonder you're so arrogant. You look like you were created by artificial intelligence to star in action movies."

"Arrogant?"

"Oh, please. You're the arrogance poster boy, and you know it. How much time do you spend in the gym?"

"None."

I scoff. "You're telling me all this sculpted muscle comes naturally? No way."

"I didn't say it came naturally. I said it didn't come from a gym. Take off your panties."

My breath catches. I glance up at him to find him looking at me with hooded eyes and dangerous intensity.

"Can we turn out the lights?"

"No. Take off your panties. But leave everything else on."

"Why?"

"Because after I make you come with my mouth, I'm going to enjoy tearing your clothes off your body."

My gulp is surely audible.

Inhaling a breath, I look down at my skirt. *Shit. What underwear do I have on? Am I wearing those ratty Walmart ones? Why didn't I listen to Chelsea when she said all my lingerie looks like I found it at a garage sale?*

"One final chance, beautiful girl. Once you take those panties off, there's no going back."

I know Cole's dark, stroking voice is meant to be frightening, but all it does is harden my resolve.

I might not be in this position if I had an extra set of batteries in the house, but I'm getting laid tonight, and that's that.

Pulling my skirt up my thighs, I hook my thumbs under the elastic of my panties and slide them down my legs until they're pooled on the carpet around my feet. Then I slip off my heels and glance up at him.

"Black. I see we had a theme for the evening. Lie back and spread your legs."

Breathless and trembling, I slowly settle back onto the mattress and do as I'm told.

Cole stands motionless as he gazes down at me. His eyes are fire. His silence is terrifying. I don't know if he's about to fall to his knees and devour me or ask if I've never heard of a disposable razor.

Instead of doing either of those things, he exhales a quiet breath and whispers reverently, "Perfect."

This feeling I have right now must be the same feeling Chet enjoyed every time he preened at his reflection in a mirror. With one simple word, Cole not only dissolved my anxiety, he also released that powerful dark femme energy Angel's always going on about.

Stretching my arms overhead, I spread my thighs wider.

Cole's searing gaze flashes up to mine. He snaps, "You're not in charge."

Because we both know I really am, I smile. "Whatever you say, boss man."

Like a predator contemplating his meal, he tilts his head and studies me. The tension grows until I'm resisting the urge to start squirming.

"You like playing with fire, don't you?"

"Seems like I'm not the only one."

"Answer the question."

"I thought I had."

"Yes or no, Shay."

Something about his intensity has my heart pounding like mad. Energy courses through my body, thrumming over my skin in waves. My nipples harden. My pussy tingles. I feel unstable, as if I'm a dangerous mix of chemicals that might spontaneously combust.

I answer truthfully. "I like playing with *you*."

Whether or not that satisfies whatever it was he was really asking, I can't tell. His blue eyes are as dark and impenetrable as the surface of a stormy sea.

He kneels between my legs, then slowly runs his hands up my spread legs from the inside of my knees to where my thighs meet my body. Staring voraciously at my exposed pussy, he licks his lips.

That simple action is so sexy, I almost moan out loud.

"You want my mouth on you?"

His voice is harsh in the quiet room. Mine is breathy.

"Yes."

"Ask for it."

He strokes his thumbs against my pubic hair, his pressure feather-light. Fighting another moan, I swallow.

"Please, Cole. I want your mouth."

When he murmurs, "Good girl," I nearly expire.

Correction. When I nearly expire is the moment his hot tongue makes contact with my tingling clitoris and gives it a firm flick. Then I moan so loudly, the girls can probably hear me downstairs.

Cole slides his hands under my bare ass and grips it as he slides his tongue back and forth in a slow, rhythmic dance over my clit. A shudder wracks my body. I close my eyes and tangle my fingers into his hair.

When I start to rock my hips in time with the strokes of his tongue, he makes a muffled sound that I recognize as a laugh.

"Don't gloat," I breathe. "Gloating is unattractive."

"Yes, ma'am," he whispers mockingly, then slides a finger inside me, making me gasp and arch off the bed. He adds another finger, and I whimper.

Okay, so maybe I'm not the one in charge after all.

Dammit.

CHAPTER 12
Cole

I f I thought her mouth tasted good, her cunt takes like
heaven.

Pulling on my hair and grinding that delicious cunt
against my face, she moans.

"Oh God, that's amazing. Your tongue is amazing. Your
fingers are amazing. This was the best idea I've ever had in my
life."

Her breathless little moans drive me crazy. My dick is so hard,
it aches.

"Yes—oh—suck just like that—*oh*—"

I love how responsive she is. How vocal. When I scrape my
teeth against her swollen clit, she jerks, crying out. I thrust my
fingers deeper inside her, and she says my name.

Moans it.

Makes it sound like I'm a superhero.

It's good this will only be for one night. I haven't even fucked
her yet, and I'm already obsessed. If I got more of her—

No. Don't go there. She can't be yours. She can never be yours.

Her pussy contracts around my fingers. Then she's coming,
crying out hoarsely, her thighs shaking and her hips jerking, the
raw sounds of her pleasure echoing off the walls.

She calls out my name again. This time there's desperation in her tone.

Lucky for us both, I know what she needs.

I snatch up her small handbag and rip it open. The contents include a cell phone, a credit card, and about two dozen rubbers. I grab one, rip open the foil packet, unzip my trousers, take my hard dick in my hand, and roll the condom on.

Then, crouched and balancing on the balls of my feet, I drag her off the bed and impale her on my cock.

Staring at me with wide eyes and wet lips, she digs her fingernails into my shoulders. Her face is red. Her thighs are open around my waist. Her expression is one of pure astonishment.

"You okay?"

"Yep," she says breathlessly. "That was just surprising."

"Why?"

"You're balancing us on your toes."

"So?"

"You say that like it's no big deal."

"It isn't."

"Oh. You're very strong, aren't you?"

"Yes."

"I should've known when I saw all the muscles. What happened to the tearing off of my clothes you were supposed to do?"

"We'll get to that in a minute. I decided I needed to fuck you first."

Her grin is so beautiful, it makes my heart skip a beat.

"Cole, you are fanfuckingtastic."

I can't help myself: I grin back at her. "You're not so bad yourself, sweetheart."

Then I thrust my hips, driving deeper inside.

CHAPTER 13
Shay

A s he's driving into me, grunting in pleasure and squeezing my ass in his strong hands while I hang on to his shoulders for dear life, I have an epiphany.

Up until now, I've been doing this stuff completely backward.

A year-long relationship with a narcissist that wrecks my self-esteem and ends in tears? Sign me up! A one-night stand with a handsome stranger? Never!

I'm a moron.

Looking between our legs as he pistons his hips, Cole growls, "Your pussy's drenched."

"You're welcome." When he glances up at me, I laugh again, feeling crazed.

"You do realize that laughing while a man is fucking you isn't the ideal response, right?"

"It's better than crying."

He grins again. I swear, the man has a drop-dead gorgeous smile. Why is he always trying to hide it?

I'm distracted by that thought because he decides to be Superman and stand straight up from a squatting position, taking me along with him as if I weighed no more than a bird.

"Wow, you're really impressive! This is the best night of my life!"

"And we've only just gotten started."

He turns around, sits on the edge of the mattress, and makes sure I'm stable before ripping open the front of my blouse. Buttons go flying.

When I gasp, he says, "Don't worry. I'll buy you a new one."

I'm not sure how that's supposed to work if we're only spending tonight together, but the question becomes unimportant when he pulls the cup of my bra aside and leans down to take my hard nipple into his mouth.

The groan that leaves me rose straight from my soul.

Dropping my head back and closing my eyes, I concentrate on the feel of his mouth against my skin while I grind my pelvis against his. His cock is big and thick inside me, his shoulders are wide and strong under my hands, and if there's a heaven, I hope one-night stands are allowed there.

"Love all those sounds you're making, sweetheart," he says against my breast, his voice a mix of pride and pleasure.

"And I love that you're calling me sweetheart. Can you please do that all night?"

"Yes. That and whatever else you want."

I'm never having another long-term relationship again.

CHAPTER 14

Cole

S hay is warm and plush in my arms, rocking her hips back and forth against my pelvis and moaning like a porn star. With her head dropped back and her nails scratching my back, she rides my cock, driving me crazy.

I never want this night to end.

I wrestle her out of her ruined shirt and toss it aside, unhook her bra and toss that aside too, then take both her breasts in my hands and squeeze them. Her sigh of satisfaction is long and loud.

"You're so fucking beautiful," I say gruffly, then latch onto one of her perfect pink nipples and suck.

"I think I have to come again. Oh God. Cole, you're incredible!"

She shudders. Her hips flex faster. I gently press my teeth into her taut nipple, and she cries out. Her orgasm is so abrupt and violent, it takes my breath away.

Obviously, her piece of shit ex wasn't taking care of business.

Crying out and shaking, she pulls my hair as she comes, giving her whole body over to it. Her pussy contracts convulsively around my cock, and I have to concentrate on not losing control.

When her breathing has slowed and she's slack in my arms, I

whisper, "We're not done yet, sweetheart." Then I roll her over onto her back and kiss her deeply.

She wraps her legs around my waist and kisses me back with so much passion, it's as if her life depends on it. When she opens her eyes and gazes up at me, it feels like an arrow shot through my heart.

No. No feelings. That isn't what this is about. Get your head straight!

I withdraw from her body, rising to stand beside the bed. I strip off the rest of my clothing, then remove her wrinkled skirt. Then, gazing down into her eyes, I say, "Give me your mouth," and pull off the condom.

And God bless her, this gorgeous woman wearing nothing but a smile obeys my command without hesitation.

She drops to her knees beside the bed, takes my dick in her hand, and starts to suck greedily on it.

It's my turn to shudder. I slide my hands into her hair and breathlessly watch her lavish my cock with her tongue. She furls it around the head, strokes it down the length, then strokes back up again. She works my shaft with one hand and cups the other around my balls, gorging on me with the most beautiful abandon.

"Good girl," I growl, making her shiver.

She strokes and sucks faster. Pleasure spreads through my entire body, starting at my cock and working its way outward in waves. My pulse goes haywire. A ragged groan breaks from my chest. I close my eyes and get lost in the feel of her mouth.

Then I hear a muffled laugh.

Opening my eyes, I look down at her. She slides my cock out of her mouth and smiles.

"Sorry. Just gloating."

"Don't make me spank you for disobedience."

A thrill in her voice, she asks, "Is that something we can do?"

"If you want to, of course."

"God, it's like I hit the lottery," she murmurs, looking dazed.

I cup her chin in my hand and say firmly, "I'm the one who

hit the lottery. You're perfect. Thank you for tonight. Now get that cock back in your mouth and keep sucking until I tell you to stop."

"Not to push this too far, but would it be weird if I call you Daddy?"

"I don't have a Daddy kink, but if you want to, then sure."

She thinks for a moment. "I don't have a Daddy kink, either, but I'm picturing Chelsea's face if I tell her I called you that all night. She'd faint."

How is she so goddamn adorable? I'm falling further under her spell with every second that passes!

But I keep my expression and voice neutral when I say, "What do you think she'd do if you told her you called me Sir?"

Her gorgeous eyes widen. "She'd die. Definitely. She'd drop dead on the spot."

Caressing her face, I smile. "I don't want to be the cause of anyone's premature death, but it might be worth it."

Never in all my life have I seen such a look of wonder on a woman's face. It's almost as if...she likes me.

When I realize how much I like her too, my smile fades and my heart sinks.

Leave it to me to have a one-night stand with maybe the one woman in all the world who might be able to understand me.

Fuck.

CHAPTER 15
Shay

Judging by the sudden pained expression on his face, Cole is only saying I can call him Sir for my benefit, but it's an ick for him. Since this night is all about good vibes, I don't want to ruin anything for either of us.

"You know what? I changed my mind. I don't want to make it too complicated. Just dick me down without any titles."

His stormy eyes regard me seriously for a moment. "You really have a way with words, sweetheart."

"Thank you." I slide his erection between my lips and flutter my lashes at him.

A slow grin takes over his mouth, transforming those full lips into something beautiful and dangerous that makes me euphoric.

Yes—that's it. This feeling he gives me...

It's euphoria.

Without warning, he grabs me by my armpits, lifts me and tosses me onto the bed, and growls, "On your hands and knees, beautiful."

I roll over and scramble into position so fast, it's a miracle I don't sprain something.

I hear foil rip. Then strong hands close around my hips, gripping them hard. Cole shoves his erection inside me, pulling me back against his body at the same time he thrusts forward. I groan in pure pleasure. He must enjoy that, because he starts to fuck me hard and deep, grunting in satisfaction.

Then he slides a hand around and between my legs, finding my throbbing clit and pinching it.

"So slippery," he whispers as I moan. "Slippery and swollen. You feel so good, baby. This pretty wet cunt is so perfect, I'm gonna fuck it all night long."

Unable to hold myself up any longer, I collapse facedown onto the mattress as he continues to thrust into me. Making fists in the sheets, I close my eyes and spread my legs wider, meeting his every thrust with a jerk of my hips.

He croons something. Praise or filth, I don't know. The words are lost under the crashing of my heartbeat and the moans slipping from my throat. All that remains is the deep, soothing sound of his voice. It washes over me, cooling my burning skin and sliding through all the brittle cracks Chet left inside me, filling those barren, empty spaces with fields of colorful wildflowers and sparkling waterfalls that quench the dark desert of my heart and turn it into a verdant paradise.

My chest grows tight. My throat closes. Suddenly—*shit*—I'm fighting the urge to cry.

I don't know how, but Cole senses it. He slows his thrusts, then stops altogether, leaning over to plant his forearm beside my head.

"Sweetheart," he murmurs, nuzzling my ear. "You okay?"

I say yes, but it means no. And he must have a lot of experience with women, because he knows. Without withdrawing from my body, he carefully takes us down to the mattress, curves his strong body around mine, and gathers me into his arms.

His mouth against my neck, he says softly, "Tell me what you need."

Chet was never this sensitive. This giving. This *wonderful*.

Eyes watering, I inhale a hitching breath. "I'm sorry. I don't want to ruin this."

"You're not ruining anything."

"I'm sure this isn't what you imagined when I propositioned you."

"Which part?"

"Me being all weepy."

His tone turns conversational. "I know it's due to my sexual prowess. I've been told it's overwhelming."

Despite the tightness in my chest, I manage a chuckle. "Your arrogance is overwhelming, that's for sure."

He gives me a squeeze and kisses my neck. His tone turns teasing. "Tell the truth. My dick is so glorious, you wanted to burst into tears of joy the moment you saw it."

"What kind of man calls his dick *glorious*? I think you're the one who's been reading too many romance novels."

He whispers, "Admit it. It's beautiful. You want to build it a shrine."

"For God's sake."

"And burn incense sticks in those little gold holders. And lay fruit and flowers all around the base as you chant it a reverent song."

"Wow. Whatever you've been smoking, I want some."

He peppers my neck with soft kisses, working his way down to my shoulder where he bites me gently. "I'm just high on you."

The sweetness of that sentiment takes my breath away. After a moment, I clear my throat of the frog in it. "That's a lyric from a song."

"Probably. I mean it, though."

I must be out of my mind, because I believe him. Heaving a big sigh, I close my eyes and turn my cheek to his shoulder. He strokes his hand down my arm, then squeezes my hip. There's a moment of contemplative silence, then he says, "We can stop now if you want."

My eyes fly open. "Are you kidding? No way! I'm not letting

one stupid little weepy moment get in the way of the best dick of my life!"

His chest shakes with silent laughter. When he's composed himself, he says seriously, "You should work for Hallmark. That would make an incredible greeting card."

Then he flexes his hips, pushing deeper inside me.

CHAPTER 16
Cole

She reaches around the back of my neck and pulls my head down for a kiss. It's a long kiss, a lingering, soulful one, and by the time it ends, both of us are breathing hard and trembling.

Looking into her eyes, I say in a husky voice, "I only want to make you feel good. Whatever you need, ask for it. If I do something you don't like, tell me. Let's pretend we've loved each other all our lives and nothing we say or do could ever change that. Let's pretend, just for tonight, just with each other, that we're where we've always belonged."

Her eyes well with water. Her voice strangled, she says, "If you keep talking like that, you'll be having sex with a sobbing mess."

I swipe a finger under her eye, capturing a lone tear. Then I kiss her nose and smile at her. "A sobbing mess with the most beautiful ass I've ever seen. Time to ride me, baby."

She lets out a little scream when I roll onto my back and take her with me. I manhandle her into position and issue a warning. "Watching you bounce up and down on my dick is probably gonna put me over the edge pretty quick, so if there's anything you need me to do to get you there with me, let me know."

She laughs. I love the way her eyes light up when she laughs. Her whole body lights up from within.

This woman is magic.

She props her hands on my chest, which is good because it distracts me from the ache inside it. She leans down and kisses me. Against my mouth, she whispers, "Okay, cowboy. Giddyup."

She arches back, giving me a beautiful view of her body. Full tits, soft belly, curved hips. Dark hair flowing around gleaming shoulders. Then she curls her hand around my dick and guides me inside her with a wicked grin.

And I want to kill her ex all over again.

The audacity of that prick. Hurting *her*. An angel with a sensitive soul, a smart mouth, and a dirty mind. I should rip that selfish idiot's arms and legs from his body, throw him off the Santa Monica Pier, and wave at him while I watch him sink into the Pacific.

Picturing it, I smile.

"My, my, now that's a devilish grin."

"You want devilish? Hang onto your hat, sweetheart, cause here we go."

I grip her hips in my hands and thrust up into her wet heat again and again, watching those gorgeous tits bounce every time our bodies meet. She shakes her hair off her shoulders and makes the single most sexy, feminine noise I've ever heard, a laughing little gasp of pleasure that pulls an answering growl from my throat.

She's soon moaning. Sinking her nails into my skin. Begging me to go faster, harder, deeper, to give her everything I've got.

"You first, baby." I press my thumb against her clit and stroke it up and down.

It might be the broken cry of ecstasy that leaves her lips that pushes me over the edge. It might be the way her thighs clench around my body. It might be the way she arches back and squeezes her own breasts, pinching her hard nipples.

Or it might be that I've caught a glimpse of how my life could be if only I were a different man.

A better man.

A man who deserves a woman like this.

Whatever the cause, my orgasm crashes into me so fast and hard, it steals my breath. I lie beneath her, convulsing with pleasure, my fingers sunk into her sweet flesh, staring up at this beautiful stranger who's given me a memory I already know I'll return to over and over for the rest of my life.

Yeah, sex is great. But connection? Real *connection*?

It's so valuable and rare, some people would kill for it.

A fact I'm all too familiar with.

CHAPTER 17
Shay

I open my eyes and look down at Cole to find him gazing up at me with an expression of such complete adoration, it makes my heart flip.

He rasps, "Goddamn, baby," then tips his head back, closes his eyes, and releases a guttural groan from deep within his chest.

My own orgasm is still pulsing through me, but watching Mr. Dark and Stormy lose control and give himself over to pleasure is so enthralling, I can't look away.

His abs are clenched. The veins in his neck are popping. His whole body strains upward into mine as he clutches my hips and shudders. He moans again, but this time the sound forms the shape of my name.

"Shay. Fuck. Shay. Oh God, sweetheart—*fuck*—"

I feel like he plugged me into a socket. Electricity surges through me, crackling hot. Along with it comes a sweet, unexpected tenderness that makes me want to kiss him all over his handsome face, take him in my arms, and promise him I'll never let anything hurt him again.

Then I give myself a bracing mental slap across the face.

Snap out of it, dummy! It's just sex!

I know it's more than that, at least for me, but I'll be damned if I'll admit it aloud. I've done enough caretaking of men for one lifetime. I've given enough of myself away for nothing in return. Tonight is about taking back my power and shoring up my battered self-esteem.

The fact that I'm using a sexy stranger with a magnetic personality and a big dick to do it is just the icing on top of the cake.

He pulls me down to lie on his chest and sinks a hand into my hair. Holding my head steady, he kisses me with searing passion, stroking his tongue against mine as he releases himself in jerks and shudders. After one final moan and a full-body twitch, it's over, and he's bathed in sweat.

And still kissing me.

It turns from desperate and passionate to slow and sweet. His big hands cradle my head. His ragged breathing returns to normal. He explores my mouth with his tongue until I'm dizzy, then tucks my head into the crook between his neck and shoulder and heaves a tremendous sigh.

He's still buried inside me. Still hard.

Closing my eyes, I smile.

After a while, he stirs. His voice husky, he says, "You okay?"

"Okay is far too weak a word for what I am right now. Job well done, cowboy."

He kisses the top of my head, releasing another long breath and a chuckle. "That was only round one, sweetheart."

"Really? How exciting."

He chuckles again. I love the sound of it, the low, leonine rumble under my ear. It sends a shiver of delight over every nerve ending. I cuddle closer to him, enjoying everything about this moment.

"You're very large. Everywhere."

His chest shakes with laughter. "Thank you?"

"It's a compliment. I like how big you are. How strong. It makes me feel—"

I was about to say safe, but stop myself, suddenly bashful. But Cole proves he's a mind reader once again.

"Good. I want you to feel safe with me."

I crinkle my forehead. "How did you know?"

He thinks about it for a moment. "Are you familiar with *Star Trek*?"

"Now that's a strange segue, cowboy."

"Is that a yes or a no?"

"Yes, I'm familiar with *Star Trek*."

"So you know who Mr. Spock is."

"How are we talking about Vulcans while you're still inside me?"

"I'm getting there."

"Get there quicker."

He gives me a soft swat on my ass. "Be quiet now."

Smirking into his neck, I say, "Good luck with that."

He sighs, then says, "We have a little bit of that Vulcan mind-meld thing Mr. Spock would do."

"But without having to touch each other's face to merge our thoughts."

"Exactly."

"So it's not at all like that Vulcan mind-meld thing. It's just telepathy."

"Are you always this argumentative?"

"I'm not being argumentative. I'm being logical."

"So that's a yes, then."

It's my turn to chuckle. "I suppose so."

He wraps his arms around my back and gives me a hard squeeze. Into my ear, he whispers, "You're so goddamn cute."

My face flushes with pleasure. My heart melts. But because I don't want to seem like too big a sap, I play it off like his praise doesn't faze me. "I'd be even cuter if my stomach wasn't growling."

"Are you hungry?"

"Famished. The girls and I didn't have supper before we went out tonight."

His tone turns disapproving. "How old are you?"

"Thirty...ish."

"Well, Miss Thirtyish, you're not very good at adulting."

"Because I didn't eat supper?"

"Because you went out for a night of drinking without putting food in your body first. You don't take care of your basic needs."

I push off his chest and sit up, smiling down at his stern, handsome face. Then I wriggle my hips and lightly scratch my nails over his abs. "On the contrary, cowboy. I'm taking care of my basic needs right this very moment."

He glowers up at me in that way of his that he thinks is terribly scary. My smile turns into a grin.

Then he's rolling me over onto my back and tickling me, and I'm screaming with laughter.

The only way this night could get better is if he left me a hundred and fifty million dollars on his way out the door.

CHAPTER 18
Cole

Her laughter is music. Especially this laugh, so different from the one I heard down at the bar with all its sorrow and sharp edges. This laugh is light and bright and peels another hard layer off my heart.

By the time this night is over, she'll have stripped it bare.

Beaming up at me, she throws her arms around my shoulders. "You give me hope for manity."

"What the hell is manity?"

"The male part of humanity."

"So you mean men."

She furrows her brows. "I have no idea what I'm saying. You just tossed my salad so well, I'm making up words."

I drop my head, bury my face in her hair, and dissolve into helpless laughter.

"Aha!" she cries. "I knew you were a big softie under all those dark thunderclouds!"

I try to stop laughing so I can scowl at her and prove her wrong, but I can't. Somehow, she found the bolted door where I keep all my vulnerable things locked behind and kicked it right off its hinges.

Nipping my earlobe, she says warmly, "You have the most beautiful laugh. I'm glad I got to hear it."

The breath I draw into my lungs burns as if the air itself is on fire. Choked by emotion, I have to keep my face hidden in her hair because I'm afraid of what she might see.

When I've gotten myself under control, I say seriously, "Thank you. I'd say something nice about your laugh too except that it sounds like a farm animal getting a tooth pulled."

She slaps my back. "Hey!"

"Too harsh? I'm sorry. It's just that I heard this injured donkey braying one time—"

"You did not!"

"—and it was eerily loud and screechy—"

"Cole! You dick!"

"—like it was dying or something, like in serious *agony*—"

"Okay, that's it! No more nookie for you!"

She tries to roll out from under me but is unsuccessful. I grab her wrists and pin her to the mattress, grinning down at her as she struggles to get free.

"You're adorable when you're angry."

She stops struggling and glares at me. "Oh yeah? As adorable as a dying donkey?"

I pretend to think. "Well, not *that* adorable. Maybe more like one of those hairless Chihuahuas? You know, how it's ugly but also sorta cute in its own scary, repulsive way?"

Fuming, she mutters, "I'll show you scary and repulsive. Put your dick near my mouth again, cowboy, and watch as I turn it into something that looks like a pit bull's favorite chew toy."

I'm setting a personal record for laughs in one month. Hell, one year.

Maybe a whole decade.

To stop her from hurling more threats, I kiss her long and deep. She responds as she always does, melting into me with a little sigh the instant our lips meet, giving herself over to me completely.

I want to fuck her again. But she needs food, so that's the priority.

Bracing my weight on my hands, I push up and slowly withdraw from her body. She groans a little, her eyelids fluttering. Then she heaves a big sigh and flings her arms out to either side on the mattress as I rise and stand at the side of the bed.

I peel off the condom and throw it in the trash can by the night stand. "I'll call for room service. What do you want?"

She answers without hesitation. "Steak. Medium-rare. A big one. Baked potato with all the toppings. Something chocolate for dessert."

"Anything green? Salad, veggies?"

"Blech. Green things are for rabbits. Do I look like a rabbit to you? No, don't answer that. I already know you think I look like a hairless Chihuahua because you're gifted with such a poetic way with words."

We smile at each other.

In another life, I would love this woman. I'd love her so much, I'd burn down the whole world just to spend an afternoon by her side.

I turn away, a band of tightness squeezing my chest.

As I call for room service, I know she's watching me. Even though my back is turned, I can feel those beautiful eyes. By the time I hang up, she's sitting upright with her knees drawn up to her chest and her arms wrapped around her legs, wriggling her toes impatiently.

"What's that look?"

"This is my inquisitive look."

"Meaning?"

"Meaning I want to ask you lots of questions because you're very interesting, but I know this is a one-night thing, so I don't want to make it weird."

Smiling, I stretch out on the mattress beside her and prop myself up on an elbow. "I think we blew past weird when you got weepy."

"Oh yeah." She brightens. "So it's okay if I ask you stuff?"

Thinking of the graveyard of bones I've got hidden in my proverbial closet, I hesitate.

She studies me. "That's a no."

I say gently, "I want you to leave this room with only good memories. If we start talking about me..."

She stretches out beside me, mirroring my posture and gazing into my eyes. "You're worried I won't like you anymore?"

"Oh, I *know* you wouldn't like me anymore."

"That bad, huh?"

"That bad."

"You could always lie to me."

I can't tell if she doesn't believe me or if she's just being sweet. I reach out and tuck a strand of dark hair behind her ear. "No," I say sadly. "I couldn't."

We gaze silently into each other's eyes. She searches my face as if she's looking for something, but I don't know what it might be.

Her voice low and soft and her eyes shining, she says, "How about this? Tell me a story. Make one up."

I frown. "About myself?"

"No, about us. Like if we met in another life, in some normal way people do. If we were introduced through mutual friends, something like that."

I answer without thinking. "I'd never allow the kind of friends I have to be around you."

She's studying me again. More closely now, her gaze sharpening. She repeats her question from moments ago.

"That bad, huh?"

"Yes. They're that bad."

"But you're not."

"I am."

"You can't be. You're wonderful."

Only with you. "You ever hear that saying, 'Birds of a feather flock together?'"

"Yeah?"

"It's true. My flock is made of predatory night birds with sharp talons and cold hearts." My voice drops. "And I'm the worst of them."

She reaches out and traces her fingertip over my lower lip. Her gaze follows her touch. She whispers, "Your heart isn't cold."

"Everyone who knows me would say otherwise."

She meets my eyes then. She meets my eyes and says something that almost destroys me.

"Then everyone who knows you is wrong, Cole. Your heart isn't cold. It's warm, and it's beautiful. You just keep it on ice so nobody can melt it."

I'm grateful that she scoots closer and presses her face to my chest, because I know I wouldn't be able to hide from those eyes of hers, those gorgeous green eyes that see straight down to the darkest corners of my black soul. I gather her in my arms and inhale several slow, deep breaths, willing my pulse to stop hammering.

"Once upon a time..." she prompts.

"Right." After a rough throat clearing, I continue. "Once upon a time, a bird of prey at rest on a tree branch saw a beautiful dove in a clearing far below."

"This clearing was in a hotel bar, I take it."

"Who's telling this story, me or you?"

I feel her smile against my chest, the curve of her cheek pressing against my heart. "You."

"Then be quiet."

"You would have made a good dictator."

When I sigh, she whispers, "Sorry."

"Where was I?"

"Two birds in a bar. I mean clearing."

"Yes. So the bird of prey sees the beautiful dove—"

"Wait, you were supposed to be telling a story of how we met as people in another life, not birds in this one."

"Are you kidding me with this?"

71

She pounds a fist on my shoulder. "I want my story! Tell it right!"

I'm laughing again, because apparently that's my new thing.

It's good we're only spending one night together. If we started dating, my reputation as a cold-blooded, ruthless bastard would be ruined within a week.

"All right, my stubborn little dove," I murmur, kissing her temple. "Here's your story. Once upon a time, the most perfect angel God ever created—"

"Now you've got a *Biblical* theme going?" she interrupts, exasperated. "First it's birds, then it's the Bible. I hate to tell you this, but you're a terrible story teller."

I roll her to her back and kiss her roughly, only coming up for air when she's trembling beneath me, sinking her nails into my back and whimpering with need.

"That's a relief, because I'm done talking. Time to get fucked again, sweetheart."

"Thank goodness. I was about to fall asleep."

We grin at each other. Then I reach for another condom, thinking the dozens she has in her handbag won't be enough.

We fuck. We eat. We fuck again, repeatedly. We talk and laugh until the morning sun creeps through the window shades. When she's yawning, her lids heavy and her beautiful eyes glazed with fatigue, I tuck her under the bedcovers and hold her until her breathing is deep and even.

Then I lie there struggling with how badly I want to stay until she's awake again.

I want to know her. Everything about her. All her secrets and fears, all the things that make her who she is. But that would mean she'd have to get to know me too...and that would be a disaster.

I'm the last thing this incredible woman needs in her life.

But because I'm selfish, I stay longer than I should, breathing in her scent, feeling the warmth of her soft body, memorizing the exact color of her hair.

Then I rise and watch her lying peacefully on the bed as I silently dress. At the bedroom door, I turn back for one final, lingering look.

Goodbye, beautiful Shayna. It was my privilege.

Maybe in another life.

My heart aching, I walk out.

CHAPTER 19
Shay

I awaken to the sound of someone knocking on the hotel room door. I don't know how long they've been doing that, but I suspect it's been a while, because each succeeding knock grows louder. I sit up in bed, groan at the soreness in my body, and look around.

Cole's gone.

Even before I opened my eyes, I knew he wasn't here. I fell asleep to the sound of his steady breathing and his solid, comforting warmth at my back, and his absence is jarring. I know we agreed to one night only, but part of me was secretly hoping he'd change his mind.

Like I have.

Obviously, he didn't.

Pushing down the disappointment, I rise from bed, grab the white terrycloth robe hanging on a hook outside the bathroom, and tie the sash around my waist. I hurry through the living room. When I peer through the peep hole of the front door, I see an unfamiliar man in a black suit standing outside in the hallway. He's holding a white garment bag in one hand.

He appears to be in his late thirties. His dark hair is shorn

74

close to his head. He's fit and broad-shouldered, with a piercing stare that could give Cole a run for his money.

On the left side of his neck, a tattoo of something I can't identify peeks out from under the starched collar of his white dress shirt.

Through the door, I say, "Yes?"

"Hullo, miss. This is for you."

His voice is deep and has a British accent. He holds out the bag. I look at it suspiciously.

"What is it?"

"A blouse, miss."

My breath catches.

"Don't worry. I'll buy you a new one."

Remembering Cole's words from last night after he savagely ripped my shirt off my body, my face grows hot and my heart starts pounding. Meanwhile, the man in the black suit stands there smiling patiently as if he's got all the time in the world.

"Cole sent you?"

"Yes, miss."

"Are you with the hotel?"

"No, miss."

"Are you...with a delivery service?"

"No, miss."

He extends his arm, giving the bag a little shake. Deciding he's not dangerous—though there's something about him that suggests he would be under the right circumstances—I open the door. "Hi there."

"Good morning, miss."

I take the bag, then stand in the doorway frowning and confused. "So you work for Cole, is that it?"

His smile grows wider, as if he's enjoying some private thought. Whatever it is, he doesn't share it. He simply says, "Have a lovely day, miss," then turns around and walks away.

Leaning out the door, I watch him go until he disappears into the elevators. Then I step back inside and unzip the garment bag. Within is an exquisite black silk blouse.

It's simple, the lines classic and clean, but it's obviously expensive. When I check the label, I almost drop the bag from shock.

The blouse is a Balmain.

It's a historic luxury French brand, renowned for the quality of its couture. Not to mention its prices. Their spring collection included a scarlet cashmere jacket that I desperately coveted but could never afford because it was thirty thousand dollars. An off-the-rack T-shirt goes for almost a grand.

I suspect this simple blouse I'm holding is priced in the thousands.

Heart palpitating, I walk back into the bedroom and carefully lay the garment bag on the bed. I stand looking at it for several moments, trying to decide what to do.

I don't know who the man was who delivered it, so I can't call him to come and pick it up. And I don't have a phone number for Cole, so I can't let him know this is much too expensive a gift for me to accept. Not that I'm seriously considering doing either of those things, because I already know I'm keeping this beautiful piece of clothing, but it makes me feel better to at least pretend to have a crisis of conscience for a moment before accepting Cole's generosity.

I should've started having one-night stands years ago.

Years! Like in my teens!

Except with my luck, those encounters would've all turned out to be with married men or escaped felons, so my lack of experience in the area is probably a good thing.

Without anyone to call to thank for this lovely item, I call Chelsea instead.

"Shay!" she shouts the instant she picks up. "I was just about to call you. Tell me everything. Was it fantastic? Did he have a big dick? Are you walking bowlegged?"

Feeling as weightless as an overfilled balloon, I smile. "Yes to all three."

I bend over to stroke the silky sheen of the blouse, lightly tracing my fingertips around the black pearlescent buttons. Then more knocking on the hotel room door distracts me.

"Chelsea, hang on. I have to get this."

I hurry to the door again. When I open it, I find a young woman in a uniform standing beside a rolling cart draped in white linens. A variety of covered dishes sit on top.

"Good morning, I'm Bettina with room service. May I come in?"

"What's all this?"

"Your breakfast, miss."

"You must have the wrong room. I didn't order food."

Bettina smiles. "The gentleman who placed the order said you'd say that. But I assure you, this is the right room."

My breath catches. *Cole.*

Into my ear, Chelsea demands, "What's happening?"

"It's room service with my food."

"Why do you sound so dazed if it's just room service?"

"Because I didn't order it. Cole did."

A pause follows. "I take it Cole's the guy you spent the night with?"

"Yeah."

"The hottie you banged ordered you breakfast? That's pretty thoughtful of him."

Remembering how he said I wasn't very good at adulting, I smile. "Yeah. He bought me a blouse too."

Her tone turns incredulous. "He took you shopping?"

"No. He ripped my blouse off me and promised he'd buy me a new one. It showed up this morning—a Balmain, no less—delivered by a guy who looked like maybe he knows how to kill someone with his pinkie."

Bettina is starting to look impatient, so I step aside and wave her in as Chelsea has a breakdown.

"Hold on a second! He had *couture* delivered to your *room*?"

"Technically, it's ready-to-wear, but yes. And it's beautiful."

"Oh my God. You lucky bitch. You should've started having one-night stands years ago!"

My laugh is breathless with delight.

"Was that a *laugh*? Wow. This Cole of yours must've really been something else."

Closing my eyes, I think of him and smile. "Girl, you have no idea."

~

I eat breakfast, shower, and dress. The Balmain blouse fits me perfectly. My mood somewhere up in the stratosphere, I float out of the hotel and take a taxi back to my apartment.

Because it's Sunday and I don't have to go to work, I decide to indulge myself and visit my favorite bookstore. I've been going there for years, and I love the owner, but I haven't had a chance to swing by in months.

I change into shorts and a T-shirt and drive out to Venice Beach with the top down, enjoying the sun on my face and the wind in my hair, thinking of beautiful dark blue eyes that could see straight through me. By the time I walk through the doors of Lit Happens, I'm grinning from ear to ear.

Cole and I might have spent only one night together, but the man has been magic for my self-esteem.

The shop is adorable. It's got a bohemian, artistic vibe, with lots of overstuffed chairs to lounge in, a little espresso bar on one side, and an assortment of stray cats that wander in and out.

And the owner is a doll. I've always thought Emery looks like a fifties movie star, all voluptuous curves, scarlet lips, and attitude. She's standing behind the counter when I walk in.

She looks up and smiles. "Hi, Shay! Long time no see."

"I know, I've been so busy! It's good to see you. Holy shit... that *ring*." Stopping at the counter, I gape at the giant diamond sparkling on her finger.

She laughs. "It's ridiculous, isn't it? I hardly ever wear it out because I don't want to get mugged, but I'm having dinner with the in-law's tonight after work. My father-in-law is so old-fashioned, he'd probably think me going without my ring was a sign I wanted to divorce his son."

"You're married? Congratulations!"

Glancing down at her hand, she blushes. "Thank you. I have to admit, married life is pretty incredible."

I don't say it, but by the looks of that ring, her husband is extremely wealthy. And by the looks of that blush she's wearing, he's a stud to boot.

"I'm so happy for you. You deserve it."

"Thank you. How about you? Still with Chet?"

It's a testament to my good mood that the mention of his name doesn't upset me. I wait for the pang of heartache to come, but when it doesn't, I say a silent prayer of thanks to the gods of one-night stands and smile.

"No, Chet and I broke up."

"Oh, I'm so sorry. Are you okay?"

"You're sweet to ask, but I'm fine."

"Judging by that secretive smile, you're better than fine. Are you seeing someone new?"

I know she's not the kind of woman who'd look down on me for having a one-night stand, but I shake my head. For some reason, I want to keep Cole all to myself. I didn't tell Chelsea the details of my evening with him, either, an omission she most likely will never forgive me for.

Or stop trying to remedy.

"I'm happily single at the moment, but I do need a new book boyfriend. Do you have any suggestions for me?"

She grins and tosses her long dark hair over her shoulder. "Of course! Follow me."

Rounding the corner of the counter, she leads me over to the romance and erotica section where she starts pulling books from shelves.

"I know you like erotic thrillers. This one's a scorcher. A

widow starts getting letters from a guy in prison who says he knows her, but they've never met. There's a twist you *won't* see coming. And here's the latest release in that mafia series with all the hot Irishmen. Oh! Okay, I can't remember if you're into stalker romance, but this one's amazing."

I crinkle my nose. "I don't know if I could ever find a stalker sexy."

Eyes shining, Emery turns to me. Her laugh is low and mysterious. "Trust me, stalkers can be *incredibly* sexy."

When she laughs again, I get the feeling there's more to that comment than just a book recommendation. "Okay. If you say so. You haven't steered me wrong yet."

We spend a few more minutes chatting about books and getting up to date, then I happen to mention how I've been thinking of making a job change.

She stares at me for a beat, gears turning behind her eyes.

"You have an accounting degree, right?"

"Yes. Good memory."

"Do you have any experience working for a CFO?"

I shrug. "I report directly to the CFO in my position now."

For some strange reason, Emery is starting to look excited. "How about a big international firm? Ever worked for one of those?"

"The company I work for is on the Fortune Global 500. Why do you ask?"

"Because a customer of mine is looking for an assistant. He's the CFO at a multinational corporation."

"Really?"

"Yes, and I think you'd be perfect." Her tone brightens. "You're exactly the right combination of tough and experienced."

"The way you say that makes me think tough might be the more important requirement."

She hesitates, quirking her lips.

"Let me guess. This customer's a piece of work, isn't he?"

"He's been through four assistants this year alone."

"Yikes. Please tell me he's not handsy."

She looks shocked by the suggestion. "No! Oh God, no, nothing like that. He's very professional. But he's..."

I laugh at the way she's trying to find a nice way to say something bad. "He's a dick."

"I was going to say temperamental. Well, no, I don't want to make it sound like he goes around throwing tantrums. It's actually the opposite. He's controlled, but in a really intense way. Like it always seems as if he's about to blow up, but he never does. He's got this supercharged energy. Most people are extremely intimidated by him."

A brief but vivid memory of the way Cole stared at me from across the bar flashes into my mind's eye.

Talk about intense and intimidating. Mr. Dark and Stormy practically invented the words.

Smiling, I say, "Sometimes people who seem the most off-putting at first are actually the biggest softies once you get to know them."

"If you're interested, I can email you the job description to see if it might be a good fit for you. Their main office is located downtown."

"Oh, you don't have to go to the trouble. I can look it up on the company's website if you tell me the name."

"It's not listed on the website. They're using a recruiting firm to try to find a match this time."

"Ah. Because they'll have to replace the candidate at their expense if it doesn't work out."

"Exactly."

"Do you have any idea what salary they're offering?"

Emery names a figure so high, I think she's joking. I laugh, but when she doesn't crack a smile and only stares at me, I realize she's not.

"Seriously?"

"Yes. The position comes with amazing benefits too. Health

insurance, life insurance, 401(k) with matching contributions, lots of paid time off, all kinds of perks."

"It sounds like the only drawback is the person I'd be working for."

She waves a hand in the air, smiling like a model in an infomercial. "Who knows? Maybe you two will hit it off immediately."

Her fake smile doesn't fool me. "Uh-huh. Or maybe I'll want to throw myself out a window after a week."

After a beat, she says, "Yeah, that's more likely. But—and this is a big but—if you can make it through a year there, you'll be able to write your own ticket for a position in any other company."

"Why do you say that?"

This time, her smile is genuine. "Because everyone in the industry knows his reputation."

"Jesus. Who is this guy, Genghis Khan?"

Ignoring that, she says, "So what do you think? Should I email you the job details?"

"I don't know, Emery. I don't want to get myself into some kind of hostile working environment."

"Oh, he's not hostile!"

When I narrow my eyes at her, she relents. "Okay, he's hostile. But it's not personal. He's that way with everyone."

"This is sounding less and less appealing by the second."

"That salary is pretty appealing, though, isn't it?"

When I make a doubtful face, she keeps trying to convince me.

"I think the problem with the other people it didn't work out with was that they weren't prepared for his...forceful personality. But I'm telling you, so you can go into it with a different perspective."

"It sounds like you know this guy pretty well."

"I do."

"Would you work for him?"

"Oh God, no, I'd kill him before lunch on the first day."

"You're doing a terrible job selling this position."

She names the ridiculously high salary again, dangling it out there like a carrot.

"What company is this job with?"

"I can't tell you."

I lift my brows. "Why not?"

"They're very private. Which reminds me, you'd have to sign a nondisclosure agreement before going in for an interview. And if you got the job, there'd be another NDA."

"Are they the Mafia or something?"

She opens her mouth, then closes it. Then, very seriously, acting as if she's telling a big fat lie, she says, "No."

I burst out laughing. "Okay, now I'm intrigued."

Looking excited, she grabs my arm. "Does that mean you'll interview?"

"No, it means you can email me the job description. It probably won't be a match for what I'm looking for, anyway, but we'll start there."

We head to the register. Emery rings up my purchases while I write my email address on the back of one of her business cards. I give it to her, we say goodbye, and I head home.

By the time I get there, Emery has already sent me an email with the position's details.

I read it over, growing more surprised by the moment.

It's exactly what I'm looking for. The duties, the responsibilities, the growth potential...they're all a perfect fit for me.

Absolutely perfect.

And she wasn't kidding about the benefits package. It's so generous, it doesn't seem real. Combined with the astronomical salary—double my current pay—it's a temptation I can't resist.

I email her back saying I'd like to interview for the position.

Thus sealing the fate that first curled its dark tendrils around me the night of Chelsea's birthday.

CHAPTER 20
Cole

It's been four weeks since the night at the hotel with Shay. It feels like four lifetimes.

I haven't been able to get her out of my mind. She lurks in my thoughts all the time, always ready to distract me with a memory of her smile, her laugh, her moans.

Her loud, lusty moans as I fucked her.

The bar where she walked up to my table is the place I'd visit several times a week after work to decompress. I've avoided it since.

I know what would happen if I saw her again.

I'd take one look at those gorgeous green eyes, and my fate would be sealed.

So, to protect us both, I drink at a different bar now. I sit alone, people-watching, pretending I'm not secretly hoping she'll walk through the door.

It's a good thing I'll never see that woman again. I wouldn't be able to concentrate on anything else.

"Excuse me, Mr. McCord. Sally Hutchinson is on line one for you."

The voice of the receptionist whose name I can never remember comes through the intercom on the phone on my desk.

Irritated by the interruption, I jab my finger onto the speaker button. "Take a message. I don't have time to talk to her."

"I'm sorry, sir, but she insisted. She says it's urgent."

Sally Hutchinson is the executive headhunter my brother Callum hired to find me an assistant. What could be so fucking urgent? What constitutes a recruiting emergency? The pool of candidates willing to work for the notoriously grumpy Cole McCord suddenly shrunk from zero to minus one?

Irritation makes my tone hard. "I said take a message."

I can almost see the receptionist wilting in her chair when she responds, her voice going from merely hesitant to downright meek. "Um. It's about, um, the opening for your assistant? She says she found someone perfect."

Perfect? Sure. I almost laugh out loud. But as that's not something I do, I growl instead.

The receptionist whispers, "I'll take a message, sir," and hangs up.

If only people obeyed my orders without question, the world would be a much better place.

CHAPTER 21
Shay

The interview process is ridiculous.

And when I say ridiculous, I mean insane.

First, I meet with a junior recruiter at the executive search agency responsible for filling the position. I complete volumes of paperwork. I sign a nondisclosure agreement. I take a barrage of tests. Once those tasks are done, I sit through an hour-long interview.

That's round one.

Round two consists of another visit to the executive search firm's office, but this time I interview with a nervous senior recruiter who seems very concerned with my conflict resolution skills. Which basically translates to "In this job, you'll have to deal with dicks."

Or one dick in particular, my potential boss.

Round three is another interview a week later, this time with the owner of the firm, a harried woman named Sally Hutchinson who asks me in a dozen different ways how I handle pressure.

"How do you prevent a situation from getting too stressful to manage?"

"How would you respond if your manager gave you negative feedback in front of your co-workers?"

86

"Can you give me an example of a time you felt overwhelmed at work and what you did to solve it?"

Each time I answer, she peers at me doubtfully from behind her glasses. After a moment of silence, she asks the same question a new way.

She still doesn't reveal the name of the company I'll potentially be working for.

Or the name of her client.

What she does do is tell me she'll send my resume to Mr. Mystery Man for review. If I pass that final hurdle, I can have the job.

"I'll need to interview with him too, I assume?"

"No," says Sally, very solemnly.

"But how will we know if it's a good match? Personality wise, I mean."

Sally sits back in her chair and removes her glasses. "Ms. Sanders, I'll be frank with you. I've worked in this field for more than thirty years. For fifteen of those years, I've owned my own firm. And in that time, I have never had a client as challenging as the gentleman for whom you'd be working."

"Challenging," I repeat warily.

"Yes. He's very demanding. He expects perfection. And he's brusque to the point of rudeness."

I say drily, "Sounds like a real charmer."

"A charmer he is not. But he is a brilliant businessman, and you can learn much from him. If you can endure his personal shortcomings, that is."

Picturing a crazed man in a business suit throwing a screaming fit in the middle of a meeting, I grimace. "Does he throw things?"

"No."

"Does he verbally harass people? Call them names, that kind of thing?"

"No. If he were violent or subjected his employees to any kind of harassment, he wouldn't be a client of mine. But I have met him, and I can tell you that he gives the impression that internally, World War III has erupted, the troops are all deserting their posts, and chaos reigns."

Thinking of Cole, I smile. "I've met someone like that. And I really liked him."

Sally arches her overplucked brows. "Did you now."

It's not a question. It's a statement of disbelief. But something about the way I spoke must convince Sally that I'm a good match for her client, because a few days later, she calls and tells me the job is mine if I want it. Then she lays a bombshell on me.

"And if you can last ninety days, I'll give you a bonus of thirty thousand dollars."

"Wow. Why?"

"Because I get paid on commission. It's a percentage of your salary. A big percentage. But if you quit before ninety days, I don't get paid at all. What do you say?"

I think of the scarlet cashmere Balmain jacket I coveted. I think of the house I'm saving for. I think about all my bills and the interest rates on my credit cards.

And I say yes.

It's the first of many times I should've said no.

After signing another nondisclosure agreement, I finally learn the name of the corporation I'll be working for.

McCord Media.

To say I'm thrilled would be an understatement.

I'm ecstatic.

McCord Media is the largest private corporation in the world. They're considered one of the most successful and influential businesses on the planet. In addition to owning a media empire that consists of newspapers, television stations, cable networks, and a film studio, they're heavily invested in real estate all over the globe.

My new position is not only a giant step up for me in salary, it's a giant step up in prestige. Emery was right: if I can last a year there, I'll be able to write my own ticket for a position anywhere else. Winning the job is a huge boost for my career.

I give notice to my current employer. I send Emery and Sally thank-you notes and flower bouquets. I buy a few new work outfits and celebrate my luck with champagne.

It must be all the euphoria I feel over the money, the power, and the possibilities for growth that make me neglect to do the most important thing of all.

Ask the name of the CFO.

CHAPTER 22
Cole

I'm sitting behind my desk poring over the company's most recent financial statement when someone knocks tentatively on my closed office door. I speak without looking up.

"Go away."

Through the door comes the voice of the receptionist whose name I can never remember.

"Mr. McCord? Your new assistant is here."

Now I do look up, and I frown.

It's five minutes past the hour. This new assistant of mine is late.

"Shall I send her in, sir?"

So the person is a she. I never know the gender of the candidates Sally sends over because she replaces their names on their resumes with a number to avoid discrimination in hiring practices.

But I'd never discriminate based on something as arbitrary as gender. Or race, religion, age, appearance, sexual orientation, or disability for that matter. Or anything else.

The only thing that matters to me is competency.

Coming in a close second is punctuality. If you're supposed to

90

be somewhere at a certain time but you're not, you can't be trusted.

Period. End of story.

I make a mental note to call Sally later this afternoon and voice my displeasure that she'd send me such an untrustworthy candidate. Right after that, I'll tell Sally she's fired.

And so is the new hire.

I call out to the door, "I'm in the middle of something," then turn my attention back to my work.

That lasts for all of ten seconds, until I hear a sound that sizzles through me like a jolt of electricity.

A laugh.

A female laugh.

Her laugh.

But it can't be. No, I'm imagining it. There's no way the unforgettable green-eyed woman is in this building. She's not standing outside my door. She's a memory I've clung to for reasons I don't want to examine, and my imagination is playing tricks on me.

Just to be sure, I push back my chair, stride over to the door, and yank it open.

There beside the meek receptionist stands Shay.

That Shay. *My* Shay. The ghost who's been haunting me for weeks now stands there in the flesh.

She turns her head and meets my gaze, instantly electrocuting me.

And because my heart is pounding and the blood in my veins has turned to fire and my chest is being crushed by an invisible weight, I do the only thing I'm capable of doing other than pulling her into my arms.

I scowl at her and thunder, "What the hell are you doing here?"

The receptionist nearly faints in terror. Pale, shaking, and wide-eyed, she presses a hand over her mouth and shrinks back.

But if Shay is as surprised to see me as I am to see her, she doesn't show it. If she's taken aback by my question or the volume at which I asked it, she doesn't react. She merely looks me up and down and sends me a faint, derisive smile.

"I'm reporting for work...boss."

Never in the history of mankind has a sentence been spoken with such disdain.

It couldn't be more obvious that I'm the only one with fond memories of the night we shared together. Judging by her expression and tone of voice, Shay regards me in the same way she might regard a cockroach who wandered across her dinner plate.

With utter disgust.

Fuck.

The last time I felt this bad, I had a bullet lodged in my gut.

CHAPTER 23
Shay

I should've known this job was too good to be true. I should've known it was all a setup.

Life only gives me a big win right before it kicks me in the teeth.

The morning started great. Riding high on a wave of excitement, I gave myself plenty of time to drive downtown, park, and check in with security. A lovely woman from human resources named Ruth met me in the vast, sparkling lobby of the McCord Media building and accompanied me to the elevator that would take us to the executive suites on the twenty-ninth floor. I'd already filled out all the new-hire forms with Sally, so I assumed it was company protocol for Ruth to introduce herself to new employees on their first day.

It soon became apparent, however, that she had something else in mind.

The instant the elevator doors closed and we began to ascend, she turned to me with a serious face and an air of urgency.

"Sally told me that she informed you of the challenges you'll be facing in your position. Is that correct?"

She put enough special emphasis on the word "challenges"

that I understood she meant my new boss but was trying to be circumspect about it.

"Yes. I've been fully prepped. I'm ready."

Her smile was small and pitying. "That's like saying you're ready to be struck by lightning, dear, but no one is ever quite ready for that."

I didn't let her cryptic statement deter me. I simply smiled back and thought of the thirty thousand dollar bonus I'd be getting in three months. "Don't worry about me, Ruth. I can handle anything. I'm unflappable."

Her expression was grave and full of doubt.

"Seriously, I'll be fine. I've gotten enough details about the... position...that I feel mentally prepared to face anything."

"That's encouraging. But please know that if you ever need to discuss any problems you may have, my door is always open."

"Thank you. But I'm sure that won't be necessary. I've dealt with all kinds of stressful work situations. I know I can handle myself."

I could tell she wanted to pat me on the head and smile at my naïveté, but she restrained herself.

Her doubt made me even more determined to withstand whatever storms my new boss might send hurtling toward me with a grace and poise everyone could marvel at.

We exited the elevator at the top floor and entered a penthouse lobby with a water feature on one side and a reception desk on the other. The view of Los Angeles through the floor-to-ceiling windows was breathtaking. Ruth introduced me to the CFO's receptionist, a birdlike brunette named Marion who seemed to be teetering on the verge of a breakdown. Her nervous tics included constant hand wringing, eyes that darted left and right as if scanning for predators, and gnawing on her chapped lower lip.

I wanted to give her a hug, but feared it might make her scream in fright.

Ruth bade me farewell and left me with Marion, who had started to hyperventilate.

"Have you met Mr. McCord yet?" she whispered.

"Not yet. First day and all."

"Oh, I know it's your first day, I just thought this time they'd make sure to let the new hire see what you'd be up against—"

When she stopped abruptly and bit her lip, I found myself wondering if I'd accepted a job with a serial murderer.

The way everyone went on about this man!

"I've got a pretty clear picture. And believe me, if he does anything inappropriate, I'll report it to human resources right away. I'm not going to let anyone mess with me."

I squared my shoulders when I said that. I lifted my chin and squared my shoulders, and poor nervous Marion looked at me like I was the bravest person she'd ever met.

At that point, I'd been warned in one way or another by no less than four women that I was walking into a minefield with a blindfold on. Also, the security guard who checked me in downstairs lifted his brows and whistled under his breath when I told him who I was starting work for today. He shared a look with the other guard sitting beside him, and they both chuckled.

So it was with an iron-clad resolve that I approached the closed door of my new boss's office. Following Marion down the hallway, I told myself that no matter what I might encounter when that door at the end opened, I'd remain calm, cool, and collected.

I'd be ice.

I'd be stone.

I'd be as I promised Ruth—unflappable.

When we stopped in front of the door, Marion knocked. "Mr. McCord? Your new assistant is here. Shall I send her in, sir?"

From within the office came the sound of a deep and displeased male voice. "I'm in the middle of something."

Marion turned to me and tittered. "Probably giving himself that enema he needs so badly."

It was so unexpected, I had to laugh.

A moment later, the door was yanked open from the inside.

And there he stood. The man I enjoyed a scorching night of dirty, unforgettable sex with a month ago. Mr. Dark and Stormy himself.

Cole.

I thought I was going to faint.

But I managed to conceal my shock and restrain the cry of joy and disbelief that wanted to burst from my chest. I stood expressionless, all that determination I'd cemented on my way here acting as support for my gelatinous backbone and weak knees.

Then Cole stared at me with a look of such absolute horror, my shock turned to hurt.

"What the hell are *you* doing here?" he shouted.

He could not have made it more obvious that the sight of me was as pleasant as having his face smashed in with a brick. Also obvious was the fact that of the two of us, only I had fond memories of the evening we shared.

Judging by his expression and tone of voice, Cole thought I gave him an incurable venereal disease.

But because I promised Ruth and poor Marion standing next to me cowering in terror that I'd be fearless in the face of this idiot's wrath, I looked him up and down like he was wearing a suit made of dog turds and replied icily, "I'm reporting for work...boss."

He looked at me as if he were going to puke.

Then he slammed the door shut in our faces.

Pressing a trembling hand over her heart, Marion said, "I'm so sorry."

For her sake, I managed a smile. "Don't be. It's not your fault. Now, why don't you show me where my desk is so I can settle in?"

Marion's eyes widened. "You're staying?"

"Oh, I'm staying, all right. And when Mr. McCord decides he's done with his temper tantrum and shows his face, please tell him I said that if he treats me with such disrespect again, I'll file a complaint with HR. And if he retaliates for that and fires me, I'll sue him. Not only the corporation, but him personally too. Will you tell him that for me?"

Marion looked at me in awe and reverence, as if I'd become her new religion.

Meanwhile, I wondered what I'd done to so offend the universe that it kept sending me these butthole men.

CHAPTER 24
Cole

I stand with my arms braced against my closed office door and try to figure out what the fuck is happening inside my body.

It feels as if I'm about to die.

That isn't hyperbole. I've been close to death several times, and this is pretty much what it feels like. The only thing missing is a pool of blood.

I close my eyes and listen to the crash of my heartbeat. I concentrate on steadying my shaking hands. I visualize a tranquil meadow and draw deep breaths. When none of that works, I spend several minutes pacing the length of my office until I've finally pulled myself together.

When I open my office door, the hallway is empty. I don't know why I expected Shay to still be standing there.

Probably hope.

I stride down the corridor and approach the receptionist at her desk. She's on the phone. When she catches sight of my face, she seems to shrink several inches.

I stand beside her desk and stare down at her, impatience gnawing at me, until she hangs up. Then I demand, "Where is she?"

"Sh-she, sir?"

"The new hire."

"Oh, uh, she went downstairs, sir. I called Simone to show her around."

Unlike my father's and brother's assistants who share the floor with us, each office accessed by a different elevator, my executive assistant sits with other administrative and support staff on the floor below.

The fewer people I have near me, the better.

I'm walking away, headed to the elevator, when the receptionist says something that stops me dead in my tracks.

"Oh, Mr. McCord? Shay asked me to relay a message to you."

I turn, narrowing my eyes when I see how she's looking at me. Is that a *smirk*?

No, I must be imagining things. This woman—what the hell is her name?—doesn't smirk. She's too scared of me to smirk.

"What's the message?"

"She said to tell you that if you speak to her with such disrespect again, she'll file a complaint with human resources."

Heat crawls up my neck and settles in my ears, where it burns. When she adds, "And if you fire her in retaliation, she'll sue," the burn spreads to the rest of my face.

"Sue?" I hiss, livid.

"Yes, sir. Sue. Both the company...and you personally."

She really relished that last part. I can tell. Now I *know* she's smirking.

This is unprecedented.

Without responding, I turn on my heel and stride away, my jaw clenched and my hands balled to fists.

Is this a setup? Is Shay planning to try to blackmail me? Did she know who I was that night at the bar when she approached me? Was the connection I've been dreaming about for weeks all a lie?

What my father's always saying is right. We can't trust anyone. Not with the position our family is in. Not with our influence, our power, our fame.

Our money.

I take the elevator downstairs and burst through the doors the moment they open.

The floor is laid out in classic cubicle style, with a main thoroughfare between a maze of desks set behind chest-height blue dividers. The whole space buzzes with activity. Phones ring, keyboards clack, voices drone at a low murmur. For someone like me, who can't concentrate without silence and hates having too many people around, the environment is a nightmare.

If I had to work in here, I'd go nuts.

I spot Shay instantly.

On the far side of the room, in one of the small, glass-enclosed offices that line either side of the floor, she stands talking with two people. One is a tall, striking redhead I recognize as Simone, our accounting manager, who's been with the firm as long as I can remember. The other person is Dylan, a senior accountant, a man in his mid-thirties with a good head for numbers and an irritating habit of laughing too much.

In fact, he's laughing right now. So is Shay.

They're laughing together.

Dylan made Shay laugh.

Something dangerous gathers into storm inside me. Seeing red, I charge across the floor with my head lowered and my scowl in place, barely noticing as people leap out of my way.

CHAPTER 25
Shay

S imone is a sweetheart. I knew as soon as she introduced herself that she and I would get along well.

This Dylan person, on the other hand, is already on my last nerve, and I only just met him.

The word "smarmy" was invented for men like him. He's looked me up and down half a dozen times in our short conversation, staring at my breasts and practically salivating over my legs. He stands too close, talks too loudly, and wears too much cologne. My nose hairs are singed from it.

If all that wasn't bad enough, he's got a laugh like a hyena's.

Or a donkey having a tooth pulled.

Pushing aside the memory of the cute story Cole manufactured about how hideous my laugh was that night we laid naked together in the hotel bed, I laugh politely at the lame joke Dylan just made and glance at Simone.

I telegraph my discomfort, which she receives loud and clear.

Thank God for women's intuition.

"Dylan, I need to spend time with Shay now to discuss her workload and get her up to speed on our current projects. Would you excuse us, please?"

"Oh sure, sure, no problemo. Shay, it was great meeting you.

Welcome aboard. My office is right next door, so feel free to drop in anytime if you need anything."

Tearing his gaze from my breasts, he jerks his chin up and winks at me. "Or if you just want to say hi."

I wonder if I can ask to be relocated, but then I get distracted by the sight of Cole barreling through the office like a charging bull, his head lowered and his jaw clenched. Startled employees scatter out of his path like buckshot.

He's headed straight toward my office.

No doubt to subject me to more of his charm. Maybe he'll spit in my face this time instead of slamming a door in it.

I turn and give Dylan a tight smile. "I sure will, Dylan. Thank you so much. It's been a real treat meeting you."

When Dylan licks his lips and chuckles, I realize he thinks I just hit on him.

If only punching a co-worker in the nose on your first day on the job wasn't frowned upon.

Cole charges through the door. He stops short, nods curtly at Simone, then turns his attention to Dylan. The glare he produces is so evil, Dylan looks as if he's about to wet his pants.

"Oh, uh. Hi there, Mr. McCord. We, uh, we were just meeting your new assist—"

"Out," interrupts Cole with a snarl.

Dylan runs off like a scolded puppy. Simone isn't so easily intimidated, however. She clasps her hands at her waist and waits with her brows lifted until Cole turns his attention back to her.

He says gruffly, "Please excuse my manners, Simone. It's been a difficult morning. I'd like a word alone with Shay."

Simone glances at me, sending me a look I understand to mean that she's within shouting distance if I need someone to call 9-1-1. Then she withdraws, closing my office door behind her.

Cole's back faces the cubicle field, so he can't see what I see through the floor-to-ceiling glass walls: a sea of people gaping at us.

Great. What a way to make a first impression. Next maybe I can barf on someone's shoes.

My face red and my heart thudding, I stand my ground under the blistering stare Cole sends me.

His voice less controlled than when he spoke to Simone, he demands, "What the hell are you doing here?"

"I believe we already established that. I'm working." Just to dig the knife a little deeper, I add a sarcastic, "Sir."

It's the wrong thing to say for several reasons, but mainly because the vivid memory of me on my knees in the hotel room with his hard dick in my hand when he suggested I call him Sir for Chelsea's benefit now sits there between us, supercharging the air.

I can tell he's thinking of it, too, because he shifts his weight from foot to foot and growls. Then he snaps, "How?"

"How what?"

"How did you come to be working here?"

"The usual method."

"Which is?"

"I was hired."

Obviously annoyed by my short answers, he demands loudly, "How did you know it was me you'd be working for?"

"I didn't."

When he only stares at me in disbelieving silence, it dawns on me that he thinks I purposely took the job as his assistant to get close to him. Not only that, he thinks my reasons for that were nefarious.

"Wait," I say hotly. "Wait just a minute. I didn't know it was you I'd be working for, okay? Nobody told me your name."

"I find that extremely hard to believe."

"I don't care what you believe. It's the truth."

He folds his arms over his chest and stares down his nose at me.

What an asshole. If murder were legal, he'd already be dead.

"Whatever story you're concocting about why I'm here, it's BS."

"Sure it is."

Exasperated, I throw my hands in the air. "I heard about this position from a friend!"

"What friend? The same one who you're planning on splitting your settlement money with when you sue me for sexual harassment?"

I already knew he was thinking something bad about why I'm here, but I didn't know how bad. This takes the cake. "You think I set you up?"

When he doesn't say a word but only continues staring at me with that same look of disdain, I have my answer.

"You *do*. You think somehow I found out who you were, and I followed you into that bar and propositioned you that night, all the while planning to get hired as your assistant so I could turn around and sue the pants off you."

"Or blackmail me, yes."

Outraged by the suggestion, I gasp.

"Well, what are the odds, Shay? You and your friends just *happened* to be at that particular bar that night? And you just *happened* to decide you wanted to demand sex from me?"

"Demand? I did no such—"

"Then, out of the blue, you show up in my office, and the first thing out of your mouth is a threat to sue me?"

He glances down at my outfit. His eyes flare. His cheeks grow even more ruddy than they were before.

"*While wearing the blouse I bought you?*"

I wish I'd put this stupid Balmain blouse down the garbage disposal. It's the nicest thing I own, and I wanted to look my best today, and now I just wish I'd shoved it down the garbage disposal where I should also shove all my pleasant memories of the evening I spent with this jerk.

"I didn't threaten to sue you. I said I'd file a complaint with HR if you continued to treat me with disrespect."

"Followed by a threat to sue."

"Okay, fine, yes, but only if you fired me in retaliation.

Which, now that I've seen you in your native environment, seems exactly like something you'd do."

He tries to interrupt, but I raise my voice and talk over him. "I shouldn't have been surprised by your behavior because literally everyone warned me about it, but given that it was you standing in the doorway and not some stuffy old guy with dandruff on his shoulders and halitosis that could kill a camel like I imagined it would be, I was. So you'll have to forgive me for playing into your ridiculous farce of a self-serving story, but in no way did I scheme to get this job."

He steps closer, lowering his arms to his sides. Now we're only a few feet apart, glaring at each other.

"All right, Shay. Then tell me. What's the name of this friend you heard about the position from?"

I can tell he thinks this is a detail that will trip me up. He thinks I'll manufacture a name from thin air, which he'll then be able to disprove as a lie because the position was never posted publicly. Or I'll give him a name of someone inside the corporation who he thinks conspired with me to trap him into a settlement and split the proceeds.

So it's with great pride and a profound sense of satisfaction that I prove him wrong.

"Her name is Emery. She owns a bookstore in Venice called Lit Happens that I've been going to for years. She said you were a customer of hers, and she thought I might be a good fit for the job."

Cole's lips part. He blinks. Then he closes his eyes, exhales heavily, and mutters, "Fuck."

Not the reaction I was expecting. "What does that mean?"

"I'm not a customer of Emery's. She's my sister-in-law."

I notice in my peripheral vision that everyone out in the cubicle field is still staring in our direction, watching our little drama unfold. *Sure hope these glass walls are soundproof.*

"Sister-in-law?"

He opens his eyes and gazes at me, nodding. "Yes. She's married to my older brother, Callum."

"Why on earth would she tell me you were her customer?"

"I assume to protect me."

That hurts my feelings a little. Does she think I'm some kind of mercenary? "Why do you need protecting?"

He drags a hand through his hair and exhales heavily. "It's just our thing. Our family thing."

"That makes not one bit of sense to me."

He turns around and paces the length of the office with his hands propped on his hips. It's a small office, so he's turning around in seconds. He paces back toward me, then makes another turn and repeats the process.

I hate myself for noticing how handsome he is. How virile. How his dark hair curls over the back of the collar of his pale blue dress shirt. How the veins in his forearms stand out.

How great his ass looks in those black slacks he's wearing.

"We're very private," he says, talking as he walks. "We have to be. You can't imagine the targets we are for every kind of scumbag out there. Scammers. Bullshit artists." His voice drops. "Kidnappers."

Kidnappers?

I recall how secretive everyone was about this job, all the nondisclosure agreements I had to sign and the hoops I had to jump through because of the company's notorious dedication to privacy, and realize with a sinking feeling in my stomach that I understand what he's saying.

The McCords are billionaires. Of course everyone would want a piece of his family's money. Of his family's empire. Of *him.*

Emery was just being careful.

I mean, I've known her for a while, but it's not as if we're close friends. We've never gotten together socially. She had every right to be discreet. In her position, I probably would've done the same thing.

Unfortunately, this clarity causes the outrage to drain from me as if a plug has been pulled. I stand there wondering if one of us owes the other an apology, and quickly decide that if he goes first, I'll follow suit.

"Oh. I see."

He stops pacing. Studying my face, his gaze sharpens. "You see what?"

"Nothing."

His expression sours. He folds his arms over his chest and gazes down his nose at me, a habit that might get him castrated soon.

"It was just a figure of speech."

"No, it wasn't."

"Yes, it was."

"I know it's inconvenient for you, but I can tell when you're lying."

"Baloney."

"It's true."

"Oh yeah? How?"

"Your voice gets strange."

"No, it doesn't."

"Yes, it does. You start to sound a little like a dying donkey."

He says it with no change in his expression or tone, but I know it's an olive branch. That little reminder of our amazing night together is his playful way of saying oops, sorry I accused you of being a calculating, gold-digging whore, let's try to play nice.

But wait—it could be a trap. He could be trying to test me to see if I'll flirt with him. Does he still think I'm only here to shake him down?

Or is he being inappropriate? Is he hoping I'll be on my knees under his desk giving him weekly blowjobs, and this is his way of hinting at it?

God, this is confusing. I have no idea how to respond. Humor? Outrage? Disdain?

Painfully uncomfortable, I resolve that if he's going to be wily and impossible to pin down, I will too. I keep my voice and expression neutral, as if maybe I'm bored by this entire conversation.

"The donkey wasn't dying. It was getting its tooth pulled."

"No. It was dying."

"I think you're remembering it wrong."

"I'm remembering it perfectly."

"You sure?"

"I'm sure."

"What color was the Chihuahua?"

"The Chihuahua was hairless."

"What kind of animal did the raptor see in the bar?"

"A dove. And I didn't say raptor, I said predatory night bird. And it wasn't in a bar, it was in a clearing."

We stare at each other. Neither of us smiles. The room feels stuffy and too small. I have no idea if we're fighting or flirting. I've had root canals more pleasant than this.

"Predatory night bird? So you're an owl."

A faint look of disgust crosses his handsome face. "I'm not an owl."

"You sure? You kinda resemble an owl."

"In what way do I resemble an owl?"

"Lots of ways. Big unblinking eyes. Stocky body. No neck."

He narrows his eyes at me. I resist the urge to stick out my tongue.

Our stalemate is interrupted when someone knocks on the door. We turn to see a young man standing outside. He's tall, handsome, and looks a lot like Cole, except he's blond. Smiling broadly, he raises a hand and wiggles his fingers in greeting.

Cole walks to the door and opens it. I can tell by the new tension in his shoulders that he's irritated by this arrival. To the man standing outside, he says brusquely, "You're interrupting."

"Yeah, I can see that." He chuckles, then leans around Cole

and grins at me. "Hi there. I'm Carter, Cole's brother. I hear you're his new assistant."

"Hi, Carter. I'm Shay. And yes, I'm your brother's new assistant, but I'm not sure for how long."

Horrified, Carter looks at Cole. His tone turns accusing. "It's not even nine o'clock! What crap are you putting this poor girl through already?"

Cole turns and gives me a lethal look. I return it with a sweet smile.

At least one of the McCord brothers is on my side.

CHAPTER 26
Cole

As always, my little brother has impeccable fucking timing.

I turn away from Shay's smiling face and tell him to get lost. Then I slam shut the door and turn back to her again.

"That's a nasty habit of yours," she notes as the door rattles in its frame.

"It's one of many. What did you mean you're not sure how long you'll be my assistant?"

Her expression indicates she thinks I'm an absolute idiot. And an asshole to boot.

Through clenched teeth, I say, "What's that look?"

"I have no idea what you're talking about."

This woman. This stubborn, infuriating woman. Drawing a deep breath, I start to count to ten. I only make it to two before I snap. "I'm not going to fire you, if that's what you meant."

"Maybe that's not what I meant."

When I only stare at her with a growl rumbling through my chest, she relents.

"Okay, that's what I meant. Are you?"

"I just said I wasn't."

"I know, but I'm giving you a chance to change your mind."

110

"Why would I change my mind?"

She gives me her you're-an-idiot-and-an-asshole look again. I suspect it will become her signature expression. I'd take her over my knee and give her a spanking she'd remember forever, but the goddamn walls are made of glass.

And she works for me now. I can't spank an employee.

No matter how much I want to.

I cross the few steps from the door to where she's standing, lean close to her face, and speak in a low, deliberate voice while staring into her eyes. "I'm not firing you. Are you going to quit?"

All sass and defiance, she lifts her chin. "No."

"Good."

When she arches one perfect brow, I amend that to, "I mean, fine. If that's your decision."

"That's my decision."

"Fine."

"Good."

"So that's it, then."

"Yes."

"So get to work."

"I plan to."

"When?"

"The minute some reasonable person who doesn't think he's an owl shows me what the hell I'm supposed to be doing."

I want to spank her so goddamn bad, my palm itches. Nobody ever speaks to me with this kind of disrespect. With her tart, airy, fuck-you tone. *Nobody.*

I'm the fucking CFO!

Something in my expression makes her smile again. Which, of course, royally pisses me off.

"Let me make something perfectly clear, Shay—"

"Ms. Sanders."

"Pardon me?"

"I prefer that you call me Ms. Sanders. To keep things professional."

If I don't end up tearing all my hair out by the time I leave this office, it will be a fucking miracle.

Also, I really want to kiss her, which is problematic on many levels. Especially as "kiss" is a euphemism for bend her over the desk, tear off her panties, shove my hard cock inside her, and listen to her scream my name when she comes.

Her eyes widen. Her lashes flutter. She clears her throat and moistens her lips. "Why are you looking at me like that?"

So you're nervous now. Good.

My smile is evil. "You don't want to know. But here's something you should know. We have a strict policy in this company about workplace relationships. Particularly relationships between superiors and subordinates. They're not allowed. Period. Understood?"

"I'm well aware. I had to read through all the HR rules and sign off on them before I started." Feigning innocence, she adds, "Why would you mention that?"

What I say is "You know exactly why."

What I mean is *Because I need to see your reaction. I need to know if you've thought of me the way I've obsessively thought of you. I need to know if you've touched yourself while remembering that night the way I have. I need to know if it was more for you than casual sex.*

Most of all, I need to know if you want to do it again.

Because if the answer is yes, the rules be damned. I already know I'd break any rule to have her again. I'd break every rule there is just to taste her mouth one more time.

Her voice cool and her composure perfect, she says, "I assure you, Cole, I won't enter into a personal relationship with anyone at this corporation. *Especially* a superior. I would never risk my position here for something so trivial as that."

I can tell she means it. She wants nothing to do with me.

Fuck.

We stare each other down for one long, crackling moment of silence, until it feels as if the air will combust.

Then I drop my gaze to her luscious lips, imagining how they looked stretched around the head of my cock. My voice comes out throaty. "It's Mr. McCord."

Forcing myself to look away from her mouth, I meet her gaze. "Like you said, Ms. Sanders, let's keep things professional."

I walk to the door and pull it open, but before I walk out, I turn back, hardening my voice. "And from now on, I expect you to be on time."

She answers without missing a beat. "I will be. Thank you for stopping by, Mr. McCord."

Without a goodbye, I turn around and walk out, determined never to set foot in her office again.

CHAPTER 27
Shay

I watch him stride through the forest of cubicles toward the elevators until I'm reasonably sure he's not going to turn around and run back in to snarl some new unpleasantry at me. Then I walk around my desk, sink into the chair, and stare at the wall, stunned.

My hands shake. My heart pounds. I'm ninety percent sure my face is the color of a tomato.

But because I've got dozens of people staring in my direction through the glass walls, I can't throw myself facedown onto my desk and scream or start shouting obscenities as I normally might. I keep it together with sheer willpower until the urge to do something dramatic passes, which is conveniently when Simone shows up again.

She knocks softly on the doorframe. "May I come in?"

"Of course. I was just..." Dazed, I look around the office. "Um. Settling in."

She chuckles. Hands on her hips, she approaches my desk. "Letting the dust settle, more likely. You okay?"

"Yes."

"I only ask because you look like you could use a stiff drink."

I meet her amused gaze and shake my head. "Is he always so..."

"Bad-tempered? Yes. You get used to it after a while. If you last long enough, he'll start to treat you like a human."

I recall how he apologized to her for his manners when he first walked in and wonder how long they've worked together to get him to that point. Probably thirty years.

"He's not violent, if that's what you're wondering. And he's not verbally abusive. He's just very intense."

"So I've been told. But there's intense, then there's Cole McCord. His poor receptionist is terrified of him."

"Marion is terrified of her own shadow. She's a lovely girl, but a poor match for that position."

"Why did he hire her, then?"

Simone smiles. "He enjoys terrifying people."

"That's just mean."

She pulls up a chair and sits opposite me, crossing her legs and folding her hands on her lap. Wearing a lovely lavender skirt suit I recognize as vintage Chanel and a pair of beige Ferragamo pumps, she's classy from head to toe.

"Some people would rather be feared than loved. He's one of them."

"Again, mean."

"Or a defense mechanism."

I study her for a moment, understanding she's trying to give me insight into our boss without getting too specific about it.

"He doesn't terrify you, does he?"

She smiles. "Nor you. Which is why I think you have a good chance of lasting here."

At least for ninety days until I get that bonus.

Sighing, I push my hands through my hair and look around the office. "I guess you should show me where to get started. I have a feeling Mr. Dark and Stormy doesn't tolerate dawdling."

I freeze, horrified that my nickname for Cole slipped past my lips, but Simone chuckles.

"That's a good one. Most everyone around here calls him the Grinch."

I say drily, "A cynical grump born with a heart two sizes too small."

"So the movie described him." Simone grows serious, her smile fading. "But the thing about the Grinch was that his heart wasn't too small. He was just unbearably lonely."

Unbearably lonely.

I recall how Cole looked at me at the bar that night we met, how his eyes were filled with such naked longing. How we bonded over our shared misery about our recent breakups.

How I told him he wasn't a villain as he described himself, he was a hero, because only a hero would break his own heart to save someone else's.

Now I feel like an asshole.

A prideful, impatient asshole who should have taken a deep breath and maybe cut the guy some slack when he overreacted at seeing me standing in his office doorway.

Me, the girl he fucked to within an inch of her life a month before.

Me, the girl he ordered dinner *and* breakfast for because he wanted to make sure I didn't go hungry.

Me, the girl he spent who knows how much money on a couture blouse to replace the one he ruined.

Me. Shay Sanders. The girl who walked out of that hotel the morning after our night together feeling happier than I had in years.

Because of him.

The man who not even five minutes ago I compared to an owl.

Good God, I told the poor man he had no neck, and I'm sitting here feeling sorry for myself? He should've fired me on the spot for insolence.

Dismayed, I look at Simone. "I think I owe him an apology for how I acted just now."

"No, you don't."

"But you weren't here. You didn't hear how I spoke to him. How rude I was."

"Trust me, Shay, it's good for him. If you were really out of line, you wouldn't still be sitting behind that desk. But if I may give you a word of advice? Don't disrespect him in front of other employees. He can't bear to be belittled with an audience. But he can take as good as he gives one-on-one. And he needs strong people around him who aren't intimidated by his overbearing persona."

I notice she said persona instead of personality, indicating Cole's bearishness is a calculated choice. One meant to keep people at arm's length.

Then I remember I told him that his heart wasn't cold, it was warm, he just kept it on ice so it didn't get hurt, and I feel like an asshole all over again.

How could I see him so clearly in that hotel room but not in this office?

Maybe it has something to do with his magical dick. I haven't had it in weeks, and my vision got clouded.

I want to bang my head against the desk.

"Thank you for the advice, Simone. I won't forget it."

"Good. Now let's get to work."

For the next few hours as she introduces me to all the work my new job entails, I do my best to focus, but Cole simmers on the back burner of my mind, his angry eyes haunting me like ghosts.

CHAPTER 28
Cole

I spend the rest of the day locked in my office strategizing the Shay Avoidance Plan.

It works like this: move to Alaska.

Because no matter how I might try to convince myself that I'll only communicate with her via email, won't attend meetings where she'll be present, and turn the other way if we happen to cross paths in the building, the fact remains that I'll know she's nearby every day, and I'll want to go see her.

I can still smell her perfume.

Kill me.

We've established that she's not going to quit, nor will I fire her. So now, I've only got one path forward.

Pretend she doesn't exist.

Which will prove extremely fucking difficult considering *she's my goddamn assistant*.

Frustrated, I pull up her resume on my computer and glare at it until my vision blurs. Then, at a loss, I pick up the phone and call my sister-in-law.

"Lit Happens, how may I help you?"

"What do you know about Shay Sanders?"

Emery laughs. "Oh hi, Cole. It's nice to hear from you. Yes, I'm fine, thank you for asking. How are you?"

"I'm sorry, I can't do pleasantries right now."

"Shocking."

She laughs again, but it's affectionate. She's used to me by now. And if she can tolerate my psychopath brother, Callum, she can certainly handle my quirks. Compared to him, I'm almost sane.

"Shay Sanders. Tell me everything."

Her tone changes from light to worried. "Oh God. Please don't tell me there's a problem already."

Yes, the problem is that I fucked her before she started working for me, and I very much want to do it again and again and again, but we have an ironclad policy against it.

Also, inconveniently, she thinks I'm a dick.

But I can't say any of that. I also don't want to lie, so I sidestep. "She said that you told her I was your customer."

"When Callum mentioned he'd contacted a recruiter to fill your assistant position, he asked me if I might know anyone. I said I'd keep an eye out, but he stressed that I should be careful. I knew what that meant. Did she seem upset about it?"

No, but she did seem upset that I suggested she's a scheming, manipulative liar.

I feel the beginnings of a headache forming a band of tightness around my skull. Then I remember I didn't have lunch because I was too busy obsessing over Shay. Closing my eyes, I grasp my temples and squeeze.

"No. Why didn't I know you referred her?"

"I don't know. When she sent me flowers to thank me for recommending her for the position, I mentioned it to Callum. I assumed he would've told you."

He probably would have, but as I avoid him as much as I avoid everyone else, he didn't have much chance.

It's not as if we're close, anyway. I might be the chief financial officer, but he's the chief executive officer, and that means he thinks I'm beneath him.

Callum's the oldest, the golden child who can do no wrong in my parents' eyes. His ego is a steamroller, flattening everything in its path.

Carter's the baby. He's most like our mother, popular and outgoing, always the center of attention. He's a genius with people and charms them with ease, an incredibly annoying characteristic for those of us who don't share it.

I'm in the middle. Competitive. Risk-taking. Misunderstood.

"How long have you known her?"

A moment of silence follows as Emery thinks. "Three years maybe?"

"And what's your opinion of her?"

"She's great."

When I sigh, Emery says drily, "God, you sound so much like Callum when you do that."

I resolve to never sigh again. "I meant what can you tell me about her that might help me understand her better?"

There's another moment of silence, but this one's different. It's long and cavernous, as if she's stunned.

"*Understand her better?*"

"Don't bust my balls, please. Just answer the question."

"I will, but you'll have to give me a sec to recover."

Scowling, I demand, "Am I really so bad?"

"You're not bad at all."

"And you're a terrible liar."

"It's just that you give the general impression you'd rather go live on Mars than deal with humans, so I'm surprised to hear that you want to understand one of us better." After a beat, she adds quietly, "Oh."

"What?"

"You like her, don't you? You're attracted to her."

It's too bad my brother married someone this smart. I would've really enjoyed having a sister-in-law who couldn't see right through me. "I'm only trying to avoid having to hire my sixth assistant this year."

"Now who's the bad liar?"

"Can we please just have this conversation without you reading anything into it?"

She laughs. "Cole, I'm a woman."

"I don't even want to know what that means."

"It means estrogen gives us psychic powers."

"Then why don't you go pick the winning lottery numbers?"

"There's no need to be sarcastic."

"It's the only reasonable response when a smart person is being silly. Can we please get back to Shay? You're making my brain hurt."

I must sound desperate, because she takes pity on me.

"Okay. You want my opinion about her? Here it is. I think she's great. And before you get all huffy and puffy and impatient, let me continue. She's one of those people you feel comfortable with right away because she's real. There's no bullshit with her. She's not trying to impress you. She's confident, but not obnoxiously so. And she's obviously bright. But she also seems really kind, which is more important."

"Kind? She told me I remind her of an owl."

Emery snickers. "She's funny too. I forgot to mention that."

"Pretty sure she wasn't joking. What else? Does she have family? Siblings? Where's she from? What does she do on the weekends? What hobbies does she have? Does she have a pet? What about pet peeves? What makes her angry? What makes her happy? What makes her tick?"

After a beat, Emery says, "Cole?"

"What?"

"Take a deep breath."

I realize I've circled my desk half a dozen times, I've got the phone in a death grip, and my voice is too loud. So I take her advice and inhale deeply, closing my eyes.

"Now sit down."

"How do you know I'm standing?"

"Because you're a McCord. You men shout best on your feet."

That makes me smile, mainly because she's right. I sink into my chair and sit back, attempting to relax. "Okay. I'm sitting."

"Good. Now, all those questions you asked me? You need to ask her."

"I can't ask her. They're too personal."

"Which is exactly why she's the one who should answer them. It's called having a conversation. And don't tell me you're not good at that, because you're doing it right now."

When I only sit there brooding in silence, she takes pity on me again.

"Here's something I *can* tell you, though. And it will give you more insight into her personality than you think."

Her voice has turned intriguingly sly. I sit up in my chair, my pulse jumping. "What?"

"The name of her favorite book."

After a moment of consideration, I say, "You're a genius. What is it?"

"*Love in the Time of Cholera* by Gabriel García Márquez."

"I'll buy a copy. Why do you think she likes it so much?"

"I'll leave that to you to interpret. But I remember something she said about it that struck me as very insightful."

"What is it?"

"She said people think it's some sweeping, epic romance, but really it's about unrealistic expectations. It doesn't ask if the hero will get the girl—it asks if he should."

I say flatly, "I hate it already."

Her laugh is soft. "Well, well. I never thought I'd see the day."

"If you're about to say something about me being human, don't. Goodbye, Emery."

"Have a wonderful day, Cole."

She's still laughing when I hang up.

I decide I can't be useful any longer today because Shay has invaded my brain like swarming bacteria. Then I feel bad for making such an unflattering comparison. Then I feel ridiculous for feeling bad, which is when I shut down the computer and leave the office.

My receptionist's desk is empty. She either left for the day or quit. I check my watch. Six o'clock. So she probably didn't quit, although I wouldn't be surprised if that happened soon.

When I hired her, I confused her fear with respect. I thought she was just being deferential. Turns out, I scare the shit out of her.

Like most everyone else, except my new assistant, who has no problem telling me off right to my face. Or threatening to sue me if I continue to disrespect her.

I think about Shay the entire ride down the elevator to the parking garage.

I think about her on the drive home.

I think about her as I stand at my kitchen counter wolfing down beef stew right from the can.

I'm still thinking about her when I change into a fresh suit, grab the briefcase that contains my weapons, and head out into the night, on my way to make another person disappear.

CHAPTER 29
Shay

I survive my first week.

The job itself is demanding, partly because there's so much responsibility, and I have to juggle several high-level projects with hard deadlines, but also because my new boss is ready with sharp questions and an unquenchable drive for perfection.

No mistake is too small for his notice. I become obsessed with tiny details, checking numbers multiple times, double and triple verifying statements of accounts, reformatting spreadsheets until they're so streamlined and functional, they could've been designed by a team of Scandinavian architects.

If my work is without flaw, my reward is silence.

If he finds a mistake, even if it's something so small as an extra space between words in a report, he flags it and requests an immediate revision.

It's exhausting. It's also exhilarating. It becomes like a game, one I'm obsessed with winning.

We communicate only via email. His arrive at all hours of the day and night, as if he never takes breaks, even to sleep. We're both short and to the point, with zero hint of impropriety. Or humor, for that matter. The emails are as dry as bone.

If anyone else were to read them, they'd think we'd never met in person and had no desire to. They'd never imagine how loudly I moaned when he was deep inside me. How I called out his name and scratched my nails down his back.

How hard he made me come.

He doesn't visit my office again. He doesn't pick up the telephone to discuss issues. He simply shoots off curt emails, which I respond to immediately, always wondering what, if anything, he thinks of me.

I think of him constantly.

I relive our night at the hotel a thousand times in my head. I calculate the odds of meeting again the way we did, as boss and employee. I wonder what strange forces were at work to bring us together, going all the way back to the first time I set foot into Lit Happens, years ago.

At the end of the week, I realize I'm being silly.

If there's one thing my disastrous relationship with Chet taught me, it's that obsessing over a man is a waste of time. Especially a man who made his intentions clear by spelling out the company policy against superior-subordinate relationships right into my face.

As I'm getting ready to leave the office late Friday afternoon, I decide to put the obsessing behind me and move on with my life.

That lasts about five minutes, until someone knocks on my closed office door.

"Come in."

The door opens to reveal a smiling young guy dressed casually in khakis and a navy-blue polo with the company logo on the shoulder. He's holding a brown kraft envelope in his hands.

"Hi. Shay Sanders?"

"That's me."

"I'm Scotty from the mailroom. This is for you."

He crosses to my desk and holds the envelope out. Now I can see that it's an inter-office memo, with a grid on the outside to indicate who the contents are for and who they're from.

On the From section, printed in precise block letters in blue pen, are the words OFFICE OF THE CFO.

Surprised, I glance up at Scotty.

"If you need to return it, just call down for a pickup. We're here from six to six." He waves and walks out.

I unwind the string from the butterfly clasp holding the envelope's flap closed and pull out a single sheet of paper from within. On it is a note hand written on corporate letterhead.

> **MS. SANDERS,**
>
> **THANK YOU FOR YOUR DILIGENCE THIS WEEK. I APPRECIATE YOUR EXCELLENT WORK AND HOPE YOU'RE HAPPY IN THE POSITION.**
>
> **IF THERE'S ANYTHING YOU NEED, PLEASE DON'T HESITATE TO ASK ME FOR IT.**
>
> **YOURS,**
>
> **COLE MCCORD**

Flabbergasted, I sink into my desk chair and read the note over and over again, slowly shaking my head in disbelief.

Thank you? Appreciate? *Yours?*

Everything about the note is extraordinary, but the sign off is a mind fuck of colossal scope. Is it "Yours" as in a shortened version of yours truly, the professional, traditional sign off to a business communication? Or is the omission deliberate, meant to signify something more meaningful, as in...*I'm* yours?

He could've said "Sincerely." He could've said "Regards." He could've said "Fuck off into eternity, you devil-tongued harlot" but instead he said "Yours."

He started off with thanks, appreciation, and hopes for my happiness, which are astonishing enough. He followed that up with an offer to assist with anything I need, along with a please instead of his typical barked order.

He also said I should ask *him* for whatever I need.

Not Simone.

Not HR.

Him.

I look up and around, half expecting to see him lurking around a corner, laughing at my shock, having a joke at my expense. But it's half past five on a Friday, and the office is empty.

I stare at the letter again, but now I'm frowning. Why the hell would he send a hand-written letter in the first place? Is his email down? Is his phone broken? Did he want me to appreciate his penmanship? And I'm still tripping all over that mysterious "Yours."

What the hell is going on?

Grabbing a blank piece of paper from the printer, I dash off a letter in response.

Mr. McCord,

Thank you for your thoughtful note. I appreciate your concern, your feedback on my performance, and also your offer for assistance.
Please be assured I have everything I need, and the position is to my satisfaction.

Sincerely,
Ms. Sanders

Then I call the mailroom and tell them I have an inter-office communication for the executive suite that needs to be picked up immediately.

Scotty shows up five minutes later. He takes the envelope and tips it to me on the way out.

I sit at my desk, wondering if I should stay or leave. What's the protocol when you're waiting to hear back on a mysterious missive sent by the guy you fucked like you were possessed one night at a hotel before you knew he'd be your boss?

What's the time limit? Ten minutes? Ten years?

I don't have to wait long, however, because Scotty returns mere moments after he left bearing the brown kraft envelope and whistling. He sets it on the edge of my desk.

"Hi again! Last run of the day. Should I wait?"

"I'm not sure yet. Can you hold on a second?"

"Course. I'll be right outside. You let me know if you need me to take anything back up."

"Thanks, Scotty."

As he ambles out, I remove the sheet of paper from the envelope. This time, the note is much shorter. It's written on the back of the one I sent.

MS. SANDERS,

I'M GRATIFIED TO HEAR YOU'RE HAPPY IN THE POSITION. PLEASE NOTE, HOWEVER, THAT YOUR SIGNATURE IS INCORRECT.

My signature? What is he talking about?

When I turn the paper over and find out, I gasp in horror.

I didn't sign my name Ms. Sanders, as I thought I did.

I signed it Ms. McCord.

Because clearly, I'm the world's biggest idiot with a gold medal for achievement in self-sabotage.

Like a teacher marking a failing grade on a student's test, Cole circled the error in red pen. My embarrassment is a boiling cauldron filled with flesh-eating piranha that I dive into headfirst.

"Scotty?"

He pops his head around the corner of the door frame. "Yep?"

"I don't have anything to send back."

"Okay. Have a great weekend!"

I know my weekend won't be great, it will be filled with regret, self-criticism, and enough whiskey to drown ten grown men, but I smile anyway. "Thanks. You too."

The moment he's gone, I dig my cell phone from my purse and text Chelsea that I need to meet her for a drink somewhere as soon as possible.

Four seconds later, she texts back the name of a Mexican restaurant in West Hollywood I haven't heard of, along with a MapQuest link.

I tell her to order me a drink if she arrives first and run out the door.

CHAPTER 30
Cole

I t's pure chance that I see Shay getting into her car in the parking garage. As chance seems to enjoy meddling where she's concerned, I'm not entirely surprised, but I have to admit that it's me who takes over from there.

I follow at a safe distance behind her white Acura as it turns onto Wilshire Boulevard and drives west.

Do I know why I'm doing this? No.

Am I going to keep doing it? Yes.

I'm not superstitious, but somehow, it feels right to watch her navigate through rush-hour traffic. I don't know if she's on her way home or somewhere else, and I honestly don't care. All I want is a glimpse of her as she gets out of the car at her final destination. A glimpse of that hair, that figure, that confident walk.

Sincerely, Ms. McCord she wrote, officially driving the final nail into my coffin. I sat staring at that name written in her pretty, feminine handwriting and got hard.

Whether calculated ploy to fuck with my head or innocent accident, it had the same effect. The small but manageable obsession I'd been nursing exploded with a bang into a giant, rampaging lust monster.

I pictured her lying underneath me in my bed at my house wearing nothing but my ring and a hazy smile of satisfaction.

An impossible fantasy, but the lust monster didn't care. I sent a short note back to her, then locked myself in the toilet and jerked on my hard dick until I climaxed, groaning her name.

It's a good thing the executive suites have private bathrooms.

She makes a right turn onto Santa Monica Boulevard. I follow. She makes another right onto Robertson, then a sharp left into the parking lot of a building with a huge painting of a calavera wearing a sombrero on the side and a sign declaring *Margaritas!* in red neon lettering.

I cruise slowly past, watch her park and run inside through a side door, then make a quick U-turn and park in the alley behind the restaurant.

Entering through the kitchen, I walk past stainless steel baker's racks and bus boys up to their elbows in dirty dishes in soapy sinks until I enter the main part of the kitchen where the cooks are. It's busy, with at least six stoves operating at once and a dozen voices shouting over each other in Spanish.

Bypassing them, I find the manager's office and walk inside without knocking.

A big Mexican man in his early thirties wearing a sleeveless Dodgers T-shirt sits at a desk too small for him, sweating in front of a computer screen.

His muscular arms are inked shoulder to wrist. His thick neck is tatted with scenes from the Bible. Hidden underneath his shirt are more tattoos of his daughter's face, quotes from scripture, his former gang affiliation signs.

From the heavy gold chain around his neck dangles a crucifix.

He looks up at me and breaks into a grin.

"Lobo! *¿Como estas, cuate?*"

"I'm good, Emiliano. It's good to see you."

He stands. We embrace, clapping each other on the back. When he releases me, I poke him in the ribs. "I'm gonna have to start calling you *flaco* if you lose any more weight. What are you down to, two-fifty, two-sixty?"

He snorts in disgust. "Eh, my lady's got me on this diet, *ese*. Fuckin' sucks. She says I'll live longer. I say I'd rather die than eat the rabbit food she keeps puttin' in front of me. A man needs a steak!"

I remember Shay lying naked on the hotel bed the night we met saying to get her a steak when I asked her what she wanted for dinner. Then our exchange right after that.

"Anything green? Salad, veggies?"

"Blech. Green things are for rabbits. Do I look like a rabbit to you?"

No, she didn't look like a rabbit. Not then and not now. She looks like a sexy, smart-mouthed siren with soulful eyes and a body I want to sink my teeth, tongue, and dick into.

The lust monster inside me pounds on his chest and lets loose a primal scream.

Emiliano says, "You here on business or to eat?"

"Business. I need to see your security footage."

"Sure thing. From when?"

"Right now. The live feed inside the restaurant."

He doesn't question it. He simply takes his seat, turns to his computer, clicks around with his mouse for a minute, and pulls up the feed. The screen is divided into six sections, each showing an area of the restaurant inside and out. He clicks around a bit more, then I'm looking at the dining room.

I scan the screen, then tap on it, indicating a table at the front. "There."

Emiliano zooms in. The screen fills with an image of Shay and her blonde friend who she was with the night we met. They're leaning toward each other over a basket of tortilla chips, engrossed in conversation.

"Turn the sound up. I can't hear anything."

"Psh. Who do you think I am, Jason Bourne? I don't got sound on this."

"How many times do I have to tell you to get a better security system?"

"I got four pit bulls. They're good enough."

"Your dogs are as mean as hamsters."

"Yeah, but nobody knows that. They look real tough. So these girls we're lookin' at. Which one's yours?"

"It's not like that."

He turns to me with a cocked brow. "You said it was business."

"It is. But I'm not moving her."

He frowns. "She's not a move?"

"No."

"So, what? We're just pervs now? Peepin' on some chick you got the hots for?"

When I give him a hard look, he chuckles. "C'mon now. You know that face don't work with me."

"Which is why I keep trying."

"So what's the deal with the blonde?"

"It's not the blonde. It's the brunette."

Emiliano turns back to the screen. He zooms in closer, squints, and purses his lips.

"One negative word, and I'll call the county health inspector to shut you down."

He waves his hand at me as if swatting away a fly. "I wasn't gonna say nothin' bad about your girlfriend."

"She's not my girlfriend. She works for me."

He peers up at me with a look of doubt.

"I'm serious. She's my new assistant. Just started this week."

"And now you're following her?"

"Yes."

"You ever heard of stalking laws?"

"You ever heard of minding your own business?"

"Yeah. It's overrated. So this is what, like, a date for you? This is how you pick up women? You gonna go peep in her bedroom window next?"

"Don't be ridiculous."

"Hey, I'm not the homie spyin' on his fuckin' secretary. *That's* ridiculous."

"She's not my secretary. She's my assistant."

"You say that like it changes anything."

I'd sigh, but as I promised myself earlier I'd never do that again, I roll my eyes to the ceiling instead.

"Oh, hey now. Check out this *guero* movin' in on your lady friend. Looks like you got some competition."

Emiliano's amused voice draws my attention back to the computer screen.

A man stands at Shay's tableside, his back to the camera. He's medium height, medium build, and blond, hence the name Emiliano called him. He's wearing a white collared shirt rolled up his forearms and a pair of black dress slacks.

There's something vaguely familiar about him. I stare at his image until he turns his head to one side and I get a good look at his profile.

It's Dylan. The one who made Shay laugh the day she started working for me. The one whose office is right next to hers.

Is this some kind of date?

He pulls up a chair at the table with Shay and her friend. He sits down and helps himself to the basket of tortilla chips. Then he says something that makes both women laugh, and I have to physically restrain myself from tearing the monitor off Emiliano's desk and throwing it through the door into the kitchen.

Looking at my expression, Emiliano whistles.

"Okay, now *that's* a scary fuckin' face, *ese*." He makes the sign of the cross over his chest. "Damn. I'll say a prayer for *guero*. From the looks of you, he'll be meetin' his maker tonight."

I don't answer. I just stare at the screen, feeling blood flow hot and vicious through every vein in my body.

CHAPTER 31
Shay

I've only been sitting with Chelsea for about five minutes before I spot Dylan at the bar. We make brief eye contact before I look away, praying he won't come over to our table. Because God doesn't like me, he comes over to our table.

"Well, well, look who's here! Hiya, Shay."

"Hello, Dylan."

"Who's your pretty friend?"

Chelsea looks him over, assesses within a nanosecond that he doesn't have the right watch, shoes, or haircut for her financial requirements, and gives him one of her not-in-a-million-years-pal smiles.

"I'm Chelsea. Hi."

Not understanding that he's already been judged and determined lacking, Dylan grins at her. "Nice to meet you, Chelsea. Me and Shay work together."

She deadpans, "How thrilling."

I've done a decent job of avoiding him this week, but there have been a few memorable run-ins. On Tuesday, he caught me in the break room getting coffee and asked if I was married. When I said no, he said maybe he'd fix that soon while staring at my chest.

Wednesday had him running to catch the elevator I was on

while the doors were closing. We rode down to the parking garage together while he told dick jokes and I thought about reporting him to Ruth in human resources.

Then this morning, he casually leaned against the frame of my open office door and asked if I'd heard of the amazing new club downtown. When I said no, he went on to describe it in great detail. It became clear after only a few seconds that he was talking about a strip club.

"Incredible decor," he said. "I'm a big admirer of good interior decorating."

Which is like saying you subscribe to Playboy for the articles.

Now he's looking back and forth between me and Chelsea like he wants to be the meat in our cheese sandwich.

Uninvited, he drags a chair over from the table next to us and sits down.

"Okay, you don't have to ignore me so aggressively, ladies. You're starting to look desperate."

We laugh politely at his dumb joke and share a pained glance.

"So how's your first week working for the Grinch been, Shay?"

I'd rather gouge out my own eyeballs than tell this moron anything negative about Cole, so I smile brightly. "Wonderful. He's really great."

Dylan makes a face. "That's not the word I'd use. Cole McCord is an asshole."

I don't like Dylan using Cole's first name. It seems too familiar and disrespectful. More than that, I don't like him calling him an asshole. That's reserved for me, and I'd never say it aloud to someone else. Especially a co-worker.

Irritated, I wipe the smile off my face and stare at him coldly. He doesn't notice. He's too busy looking at Chelsea's cleavage.

"Cole?" she says, munching on a tortilla chip. "Why does that name sound familiar?"

I send her a meaningful look. She falls still, then her eyes widen. She mouths *No!*

Luckily, Dylan decides then to ask us if he can buy us a round of drinks. Wanting to get rid of him, I say no thanks and hope he'll go away, but Chelsea never misses the opportunity to take advantage of her pretty-girl-free-drinks privilege and says yes.

"Two skinny margaritas, please. You're a doll."

"Be right back, ladies."

He rises, puffs out his chest, and looks around to make sure everyone nearby sees he's got two women at his table as if we're his harem.

The moment he's gone, Chelsea leans forward and hisses, "Cole? *The* Cole?"

"The very same."

"What the fuck, bitch? How did you not tell me this before?"

"I only found out the day I started that he was my boss."

"You've been working there for a week already!"

"I know, but we haven't talked all week."

"You should've called me first thing Monday morning! You twat! I hate you!" Eyes shining with excitement, she leans closer and lowers her voice to a whisper. "Tell me everything."

I give her a brief overview of the situation, starting with Cole slamming his office door in my face and ending with me accidentally signing off as Ms. McCord on the inter-office memo. When I'm done, she slumps back into her chair and stares at me in amazement.

"What are the odds that you end up working for the same guy you had a one-night stand with?"

"Astronomical. I blame you for the whole thing."

She laughs. "And you're welcome."

"No, I'm not welcome. It's a disaster."

"Does anyone else know?"

"Nobody. I'm taking it to my grave."

"So I can only tell Angel and Jen."

"*Nobody*, Chelsea. This is too problematic."

"How is it problematic?"

"I fucked my boss!"

137

"So?"

"So it's unethical."

She scoffs. "It's not like it was intentional."

"Oh, it was intentional all right."

She grabs my wrist, gasping. "Wait, did you do it again?"

"No. And we won't because there's a strict company policy against it. Plus, I don't think we like each other."

"Who cares if you like each other? The man is smoking hot and left you walking on clouds! Get back on that baloney pony and ride it into the sunset!"

I shake my head in disbelief. "You're the epitome of romantic. Let go of my wrist."

She does, only to pick up another tortilla and chomp on it. Juicy gossip always makes her hungry.

Dylan returns with two margaritas and sets them on the table. "House specials, ladies. Drink up. I'll be right back. Gotta get my beer."

As soon as he's out of earshot, Chelsea starts in again. "I'm literally going to kill you for making me wait to hear this. How do you want to die?"

"Shut up."

"I know, I'll call up your hot boss and ask him if he could please fuck you to death." She makes a goofy face and mimics humping.

"What are you, twelve? Stop that."

"Listen, you know it's inevitable."

"What is?"

"You riding his dick again."

"Not gonna happen."

"It's totally gonna happen. There will be so much sexual tension in that office, you'll be bouncing off the walls."

"He works on a different floor. And he's been ignoring me. He doesn't want to do it again."

"Honey, that man bought you two meals and a Balmain blouse. Trust me on this. He wants to bone you."

"Who wants to bone you?"

Chelsea and I pull apart and look up in horror at Dylan, standing over us, holding a sweating bottle of Modelo.

He tilts his head in my direction and winks. "Were you two just talking about me?"

It's a good thing I haven't eaten anything yet. It would be all over his shirt.

"Haha." I grab the margarita and suck it down, wishing the ceiling would fall on his head.

He takes his seat again, makes himself comfortable, and launches into a rant about potholes, of all things. Apparently, he's on some minor local political committee tasked with surveying all the potholes on the west side. This makes him feel very important, as evidenced by how many times he says, "It's a really big deal."

Chelsea eats tortilla chips in polite silence and pretends to listen, while really she's counting down the minutes until her goodwill, purchased with margaritas, expires.

Judging by her glazed eyes, I think he's got about thirty seconds left.

"Wow, you really went through that drink! I'll get you another one."

Grinning one of his obnoxious grins at me, Dylan stands and heads back to the bar.

When he's gone, Chelsea groans. "Oh my God, that guy could euthanize animals with his personality. He should go work for a vet."

"That would be inhumane treatment. Let's order some food. My stomach's growling."

Not only is my stomach growling, my head feels weird. It's probably a side-effect of inhaling Dylan's cologne.

We flip through the menus the hostess left with us when we were seated and decide on two entrées we'll share because we always eat off each other's plate. Chelsea flags down the waitress, and we order.

Then, like a recurring rash, Dylan comes back. He holds out a fresh margarita to me with a flourish, as if it's a Christmas present he spent all winter making.

"Thank you."

"You're so welcome."

He takes his chair and watches me as I'm taking a sip. His grin is gone now, and his energy is different. More intense.

"You're really hot. But you already know that. I can tell by the way you strut around the office with your nose in the air."

Chelsea snorts. "Slow down, tiger. You can't pour on the charm all at once, she'll faint."

I set the drink on the table and turn to him with my brows lifted and a challenge in my voice. "*Excuse* me?"

Proving himself the charmless dirtbag he is, he doesn't back down or try to pretend he was joking. He only shrugs, as if I'm lucky to be the recipient of his attention, and doubles down.

"It was a compliment."

"Sure didn't sound like one."

"I like confident women."

"Seems like what you like is to tear them down."

He looks straight into my eyes and smiles. "Or tear off their clothes."

Warmth blooms over my chest. I'd say it was anger, but I'm also slightly dizzy, and my stomach has turned sour. I look away from Dylan and focus on Chelsea.

She has a strange, fuzzy halo around her head.

She frowns at me. "You okay?"

"I think I need to go to the restroom. I'll be right back."

I stand, surprised to find I need to hold onto the table for support as I rise. My legs are shaky, and my heart's beating too fast. Making my way slowly across the restaurant, I try to remember what I had for breakfast and lunch. I must've eaten something bad.

I make it to the ladies room, turn on the spigot at the sink, and splash cold water on my face. My reflection in the mirror looks dazed. My color is awful. Even though I'm roasting hot, my complexion is gray.

I shut off the water and lean against the sink. Closing my eyes, I inhale a few deep breaths. It doesn't help. The pulsing ranchera music piped through the ceiling speakers is making my dizziness worse.

Drying my face with a paper towel, I fight to stay steady. On my way out the door, I stumble and wind up banging into the wall.

I stand there for a few moments in the dim corridor by an old, inoperable pay phone, sweating and hyperventilating, wondering what the hell is happening to me. I feel as if I've had ten shots of tequila.

Closing my eyes again, I swallow down the hot bile rising in the back of my throat.

"There you are. You all right, Shay? Here, let me help you."

The voice is Dylan's. Smooth and low, it comes to me as if from very far away. A strong hand curls around my upper arm and squeezes.

"I'm okay, really. I just need...I need..." I don't know what I need. I can't think. My brain isn't working right.

"You should probably go home and get to bed. You look really sick."

When I open my eyes, my vision is blurry. I try to push off the wall, but don't have the strength.

My lack of strength soon doesn't matter because Dylan peels me off the wall and starts to lead me in the opposite direction down the corridor from where I came, toward an exit door at the end.

"Wait. Hold on. Dylan, get Chelsea. I need Chelsea."

He winds his arm around my shoulders and propels me forward, shushing me when I make a small cry of distress. I stumble again, losing my balance, but he catches me, grabbing me roughly and pulling me against his chest.

"Only a few more steps," he coos into my ear. "We'll get you home safe and sound, Shay. My car is right outside. I'll take you there."

Why can't I feel my legs?

It's the last thought I have before my vision goes black, and I fall forward into nothingness.

CHAPTER 32
Cole

Staring at the video feed of Chelsea sitting alone at the table in the dining room, I check my watch again.

"What's taking so long?"

Emiliano shrugs. "Women take forever to piss."

"Only when they go to the bathroom together. Why don't you have a fucking security camera in the back hallway?"

"I do. It's out."

"Jesus Christ."

"What, you think I'm made of dough, *ese*? That shit don't grow on trees."

"You sound like my father. I'm buying you a new security system next week."

He chuckles. "Could use a new truck while you're at it."

I mutter, "Why don't you throw in a boat?"

"You can get me that for my birthday. I'll send you the link to the one I want. It's got purple lights underneath that make it glow in the water. *Esta bien chido*."

Aggravated that Shay hasn't reappeared on camera, I check my watch again. "What other angles do you have? Can we see from the other direction?"

He clicks around a few times, bringing up different views of the main dining room, the bar, and the entrance.

"Wait, go back to the bar. Yes, there. Stop."

I scan the crowd at the bar, but Dylan isn't among them. He got up a minute or so after Shay left the table, and I assumed he went back to the bar for more drinks. But he's not there, and he's not at the table either.

A familiar feeling raises the hair on the back of my neck.

It's a heightening of all my senses at once. A sharpening. My surroundings come into brighter focus, my breath quickens, and all my muscles tense.

Shay might be talking with Dylan in the back. She could be flirting with him, or simply chatting about work. I have no way of knowing if they arranged to meet here for drinks, which is the most likely scenario given that they work right next to each other and have probably bonded over a mutual dislike of me.

But an animal that always slumbers beneath my skin has blinked open its eyes, sniffed the air, and started to growl.

When I speak, my voice is low and tense. "Show me the entry to the hallway again."

He clicks to the view of a dark rectangle flanked by potted palms. The lighting is bad down the corridor that leads to the restrooms, but it's enough to show that Shay isn't on her way out.

"Show me the parking lot."

"You think she ditched her friend?"

"No."

He shoots me a glance, examines my expression, then changes the image on the screen to show the restaurant's parking lot.

Stumbling over her own feet, Shay clings to Dylan as he drags her across the asphalt toward a blue sedan parked near the back.

I'm out the door before Emiliano can even blink.

I charge through the kitchen, burst out the door I came in through, bolt around the side of the building to the parking lot, then sprint at top speed toward the blue sedan.

Dylan has the back passenger door open. He's trying to force

Shay inside with one hand on the top of her head as he pushes her to a sitting position.

"Hey!"

Dylan looks up and around. Spotting me, he freezes. I skid to a stop two feet away from him and get into his face, breathing hard.

"Hi. Going somewhere?"

He swallows and glances down at Shay. "Oh hi, Mr. McCord. Uh, yeah, we were just...just leaving."

I look at Shay. She's sitting upright on the back seat with her eyes open, but she's totally out of it. Damp tendrils of hair cling to her forehead and neck. Her breathing is rapid and shallow. Her pupils are dilated, and her head lists to one side as if it's too heavy for her to hold up.

I've seen this before. Too many times to count.

When I look back at Dylan, a snarl of fury rumbling through my chest, he turns white.

"She asked me to take her home. She's sick! Look at her!"

"Oh, I fucking know she's sick, my friend. But you're not taking her anywhere."

Fear plain on his face, his gaze darts between me and Shay. I see the wheels turning behind his eyes, excuses and lies tripping all over each other on their way out of his mouth.

"Sh-she really had a lot to drink. I was just trying to be a good friend. I just wanted to help."

"One more fucking word, and I'll rip your tongue out of your mouth. Move."

I shove him so hard, he falls on his ass. As I pull Shay gently from the car, he scrambles to his feet, then runs to the front of the car and crouches there, shaking.

Shay mumbles something incoherent as I gather her into my arms. "Come on, sweetheart. I've got you. Lean into me."

I carry her quickly across the lot to the restaurant. Her head lolls back. Her eyes slide closed. She's boneless in my arms, like a ragdoll.

Fuck.

Kicking the door open, I carry her inside and back to Emiliano's office. He's already on his feet, spreading a blanket over the battered leather sofa against the wall.

"What do we got?"

"Spiked."

"Doc?"

"Yes. Tell him to hurry."

He pulls his cell from his pocket and jabs his thick finger onto the screen, dialing a pre-programmed number with one touch. As I lower Shay to the sofa, he speaks a few quiet words into the phone in Spanish. Then he hangs up.

"Here in fifteen."

My relief is instant. Considering it's a Friday night, traffic is worse than usual. The ten-mile drive to the beach from here could take an hour. "That's fast."

"Got lucky. He was on his way to see the Lakers at Staples Center."

"They don't call it that anymore."

"Fuck if I'm callin' it Crypto-dot-com center. That's fuckin' stupid. Need a bucket?"

"Yes. Then go get her friend."

He turns, pulls a waste basket out from under his desk, and sets it on the floor next to the sofa. Then he leaves, closing the door behind him.

"Shay. Sweetheart, open your eyes. Can you hear me?'

She mumbles something about her head.

"I know, sweetheart. I'm going to help you with your head, okay? Let me roll you over a little bit."

Careful to support her neck, I roll her to her side, adjusting her head on the cushion. Then I slide the bucket in range and gently grasp her jaw.

"You have to throw up now, baby. You understand? We have to get the bad stuff out of your system."

"Bad stuff," she whispers, her voice faint and scratchy. "'Kay."

I'm encouraged that she's responsive. Being as gentle as I can, I open her mouth and stick my finger all the way in.

She jerks and retches, grimacing.

"I know, baby. Do it for me. You can do it."

Hating myself for hurting her but knowing it's necessary, I shove my finger deeper.

This time, she heaves, makes a sound like she's dying, and throws up. I pull my hand away and hold the basket in place as she vomits into it, coughing and spitting.

I focus on holding her steady as she continues to retch until there's nothing left to come up. Then she collapses back against the sofa, groaning.

I pull off my suit jacket, use it to wipe off my hand, and toss it aside. Holding her wrist, I take her pulse. It's fast and weak, but steady.

I go into the small bathroom attached to the office, wash my hands, and wet a hand towel. I use it to clean Shay's face.

As I'm wiping off her chin, her lashes flutter. She opens her eyes and whispers my name.

"Yes, sweetheart?"

She mumbles something about riding a pony. I have no idea what she's talking about, so I smooth my hand over her damp forehead and hope the doctor isn't delayed.

Emiliano returns with the blonde in tow. The second she spots Shay on the sofa, she drops her handbag on the floor and rushes over, pushing me aside as she sinks to her knees.

"What happened?"

"Her drink was spiked."

She lifts one of Shay's eyelids and examines her pupil. She takes her pulse at the vein in her neck. She adjusts the collar of Shay's blouse, then kisses her forehead. Then she stands and turns to me with a thousand suns exploding into supernovas of hatred in her eyes.

"If you did this to her, I'll lock you inside your house, set it on fire, and watch you burn. And that's not a threat, motherfucker. That's a promise."

Emiliano and I share a glance. I can tell he's as impressed as I am.

"I'd never hurt her, Chelsea."

If she's surprised I know her name, she doesn't show it. She just stands there staring at me like some bloodthirsty Viking queen about to launch a war.

"Emiliano, check out the security feed for the last hour at the bar. Keep your eye on *guero*."

"Sure thing." He sits at the desk and starts clicking around on his computer.

Chelsea is still staring bloody murder at me. She shows no signs of panic or fear, or any of the other stress reactions people usually exhibit in these kind of situations. I think if she had a sword in her hand, I'd already be decapitated.

I say gently, "It wasn't me. I'm her boss—"

"I know who you are," she cuts in. "I remember you."

"I remember you too. Shay called you a dangerous creature."

"That's because she knows what I'm capable of. And let me tell you, boss man, if me, you, and big *papi* over there get into it, I'm the only one who walks out of this office alive."

Chuckling, Emiliano says, "I'm really starting to like this girl." Me too.

I hold up my hands in surrender. "I hear you. Okay? We're good."

After a moment of narrow-eyed doubt, Chelsea decides she'll let me live for a moment longer.

"Walk me through what happened. She left the table to go to the bathroom. Ten minutes later, big *papi* comes to get me and brings me back here. She's passed out on the sofa, and you're hovering over her like some psycho who wants to make a suit out of her skin."

Emiliano chuckles again.

Ignoring him, I tell her everything that occurred since I came in the restaurant. When I'm done, she folds her arms over her chest and gives me a slow, calculated once-over.

"You watched us on the security cameras."

The way she says it sounds really bad. Emiliano thinks so too, because he throws me an I-told-you-so look over his shoulder.

"Yes."

"So you followed her here from work."

Jesus, she's sharp. I should hire her.

"Yes."

"Why?"

"Because I saw her getting into her car in the parking garage. Because I wanted to know where she was going. Because I couldn't help myself."

She steps closer, demanding, "And because what else?"

"Because I haven't stopped thinking about her since we met."

"You like her?"

"I more than like her."

She searches my face with the unblinking focus of a hawk in a tree searching for mice in the bushes. I let her look. I don't have anything to hide.

At least where Shay is concerned.

Into our standoff, Emiliano says, "Got it. That *pinche puto*."

Chelsea and I turn to see a slow-mo image on his screen of Dylan taking a tiny vial from the pocket of his slacks. He hides it in his palm. When the bartender sets two drinks in front of him, he passes his hand over one of them, tips it quickly, then picks up both drinks and turns away.

Emiliano huffs. "*Guedo*'s done that before. He's good at it."

Watching the screen with glittering eyes, Chelsea says softly, "That wasn't GHB or Rohypnol. It worked too fast. I'm thinking ketamine."

I agree, but I'm interested in how she knows. "You in law enforcement?"

"I'm an ER nurse."

That explains the battle-hardened nerves. "I've got a doctor on the way to take a look at her."

"You have a doctor coming *here*? No, she needs to get to the hospital."

"If she goes to the hospital, they'll test her for drugs."

"Exactly."

"There will be a police report."

"That's what we want!"

"No, it isn't. Let me tell you why."

With thinned lips and flared nostrils, Chelsea stares at me for a beat. She glances at Shay lying quietly on the sofa, then looks warily back at me.

"I'm listening."

"Dylan passed an extensive background check when he was hired. It's a process everyone goes through. If HR discovers any hint of impropriety in your history, you don't get the job. I'm talking criminal convictions, but also arrests that don't result in a conviction. Charges that were brought but dropped. Lawsuits. Settlements. Liens. Credit. References. Education. Social media profiles. Everything."

"What's your point?"

"He's squeaky clean."

"He's a scumbag! You saw that tape! We'll give it to the police and get him thrown in jail!"

"Maybe. Maybe not. He has no priors. No criminal history of any kind. He's a smooth-talking Caucasian male with a sympathetic face. The court system is historically lenient on people like him. And he can afford to hire a very good attorney. Best case scenario, he gets sentenced to a few years but probably doesn't spend any time in prison."

She mulls it over silently for a moment. "Community service, not conviction."

"Yes. Which means he's free to do it again."

She turns away, props her hands on her hips and stares silently down at Shay on the sofa. Then she turns back to me.

"I assume you have an alternative."

"Yes."

"Which is?"

"I'll take care of him."

She scoffs. "What, you'll demote him to the mail room?"

"No. That isn't what I mean."

"Then what do you mean?"

I gaze at her steadily but remain silent.

She lifts her brows and looks at Emiliano. "Is he serious?"

"As a heart attack, *mami*."

She reassesses me, looking me up and down. Then she folds her arms over her chest again and cocks her head. "You'll take care of him."

"You heard what I said."

"How will I know? Will it be on the news? Local Business Mogul Buries Scumbag in the Desert?"

"It won't be on the news. And it won't be in the desert."

After a moment, she laughs. "You're joking."

"You know I'm not. But if it helps you feel better, you're welcome to think that."

When she only stands there staring at me in disbelieving silence, I say, "Let me ask you a question, Chelsea. How many girls have you seen pass through your ER in Shay's condition?"

"You know the answer to that."

"And how many rape victims? Assault victims? Domestic violence victims?"

Her jaw works. She swallows. Her voice comes out low. "You know the answer to that too."

"And how many of the men who abused all those women got the punishment they deserve?"

"A few."

"Too few. Most of them walk, and the abuse escalates until somebody's dead."

Anger flashes in her eyes. Her voice rises. "So what? You're some kind of billionaire vigilante who crunches numbers during the day and fights crime by night?"

"I don't fight crime. I solve problems."

She throws her hands in the air. "Oh, for God's sake, this is ridiculous." She turns to Emiliano. "Are you listening to this lunatic?"

He turns in his chair and gazes at her, thoughtfully turning his gold crucifix over in his fingers. "Not everybody who does bad things looks like a bad person. Same as not everybody who looks good is good. Nothin's black or white. Whole world's just shades of gray, *mami*. We're all on the spectrum."

She says flatly, "Great. I've got a nutjob rich dude on one hand and a gangster philosopher on the other."

"Former gangster. But look at you, for example. *Eres muy bonita*, like a Barbie doll, pretty smile and perfect hair. But you got some claws on you, don't you? Under all that pretty there's a savage little beast who'd slit a man's throat for hurting her friend and sleep just fine at night after."

She slowly turns and looks at Shay. A strange look crosses her face. "I might not sleep fine. But I'd sleep."

Emiliano's cell rings. He answers it, listens, then disconnects. "Doc's here. Should I send him in?"

Chelsea and I look at each other.

"It's up to you."

"If I say no?"

"We take her to the hospital."

She stares at me for a long time, then exhales and nods. "Okay, boss man. We'll do this your way. But if her condition worsens, she goes straight to the ER."

"Agreed."

Sitting next to Shay on the sofa, she rubs her arm gently. I motion for Emiliano to bring the doctor in. He leaves the office, closing the door behind him.

Her attention still on Shay, Chelsea speaks in a low voice.

"My little sister had a Dylan once. In college. Mr. Popularity, everyone thought he was so great." She pauses to brush a strand of hair off Shay's pale cheek. "But she didn't have someone like you to look after her. She woke up the next morning bleeding, covered in bruises, with only a vague memory of the night before. Thank God she couldn't remember everything. With the condition she was in, he brutalized her in ways she didn't want to know."

Her voice drops even further. "Of course, no one believed it wasn't consensual. She was the bookish little scholarship girl. He was the star athlete. He wouldn't have to force himself on someone like her, right? He could have his choice of girls. But the thing with guys like him and Dylan is that they don't like choice. They like force. They don't give options, they take them away, and they get off on it. So whatever you plan on doing to that piece of shit Dylan..."

She turns to look at me. Her eyes glitter with unshed tears.

"Make it hurt."

"I will. I promise."

"Good."

After a moment, I say, "How's your sister now? Did she make a full recovery?"

"Ashley killed herself on the anniversary of the assault."

"Oh fuck. I'm so sorry."

"Me too. She was eighteen years old. A kid. He stole her innocence, he stole her reputation, then he stole her whole life. Her whole future. And he walked. He's married now. Has two girls of his own."

She turns back to Shay. She takes her limp hand and tenderly squeezes it. Her voice hardens. "I'll wait until they're grown to pay him a visit."

Silent, watchful, and moved, I stay until the doctor arrives and says Shay will recover in a few hours.

Then I head back to the office to look up Dylan's address.

CHAPTER 33
Shay

I wake up in bed in my room with a throbbing headache and a vague sense of doom hanging over me like thunderclouds.

It's morning. Sunlight streams through the windows. Birds chirp in the tree outside. My mouth tastes like the final resting place of a dead rodent.

"Hey, sleepyhead."

Chelsea sits in the overstuffed chair next to my dresser. Her feet are bare. Her legs are tucked up beneath her. She has dark circles under her eyes, her lids are heavy with fatigue, and her shirt is wrinkled.

"Hey. What are you doing in that chair?"

"I slept here."

"Why?"

She studies me for a moment. "What do you remember about last night?"

"Last night?" I furrow my brow, trying to remember. "I left work around six, I think. Got in the car and drove..."

I wait for it to come, but there's nothing. My mind is blank.

Panic sets in.

I sit up too fast, and the room starts to spin. "Shit. Oh God. I

154

feel awful. Did we go out? Did I have too much to drink? I can't remember anything."

Chelsea unfolds her legs and crosses to the bed. She sits on the edge of the mattress and squeezes my hand. This is when I realize I'm still dressed in the clothes I was wearing yesterday at work, and my panic spikes.

"You're okay," she says, her voice soothing. "You're safe now."

"The way you say that makes me really nervous. What happened?"

A floorboard creaks.

Cole appears in my bedroom doorway, looking serious and disheveled. His jaw is shadowed with scruff, his shirt is stained, and his hair is a mess. He looks as if he's been rolling around in the woods fighting bears.

He's never looked more handsome.

My mouth goes dry from fear.

"Why are you here? Did I do something wrong? Was there an accident? Why can't I remember anything?"

Chelsea stands, leans over and kisses me on the forehead, then straightens.

"Cole will explain. I'm going home to get some sleep. Call me if you need me. And remember that I love you, no matter what."

She turns and walks away, stopping briefly to share a wordless look with Cole. He rests his hand on her shoulder for a moment, then she walks out, leaving me confused and hyperventilating.

He takes the chair Chelsea vacated. He leans over, rests his forearms on his knees, clasps his hands together, and gazes silently at me.

Terror makes my voice high. "Oh my God, did I kill somebody or what?"

"No. You didn't do anything wrong."

Relief floods me. My frantic heartbeat slows. Then I notice a few more details about Cole's appearance, and it surges again. "Why are your knuckles all scraped up? Is that *blood* on your shirt?"

"Look at me."

When I meet his gaze, his eyes are dark. So dark, they look more black than blue.

"You met Chelsea at a Mexican restaurant after work last night. You drank a margarita that had been spiked with drugs."

"*Drugs?* Oh God."

"Take some deep breaths. You're hyperventilating."

I do as he orders, sitting there with my head pounding and my heart throbbing and a sick feeling saturating every part of me. "Someone drugged me? Who would do that?"

"Dylan."

I'm not sure I heard him right. "Dylan from the office Dylan?"

"Yes."

"How do you know?"

"Security cameras recorded it."

When he doesn't offer more, I go from feeling sick to feeling stabby. "I'm sorry, you're going to have to tell me more than five words at a time. Tell me the whole story, start to finish, and don't leave anything out."

He doesn't move a muscle or change his tone. He gazes straight at me as he speaks.

"All right. Keep breathing. I saw you get into your car when you were leaving the office and decided to follow you. I did that because I've been obsessing over you since the night we spent together, and it got worse this past week. Then you signed the memo with my last name instead of yours, and I lost my mind. I tailed you in my car, and when you went inside the restaurant, I followed you in there too. I know the owner. He's an old friend. We work together sometimes. I asked him to let me watch you on his security cameras. I want you to know that he didn't like that idea, he didn't approve, and he was right, but I made him do it anyway. I wanted to see you. I *needed* to see you, to see what you were doing and who you were with."

He pauses. "You're not breathing, Shay. Deep breaths."

Stunned, I suck air into my lungs until he's satisfied I'm not going to faint. I'm not so sure about that myself, but he starts talking again, so I focus.

"I owe you an apology for my behavior. I know better. I *am* better, but last night, I wasn't. Stalking, spying, it's inexcusable. I can't tell you how ashamed I am for that. And for raising my voice to you, slamming doors..."

He closes his eyes and draws a slow breath. "You have my word I won't do any of that again."

After a long moment, he continues, his voice lower.

"You went to the bathroom and didn't return. I became suspicious, so I had Emiliano check all the camera's views. One of them showed Dylan dragging you through the parking lot to his car. I stopped him and brought you back into the restaurant. I called a doctor, then called Chelsea into the office. When the doctor arrived, they examined you, took your vitals, and determined you were stable and whatever had been given to you would be metabolized by your system within hours. We decided to bring you home and watch you here. Which is what we've been doing until now."

I know my mouth is open. I know my heart is still beating because it hurts. That's pretty much all the knowledge I have, so I sit gaping at Cole until the blood that drained out of my head starts to creep back into it, and I can speak again.

"You...you've been obsessing over me?"

"Yes."

I love that he doesn't look away, flinch, or deny it. I know he doesn't want to admit it, but he does anyway, and that gives me the courage to continue.

"And...you followed me."

"Yes."

"You watched me."

"Yes."

My throat closes. My chest gets tight. My eyes begin to water, and it's hard to speak because I'm so emotional. "Dylan drugged me. He was taking me to his car, but you stopped him."

"Yes."

"So...basically...you saved me. You saved me, Cole. That's what you're saying."

He hangs his head, exhales, and drags his hands through his hair. Looking at the floor he says, "I'm not a hero."

"If you hadn't been there watching me, what would've happened?"

He lifts his head and gazes at me with dark eyes but remains silent.

"Dylan didn't drug me and try to get me into his car so he could take me on a sightseeing drive."

"I'm not a hero."

"Stop saying that. You *are*."

He leaps to his feet and starts to pace at the end of my bed, hands on his hips, jaw clenched, eyes flashing. I watch him for a moment, wondering why he's so agitated.

"You said you 'stopped' Dylan. What does that mean?"

"I shoved him."

I take in his raw knuckles, his wrinkled slacks, the stains on his shirt. "You shoved him."

"Yes."

"Into a hole you dug?"

He stops pacing and looks at me but doesn't answer. His blue eyes are fathomless.

"Cole?"

"Yes?"

"What happened to Dylan?"

After a moment of hesitation, he speaks. His voice is deadly soft.

"He was fired."

We stare at each other across the room. I think of Chelsea, how she looked at me when I woke up. The darkness in her eyes. The resolution, like we'd passed a milestone we couldn't go back from.

I remember how Cole touched her shoulder when she left. The glance that passed between them like they a shared a secret.

And I understand that being fired by Cole is on a whole other level than his human resources department can handle.

I wait for shock or fear to come, or any negative emotion at all, but the only thing I feel is a twinge of relief that I won't have to deal with that sleazebag Dylan anymore.

One door closes, another opens, and now Cole and I are on different ground than we were before.

Shared ground.

Strangely, it feels as if I've finally found my footing.

I say quietly, "They'll find out. The police. Whatever you did, they'll find out."

He mistakes my meaning. Moistening his lips, he looks away. His voice turns gruff. "You want to talk to them. I understand."

"No, listen to me. I don't care about Dylan, I care about you."

He snaps his head around and stares at me in crackling silence, his eyes ablaze.

"Those security cameras will have recorded you coming and going from the restaurant. Him too. If he's missing, it's only a matter of time before the police start tracing his steps, asking people where he went, getting footage from traffic cameras... Why are you looking at me like that?"

"You don't care about Dylan?" He says it slowly, like he can't quite believe it, his mouth moving over the words as if they're from a foreign language.

"The only thing I care about is that you're okay."

Our held gazes are an invisible chain of molten fire between us, heating the air, burning with urgency. I want to leap out of bed and run to him, but I don't have the strength.

"You're not thinking straight."

"I am. I knew that guy was wrong from the second I met him. A predator. And we both know I'm not the first girl he tried that with. As far as I'm concerned, good riddance."

Cole stares at me, dark brows drawn together, eyes piercing, every inch of him taut.

"If you're about to say I'm not thinking straight again, you'll regret it."

In contrast to his feral energy, his voice is soft and stroking. "I wasn't about to say that."

"Good. Did Chelsea tell you about her little sister, Ashley?"

"She did."

"And are you and Chelsea friends now? Because I need you to be."

"Why?"

"My bestie has to like my boyfriend."

He closes his eyes, exhales, and shakes his head. "We can't have a relationship, Shay."

"You just admitted you're obsessed with me. Personally, I think that's a fantastic baseline to start a relationship with."

He opens his eyes and scowls. "It's not. It's unhealthy. And you're conveniently leaving out all the other things that aren't so fantastic."

"Like that you did something to protect me?"

"Most people would consider that 'something' immoral. Not to mention illegal."

"I'm not most people. Are you going to come over here and kiss me or not?"

"No."

I lie back down, close my eyes, and sigh. "Probably not a good idea anyway. My breath is disgusting."

When the silence continues on too long, I sneak a peek at him. He's standing in the same spot, staring at me with a mixture of disbelief and confusion on his face.

"What?"

"It's just..." He shakes his head. "You and your girlfriend Chelsea are two of a kind."

"You haven't even seen us in action yet." I close my eyes again.

After another long moment, the mattress dips on my right side. A strong hand tenderly smooths my hair.

He orders, "Stop smiling."

"I can't help it."

"We're not going to have a relationship, Shay."

"I don't care how sternly you try to say that, it still sounds like BS."

"It's not BS."

"Oh, come on. You're obsessed with me. How long do you think you can hold out before you're sending me diamonds and roses and writing me love songs?"

He makes a small huff of amusement. "Are you always this..."

"Charming? Adorable? Irresistible? Yes."

"I was going to say stubborn."

"Oh. Yeah, pretty much. You should also know that I'm incredibly impatient. It's one of my biggest personality flaws. That and I can be moody. Especially around my period. I'm only telling you that so you'll be prepared."

His fingertips trace my hairline, my cheekbone, my jaw. His touch is so gentle, I shiver.

"I can't do relationships, Shay. My life is too..."

When he's silent too long, I prompt, "Messy?"

"Dangerous."

I open my eyes and look at him. Gazing down at me, his eyes full of emotion, he's so goddamn handsome, it's dumb. And the way he looks at me makes my heart start to thud.

"How is your life dangerous?"

"It just is."

"You won't tell me?"

"I can't. It would put you at risk."

"Risk of what?"

He doesn't answer. He simply watches the path his fingertips take as they trace my eyebrow then follow the curve of my ear.

"The night we met, you said you'd just gotten out of a relationship."

"That was different."

"So you can have one, just not with me."

"It's company policy."

"Your family owns the fucking company."

"Which is why it's even more important that we honor the rules."

"Are you kidding me right now? You know half the people in that building are banging each other."

"Still. It's company policy."

"Mention that again, and I'll punch you right in your nose."

He leans down suddenly and buries his face in my hair. He inhales deeply, then exhales and sighs in contentment. His shoulders relax.

I wind my arms around them and turn my cheek to his, lowering my voice to a whisper. "Things are different now. Do you actually think we can go back to ignoring each other at work after this?"

"We have to try."

"Oh, really? The way you're sniffing my neck would indicate otherwise."

"Don't be stubborn about this. Let it go."

"No. Sorry."

"You're not sorry."

"You're right, I'm not."

He burrows closer, sliding his arms under my body so he can squeeze me hard against his chest. We lie like that for a moment, just holding each other, until he murmurs, "I should let you rest."

"No, you should give me an orgasm."

"Goddammit, woman."

"Stop trying to control me. You know I'll win."

He releases me and stands. Then, because it seems to be the way he gets his exercise, he starts to pace again. I prop myself up on my elbows and watch him until I start to get tired.

"Hey. Handsome."

He shoots me a tense sideways glance but doesn't stop pacing.

"How about this? Let's not call it a relationship. We'll call it a situationship instead."

His look sours.

"Fine, it doesn't have to be categorized. We won't call it anything. It will be The Thing That Must Remain Nameless. And we'll be very circumspect around the office so no one will know. I'll even pretend to hate you. Everybody will believe me because you're pretty awful."

He stops pacing. "I'm *awful*?"

"Yes."

"Like how awful?"

"Like so bad your nickname is the Grinch. Oh, look, there's that face you make when someone tells you some truth you find annoying."

"I'm not making a face."

"You are. It's like, 'Ew, smelly peasant, get out of my way with your rotting teeth and dirty rags, can't you see the king of the universe is passing through?' Like that. Super arrogant and scornful. I've thought more than once that you must practice it in front of a mirror."

He gazes at me in agitated silence, jaw working, eyes narrowed. Then he drops his head and starts to laugh.

"Does this mean I win?"

"No, funny girl, it doesn't. But it does mean I'll make you breakfast. In the meantime, lie there and think about all my red flags that are waving in your face. Then make the right decision."

"I'm not changing my mind, Cole. Like it or not, I'm your girlfriend now."

Shaking his head, he walks out of the room.

CHAPTER 34
Cole

I'm cooking scrambled eggs in a saucepan I found under her stove, watching my hands shake and marveling at it.

I'm never unsteady like this, but I know it's not because of what I did last night.

It's because of her. The effect she has on me.

"Like it or not, I'm your girlfriend now," she declared, as if it was a court ruling. As if it was inevitable. Final.

As if it wasn't the worst decision she'd ever make.

Yes, I fantasized about her a million different ways before now. And yes, I wanted to know her better. But I didn't know how her instant acceptance of what I'm capable of would feel. I didn't know how it would move me.

Looking into her eyes as she said she didn't care about Dylan, only about me, something heavy and profound shifted inside my soul, like tectonic plates moving under the surface of the planet, reworking how everything looks above.

She didn't cry. She didn't scream. She didn't accuse me of being a monster. She simply heard the awful truth and accepted it with a grace I don't deserve.

Then she shoved a stake in the ground and claimed me as her territory.

I've never met anyone like her.

I'm not sure if she's a blessing or a curse.

My cell rings. I fish it from my pocket, glance at the screen, and put it to my ear. "Killian. I wasn't expecting to hear from you."

"And I wasn't expecting to hear you eighty-sixed one of your employees, but here we are."

It shouldn't surprise me that he knows. Killian Black always knows everything. What's surprising is that he's calling me about it.

He usually stays out of my way, working mainly with Callum and my father, who both think I'm ignorant of their business relationship with the notorious former head of the Irish mob. He supposedly died years ago but is alive and well and running a thirteen-member cabal of powerful families like mine who work alongside—but mostly around—international law enforcement.

Suffice it to say, I'm not ignorant. But it benefits me to let my family think so.

"That a problem for you?"

"No."

"Good."

"The problem is your brother."

I scoff. "What's Callum done now? Hacked a government satellite to spy on his wife?"

"Not Callum. Carter."

I frown. My younger brother isn't involved in anything more problematic than throwing too many cocktail parties on his yacht and trying to write them off as company expenses.

"What's happening with Carter?"

"He met with the executive team at TriCast."

Killian might as well have kicked me in the stomach for how my body reacts to hearing that sentence. My breath is knocked out of me. I almost drop the spatula I'm holding from shock.

"*TriCast?* They're our biggest competitor. We hate each other. Why the hell would he meet with them?"

"Because they're tired of being in competition, mate. They made him an offer to acquire."

"Acquire? As in *us*?"

"Aye."

"Does my father know?"

"No. Nor Callum. Carter did this on his own."

Infuriated that my brother would be so reckless, not to mention underhanded, I snap, "That little fucker. I'm gonna rip off his dumb Ken doll head."

"It's only a matter of time before it gets out. A McCord taking a meeting with the board of TriCast will get people thinking you've got problems internally. Financial problems at least. Thought you'd like to know so you can be ready to spin it in your favor."

"I appreciate it. Out of curiosity, why didn't you call Callum about this?"

He chuckles. "Don't take this the wrong way, mate, but your older brother's as likely to throw Carter off a roof as he is to have a heart-to-heart talk with him about loyalty. I didn't want to be the cause of the lad's premature death."

"Good point. Thank you, Killian."

"You're welcome. And your new lass is a firecracker. Best of luck."

He disconnects, leaving me standing there wondering if the last time I saw him, he implanted me with some kind of microscopic GPS device with an audio-video component.

I wouldn't put it past him.

"Hi."

Shay stands by the refrigerator, watching me. She changed out of her wrinkled work clothes and is wearing a short robe now, a black silk one that shows off her legs and bare feet to perfection, along with every beautiful curve.

I slip the phone back into my pocket and try to pretend the sight of her isn't devastating. "Hi. What are you doing up?"

"I heard your voice, so then I missed you. I think the eggs are burning."

Looking back at the saucepan, I flip the eggs over with the spatula and inspect the results. "Depends on your definition of burning."

"I didn't realize the word had multiple definitions."

"Sure it does. Like girlfriend does. Could mean a friend who's a female, could mean something else entirely."

As I turn off the gas and move the pan to a cool burner, she walks closer, smiling.

"Hmm. Sounds complicated."

"It is."

"It doesn't have to be."

"It still is."

"If I try to tuck myself under your arm, will you push me away? Just checking first to see how much resistance I'll be met with so I can prepare a counteroffensive."

When I sigh, she sneaks over and pulls my arm around her shoulders. Turning her face to my chest, she winds her arms around my waist and smiles wider.

"You're trouble," I murmur, pressing a kiss to her forehead.

"Says Mr. Trouble himself. By the way, I brushed my teeth."

"Congratulations."

"I'm only telling you that so you won't be afraid to kiss me. I had dragon breath, but now it's all sweet. Here, check." She tilts her head back and purses her lips.

She's so fucking cute, I just want to bite her.

"We can't have a relationship, Shay."

She stares up at me with soft eyes and lifts a hand to my cheek. "We already are. Now kiss me before I get irritated with you and the mood is ruined."

"It's so interesting to me how you always think you're the one in charge."

"And it's so interesting to me how you think I won't get what I want."

She rises up on her tiptoes and presses her lips to mine. I gently push her back down, then grab a small chunk of warm eggs from the pan and hold it up to her mouth.

"Eat."

Without breaking eye contact or objecting to me issuing orders, she opens her lips and allows me to feed her.

Her pink tongue, her sweet mouth, her teeth scraping my fingertips—fuck.

I'm getting hard.

She chews and swallows, then smiles up at me. "You should see your expression right now, handsome. It's something else."

I love how she calls me handsome. I love how she challenges me. I love how she's not afraid of me, even though she should be, even though I've given her more than enough reason to.

I love everything I've seen about this strange, stubborn woman. And if I'm not careful, I'll soon be in too deep to let her go.

Without consciously deciding to, I kiss her.

She presses her body against mine and kisses me back, matching my intensity, rubbing her breasts against my chest. I hold her head in my hands and feast on her mouth.

When the kiss ends, and we're both breathing hard, she whispers, "I've been needing that for weeks. I haven't stopped thinking about you since that night we spent together. I've made myself come so many times thinking of you. I imagined my fingers were your tongue, and every time I climaxed, I called out your name."

I groan. How is she so perfect?

But I can't get distracted. She needs to rest and eat. She needs to recover. What she doesn't need is me pawing her like the selfish lust monster inside me wants to.

Looking at my face, she says firmly, "Whatever you're thinking, stop it."

"I was thinking I need to let you rest."

"Like I said, stop it. And don't growl at me either. You don't intimidate me."

Trying not to smile, I frown instead. "You need food, Shay."

Rubbing against me, she breathes, "So feed me."

"I didn't mean it like that."

"I know you didn't. Damn, I never imagined watching a man fight his desire for me could be so hot."

Sliding a hand into her hair, I curl my fingers into a fist and hold her head immobile as I stare into her eyes. "You. Will. Eat. Understood?"

"Sure. Hey, guess what?"

"What?"

"I'm not wearing any panties."

The little devil knew exactly what that would do to me. We stare at each other as my dick throbs.

So it's war.

Challenge accepted.

I take another chunk of eggs from the pan and lift it to her lips. She instantly opens her mouth and accepts it, which makes my dick throb again. When she swallows and sucks on my fingers, I exhale an uneven breath. Then she slides a hand between my legs and gently squeezes my hard shaft.

When I tighten my hand in her hair as a warning, she whispers, "I promise I'll be good and won't do anything else."

"You're a liar."

"Yes. Feed me more eggs, please."

My heart races. My head pounds. My balls ache. It's as if she has the button that operates my adrenaline, and she keeps pushing it over and over again.

I take another fingerful of eggs from the pan. When she opens her mouth for them, she strokes her hand up, squeezes the crown of my cock, then strokes down the length again. She chews and swallows, all the while looking into my eyes.

I pull my fingers from her mouth and loosen the tie on her robe. It parts, revealing her naked breasts, her soft belly, the curve of one plush hip.

I stare down at her hard nipples, listening to her hitching

breath and watching the pulse flutter at the base of her pretty throat, and realize that what I want from her is the truly dangerous thing.

I want to own her, body and soul.

Even more than that, I want her to own me.

I want to be the only man who makes her laugh, the only man who makes her pulse fly, the only man who fucks her. The one who dries her tears and holds her hand. The one who takes care of her. The one she dreams about and fights with and makes up with. The one she promises herself to. The one she loves above anyone else.

And the force of how much I want all those things staggers me.

This isn't who I am.

Or at least it wasn't, until I met her.

I pull away abruptly. Then I yank her robe together, tie the sash around her waist, and pick her up in my arms.

As I'm carrying her back to her bedroom, she sighs. "Oh look. Mr. Dark and Stormy's back."

"You need to rest. So that's what you'll do." Striding through her bedroom doorway, I carry her to the bed and gently set her down on the mattress. Then I pull the covers up all the way to her chin.

She stares up at me in obvious disappointment, shaking her head.

"Not a word. I'm going to get you a glass of water, which you'll drink. Then you'll sleep. And when you wake up, I'll feed you a proper meal."

Her look of disappointment turns to one of hope.

"Not that kind of meal. Christ. You're worse than I am."

She smiles. "Thank you."

"It wasn't a compliment."

Yawning, she closes her eyes. "You silly man. Of course it was."

Within seconds, her breathing slows. She makes a small sound in her throat and turns her cheek to the pillow.

Then I'm standing there watching her sleep, counting all the reasons I should walk out and never return, fighting with myself to do the right thing and leave this beautiful woman in peace.

I can't have her. Not the way either of us wants. It's an impossibility.

My chest aching, I leave the room, closing the door quietly behind me.

CHAPTER 35
Shay

When I open my eyes again, I can tell by the way the light has changed that it's late afternoon. I sit bolt upright in bed, my heart hammering. Then I throw off the covers and run to the door.

I know as soon as I open it that he's gone.

I walk around my apartment anyway, sniffing the air. Cole's scent lingers, a ghostly reminder of the man who saved me from disaster.

On the kitchen table, he left a full glass of water. Beside it on a plate is a turkey sandwich on wheat bread, and beside that is a note.

> MS. SANDERS,
> PLEASE EAT THE SANDWICH I MADE FOR YOU AND DRINK THE WATER. THEN DRINK ANOTHER GLASS. I'LL SEE YOU MONDAY MORNING.
> YOURS,
> MR. MCCORD

Oh it's like that, is it? We'll see.

I crumple up the piece of paper and toss it into the sink. Then I sit at the table and stuff the sandwich in my mouth because I'm starving, all the while thinking about Cole. When I'm done eating, and I've polished off the water, I rise and take the crumpled note out of the sink. I flatten it carefully on the counter, smoothing the bent edges. Then I go into my bedroom and stash it in my underwear drawer.

I don't know why, but it feels important that I keep it.

Then I call Chelsea. She answers on the first ring.

"Hi. You okay?"

"Yes. You?"

"Yes."

We sit in silence for a moment. Then she says, "Is he still there?"

"No. I went back to sleep, and when I woke up just now, he was gone."

"How are you feeling?"

"Good. Better than this morning. No more headache, and my stomach's solid."

"I meant emotionally."

I take a moment to think about it, then answer honestly. "Surprisingly steady."

Her soft exhalation lets me know how worried she's been about me.

"What about you?"

"Bitch, I've had twelve mental breakdowns in the past hour alone. I still can't wrap my mind around it."

"I want to know everything that happened on your end since I got to the restaurant last night. Go."

She draws a slow breath, then spills the tea in one long, uninterrupted monologue, barely pausing to inhale. When she's done, I have more questions than when she started.

"Who's this Emiliano character? How does Cole know him?"

"No idea. We didn't get to that."

"He told me they were old friends. Said they work together sometimes."

"Work together," she repeats, her voice thoughtful. "Interesting."

"What was he like?"

"Smart. Tough. Looks like somebody who could break all your bones, but talks like Socrates."

We're quiet for a moment, until she says, "I think we should agree that whatever Cole told us both about Dylan, we don't share with each other."

"Why?"

Her tone darkens. "The less we know, the less we can tell the police if they come asking."

A chill runs over my body, leaving goose bumps on my skin. "I'm worried about them too. I told him they'd start looking at traffic cameras, interviewing people if..."

I don't have to say it. She knows what I mean.

"Yes. What was his response?"

"Seemed like he didn't care. He was too focused on convincing me we can't have a relationship."

"That sounds extremely rational."

"I don't care if it's rational."

"You should."

"Well, I don't. And don't tell me you don't like him, because I know you do."

"It's not about whether or not I like him. It's about whether or not he's good for you."

"So you do like him."

She sighs. "For fuck's sake."

"I like him too, Chelsea. A lot. A really, really lot."

"You liked Chet a really, really lot too."

"Please. They're not even in the same ballpark!"

"I know. But this guy is...complicated."

That makes me laugh. "You think?"

"Don't be blasé about this. Whatever kind of 'work' he and Emiliano do together, I'll bet my left arm it isn't something legal."

"What, you think he runs drugs or something?"

She thinks for a moment. "No. I think they're a couple of do-gooders."

I make a face at the phone. "What does that mean?"

"I don't know exactly. All I can tell you is the vibe I got. The two of them are tight, that was obvious. Emiliano said he was a former gang member, and a lot of guys who get out of gangs dedicate themselves to helping other people. Community outreach, educating kids about the dangers of the lifestyle, that kind of thing. And Cole knows all about the court system, how it handles guys like Dylan, how abusers don't usually get the sentences they deserve. I don't know how the two things are connected, but I bet they are."

I think about how ashamed Cole was that he followed me and watched me on the restaurant's cameras. How he apologized and said it was inexcusable.

I think about how much anger he tries to keep bottled up, how it leaks out all over the place despite his best efforts. In his scowls, his arrogance, the slammed doors.

I think about how someone like him—rich, privileged, on top of the world—would know how abusers slip through the system.

And I wonder what would make a man in Cole's position endanger his entire life to get rid of one.

This is bigger than me and Dylan. This goes back much longer.

Maybe Cole lost someone the way Chelsea has.

"So what do we do now? Investigate? Stake out the restaurant?"

"No, we don't stake out the restaurant, idiot! We leave it alone!"

I sigh heavily and roll my eyes to the ceiling. "Chelsea. You're forgetting who you're talking to."

Her voice turns dry. "Oh, I know who you are, dumbass. I'm just trying to talk some sense into that thick skull of yours."

"Yeah, let me know how that goes. In the meantime, I'm going to make a plan."

"If this plan involves going back to the restaurant, forget it. You can't be seen there now. Neither of us can."

"But I want to talk to Emiliano."

"Do you also want to get arrested for being an accessory to a crime? Use your brain! Whatever Cole did to Dylan, it was bad. You saw the condition he was in. You don't get someone's blood all over you by giving them a friendly pat on the cheek. So if anybody asks, we had tacos and a margarita, we never saw Dylan or Cole, and we drove home separately and went to bed. End of story."

"But the security cameras in the restaurant, the traffic cameras on the street. There's evidence we were all there if anyone looks."

"Cole's a billionaire. His buddy's a former street thug. They're men who can get things done. Between the two of them, I'm sure they've already gotten rid of the evidence. But just in case they haven't, we have to be careful."

A sudden memory assaults me. It was the day I was in Lit Happens, talking to Emery about the job. Something she said made me joke that the person I thought then was her customer was in the Mafia. The way she looked askance at me, the way she hesitated before her unconvincing denial...

Holy shit. Was I right?

But no, that can't be it. The Mafia isn't filled with do-gooders. I mean, I don't think so. Not that I have any experience in the area.

"Promise me you won't go back to the restaurant, Shay. I mean it."

"I promise."

"Promise me you won't call, either."

"I promise."

After a pause, she says, "Why don't I believe you?"

"I won't do anything except see if I can get Cole to open up a little."

Her laugh is dry. "You mean you're going to make it your life's mission to interrogate him. Poor bastard."

"Whose side are you on here?"

"Yours. Always." She sighs. "So if your billionaire boyfriend does anything to hurt you, I'll be obligated to make his existence a living hell."

I smile because calling him my boyfriend is her way of saying she approves. "I love you, Chelsea."

"I love you too, you nonsensical twat. Now please rest and take care of yourself. I'll check in with you tomorrow, okay?"

"Okay. Bye."

After we disconnect, I stand looking out my bedroom window into the golden afternoon beyond and let my mind wander until eventually all thoughts have gone quiet, and there's only one burning question that remains.

Cole McCord...who are you?

CHAPTER 36
Cole

I t's six o'clock Monday morning. I'm sitting behind my desk at the office, reading the final chapter of *Love in the Time of Cholera*.

I have never been this depressed.

It's not only the novel's overarching theme, which is that love is a plague comparable to cholera and people in love suffer from a mental disturbance. It's that I haven't been able, even for a single moment, even while reading, to stop thinking of Shay.

I'm like Florentino, the main character in the book, who becomes so obsessed with his beloved that he eats flowers and drinks cologne in an attempt to replicate her scent. I read that passage and thought, *Sure. I can see it. I'd eat Shay's panties if I had a pair.*

Then I threw the book across the room.

I want to do the same thing now as I finish the fucking thing, because after days of reading, I've arrived at the end, only to discover that the misunderstandings and obstacles that stand in the lover's way take *fifty fucking years* of torture and longing to overcome.

I should've known in the beginning when he asked permission to court her and right then a bird shit on her embroidery work that we were in for some serious anguish.

If a bird shits anywhere near me today, I'm changing my name and moving to the South pole.

Worst of all is that the "hero" of the novel is both the protagonist and the antagonist. Talk about red flags. This guy invented them. I honestly can't tell whether he's madly in love or just mad.

The heroine, on the other hand, is all Shay.

Proud, stubborn, headstrong, independent, this broad Fermina knows what she wants and won't stop until she gets it. Her husband, Dr. Urbino—yes, she marries some other guy before her and old Florentino get together a million years later—tells her she can't have any pet that doesn't speak, so she goes out and gets a talking fucking parrot.

He thinks he's being all clever because he doesn't like animals but doesn't want to seem unreasonable so he sets an impossible bar, then she says, "Oh yeah? Hold my beer."

Shay to a T.

The guy you had a one-night stand with turns out to be your new boss?

Don't let him get the upper hand. Tell him he looks like an owl.

The new boss makes one of your co-workers disappear?

Declare the boss your boyfriend and try to seduce him.

It's insanity. All of it. Me, her, this goddamn book.

I toss it aside and stand, stretching my legs. It's too early for whiskey, so I make myself a coffee in the built-in coffee maker in the wall behind my desk and drink it as I pace the length of the office and try to clear my head.

The city is gray today. The thick marine layer blocking out the sun stretches all the way from the beach to downtown. I gaze out the windows as I pace, thinking of green eyes and tragic love stories, and remind myself for the hundredth time that she can't be mine.

But goddamn. I've never wanted something more. I'm obsessed with her.

She's my plague of cholera.

A knock on my office door distracts me. The receptionist doesn't get in until eight, so I'm forced to deal with the interruption myself.

When I open the door, I find Scotty from the mail room standing there with a brown kraft envelope in his hand.

"Morning, Mr. McCord. This is for you."

He holds it out. I take it, wondering who'd be sending me something so early. Aside from the mail room guys and security, I'm almost always the first one in.

"Thank you, Scotty."

When he blinks, I realize he's surprised I know his name. Then I remember Shay admonishing me for being awful around the office and decide to pretend I'm human.

"And good job, by the way."

Scotty pulls his brows together. "On delivering your envelope?"

This is why I don't talk to people. This right fucking here. "I meant overall. You're doing a good job. Keep up the good work."

Then I close the door in his face so I don't have to see his expression of confusion anymore.

At least I didn't slam it. Shay would be proud of me for that.

I unwind the little red string from the envelope's clasp and pull out a sheet of paper.

Dear Mr. McCord,

I have a few questions about the quarterly financial report you asked me to prepare for you. Would it be possible to schedule a brief meeting with you today to go over them?

Sincerely,
Ms. Sanders

I didn't ask her to prepare a quarterly report, the sneaky little thing. She just wants to talk to me. And whose dumb idea was it that we communicate via inter-office memo anyway?

Oh, yeah. Mine. Because when I started reading *Love in the Time of Cholera* last week, that idiot Florentino was sending love letters to Fermina, and I knew it was Shay's favorite book, and it seemed romantic.

Now that I've finished the novel, hand-writing letters seems like only something a man with no self-control and an unhealthy fixation on a woman who'll cause him fifty years of angst would do.

I told her those romance novels were bullshit.

I pick up the phone and dial her extension.

"Shay Sanders speaking."

"Good morning, Ms. Sanders."

She exhales the smallest, shakiest breath, then clears her throat. "Good morning, Mr. McCord."

"What are you doing in so early?"

"Trying to get a head start on the week, sir. Also...I couldn't sleep."

God, her voice. Why does her voice do things to me? It's not like it's throaty or seductive. It's just *hers*.

I'm so fucked.

"I'm sorry to hear that. Try magnesium."

After a beat, she says tentatively, "Pardon?"

"Magnesium. It helps with sleep and anxiety."

"Oh. Um. I will. Thanks for the tip."

I close my eyes, pinch the bridge of my nose, and scream at myself internally for being a giant, useless, plague-infected fool. "No problem. About that report—"

"Yes," she interrupts. "I really need your help with it. It's been giving me some problems. Could I come up to your office for a few minutes to speak with you about it?"

When I don't respond because I'm struggling with how much

181

J.T. GEISSINGER

I want to see her versus what I know is right, she whispers, "Please?"

Please. Never has a single word had such an effect on my body.

I close my eyes and attempt to banish the image of her begging me to let her come as I drive into her cunt from behind. Bent over my desk, her skirt pushed up over her perfect ass, my hard dick dripping with her—

"Yes," I say too loudly. "Now. Come up now. Immediately."

I slam the phone down and exhale a hard breath.

Fucking hell. This has disaster written all over it. Next thing I know, I'll be eighty-five years old, and Shay and I will finally be going on our first date.

I pace until I hear a knock on the door. The moment I open it and I see her face, I know I've already lost.

I pull her inside by her wrist, close and lock the door, take her in my arms, and kiss her.

CHAPTER 37
Shay

The kiss catches me completely off guard.

Expecting to be met with some cold, professional version of Cole who'd tell me again that there could be nothing between us, I steeled myself on the elevator ride up. I was ready with my arguments. I had all my speeches prepared. We had to work something out so we could be together, and that was it.

Then he opened the door and fell on me like a starving man.

His mouth is hot and demanding. His tongue delves deep. He holds me against his body with his arms wound tightly around my back and drinks from my mouth until I'm dizzy.

Then he sets me firmly away from him and steps back, shaking his head.

"We can't do this, Shay."

Unsteady and breathing hard, I take a moment to gather my wits and try to understand what he's saying. "You mean here? We can't do this in your office?"

"No. I mean at all."

Hurt by his words and the hardness in his voice, I turn and walk away. "I'll pretend I didn't hear that. And before you open your mouth again, let me tell you something..."

I stop a few feet away from his desk and stare at the copy of

Love in the Time of Cholera sitting on the blotter. When I turn to look at him, he sighs and drags a hand through his hair.

"I thought you didn't like romance novels."

"I don't."

"Then why is that book on your desk?"

"It's a long story. How are you?"

I take a moment to inspect his expression. It's intense. Worried. Yearning. Ambivalent. He stands with his back ramrod straight and his head slightly lowered, arms at his sides, legs spread apart, hands flexed. He looks like he's fighting himself not to break into a run, grab me, and kiss me again.

Folding my arms over my chest, I stare at him. "I'm well. Thank you for asking. You?"

"Fine. Thanks."

His intense gaze rakes up and down my body. He licks his lips and shifts his weight from foot to foot.

"Cole, if you seriously think you can act like there are no feelings between us, and we're just going to go about our lives as if nothing ever happened, you're not as smart as I thought you were."

"I never said there were no feelings. I said we can't do anything about them."

I look at him in his beautiful navy-blue suit with his gorgeous face and his strong body, and wonder how such a perfect specimen of a man could be this absurd.

"So you're planning on spending the rest of your life alone, is that it?"

"Yes."

"You're an idiot."

"Also yes. You look beautiful today. I love that color on you."

"Color? I'm wearing black."

"It's perfect. You're so perfect, I could go blind."

I can't help it. Despite my hurt and confusion, I smile. "You know, for someone who's trying to convince me we can't have a relationship, you're doing a terrible job."

"I don't want you to think it's because I don't want you. I want you like I've never wanted anything. But I'm not good for you, Shay. I'm not...good."

My heart is a sucker for this man. He stares at me with such seriousness on his face and in his eyes and voice, trying to tell me why we can't be together, but I can barely hear him over the pounding of my pulse. It's a roar of *kiss me kiss me kiss me* in my ears, deafening me.

I sit on the edge of his desk and close my eyes, trying to block it out.

A moment later, he strokes a hand over my hair.

"Are you really okay?"

His voice is soft, close to my ear. I nod but don't open my eyes because I want him to keep touching me.

"I'm sorry you couldn't sleep. Was it because of me?"

I nod again, inhaling his scent and enjoying his body heat. He must be standing very close.

"Shay. I'm so sorry."

"It's okay."

"It's not. I don't want to be the cause of your sleepless nights."

"It wasn't a bad thing. It was just that I woke up and remembered you called me baby the other night. You called me baby when you were taking care of me, just like you did that night at the hotel."

There's an electric pause before I open my eyes and look up at him. He's inches away, gazing down at me with ravenous eyes, his hand on my hair, his lips parted. The pulse in the side of his neck throbs.

I flatten my hands on his chest and whisper, "I want you to call me that again but while you're inside me."

Because I've got my hands on his chest, I feel his reaction to my words. His heartbeat starts to gallop, and his abdominal muscles tense. He draws a sharp breath. He gathers my hair in his big hand and makes a fist around it.

That simple gesture gets me so hot, I almost moan out loud. I stare up at him with my pulse flying and my nipples hardening, begging him with my eyes to put his mouth on mine.

Eyes burning, he breathes, "What are you doing to me?"

"The same thing you're doing to me. Please, Cole. Please kiss me. You can send me away after that. I promise I'll go if you ask me to, but please just kiss me again before I lose my mind."

His lids flutter. His voice turns gruff. "Stop begging. You're fucking killing me."

"Please."

He closes his eyes and groans. I stand, slide my hands up his chest and wind my arms around his shoulders, then brush my lips over his with feather-light pressure. Against his mouth, I whisper, *"Please."*

His voice turns guttural. "This is a dangerous game you're playing."

"It's not a game."

His erection is stiff against my hip. His breathing is erratic. I know he's close to snapping and losing control of himself. He's right on the razor's edge of letting go and crushing his mouth to mine.

So to try to push him over, I lick his lips from one corner of his mouth to the other, the stroke of my tongue whisper soft. Then I ever so gently take his lower lip between my teeth and bite down.

He reacts so fast, I can't comprehend how it happens.

In a whipcrack move, he turns me around and pushes me face-down onto his desk. I'm bent over the edge of it, my breasts flattened on his blotter, my bottom pressed against his crotch as he stands behind me.

With one hand on my hip and the other curled around the back of my neck, he leans over and speaks into my ear in a voice so hot and rough, it makes my legs shake.

"You don't want me to lose control of myself, pretty girl. You don't want me to let the monster off its leash. I played nice that night we spent at the hotel, but nice isn't what I am. I keep telling you I'm not good, but you refuse to listen."

I'm shaking with excitement. I can't catch my breath. My panties are soaked, and he hasn't even touched me yet. I think if he pinched one of my hard nipples, I'd spontaneously combust. ˙

"You are good. You *are*."

He growls in frustration. Yanking up my skirt, he spanks my ass several times in quick succession. The blows are sharp and stinging. Then he pulls my skirt down, hauls me off the desk, and leads me to the door with his hand around my upper arm.

He pulls the door open. He pushes me through it. I spin around and gape at him, my face hot, my pussy wet, my ass burning.

Without another word, he shuts the door in my face.

I flatten my shaking hands on the door, then rest my forehead against it, trying to catch my breath and calm the butterflies in my stomach.

My entire body sizzles with need. I might light this entire building on fire from how hot he made me.

After a few moments, I hear his gruff voice. "Don't make me open this door again. Go."

"So that's it?"

"That's it."

"You get to decide unilaterally?"

"Yes."

"And you think I'm just going to roll over and let you do that?"

"Yes."

"I'm not giving up, Cole."

"I'll hire a new assistant if I have to."

"No, you won't."

He doesn't answer for so long, I think he must've walked away. But then I hear a heavy exhalation.

"You're right. I won't. Go back to your desk, Ms. Sanders.

This conversation is over. And stop reading those goddamn romance novels!"

I stand there listening to him breathe raggedly. He mutters a curse. I picture him dragging his hands through his hair, fighting with himself not to open the door and pull me back inside again so he can kiss me, and I fall for him a little more.

"I don't care if you're a monster, Cole. Whatever you are, good or bad, I want you."

He growls, "You don't know me."

"I know you're not a narcissist like Chet. And I know you care about me."

"Why do you have to be so goddamn persistent? Why can't you just believe that I have your best interests at heart when I tell you to walk away?"

"Because you made the mistake of giving me everything I needed the first night we met. Because the more I see of you, the more I want. And because I decide what's in my best interests, not you. And by the way, if that little show of dominance was meant to scare me, it had the opposite effect. I'm ten seconds away from an orgasm. Have a good day, Mr. McCord."

I turn around and walk shakily toward the elevators but decide to take the stairs instead. I need a moment to put myself back together before I return to my floor. I'm not sure if anyone else has arrived yet, and I'm a mess. So I turn and head to the Exit door on the other side of Marion's desk. It leads to the stairwell between floors.

I step onto the concrete landing and into the cool, echoing hallway, but before the door closes behind me, Cole barges through it.

CHAPTER 38
Cole

She shouldn't have said I gave her everything she needed. She shouldn't have said she wants me, good or bad.

She shouldn't have said that thing about being ten seconds away from an orgasm either.

But she did, and now both of us are fucked because the monster inside me has smashed its chains.

I push her against the raw cinder block wall and take her mouth, thrusting my tongue inside so I can taste her. She's sweet, soft, warm, delicious...that surprised little moan coming from the back of her throat makes me even harder.

My hands rove all over her body, squeezing her tits, her waist, her succulent ass. I break the kiss to pull her skirt up her thighs and drag her panties down to her ankles. When I straighten and look at her, she's all wide-eyed and trembling, her cheeks red and her pretty mouth wet.

I put one hand in her hair and the other between her thighs and take her mouth again, kissing her greedily as I fondle her cunt.

She's slippery and hot, the bud of her clit swollen. She wasn't lying: she's ready for me.

When I thrust a finger inside her, she shivers. I add another and she moans.

I put my mouth next to her ear and speak through gritted teeth. "You're gonna be quiet, baby. You're gonna be a good girl and take my dick right here in this stairwell, and when you come, you're not gonna make a fucking sound. Understood?"

She nods, biting her lip.

"Belt."

She fumbles trying to unclasp my belt because my hand is still between her legs, and I'm finger fucking her, and she loves it.

"Zipper."

She undoes the button on my fly and pulls the zipper down.

"Cock."

She slides her hand into my briefs and pulls out my stiff shaft, squeezing it at the base. Her hand feels so good around me, I have to stifle a groan.

"Now slide your leg up and open your mouth."

She does as she's told, sliding her bent leg up to my waist. I pull my fingers out of her cunt and push them into her mouth. She automatically starts to suck, her lids fluttering closed.

Goddess. She's a fucking goddess. How did I ever think I could resist?

When she's cleaned the wetness off my fingers, I order, "Now get that cock inside you."

Trembling, she guides me as I press my hips forward. The moment slick heat envelops the head of my dick, I grab her hips and thrust.

She gasps and arches back. Her body presses against mine. She doesn't cry out, but she sinks her nails into the muscles of my back and shudders.

I slide my hands under her ass and bite her throat as I thrust again, driving deeper inside her soaked pussy. She's tight, hot velvet, and I can't get enough.

She says my name so softly, but the pleasure in her voice has a profound effect. It drives me crazy. I thrust into her over and over, my fingers sunk into her flesh and my heart racing.

When I lean down and bite her hard nipple through her blouse and bra, she stiffens. Her pussy contracts around my cock.

She likes that.

I bite down harder.

She orgasms with a full-body jerk, then begins rocking her hips frantically as her cunt convulses around me. I hold her weight as she sags against the wall. She whispers my name again, and it's my undoing.

I empty myself inside her, giving her everything I shouldn't, including my black heart and my wasted soul.

CHAPTER 39
Shay

Still sunk deep inside me, Cole kisses my neck, then speaks in a voice so deep and raspy, it sounds like he's swallowed gravel.

"Good girl."

Panting, delirious, and still convulsing in pleasure, I cling to him as he kisses my jaw.

I'm not even really holding myself up. I'm balanced on one tiptoe, but Cole's supporting almost all my weight in his hands. It's a good thing, too, because I'm dizzy and shaking, my legs newborn-colt weak.

He takes my mouth. The kiss is deep and passionate, but not as rough as when he first burst through the stairwell door. He's breathing as hard as I am.

When I open my eyes, his are already open. The look of adoration in them makes me weak all over again.

"You're so beautiful," he whispers raggedly. "I've never seen anything as beautiful as you are, baby. You're a fucking work of art."

He presses his lips to mine in a sweet, soft kiss that's somehow even more breathtaking than his passionate ones.

I'm not sure I could speak even if I wanted to. So I remain

silent as he gently withdraws from my body, steadying me when I wobble. I stay quiet as he fixes his clothing, pulling up his zipper and clasping his belt. He squats down to retrieve my panties, and I use his shoulders for balance as he pulls them up my legs. He stands, slides them up my hips and into place, and rearranges my skirt, smoothing the wrinkles.

Then he grasps my chin and looks into my eyes.

"Don't clean up."

I moisten my lips and shake my head, not understanding his meaning.

"Don't wipe my cum out. I want you to sit at your desk all day, wet and sticky, thinking about me. Tell me you will."

What is it about his voice that makes me want to roll over and do tricks for him like some obedient little puppy?

"Yes. I will."

He smooths my hair, kisses my forehead, then takes my hand and leads me down the stairwell to the twenty-eighth floor. Our footsteps echo off the walls. The fluorescent lights flicker. I'm so disoriented, I feel as if I'm having an out-of-body experience.

When we reach the landing, he turns to me and kisses me again.

"Are you okay?"

"Yes. No. I have no idea. What just happened?"

He pulls me into his arms and nuzzles his nose into my hair. "You know what happened."

"I mean what does it mean? Ten minutes ago, you were insisting I walk away from you."

He takes my face in his hands and gazes deep into my eyes. "And you should."

When he doesn't add anything else, I sigh. "Remember how I told you at the bar that first night that you were the most annoying man I'd ever met?"

His full lips curve upward into a smile. "I remember everything. Now get to work."

Lowering my voice, I say, "What if someone asks me about Dylan? What do I say?"

"No one will ask about him."

"How can you be so sure?"

"It's taken care of."

"Oh, great. Could you be a little more cryptic? That wasn't halfway mysterious enough."

He kisses my forehead, then each cheek, then my lips, like some kind of formal Mafioso blessing from the movie *The Godfather*.

"You don't have to worry about anything, baby. You don't ever have to worry about anything again."

He opens the door and gently pushes me through it. Then he turns away, letting it close behind him with a metallic clang.

I stand there listening to his footsteps recede up the cement stairs with that out-of-body feeling again, as if I'm watching this all unfold in a dream.

"You don't ever have to worry about anything again."

What could that possibly mean? It could be anything from forcing a lobotomy on me to paying off all my credit cards and my car loan.

The cubicle field is still empty. The clock on the wall reads six thirty, so I've got plenty of time before anyone else shows up. Unsteady, I head to the ladies room to fix my hair and makeup. Then I go back to my office and sit at my desk.

It's now six thirty-seven, and I have no idea how I'm going to get through this day.

Deciding to get a cup of coffee, I head into the break room. I'm surprised to find Simone standing at the counter, making a cup of tea. Wearing a gorgeous emerald green suit that flatters her creamy complexion, she looks up and smiles.

"Good morning, Shay."

"Good morning. You're here early."

"I like to get an early start on Mondays. How was your weekend?"

I freeze, then force a stiff smile. "Great. Yours?"

She shrugs, dunking the tea bag up and down in her mug. "Relaxing. I read, got caught up on Netflix. Puttered around in the garden. By the way, Dylan quit unexpectedly over the weekend, so you might have to take over some of his workload until we find a replacement. I'll try to make it as little as possible. I know you've got your hands full already."

My breath catches. My heart skips a beat, then starts to thud. I swallow nervously.

"Dylan quit?"

"Mmm. Left me a voicemail. Not very professional, but not all that surprising. He's been having some issues for a while."

My mind races. I'm not sure how I'm supposed to act calm and collected when everything inside me is tumbling around in screaming turmoil, but I manage to eke out a word.

"Issues?"

She removes the teabag, wrings it out with a spoon, sets it on a small ceramic holder shaped like a four-leaf clover on the countertop, then picks up the mug and looks at me.

"Interpersonal problems with the staff. He wasn't well liked. I'm sure he won't be missed."

Her voice is smooth, but her stare is pointed. She sips her tea, gazing at me over the rim while I try very hard to make my face an emotionless mask.

She knows.

Not only that, but she also delivered a fabricated story about him quitting over voicemail without batting an eye, which is impressive in several ways, but mainly because she can claim to have accidentally deleted it if anyone in law enforcement asks to hear it.

I concentrate on keeping my breathing steady. Holding eye contact with her is one of the most difficult things I've ever done. "I see," I say quietly. "Well. I...I'm happy to help in any way I can."

She lowers the mug and smiles. "Thank you." Then she walks

to the door, pausing briefly to touch me on the shoulder as she passes.

It's the same brief touch Cole gave Chelsea Saturday morning at my apartment.

The acknowledgment of co-conspiracy.

I can't decide if that makes everything better or so much worse.

～

In the copy room after lunch, I overhear two female junior accountants talking about Dylan.

"Thank God he quit. He creeped me out."

"I know, right? Me too. He kept asking me out for drinks, even after I told him I have a boyfriend. He actually had the nerve to say my boyfriend didn't have to know."

"Michelle said he cornered her in the parking garage one night. Really scared her."

"What happened?"

"She was working late. Came out to find him waiting for her by her car. Nobody else around, just him lurking there. He'd parked behind her, blocking her in. Had his passenger door open like he was going to push her inside."

"No!"

"Yeah. I guess one of the security guards got off the elevator to do his rounds right then and it spooked Dylan. He got into his car and drove away without a word. Michelle felt silly after because nothing happened so she didn't say anything to anyone, but when she found out this morning from Kayleigh that he tried the same thing with her, they both freaked out. Now everybody's talking about what a perv he was."

I keep my head down and my eyes on the copy machine as the girls walk out of the room together. When I pick up the stack of papers from the tray, my hands shake.

~

As I'm driving home that night, my cell phone rings. It's a number I don't recognize.

"Hello?"

"Hi, baby."

It's Cole. I'm so shocked, I almost drive off the road. "Oh hi!"

"Why do you sound so surprised to hear from me?"

"I never gave you this number."

"Did you really think it would be hard for me to get?"

"Riight. You being ruler of the universe and everything. I miss you."

There's a pause. Then he speaks again, his voice softer. "How do you do that?"

"Do what?"

"Make my heart flip."

Smiling, I check the rear view mirror before changing lanes. "Just lucky, I guess."

"What are you doing right now?"

"Driving home. You?"

"Sending a text to my personal shopper."

"You have someone who buys your clothes for you?"

"No, I have someone who makes my clothes for me. My personal shopper handles everything else. What size dress do you wear?"

"Woah, cowboy. That's a very personal question."

"You spent all day dripping with my cum. That's pretty personal too."

Remembering our tryst in the stairwell this morning, my cheeks warm. "Good point. Why do you need my dress size?"

"Because we're having dinner tonight. I want to buy you something special."

"We're having dinner?"

"Yes."

"I don't recall being invited on a date."

"Was my dick inside you today or not?"

"Yes, but your dick was inside me weeks ago at the hotel too, and I thought I'd never see you again after that."

"You thought wrong. We're going on a date tonight, and I'm buying you a dress."

Grinning, I tease, "Maybe I'm busy."

A noise like the rumble of thunder comes through the speakers. The king of red flags is displeased.

"Fine, I accept your noninvitation to dinner. And it's very generous of you to want to buy me a dress, but you don't have to do that. I have plenty of things to wear. I'm a bit of a clothes horse."

"I wasn't asking permission. Tell me."

Gauging by the tone of his voice, I know I won't win this, so I relent and tell him. When he asks for my shoe size next, I tell him that too. Then I laugh. "And my ring size is six, cowboy, in case you were wondering."

When that joke is met with stony silence, I cringe, mouth *Fuck*, and change the subject. "So where are we going to dinner?"

Over the car speakers, his voice is velvet soft. "Do you want me to buy you a ring, Shay?"

Time number two of almost driving off the road. I swerve so close to the car in the next lane, the driver honks his horn and screams at me. I better end this phone call before I cause an accident.

"Um. Um."

"That's not an answer."

"I mean...it depends what kind of ring. If you're thinking like a chastity ring, the answer's no."

He chuckles. "Got it. No chastity rings. Not that I'd ever give you one of those anyway. Fuck, you're adorable. I'll be at your place at seven to pick you up."

He disconnects without a goodbye.

My apartment in Mar Vista is a thirty minute drive from downtown. By the time I arrive, I've gone over our conversation in my head about four thousand times. I also called Chelsea to further deconstruct it, but only reached her voicemail.

I'd call Jen or Angel, but after last Friday night, Chelsea's the only one I'll talk about Cole with.

And I already know there will be a lot to talk about.

I park, rush inside, and shower. As I'm putting on lipstick, my doorbell rings. When I open the door, lo and behold, it's the same mystery man in a black suit with the peekaboo neck tattoo who delivered the Balmain blouse to me at the hotel weeks ago, the hottie with the British accent.

I'm so surprised to see him, I blurt, "You!"

He must be used to women reacting to him in strange ways, because he simply smiles that secretive smile of his and holds out the long black garment bag he's holding.

I take it from him, hold it to my chest, and look him up and down.

Despite his expensive suit and tidy buzz cut, he's got a macho swashbuckling pirate thing going on. He seems like the kind of man who could drink ten other men under the table and still have enough strength for a sword fight and a lusty romp in bed with a saucy wench. All he's missing is a little silver ring in one ear and a tricorn hat with a jaunty feather.

I compose myself and offer a more reasonable greeting. "Hi there."

"Hullo, miss."

"So you're bringing me clothes again."

He inclines his head. That looks secretive too. There's something so interesting about this guy, but at the same time, he's more than a little scary.

"Do you have a name?"

"Axel, miss."

"That's a pretty badass name."

"Thank you, miss."

"I'm Shay."

"I know who you are, miss."

"Of course you do. And you don't have to keep calling me miss, not since we're on a first name basis now and whatnot."

He tilts his head, clasps his hands in front of his crotch, and considers me so intently, I think he might be mapping the neural network of my brain.

"Out of curiosity, if I ask you what else you do for Cole besides deliver women's clothing, would you tell me?"

"No, miss."

"Of course not."

"Will you tell me what that tattoo is on the side of your neck?"

"No, miss."

"I didn't think so."

"Have a good evening, miss."

"You too, Axel. Try not to kill anyone with your pinkie."

"Never with my pinkie, miss." He smiles, then turns and melts into the night.

I really want to introduce Chelsea to this guy and get her take on him. I bet she could crack his code in five minutes flat.

Hurrying back inside, I lay the garment bag on my bed and unzip it. Inside is a stunning red crepe dress. I peek at the label.

Valentino.

Breathless, I remove my robe and toss it onto the bed, then carefully take the dress off its padded hanger. It's sleeveless and low-cut, with exquisite beaded detailing around the hem. When I slip it on and zip it up, it hugs my body like a second skin. I turn and look at myself in the full-length mirror next to my dresser.

Simple yet effortlessly glamorous, the dress hits mid-thigh, showing off my legs.

I love it.

Just as I'm stepping into a pair of strappy champagne heels, my doorbell rings. I glance at the clock on the nightstand to check the time. He's five minutes early.

I close my eyes for a moment and inhale a deep breath to calm my nerves before heading to the front door.

CHAPTER 40
Shay

Unsmiling, he stands on my doorstep wearing a perfectly fitted black suit and a white dress shirt open at the collar, no tie. His hair is tamed and shining. His blue eyes are dark and piercing. His energy is crackling hot.

He looks like a Grimm brothers version of Prince Charming, more dark and dangerous than Disney's and sexier by a mile.

Feeling shy, I say, "Hi. Thank you for the dress. It's really beautiful."

"You're the one who's beautiful."

He pushes the door open, kicks it shut behind him, pulls me into his arms, and takes my mouth like he's been starving for it, kissing me so hard, I'm bent back at the waist. I break the kiss, laughing, but he doesn't let me escape. Instead, he presses his cheek against my neck and hugs me tighter.

"Wow! I guess you missed me."

Sliding a hand down my back, he squeezes my ass. His voice turns gruff. "I can't stop thinking about you."

"Lucky me."

He turns his head and meets my eyes. "No. Unlucky you. But I'll do my best to make up for it."

My arms wound around his strong shoulders, I smile up at him. "I'm glad you're here. Don't ruin it by being obnoxious."

"I'm never obnoxious."

"The way you talk about yourself like you're some kind of unnatural beast that should be locked in a basement is. I don't like it."

He lowers his head, gently bites my jaw, then murmurs, "I am an unnatural beast. Just because you don't see it doesn't mean it's not true."

"Don't make me kick your ass. I haven't even had dinner yet."

He gives me a firm closed-mouth kiss, then sets me away from him and looks around my living room, his gaze curious and sharp. Before I can say anything, he stalks off toward my bedroom and disappears inside.

I prop my hands on my hips and call out, "Yes, I'd love to give you a tour, Cole. How polite of you to ask. We'll start in the bedroom."

He makes a pass by my open door then disappears again. I stand in the living room tapping my toe until he comes out, smirking.

"Why do you look so pleased with yourself?"

"I took a pair of your panties out of your laundry basket."

Heat creeps into my cheeks. "Ah. How very psychotic of you. Do you always steal dirty laundry on a first date?"

"Never. But I want to be able to smell you when you're not near me. I'll keep them in my desk drawer at the office. And this isn't our first date." His smirk deepens. "On our first date, I fucked you all night long, princess."

My pulse goes haywire. I look at him, so sophisticated in that suit, so distractingly handsome, and think his elegant exterior is so deceptive.

His true nature isn't quite as civilized.

"I'm not a princess. I'm a queen. Get it right, stud, or I'll give you one of those haughty looks you're always throwing around."

"Oh no," he says with mock fear. "Not the haughty look."

"Yeah. It's pretty devastating."

"You don't seem devastated."

"That's because I'm a badass. Which reminds me, your personal shopper is a super interesting guy."

Lifting his brows, he strolls closer. "Interesting in what way?"

"In all the ways. How long has he worked for you?"

His gaze drops to my mouth as he approaches. "Axel and I have known each other for a while."

I say brightly, "Oh look, another cryptic evasion masquerading as an answer! You're very good at dodging questions, Mr. McCord."

"And you're very good at busting my balls, Ms. Sanders. That wasn't on your resume."

He reaches out, takes me by the shoulders, and pulls me against his chest. I wind my arms around his back and smile up at him. "This is better than when you're pretending we're not going to have a relationship."

"I wasn't pretending, I was being protective. And I haven't said anything about a relationship."

"Seriously? You just stole a pair of my dirty panties. We're totally in relationship territory now. Wait, sorry —situationship."

When he purses his lips in displeasure, I sigh.

"You know what? You're right. We'll just have an ongoing series of one-night stands and pretend we don't know each other the rest of the time."

He strokes his thumb over my cheekbone and gazes at me in pensive silence for a moment. Then he says something that makes me want to do more than bust his balls—it makes me want to take a hammer to them.

"That's exactly what I was thinking."

"I was joking!"

"Let's not get into this right now. I need to feed you."

"You know, if I were a few years older, being around you would put me at extreme risk of cardiac arrest."

He brushes my lips with his. "Because you're so attracted to me?"

"Nice try. No, because you're bad for my blood pressure."

Into my ear, he whispers, "Is that what you think when I'm buried inside you, and you're clawing my back and moaning my name? That I'm bad for your blood pressure?"

His words evoke a memory of this morning in the stairwell, and a small, involuntary shudder runs through me.

He chuckles. "That's what I thought."

"Don't be smug. I hate smug."

"Yes, ma'am."

"And don't be sarcastic either."

Squeezing me tighter, he chuckles again, his breath warm on my neck. "So many rules. Are you ready to go?"

I say drily, "Sure. Just let me grab something sharp to poke you with first."

"You don't need anything else. You've already got that tongue of yours."

"Ha. Touché, Mr. McCord. Touché."

His SUV is big, black, and luxurious. He has to help me into the passenger seat because it sits so high. Then he buckles me in, kisses me, and slides his hand up my bare thigh.

"It's taking all the self-restraint I have not to bury my face between your legs and eat your pussy, baby, because I love the way you smell and taste. But after dinner..."

He smiles, looking straight into my eyes.

My nipples harden. My heart pounds. I want him to do it right now, and I don't even care that we're in a public parking lot.

"Dessert, then," I say, amazed at the effect he has on my nervous system.

He closes my door and gets behind the wheel. As soon as we pull out of the driveway, he takes my hand. We drive through the city holding hands, and if I stare at his profile too much, he doesn't seem to mind it.

"You're very handsome. But of course you know that."

He glances over at me. "I don't see myself the way you do."

"You should. It's an incredible view."

He lifts my hand to his mouth and kisses my knuckles. "You're being sweet."

"I'm being honest. You're the best-looking man I've ever met."

"You should see my brother, Callum. Then tell me what you think."

Intrigued, I turn toward him. "Is he Emery's husband?"

"Yes."

"I haven't seen him around the office. I met Carter the first day I started, but not since."

His voice turns dry. "Count your blessings."

"You don't get along with them?"

"Everyone assumes it would be so great to work for a family business until they actually do work for one, which is typically when they realize they can't stand the people they share DNA with and start to wish they were adopted."

I'm taken aback by the bitterness in his voice. I stare at his profile, watching a muscle flex in his jaw, and wonder what his father is like. From the sound of it, their relationship isn't exactly warm and fuzzy.

"Does your mother have much involvement with the company?"

His features soften at the mention of his mother, and so does his voice. "Not in the day-to-day operations. But my father can't make a decision without her."

"How long have they been married?"

"More than forty years." He glances over at me. "What about your parents?"

"They divorced when I was ten."

"I'm sorry to hear that. Are you close with them?"

I look out my window into the city passing by the windows, at the starless evening sky, focusing on them instead of the sudden tightness in my stomach. "My dad, yes. He's in Oregon now with his new wife. We get together on holidays."

When I don't continue, he squeezes my hand. "And your mom?"

"She lives in Vegas. We speak on the phone occasionally, but..." I have to clear my throat before continuing. "We're very different people."

"How so?"

I wasn't expecting him to ask that. Most guys would leave it alone, guessing from my tone that I don't want to get into it. But I have Cole's full attention now. I'm not even looking at him, but I feel it. How the air has charged. How he grips my hand a little harder.

"She drinks a lot. And when I say a lot, I mean she starts around noon and doesn't stop until she passes out. She's got congestive heart failure now, but even that hasn't made a difference in her drinking habits."

Cole lifts my hand to his lips and kisses it again, pressing his mouth against my skin for a long moment.

"I'm sorry."

"Thank you. It is what it is." Sighing, I lean my head against the headrest and close my eyes. "I blame her boyfriend."

"Why's that?"

"He beats her up. They've been together since her and my dad separated. I keep begging her to leave him, but she won't. I've tried everything I can, but people have to want to take part in their own rescue. So now I just let her be and wait for that phone call in the middle of the night from the police that I know will eventually come."

After a moment when I realize Cole hasn't said anything, and his silence has gone from attentive to tense, I'm horrified.

What was I thinking? He tells me his parents have been married forty years, and I match it with *that*?

My cheeks burn with embarrassment. "Sorry. That was a lot."

"You don't have to apologize. Thank you for telling me. I'm glad you did."

I glance over at him. His jaw is hard again, and he's wearing an expression that's obvious even in profile. He doesn't look glad.

He looks murderous.

But thankfully, he changes the subject so neither one of us have to tiptoe through that mess anymore.

"What about sisters or brothers? Any of those?"

"I'm an only child."

"Lucky."

"Growing up, I always wished I had a sister. Maybe that's why Chelsea and I are so close. We've been friends since high school."

He looks at me for a long moment before turning his attention back to the road. "You two must share everything."

"Yes. Well, not *everything*."

His voice drops. Without looking at me, he says, "I don't mind if you talk to her about me. I know she's important to you. And I trust both of you."

"Really? You trust us?"

"Yes."

"But you only met her the one time. And you and I haven't exactly spent a lot of time together either."

"I know people. When they're good, when they're bad, when they can be trusted, and when they can't. And both of you can be."

I study his profile, fascinated by him but also confused. "Did you get all this insight into human nature in business school?"

His lips lift in a brief, enigmatic smile that looks very similar to the ones his pal Axel produces. "Not exactly."

When I stare at him silently for too long, he chuckles. "Don't overthink it."

"I wouldn't have to if you tell me what you mean."

"Some other time."

From the way he says that, I get the distinct feeling that time will never come. But I don't insist.

We spend the next thirty minutes talking about safer topics. Movies, music, travel, food, books. He knows something about everything. He's visited every city I've ever wanted to visit, and describes them in such detail, I can picture them as if I've been there. I'm so caught up in our conversation, I forget to ask him where we're going, but then we turn off Sunset Boulevard onto Beverly Glen.

"Are there restaurants up here? I thought this area was all residential."

He smiles. "The best restaurant in LA is at the top of the hill. It's got an incredible view of the Valley on one side and the Santa Monica Bay on the other."

We follow the winding road up the hill, every house we pass getting larger. Eventually, the only thing I see of them are rooftops set far back behind gates. Then we pull up to an enormous stone guard gate. We slow, Cole lifts his chin to the uniformed guard who appears at the window, and we pass through.

The same thing happens at another guard gate fifty feet in.

Wherever we're going, it must be exclusive. The property up here is among the most expensive in all of Los Angeles, and judging by the size of the homes we're now passing, they're filled with celebrities and the uber-rich.

We stop in a driveway flanked on either side by huge palm trees and stone statues of lions. The black iron gate is massive, spanning the width of the driveway and continuing along the street on either side. I can't see what's beyond the gate because of all the trees and shrubs lining it, but then it opens and we drive through, revealing the building beyond.

Estate, rather.

It's a home, an impossibly beautiful Italianate style mansion awash in soft light from landscape lighting hidden among lush greenery.

"Cole?"

"Hmm?"

"This isn't a restaurant."

His laugh is soft and pleased. "Ah, that sharp intellect of yours, Ms. Sanders."

We pull through the gates and drive into a large motor court with a central fountain. He parks the car in front of an arched stone entryway, kills the engine, then turns to me.

"I hope you like Asian fusion food. Wolfgang made his famous Shanghai lobster for us."

"Wolfgang? As in *Puck*?"

He winks at me. "Hope you're hungry." He exits the car and comes around to my side, opening the door and waiting as I unbuckle my seatbelt.

Then he takes my hand and leads me inside his home.

CHAPTER 41
Shay

The place is incredible.

The foyer has vaulted ceilings and walls of windows that showcase incredible canyon and city views. A pair of curved limestone staircases rise elegantly to the second floor. The white marble floor gleams.

Holding my hand, Cole leads me through the entrance into the main living area, which is even more grand. Acres of dark hardwood floors are offset by white furniture and walls hung with oil paintings. There's a bar room, a library, a formal dining room, a screening room, and a wine cellar, and that's just the first floor.

As I stand in wide-eyed wonder gazing through the windows at the huge backyard pool surrounded by a lounge area with harlequin pattern pavers inset with squares of grass, Cole squeezes my hand.

"What do you think?"

"It's like a fairytale castle. Who else lives here with you?"

"Nobody."

I turn and look at him. In the warm ambient lighting, his features are softer. Maybe it's my imagination, but his demeanor is softer too, as if by merely walking through the front door of his home, he shed a few of his hard layers.

"You live here alone? This place must be like ten thousand square feet."

"Fifteen. On six acres." He turns and gazes out the windows into the night. "I wish it were twenty, but I can't find any parcels that big in the city. There's a place in Montecito that's two hundred and thirty acres that I'd love to buy, but the owner won't sell."

I furrow my brow in confusion. "Why do you want that much space?"

"Same reason wild animals need a lot of space."

"To roam?"

"So they don't have to bump into each other."

"Don't you get lonely?"

He answers after a contemplative moment, his voice soft. "All the time."

I remember what Simone said the day I started work and slipped and called him Mr. Dark and Stormy. She said everyone at the office called him the Grinch, but the thing about the Grinch was that his heart wasn't too small. He was just unbearably lonely.

This man is a mystery. He longs for connection, but purposely keeps himself separate from the only place he can get it. Other people.

"Hey. Handsome."

He glances at me.

"Thank you for bringing me here. It means a lot to me."

Blue eyes shining, he reaches out and caresses my cheek. He murmurs, "Beautiful Shayna. Thank you for coming. I love having you here."

Emotion swells in my chest, expanding until it's hard to breathe. I want to look away from him to hide, but I can't. The force of his gaze is too powerful.

I don't know what it is about him, but I'm drawn to him in a way I've never been drawn to anyone else. To his mysteries and his moods, his longing and his loneliness, all the parts he keeps hidden from everyone for reasons yet unknown.

I know he's got secrets. I know he's not perfect. But I've never known anyone I wanted to understand more.

"I could get addicted to the way you're looking at me right now," he says, his voice throaty.

"If I ask you something, will you answer honestly?"

"I'll always be honest with you."

"When you're not sidestepping, you mean."

That earns me a smile. "What's the question?"

"Can I trust you not to break my heart?"

A look of pain crosses his features. He closes his eyes and exhales a quiet breath. When he opens his eyes again, they're filled with anguish.

"Why do you think I keep saying we can't have a relationship?"

That shouldn't hurt as much as it does. I almost wish he'd lied to me. But I guess that's what I get for asking the question.

I look away, out into the night. "Okay," I whisper around the lump in my throat. "Fair enough."

"Shay—"

"No, let's not ruin this. We have tonight. And we have Shanghai lobster. And if you're very, very good, I'll let you convince me that we should go skinny dipping in that enormous pool."

He gathers me into his arms and hugs me, pressing his face against my neck. We stand like that for a while, holding each other and breathing, until I feel tears well at the corners of my eyes and pull away.

He's already breaking my heart, and we haven't even eaten dinner yet.

Taking my hand, he leads me through a set of open French doors onto the terrace. The air is warm and still, perfumed by the cascading honeysuckle vines climbing the balustrade. We sit at a small round table draped in white linen and set with fine china and crystal. White tapers in silver holders add a romantic glow to the setting.

Overwhelmed, I take in the view.

"You're quiet," observes Cole, spreading a linen napkin over his lap.

"I'm processing."

He nods, accepting that answer without pressuring me for more. Then he pulls his cell from his jacket pocket and dials a number. To whoever answers on the other line, he says, "We're ready."

He disconnects, shuts his phone off, and slides it back into his pocket. Then he takes my panties from another inside pocket and holds them to his nose. Looking at me, he inhales deeply.

Embarrassed, I shake my head and look away.

"Don't be shy."

When I glance back at him, he's grinning.

"You're strange."

"You told me that the night we met. Do you remember?"

"Yes, and I was right. Put those away, please."

He folds them carefully and places them in the outer breast pocket of his jacket, arranging them until the panties look like a pocket square.

"I don't want to know how many times you've done that before, but you're entirely too good at it. Please don't tell me you'll wear them into a meeting."

"Oh, these are coming with me wherever I go."

He laughs at my expression. I love his laugh, open and unguarded, loud and happy. The sound thrills me. I sit and stare at him, mesmerized.

Eyes glowing, he leans across the table and takes my hand. "There's that look again."

"What look?"

"The one I'm addicted to."

"The one you said you *could* get addicted to, you mean."

"Apparently, one hit was all I needed."

Blushing, I look down at the table. "You're just laying it on thick because I said that thing about skinny dipping."

"You know I'm not."

I glance up. Our gazes lock. My nervous system slams into high alert and starts lighting my body parts on fire. How does he do this to me?

"You're so fucking beautiful. Goddamn, Shay. Goddamn."

His voice is low and vehement, and his eyes are shining. I wish I could take a picture of his face so I could remember him at this moment, so I could look at it when things get rough between us, which I know they will.

I whisper, "Thank you."

He leans over and kisses my knuckles just as two young men arrive at our tableside. They're wearing long-sleeved white dress shirts, black slacks, and black vests with the word *Spago* sewn in white lettering on the chests.

"Good evening," says the taller blond one. "I'm Brett. I'll be serving you this evening. Christian is assisting me." He nods toward his companion, a slender young man with a beautiful smile and big, dark eyes.

Cole leans back into his chair, crosses his legs, and folds his hands in his lap. He watches me with unwavering intent as our servers set plates of food in front of us and pour wine into the crystal goblets.

Brett gestures toward my plate. "For our first course, we have pork belly dumplings with black vinegar, chili oil, and ginger, paired with Wolfgang's favorite dry Austrian Riesling. *Bon appétit.*"

They withdraw, leaving me more overwhelmed than before.

Because of course he would, Cole notices.

"What's wrong?"

"Nothing's wrong. This is just...incredible. You went to a lot of trouble. I hope you don't think I'm the kind of girl who wouldn't be happy getting takeout from a pizza joint."

His voice turns soft. "I know what kind of girl you are. And don't worry about the effort. It's my pleasure."

"Still, Cole. This is a lot."

"It's worth it just to see your expression."

"Well, thank you. For everything. But don't think I expect—"

"I'm going to give you things," he interrupts. "Nice things. Things you deserve, things it will make me happy to give you because I know you'll appreciate them, but also selfishly because I know how good it will make me feel to provide them for you."

I exhale a shaky breath, wishing I didn't feel so unsteady. "Okay, but don't be disappointed when you come over to my place and I serve you SpaghettiOs from a can."

"Are you kidding? They're my favorite."

Smiling, he picks up his wine glass and takes a sip of wine. I do too, glad for a distraction from the whirlwind of emotions crashing through me. Then I decide to be bold and just say what's on my mind.

"I'm not sure how this is supposed to work. You don't want a relationship, but you want to give me things. You said I don't ever have to worry about anything again, but you also said that thing about only having a series of one-night stands."

"You said that. I just agreed with it."

"You know what I mean."

"Eat your dumplings before they get cold."

Another sidestep. How annoying. I keep that thought to myself as I pick up my fork and stab a fat little dumpling. I'm aggravated for all of ten seconds until I start to chew, and the flavors explode on my tongue.

"Oh. Oh my God. This is...holy wow, this is good."

"Holy wow?" he repeats, chuckling.

"Don't make me throw a dumpling at you."

"You can throw anything you want at me, baby."

His voice is so soft and stroking, his eyes so warm, it makes me shiver. I drop my gaze to my plate to avoid giving him a glimpse of everything I'm feeling. If he does, he lets it go without comment, instead pausing to take another sip of his wine.

We finish the first course in comfortable silence. Well, he seems comfortable. I'm bursting with questions I have to swallow along with my food. The second course arrives just as I'm about to ask him about Axel again, which hopefully would give me an opening to ask about Emiliano...and then everything else.

Christian clears our plates. Brett sets two new ones in front of us.

"Shanghai lobster with curry sauce and crispy spinach. *Bon appétit.*"

Bemused, I watch him leave. "Do you think he gets in trouble if he doesn't say *bon appétit* every time he sets a plate in front of someone?"

"It's just a fine dining thing. Oh shit."

Surprised by the sudden change in his tone, I look at him. "What's wrong?"

"I never asked if you like lobster."

"You're right. You didn't."

He waits for me to continue. When I don't, he raises his brows. "Well?"

"I'm allergic, actually. Deathly allergic. I break out in hideous hives."

When I spear a succulent chunk of lobster and dip it into the little pot of melted butter, then pop it into my mouth, his expression sours.

"Smartass."

"Guilty. Oh God, this is even better than the dumplings!"

He looks at the glob of butter I feel dripping down my chin and licks his lips.

"Make sure to save some of that butter."

"Why?"

He smiles. "I'll need it for later."

"You planning on having toast for dessert?"

"I'm planning on having you for dessert. Right over there, on that lounge bed."

I glance over at the grouping of furniture nearest to us on one side of the pool. Four striped chaise lounges sit at the edge of the pool. A long sectional sofa and a pair of big arm chairs are arranged behind them.

Beside a lit firepit next to those is a large, comfortable looking lounge bed draped in white throws and mounds of pillows.

He grins a wolfish grin. My heart flutters.

"Pardon me, Mr. McCord, but this is strictly a business relationship, remember?"

Eyes flashing, he growls, "What I remember is how wet your pussy was when I fucked you in the stairwell, Ms. Sanders. How you said my name. How hard you came on my dick."

My fluttering heart starts to pound, my nipples start to tingle, and a flood of warmth spreads between my legs. I fidget in the chair, confused by his unpredictable mood changes but incredibly turned-on by his words.

Unsure of how to respond, I stuff more lobster into my mouth.

Cole's laugh is soft and pleased. "You're adorable."

"Don't make fun of me."

"Never, beautiful girl. Never."

When I glance up at him, I find him smiling at me with a look of adoration.

Every minute I spend with him, I grow more confused.

And turned on.

But mostly confused.

What's the big deal about relationships with him? What's he hiding?

"How are you enjoying the lobster, madam?"

I jump in surprise. Brett has appeared from thin air at our tableside. He looms over me, his hands clasped behind his back, his gaze inquisitive.

I press a hand over my racing heart. "Oh, it's wonderful. Just amazing. Thank you so much."

Smiling, he nods and withdraws again.

Cole chuckles behind his fist.

"Give me a break, handsome, I'm coping as best as I can over here."

"Hmm. Then maybe you need a change of seating."

He stands, pulls me to my feet, then takes his chair again, pulling me down with him so I'm sitting on his lap.

He kisses my neck. "That's better. Mmm, you smell delicious." He reaches up and fondles my breast, pinching my hard nipple through the fabric. "You feel even better."

"You'll ruin the dress," I protest breathlessly, looking around to make sure one of the waiters isn't in sight.

His kiss turns to a bite. He moves his hand from my breast down to my thigh and pushes the hem of my skirt up. When he slides his hand between my legs, he growls in approval.

"You didn't wear panties, you dirty girl."

"I didn't know you were such a collector or I would have."

He chuckles, moving his mouth down to my collarbone as he lazily rubs his hand over my flesh, petting me but not sliding his fingers inside. He strokes his fingers all around then firmly pinches my labia, sending my pulse into overdrive.

Into my ear, he says, "Ask me to finger fuck you, baby."

"Here? Now? But the waiters—"

"We won't be disturbed. Ask me."

He bites my throat again, harder this time, his hand still stroking back and forth between my thighs. My nipples are so hard, they ache. My pulse is flying, and I can't catch my breath.

His voice turns rough. "You're already soaked, pretty girl. It's all over my hand. Ah, God, you're so fucking perfect. You need me to finger fuck you, don't you? You need me to make you come."

Rocking against his hand, I manage a breathless, "Yes."

"Ask me. Say please."

I love the dominant side of him. This commanding, bossy side that comes out when he's turned on. My excitement makes my voice shaky.

"Please, Cole. Finger fuck me. Make me come. Please."

He thrusts a finger inside me and takes my mouth, kissing me hard, inhaling my whimper and returning it with a deep grumble of pleasure that excites me even more. I grab his face and kiss him back as I ride his hand.

When I moan into his mouth, he breaks away and orders, "Open your eyes. Look at me."

My lids drift open. He gazes at me with eyes like fire as he adds another finger to the first and starts to stroke my clit with the pad of his thumb.

The sound I make comes from deep within my chest.

"Keep looking at me, baby. Don't look away. Spread your legs wider. That's it. Fuck yes, that's it."

I whisper his name.

He tugs on my swollen clit, making me jerk and moan in helpless pleasure. Then he starts to thrust his fingers in and out, deeply and firmly, his strong fingers delving into my core, sending shockwaves of pleasure throughout my body.

"Oh God. Oh God, Cole. Cole..."

"Give it to me, baby. Give it to me now."

I fall over the edge looking into his eyes, surrendering to this strange magic we weave every time we're together and hoping that in the end this spell he's cast over me will be made of more light than dark.

Hoping, but not quite believing it will.

CHAPTER 42
Cole

She gasps. Her sweet cunt clenches around my fingers. Then she stiffens and groans.

She orgasms looking into my eyes.

Any thought I had of resistance is stripped away. I melt for her. I burn. I break. She's the most perfect thing I've ever known. The way she gives herself to me completely leaves me shaking.

She drops her head back against my shoulder and groans again. Her body jerks. Her pussy throbs and convulses rhythmically around my fingers. My cock is so hard and desperate to get inside her, it hurts.

And she keeps saying my name, over and over, this whispered chant that makes me feel like a king or a god, big and powerful, capable of anything.

Of creation as much as carnage. Of love as much as hate. Of good instead of all the bad hidden inside me, the bad that always turns lighter and breathes easier when she's near.

After a moment, her body relaxes. Her lids slide shut. Panting, she licks her lips and reclines against me, lush and satiated, her head on my shoulder, her breathing ragged.

She's so wet, my whole hand is slick.

My heart aching, I kiss her cheek and whisper into her ear, "If I fall into you, promise you'll catch me."

When she opens her eyes, they're hazy with pleasure. She rests her hand on my cheek and smiles an angelic smile. "I'll catch you, handsome. I promise."

To lighten the moment and deal with the crushing pressure inside my chest, I make a weak joke. "It might hurt. I weigh a lot."

"I'm stronger than I look."

She kisses me sweetly, sighing against my mouth as I withdraw my fingers from her body. Then she watches, her cheeks growing red, as I leisurely lick each one clean of her juices, savoring her taste.

"That's downright carnal."

"I'd eat you for every meal if I could."

"That can be arranged, handsome."

"I need to fuck you, but you need to eat first."

"Yes please to the first thing and a delay to the second."

"It's not a negotiation, beautiful. Stand up."

I help her rise, steadying her when she wobbles. Then I help her sit, place her napkin on her lap, give her a deep, passionate kiss, and return to my chair.

She stares at me across the table as I gulp wine, trying to pretend my hands aren't shaking.

Fuck. What she does to me. She's an earthquake, and I'm a creaky old wood building with no supports in its foundation. The woman leaves me in rubble.

"Okay, handsome. Have it your way."

I smile. "What other way is there?"

We eat. Crickets serenade us. A warm breeze whispers through the trees. Our gazes keep finding each other, catching and holding for brief moments, breaking apart only to catch and hold again. The servers take our plates and bring something new that I eat without tasting because I'm too caught up in her to notice anything else.

Finally, the meal is over, and the table is cleared except for our wine glasses and one little pot of melted butter I insisted stay. The servers bow off, leaving us alone on the terrace.

The moment they're gone, I turn to Shay. "Take off your dress. Leave the heels on. Let me look at you."

Her breath catches. Her fingers tremble on the stem of the wine goblet. She licks her lips, takes another sip of wine, then rises, placing her napkin aside.

Without a word, she unzips the dress and shimmies out of it, draping it over the back of her chair.

Then she stands there staring at me wearing only moonlight, heels, and a small, shy smile.

My heart hammering and my dick like steel, I say gruffly, "No bra either."

"I didn't want to ruin the lines of the dress."

I hold out my hand. "Come here."

She moves over to me slowly, giving me time to savor it. My eyes drink her in. Gleaming skin and full breasts, long legs and dark hair, movement like lines of lyrical poetry.

I'm obsessed with possessing her.

Not only her body, but her heart. Her mind. Her soul. I want to devour this woman. Brand her. Mark her as mine and mine alone.

The fact that I can't makes it all so much more powerful, and so much worse.

"Bend over the table in front of me."

I move the chair back and spread my legs so she can get between them. Then I watch as she obeys me, lowering her chest onto the tabletop and presenting me with her round, perfect ass.

Starting at her ankles, I stroke my hands up to her thighs. "Spread your legs wider. Show me that pussy."

Legs quivering, she does as she's told. Sitting in my chair, I've got a beautiful view of her body, shoulders and back and her exposed cunt, plump, pink, and glistening.

And the sweet little knot of puckered flesh between her ass cheeks.

"Cole?"

"Hush."

She rests her cheek against the tablecloth and shivers. When I run my fingertip along the seam where her pussy meets her thigh, she inhales a soft gasp.

I lean down and bite her succulent ass. "I said hush, baby. Not another sound out of you."

I want to fuck this ass. I want to taste it. I want to lick it. I want to hear her moan as I drive deep inside, reaching around to pinch her nipples.

What I do instead of any of that is pick up my wine, sit back in my chair, and enjoy the view.

It's fucking spectacular.

She wriggles her ass, making my dick jump. I say, "You're not in charge, sweetheart," and spank her once, lightly, with an open palm.

Her small, breathless whisper of, "Harder," is such a turn-on, I almost break and yank my hard cock out from my trousers and plunge it inside her. But I control myself, opting instead to have a little fun with my obedient beauty while she's still being obedient.

Knowing her, it won't last long.

I tip the wineglass over her bottom and allow a small stream of wine to pour over her ass and pussy. Then I lean in and greedily lap it up, sucking on her lips and swirling my tongue around that puckered bud.

She moans, and I chuckle. "Bad girl. So bad."

I spank her again, loving how her ass jiggles as I strike it.

"Cole," she whispers breathlessly. "Please."

She wants more, and so do I, but she keeps forgetting who's in charge. So I take my time pouring more wine over her, stroking her wet clit and licking her ass until she's moaning and rocking her hips.

I stand and move around the table so I'm near her head. I take off my jacket and lay it over the back of the chair over her dress, then unbuckle my belt and unzip my trousers. I take my stiff dick in my hand.

"Suck me while I give you the spanking you're begging for."

Without a second's hesitation, she opens her mouth.

"Good girl."

I guide my erection past her lips. She moans around it and closes her eyes. I slide a hand under her head to support it as she takes me down her throat. In the moonlight, I see goose bumps form all over her back, and that simple evidence of her pleasure and emotion drives me wild. It makes me feel like an animal.

I lean over and spank her smartly until both her cheeks are pink. When I stop, I'm panting with excitement. Her pussy pulses under my fingers when I fondle it.

"You want me to fuck this, don't you, baby?"

She moans around my cock again.

My laugh is dark and pleased. "I know you do. Keep sucking."

I dip my fingers into the small pot of melted butter, hissing in pleasure when the head of my cock touches the back of her throat. Then I slide my buttered fingers between her ass cheeks and stroke them over her anus as she moans louder, urging me on.

I whisper, "Such a greedy little girl," and sink my finger into her ass.

She whimpers.

I stare down at her as she works on my dick, pausing at the crown to swirl her pretty pink tongue around it then sliding her lips over the shaft, straining forward to take as much as she can as I finger fuck her.

When I speak, my voice is guttural. "I'm gonna come in this ass, baby. I'm gonna fuck your sweet cunt first, but then I'm gonna come deep inside your ass. And I want to hear you scream my name when I do, understand me?"

Without waiting for an answer, I withdraw my finger from her ass and my dick from her throat, then flip her over and pick her up in my arms.

I carry her across the pavers and around the fire pit to the lounge bed. She clings to my shoulders, gazing at me with wide eyes and parted lips, breathing erratically. When I kneel on the edge of the bed and lay her gently down, she kicks off her heels and lies with her arms flung over her head as I strip out of my clothing.

The firelight casts a golden glow over her bare skin. Lying there nude on the pillows and soft throws, her nipples hard and her chest rising and falling rapidly, she looks untamed and beautiful, a wild thing I caught in a forest and brought home to eat.

It's thinking these ridiculous romantic thoughts that makes me realize how deep in I already am. I asked her to catch me if I fall, but the reality is that I've already fallen.

Now it's only a matter of discovering how badly I'll shatter when I hit the ground.

I kneel between her spread legs, then lower myself on top of her, balancing my weight on my forearms. We stare silently at each other as she reaches between our bodies and takes me in her hand.

Supporting my weight on one elbow, I squeeze her breast, then lean over to capture a hard nipple in my mouth. When I suck on it, she shudders.

I go back and forth between each breast, licking and sucking her taut nipples until she's panting and writhing beneath me, sliding the head of my cock up and down between her soaked pussy lips, urging me forward with her hips in a wordless plea.

When I know she's about to break and beg, I kiss her and thrust inside.

She surges up against my chest with a muffled cry and throws her arms around my shoulders and her legs around my waist. I fuck her deep and hard until her thighs are shaking and she's clawing my back.

She climaxes, crying out into my mouth. I swallow her cries and fuck her through her orgasm until my balls are aching with the need for release.

Then I withdraw from her, roll her onto her stomach, stuff pillows under her belly so her beautiful ass is tilted up, and position myself between her legs. With my chest to her back, I lower my head and put my mouth against her ear as I press the head of my cock against her ass.

"Ready?"

"Yes!"

A slow push, a moment of resistance, her soft cry of pleasure or pain. Then her body submits to me, and the engorged head of my cock slides inside tight, oiled heat.

She shudders and buries her face in the pillows, moaning my name.

Breathing hard and sweating, I fall still for a moment, giving her time to adjust to me. I kiss her shoulders and neck, nuzzle my nose into her hair.

When I feel her relax, I flex my hips slightly, pressing forward, shaking with the need to plunge deeper but holding back to make sure she's okay.

Then she jerks her hips up suddenly, thrusting me all the way inside.

The moan that slips past my lips is low and broken. I think I might pass out from pure bliss. I breathe, "Fuck," and moan again.

"You keep telling me you're in charge, handsome, but we both know who the real boss is."

I drop my forehead to the space between her shoulder blades and laugh softly, enjoying the moment, the firelight, the smell of her hair and skin. "You're right, baby. You're always right."

"Really?"

"No."

Sliding a hand between her legs, I stroke her clit as I thrust into her. I play with her pussy and fuck her ass until she orgasms, screaming my name, and neither one of us cares who's in charge anymore.

I follow her over the edge wishing I were a different man without skies full of secrets and oceans of blood on his hands.

CHAPTER 43
Shay

Groggy with afterglow, I lie quietly in Cole's arms, enveloped in his warmth and strength. Sweat cools on my skin. The fire paints the yard in dancing patterns of light and shadow. His heart throbs beneath my ear with the strong, steady beat of a drum, and for once, my mind is still.

I don't know what lies beyond this moment. All I know is that he feels like home to me in a way I never expected any man could feel.

It's terrifying.

As soon as that realization hits, my quiet mind explodes into a tornado of questions, worries, and imagined outcomes to this nonrelationship of ours, each one progressively worse.

He rouses, turning his head to kiss my hair. His voice is a husky murmur. "You okay?"

"Yes. Why?"

"You're thinking."

"God forbid."

"Exactly. Hence the question."

Sighing, I close my eyes and snuggle closer to him. "This morning in the stairwell."

"What about it?"

"We didn't use protection."

I wait for him to say something, but he doesn't, so I continue. "What I meant was we should probably talk about contraception. Assuming we're going to keep doing this, which I hope we will."

He inhales a slow breath, then exhales quietly, gliding his fingertips up and down my arm. He kisses my head again, then pulls me on top of him, arranging my body on his so I'm using him as a big pillow. He pulls one of the soft furry throws over my back, then puts a hand on my head and tucks it into the space between his neck and shoulder, keeping it there when he speaks.

"I take it you're not on the pill."

"I didn't say that."

"So you are on the pill?"

"Yes. I never stopped after Chet and I broke up."

After a pause, he says, "Ah. This conversation isn't really about contraception."

"I'm not accusing you of not disclosing that you have an STD, if that's what you're thinking."

"What I'm thinking is that you're looking for answers about our situation that I can't give."

A lump forms in my throat. Hurt gathers into a sick little ball in my stomach. I wish I wasn't so emotional, but that's like saying I wish the sky wasn't blue. Nothing can be done about it.

Why do I keep getting ahead of myself with this man? Why am I already in so deep? I know whatever shape it will take between us will be messy, so why am I setting myself up for the heartbreak that's almost certainly coming?

Oh yeah, because I'm a stubborn, foolish romantic who never learns the lessons the universe keeps trying to teach me about the real cost of love.

He's right. I should stop reading romance novels.

"Can I ask one question?" Without waiting for a response, I hurry on. "Why would you say you'd buy me a ring if we can't have a relationship?"

"I asked if you wanted me to buy you a ring, not that I would."

"I see. Pardon me while I lie here and die of embarrassment."

"Shay. Love. Why can't we just take this one day at a time?"

I'm hurt and angry, but he called me love, so it shaves a hair off my angst. I lie on his chest and try to reason with myself that I'm asking for too much too soon, but then I get mad all over again.

"Hey, remember a little while ago when you asked me to promise I'd catch you if you fell into me? I guess I must've taken that the wrong way. You were actually talking about falling into my vagina, correct?"

He rolls over, pinning me underneath his heavy body and staring down with blazing intensity into my eyes.

He growls, "You know what I meant, and it wasn't falling into your goddamn vagina."

"So you were alluding to falling in love with me."

"Would you like me to draw you a picture?"

"There's no need to be snarky. Nice sidestep, by the way. You're incredibly good at those."

His lips thin. His eyes narrow. Thunderclouds gather over his head. All of that might convince me to drop the subject, except I just decided that I've had enough of dancing circles around each other.

"Okay, Cole. I'm just gonna go ahead and ask because I don't love the whole cloak-and-dagger thing you've got going. What are you hiding? Do you have a wife stashed away somewhere? A girlfriend you haven't told me about? A bunch of kids?"

"No, no, and no. And now we're going to go upstairs, shower, and go to bed."

Nose to nose, we stare into each other's eyes. I can tell he really means this is the end of the discussion. He won't answer any more questions. He won't give me more than he already has.

Maybe ever.

He waits silently as I wrestle with dueling desires to let it go and see where time takes us or get up and walk out of his house and his life for good.

Instead of either of those choices, I lob the tennis ball back onto his side of the court.

"Okay. I believe you. And I'll leave it alone for now. But here's something I want you to think about, especially in light of what happened Friday night and the things you apologized for afterward, namely things you weren't proud of like slamming doors and raising your voice."

I pause to make sure I've got his full attention. I do, so I continue.

"There's a fine line between privacy, which is everyone's right, and controlling the flow of information, which is something bad guys do."

His response is instant. He delivers it in a low, calm tone while staring right into my eyes.

"Believe me, I'm very aware of the behaviors of abusers. And if we were in a committed relationship, I'd tell you everything. No part of my life would be hidden from you, and I'd expect the same in return. But as I keep telling you, *I don't do relationships*. There are reasons for that, very valid fucking reasons, but the primary one is because being with me isn't safe. Not because I'd harm you in a physical or emotional way, but because my lifestyle is dangerous. That isn't an exaggeration. It's dangerous, Shay, and what you've encountered so far with how I handled Dylan is only the tip of the iceberg. So yes, I want you, and yes, I'm falling for you, but because I know what I-know, I can't let it go farther than this."

My throat closes. My pulse races. My shame is a bottomless well that I throw myself into headfirst.

He's flat-out telling me that this is it. Random hook-ups at his convenience.

No commitments, no questions, just sex.

I shouldn't be so hurt. It's not like he hasn't been saying this since the beginning. I just haven't been listening.

"I understand. I think I'd like to go home now."

"Shay, please listen—"

"No, you listen, Cole. I hear you. I get it. And how you want to live your life is totally up to you. But you know what? I deserve better than late night bootie calls and an uncommitted heart. So yes, this has been amazing, and yes, I'm completely gaga over you, but you need to let me up now because I'm going home."

He closes his eyes and mutters, "Fuck."

Then he exhales heavily and rolls off me.

I stand, grab my heels, and walk across the grass-lined pavers to the terrace, where I grab my dress off the chair and step into it. As I'm zipping it up, he approaches, naked and stupidly beautiful, his face pained.

He watches me slip into my heels, then suddenly pulls me into his arms.

In a raw voice, he begs, "Stay. Please."

When I don't answer, he squeezes me tighter. "I'll take you home in the morning. Just stay with me tonight, baby. Please stay with me."

The vulnerability in his voice melts my fragile resolve. I rest my cheek against his chest and close my eyes, trying to keep the pain from my voice when I speak.

"Okay. Just for tonight. You've got me until the sun comes up, handsome, then I turn into a pumpkin."

He kisses my neck. Without another word, he picks me up and carries me inside.

CHAPTER 44
Cole

She's silent as I carry her through the house and up the stairs to the master, but every so often, she releases a soft, sad sigh.

I know she's not aware she's doing it, but it kills me all the same.

I should've stayed away. I should've been stronger. I should've known that whatever forces that led to her standing in my office doorway on her first day as my new assistant were dark and twisted because whatever Fate has in store for me, I've always known it's bad.

There are no such things as coincidences.

Shay was put in my path to remind me of everything I can never have. To remind me there's a reason I stay away from people. A reason I don't get close. A reason that's bigger than my own selfish desires, no matter how strong those desires might be.

I made a vow that my life would be spent in service to something bigger than me. A vow I've kept for a long time. But she sat down at my table at the hotel bar weeks ago and smiled at me, and I've thought of nothing else since.

I want so badly to be the man she needs. But the only thing I can give her is uncertainty.

Like she said, she deserves better.

I carry her inside the master bathroom and set her down. I strip off her dress. As she uses the toilet, I turn on the shower and get the water to a nice temperature, then take her in my arms when she steps in.

We stand in silence together letting the warm water flow over our skin. Our heads bowed, our arms around each other, steam rising in billowing clouds that gently caress us...the moment feels holy.

That is, if I knew what holiness is.

Then she takes a breath and grabs a bar of soap from the niche in the wall. Holding it out to me, she smiles.

"Okay, cowboy. You got me pretty dirty. Better clean me up."

And my heart breaks. It just fucking breaks. For her, for how brave and sweet and wonderful she is, and for me too, because no man should be given everything he's ever wanted when what he wants is exactly what he can't have.

I take the bar of soap from her hand, force a smile, and resolve that I won't ruin our last hours together by being maudlin. "Yes, ma'am. Tell me where you want me to start."

She goes up on her toes and kisses me.

I kiss her back, trying to pretend the mist in my eyes is from the shower.

After the shower, I dry her off and carry her into bed. She laughs at me, protesting that she knows how to walk, but I know this will be the last time I can do this, so I do.

I make love to her again. It's different than before, softer, sweeter, and devastatingly powerful.

Probably because we both know it's goodbye.

She falls asleep in my arms. I lie awake, watching the play of shadows on the ceiling, aching for all the moments we won't get to share. I finally drift off to sleep, only to awaken with a jolt sometime later.

The room is dark and silent, but I sense someone watching from the shadows.

I listen hard, my ears and eyes open, my pulse jagged. My old friend paranoia has me questioning everything—the hum of the air conditioning, the creak of a floorboard, the rustle of a tree branch outside the window.

Then I hear a distant ringing and realize what woke me.

Careful not to disturb Shay, I rise and walk naked to the closet. I grab a pair of sweats from the dresser and pull them on in the dark. Then I head out of my bedroom and down the hallway to my office, where the cell phone on my desk continues to ring.

It's the burner I use for business, the number which only dangerous or desperate people have.

"*Yonige-ya.*"

A male voice with a British accent answers me. "You on your way?"

It's Axel. I frown. "Way where?"

"We have a move tonight."

Fuck. Not tonight, of all fucking nights.

"Since when?"

"Since Tuesday of last week. I sent you the package." He pauses. "Don't tell me you forgot."

That's exactly what happened, but I'm not about to admit that my attention has been otherwise occupied. "Got my dates mixed up."

"You don't get your dates mixed up." Another short pause. "She with you?"

I can't help the growl that rises in my throat. "None of your fucking business."

He chuckles. "That's a yes. Look at you, having a sleepover. I'd ask if you were out of your mind, but I already know the answer."

"Fuck you, Axel."

He doesn't take offense. He knows it's myself I'm frustrated with, not him.

"I love you too, bruv. I'll send you the address again. You've got twenty minutes to get to Van Nuys. It's gonna be tight."

He disconnects, leaving me cursing.

Moving fast, I return to the bedroom and dress in the dark. My eyes have adjusted, so I can easily find what I need. I grab my briefcase, dash off a note for Shay in case she wakes up, and leave it on my pillow.

I stare at her silently as she sleeps for a moment. It's almost impossible to leave her, but I must.

The 405 is unnaturally quiet tonight. One bit of luck. I speed down the freeway into the Valley, my foot jammed against the gas pedal, my mind sharp, and my hands steady.

I'm in go mode.

I've done this so many times before, it's as automatic as breathing.

I park three blocks away and walk the rest of the distance. The streets are empty. The neighborhood is worn around the edges, mostly apartment buildings built after the last world war, strip malls with liquor stores and laundromats and the random fast food drive-through on a corner.

It's not always like this. I've moved women from wealthy neighborhoods too. Money solves some problems but amplifies others.

A black Sprinter van with fake plates idles across the street from the four-story apartment building I'm headed to. Axel is behind the wheel. He spots me and gives me a thumbs-up.

Then I'm standing in front of apartment 2B, lightly knocking.

The woman who opens the door is slightly built, with frizzy brown hair and a chalky complexion. Her sweater is threadbare and her shoes are old too, but the purple bruise on her cheekbone is fresh. So is the cigarette burn on the back of her hand.

The little girl with the big brown eyes hiding behind her and clinging to her leg has bruises around her throat in the shape of fingers.

"Hello, Theresa. Are you ready?"

She nods, opening the door wider to let me in.

When I step inside, I smell cigarette smoke and stale beer. The living room is small but tidy. A single light burns in the hallway that leads past the kitchen. Down that hallway behind a closed door, a television blares.

Good. Ambient noise masks all kinds of nastiness.

Unless, of course, he starts screaming. Which they sometimes do. Then I'll have to get creative. A crushing blow to the windpipe usually does the trick.

I close the door behind me and turn to Theresa, who's chewing her thumbnail and hyperventilating. I keep my voice low and soothing because I know her nerves are shot.

"I'll be out in less than five minutes. Then I'll take you across the street to my associate who's waiting. He has all your paperwork. IDs, passports, plane tickets. He'll take you to the airport and get you on the flight. When you arrive in Vancouver, you'll be met by another of my associates who'll assist you from there."

"How will I know how to find him?"

"It's a she. Her name's Kiyoko. And she'll find you. Just stay inside the terminal. She'll give you money and the keys to a car and your new apartment. You have my number if you need it."

Theresa nods. She licks her lips, glances down the hallway, then looks back at me. Her eyes fierce, she whispers vehemently, "God bless you."

Too late. The devil already did.

"Remember, you can never contact anyone you know again. Your life here is over. Theresa Davis and her daughter no longer exist."

She nods, but I'm already turning away. I walk silently down the hallway, stop at the closed door, and remove my gloves from my briefcase.

Then I open the door and walk inside.

A sweating man in boxers is propped up on pillows in bed. He's balding, shirtless, and overweight, eating potato chips from a small pile on his chest and smoking a cigarette. Empty beer cans litter the nightstand and floor next to him.

Not all abusers are such slobs. Like Dylan, most of them appear respectable. It's one reason they get away with so much.

Good people don't believe that evil can look pretty.

The man on the bed jerks upright and tries to hide his fear behind a snarl. "Who the fuck are you?"

I let him sit with that fear for a moment, just a small taste of the terror Theresa and her daughter have lived with for years. "A friend of your wife's."

I smile and close the door behind me.

CHAPTER 45
Shay

The note is written in Cole's handwriting. The words make sense, but the underlying message is confusing.

> BABY,
> IF YOU WAKE UP AND I'M GONE, DON'T WORRY. I HAD TO TAKE CARE OF SOME WORK. I'LL BE BACK IN A FEW HOURS.
> I ADORE YOU,
> COLE

Standing at the side of the bed wearing a white dress shirt of his that I found in his closet, I read the note over again. Uneasiness is a hungry sewer rat gnawing holes through my stomach.

Everything about this is strange. Him leaving me here alone, the "work" he had to take care of, that sign off.

Especially the sign off. He's expert at turning the closing of a letter into mind fuckery.

So he adores me but doesn't want to commit to me. He adores me but doesn't answer my questions. He adores me but keeps me at arm's length distance while dropping masterpieces of mystery such as, "Being with me isn't safe."

I look around the room, at all the expensive furnishings and the artwork and the elegant décor, and say into the silence, "This is bullshit."

I want to ransack his closet, but I don't. I want to rifle through his drawers, but I don't. I want, badly, to find some evidence of whatever it is he's hiding from me, but I decide to respect his privacy instead.

Barefoot, I head downstairs to the kitchen. The overhead lights blink on automatically, which is convenient but also weird. It makes me wonder if the house is operated by artificial intelligence, then I get creeped out that maybe a sentient computer is spying on me from behind the walls.

The contents of the massive stainless steel fridge are bizarre. Two dozen hard boiled eggs in a bowl, seven identical prepped containers of sliced steak and mashed sweet potatoes, and four glass jars of beige liquid that look like protein shakes are arranged separately in symmetrical rows on each shelf. The cheese and vegetable drawers are empty, as are both doors.

There are no condiments, no snacks, no desserts in the freezer.

The only thing in ample supply is cold air.

I open one of the protein shake jars and sniff, instantly regretting it. The contents smell like dirt and cabbage, which means it's probably healthy. I replace it and grab one of the containers of steak and potatoes, then rummage around in drawers until I find a fork.

Standing up at the kitchen island, I eat cold steak and get more upset by the second.

He left me here alone.

He *left* me.

I'm in the middle of angrily chewing filet when Cole walks through the door.

Like a mortician, he's dressed entirely in black. Suit, shirt, tie. The gray leather briefcase he's holding has a strange dark smear across the top and side, along with a splatter pattern that looks like abstract art.

He sets the case on the counter beside the fridge, then turns to me, his expression blank.

"Hello."

"Hi."

"Are you okay?"

"Yes. Are you?"

"Yes."

His energy is odd. He appears calm, but it's like the calm that comes after a really hard workout when you've spent yourself physically, leaving your mind clear.

The knuckles of both his hands are black and blue.

My heart starts to pound. I slowly set the fork down, staring at those bruised hands and the healing scrapes from the other morning when he said Dylan was fired, most of which have reopened and are oozing blood.

"Cole?"

"You don't want to know."

"That's funny, because I was just thinking that I do."

He doesn't reply. He only stands staring at me with his odd, unnerving calm.

"You told me you trusted me."

"I do."

"So tell me what this work thing was that was so important you had to leave in the middle of the night and left your hands in that condition."

"It was a personnel issue."

"A *personnel* issue. Like Dylan's was?"

He says nothing.

"What were you out doing in the dark while I was here sleeping? Tell me."

Still nothing. A faint whiff of cigarette smoke reaches my nose.

His strange calm has infected me, because I should be freaking out, but I'm not. The only physical reaction I have so far is an accelerated heartbeat.

"I didn't know you were a smoker, Cole."

"I'm not."

"Just went out to punch some trees, did you? Box a few rounds with a buddy at the gym?"

"No."

"So what, then?"

"I can't tell you."

"Why?"

"Because I can't have you hate me. It would end me if you hated me. I can handle anything but that."

I stare at him, so calm and handsome, so odd and enigmatic, and so obviously dangerous it permeates the air all around him, and realize that this man standing in front of me is capable of anything.

Including extreme violence.

I knew it before, but now I know it in a different way. Not only is he capable of violence, he goes out and looks for it. He walks around with it in the darkness, holding its hand. He prepares for it, evidenced by that case with its ominous smear and whatever tools of mayhem it contains.

And, if I'm not mistaken, there's a part of him that enjoys it too.

My voice is quiet in the stillness of the kitchen. "Did you kill someone?"

He stares at me, his body still, his blue eyes glittering.

His silence speaks volumes.

I wait for the fear to come. Or the shock. Neither arrives. Which means I'm too far down this rabbit hole to find my way out.

I'm in love with him, monster or not.

Holding his gaze, I say, "I'll never hate you. No matter what you've done. No matter if you keep doing it. I won't hate you because I can't, Cole. My heart won't let me. So whatever happened tonight, it doesn't change how I feel. Maybe it should, but it doesn't, and that's the truth."

Finally, his odd composure breaks. He closes his eyes, clenches his jaw, and swallows. His right hand trembles, then falls still. His voice turns raspy. "You can't mean that."

"You know I do."

"You don't know what you're saying."

"I really hate it when you're patronizing. Let me ask you something. Final question about this, I promise."

He opens his eyes and stares at me. His gaze burns me down to the marrow of my bones.

I point at his hand. "Did you do that to someone bad? Yes or no."

This time, his answer is immediate. "Yes."

"That's what I thought. Now, are you hurt anywhere on your body other than your hands?"

When he shakes his head, I exhale in relief.

"Good. Now that we've got all that covered, let's share this steak, then go back to bed. I don't know about you, but I'm exhausted."

When he doesn't budge an inch, I start to lose patience. "Don't just stand there staring at me like I'm speaking Latin. Come over here and get some food in your stomach."

When he still doesn't move, I stab a piece of filet and bring it over to him, holding it up near his mouth.

Brows knitted, he stares at me.

"Please don't make me do the choo-choo train noise to get you to open your mouth. It would be humiliating for us both."

He takes the fork from my hand, sets it aside on the counter-top, and cups my face in his hands.

"This isn't a fight you're going to win. We can't be together."

"I didn't say anything about us being together. I said eat the steak."

When he doesn't respond, I close my eyes and sigh. "Look. Nothing's changed. The whole thing is impossible. I realize that.

You'll take me home in the morning, and we'll go back to living our separate lives and pretend there's nothing between us when we see each other at work. But for right now, just *eat the fucking steak.*"

I open my eyes and meet his burning gaze. "Okay?"

His expression is indescribable. Sometimes there aren't words for things, and this is one of them.

I know he's not angry with me. It's more like he met someone from an alien world who he's desperate to understand but can't because he doesn't speak their language.

"I know it doesn't make sense. I don't get it either. It's just how I feel. You could ask me to be the driver of your getaway car, and I'd say yes. You could ask me to lie to the FBI, and I'd say yes. Just please don't ask me to help you bury a body because digging a big hole sounds really hard, and my arm strength isn't what it should be."

He swallows. He shakes his head. It's obvious he's struggling.

So I turn to the counter and pick up the fork. I slip the piece of steak off the end and hold it to his lips. "Eat, honey. It will make me happy."

He opens his mouth and accepts the meat, then stands there looking electrocuted as he chews.

"I like it when you're obedient."

"Don't get used to it."

"I won't. Want another piece?"

Staring at my lips, he nods.

I grab the container from the island, then go back and stand in front of him, holding another bite of filet. I lift it to his lips. He opens his mouth and takes it.

We stare at each other in blistering silence until he's swallowed.

"More?"

He nods.

When I lift the meat to his mouth this time, he puts his hands around my waist and pulls me against him. I give him the steak, watching the pulse throb in the side of his neck. His cock is growing hard against my hip.

I whisper, "You like me feeding you."

"Yes."

His voice is husky. His breathing is erratic. His pupils are dilating fast.

He's a man who does bad things in the dark as if it's another day at the office, returning home a little tired but composed. But show him some tenderness, and he crumbles like a sandcastle under a crashing wave.

Like my heart is doing, watching him fall apart for me.

I set the container on the counter, turn back to him, slide my hands up his chest, and look into his eyes.

"I think you're beautiful. All your parts. All your broken pieces. They're beautiful to me, and so are you. So if I never get the chance to tell you again, I'm telling you now that if you and your monsters ever decide you need a home, you have one in me."

He doesn't answer. I didn't expect him to.

He's too busy fighting his demons.

I hand feed him the rest of the meat in the container, then we go back upstairs to bed.

CHAPTER 46
Cole

N ear morning, it starts to rain.

I lie awake as I have been for hours. Shay slumbers peacefully beside me. I'm on my back. She's on her side, holding me, one leg flung over mine, an arm across my chest, her head resting on my shoulder.

She knows what I am yet still she sleeps like a baby. Sleeps and holds me like I'm the one who needs protection, not the other way around.

How is it possible?

What does it mean?

She's not mentally impaired. She's not in denial. She's not anything but completely accepting, and it makes not one bit of fucking sense.

Emiliano calls me the wolf.

My employees call me the Grinch.

Axel calls me the Evaporator. Bruv, British jargon for brother, when he's feeling generous.

Other people call me by other names, none of them flattering, but Shay calls me honey and beautiful and feeds me steak from her fingertips as if I'm an injured animal she brought home to nurse back to health.

It can't be this easy.

Things like this don't exist between people like us.

Do they?

I turn my head and look at her, sleeping so soundly. Trusting me. *Me*, the man who walked in from the night with another man's screams still echoing in his ears. She looked at me, and she knew, and she did the impossible.

She accepted me.

Again.

With rain pattering against the windows, I rise from bed, careful not to disturb her. Then I go into the closet, pull the burner from the inside pocket of my suit jacket, and call Axel.

As always, he answers after one ring. He might be the only man on earth who sleeps less than I do.

"Hullo, bruv. Everything's green on my end. You solid?"

"No."

I exhale and drag a hand through my hair. The most patient man I've ever met, he waits in tolerant silence for me to get my shit together.

"I need you to talk some sense into me."

"About what?"

"Shay."

This time, his silence is surprised. We've known each other long enough that I can tell the difference. But still he waits for me to speak first.

"I...I'm...fuck." I blow out a hard breath and admit the truth. "I'm done for."

His voice low, Axel says, "You can't be serious."

"That's the thing. I am."

"She's a civ."

"No shit. Doesn't change anything."

"And she works for you."

"Still doesn't change anything."

"Bollocks. If you really care about her, you walk away. We don't get the white picket fence. Not us."

I already know, but I'm desperate enough to argue.

"Why does it have to be a white picket fence? Why can't it be something else? Why can't it be like some Wes Craven version of *Pride and Prejudice* where Mr. Darcy murders people instead of sneering at them and Elizabeth Bennett grinds up the bones and uses them to fertilize her roses?"

"Listen to yourself. I'd be laughing hysterically if I knew this wasn't a joke."

"You're British. You don't do anything hysterically. The best you can manage is a scathing comeback."

"You say that like a good scathing comeback isn't art."

"Help me, Axel. I need help, and I need it now, because I'm ten seconds away from going into the other room, shaking her awake, and asking her to marry me."

"Bloody hell. How long have you known this girl, four minutes?"

"Four minutes can be a lifetime with the right person."

"You're daft."

"No, I'm in love."

"Same thing."

I think of Florentino from that wretched book *Love in the Time of Cholera*, how he spent fifty years pining over Fermina before they finally got together, and wish I'd never learned to read.

"Killian Black has a wife. Why can't I?"

Axel's voice turns sour. "You're not Killian Black."

"Nobody is. That's my point. If the most dangerous man on the planet can put down roots, there's hope for the rest of us."

"You and I can't put down roots because we'd poison the soil."

I grimace at the phone. "We're not that bad."

"I disagree, lover boy, but let's play this out. You put a ring on her finger, you move her in, you play house. What happens when she wakes up in the middle of the night and you're gone, then you stroll through the door with blood on your hands? You think she won't run as fast as she can? Because that's exactly what will happen. You're only setting everyone up for heartbreak. And prison time for you when she goes to the police."

"She won't run or go to the police."

He scoffs. "That's hope talking, not logic."

"No, it's experience."

This time, his silence is stunned. "She knows?"

"No details, but enough to understand she's not dealing with Mary Poppins."

Another stunned silence. "*You're telling me this bird is okay with it?*"

"She told me she thinks all my broken pieces are beautiful."

"Bollocks!"

"Swear to God."

"You're making it up!"

"That's what she said, Axel. Verbatim."

He snorts in disbelief or disgust. "So she's as daft as you are!"

"Then she fed me filet mignon from her fingers and said if my monsters ever need a home, they have one in her."

"Christ on a cracker!"

I'm taken aback by his shouting. He never raises his voice. The closest I've seen him come to losing his temper is once at a coffee shop when the server gave him green tea instead of Earl Grey. His look of scorn was so savage, the poor girl nearly burst into tears.

"This is the most worked up I've ever heard you."

"I've never had to deal with this much insanity before. And that's saying something, considering I worked at a psychiatric hospital for five years."

"You worked at a psychiatric hospital?"

"Why do you sound so surprised?"

"You're the son of nobility. What aristocrat lets his son work in an asylum?"

"Well, I didn't ask bloody permission did I?"

"There's no need to shout."

There's some indiscernible muttering, then he comes back on the line more composed. "Look. If you think you and Little Miss

Sunshine have a shot, you're off your bloody rocker, but I won't be the one to ruin such a cheery mutual delusion. You can do that yourselves."

Hope blossoms in my chest. "So you're saying I should keep seeing her?"

His sigh contains centuries of British contempt for stupidity. "You're a wanker."

"Agreed. Before you hang up on me, I need to find someone."

"Thank Christ, we're back to the real world. What's the name?"

"Don't have a name."

"Address?"

"Don't have that either."

"What've you got?"

"Nothing."

"Perfect. Make my job a little harder, why don't you?"

"You can manage it."

"Of course I can. They don't call me Hound Dog for nothing."

I chuckle. "It's hilarious that you think you got that nickname because you're so good at tracking."

He sounds offended. "What the hell other bloody reason would there be?"

"A hound dog is slang for a promiscuous man, idiot."

"Pfft. I'm not promiscuous."

"How many women have you slept with so far this year?"

After a beat, he says, "Fine. I'm promiscuous. Don't slut shame me."

"Nobody's slut shaming anybody. I'm just pointing out that your nickname has more than one meaning."

He mutters, "You Americans and your barmy slang. It's like you're all dead from the neck up."

"*Our* slang is bad? You should listen to yourself some time. Back to the person I'm looking for. She lives in Vegas."

"Lotta people in Vegas, mate."

"Yes, but only one of them is Shay's mother."

"What's she got to do with anything?"

"She's got a boyfriend who needs attention."

"Ah. So then it *is* true love with you and the bird."

"Why do you say that?"

"Haven't you read any Shakespeare? Nobody unalives their father-in-law unless it's true love."

"He's not my father-in-law. He's just some scumbag abusive boyfriend."

"Call it what you want, tosser, if it's your bird's mum's bloke, he's your father-in-law."

"Sometimes I have no fucking idea what you're saying."

"Now you know how I feel half the time when I'm talking to you. If I'd known when we met all those years ago at boarding school that you'd turn out to be such a stupid sod, I never would've saved you from getting your arse beat by those upperclassmen."

"That's a nice bit of revisionist history there, but it was *me* who saved *you*."

"Oh, that's just wonderful. Not only have you lost your mind over this bird of yours, you've lost your memory too."

"Just get me the information, you sarcastic bastard. Shay's last name is Sanders."

Muttering an oath, he hangs up on me.

I set the phone on the dresser, take a moment to breathe, then go back into the bedroom and climb into bed.

I fall asleep curled around Shay's body, debating whether or not I should water the seed of hope that germinated in my chest after my call with Axel or stomp it underfoot.

CHAPTER 47
Shay

I wake up disoriented and sweaty, struggling for breath under a heavy, immoveable weight.

"Cole, wake up. You're smashing me."

Lying on top of me as silent and still as a coma patient, he doesn't respond. I poke him in his ribs, which doesn't get a response either, so then I try to push him off, which I should've known would be a complete failure too, as the man weighs five thousand pounds.

If I can't get him off me soon, I'll suffocate.

So I resort to guerrilla tactics. At the top of my lungs, I shout, "Fire!"

He jerks and leaps up, then stands naked at the side of the bed, wild-eyed and bristling, his hands in a karate-chop pose I've only ever seen characters in bad television dramas do.

"What's wrong? What's happening?" He looks around the room as if he's expecting the walls to start churning out ninjas, then hollers to no one, "I'll kill you with my bare hands!"

It's so funny, I start laughing and can't stop.

He looks over at me convulsing on the bed. "What are you laughing at?"

"You look like you're auditioning for *Charlie's Angels*!"

He stands straight, drops his hands to his sides, and gives me an evil glare.

I roll over and laugh into the pillow until my stomach hurts, and I'm crying.

"Very funny. Ha ha. I'm glad you think I'm so amusing."

When I roll to my back again, he's still glaring at me, except now he's got his arms folded over his chest.

Gasping for breath, I say, "Oh God, that was amazing. You should've seen yourself. If there really was a fire, you could've put it out with your terrifying karate hands."

After another moment of narrow-eyed annoyance, he leaps on top of me with a roar and starts to tickle me, digging his fingers between my ribs.

"No! No tickling!" I scream, which only makes him tickle me harder.

When I shout, "Mercy!" he relents. Capturing my wrists, he presses my arms over my head and holds them against the pillow as he smiles down at me, his eyes soft and warm.

"Hi."

"Hi yourself, sensei."

"You spent the night."

"I did. And narrowly escaped death by crushing with some fast thinking."

"Yes. That's what I admire most about you, by the way. Your brain."

"If brain is a euphemism for boobs, I believe you."

We grin at each other until he dips his head and kisses me. The kiss is slow, soft, and intimate. It leaves me breathless. Against my mouth, he murmurs, "Your boobs are nice too."

"*Nice?* Excuse me, but these puppies are spectacular."

He rubs his cheek against my chest, grumbling in pleasure like a lion. Through his shirt I'm wearing, he sucks on a nipple until it's peaked, and I'm even more breathless than before.

His knees are planted on the mattress on either side of my

hips. Between his spread legs, his cock is already stiff, bobbing as he moves to my other nipple.

"Cole?"

"Mmm."

"You seem like you're in a good mood."

"I am. Try not to ruin it by talking."

"I'm not talking. Who's talking? Not me."

"Don't try to read my mind either."

"Okay. So I shouldn't ask you why you're in such a good mood?"

"Only if you want me to stop doing this."

He lightly sinks his teeth into my nipple. I groan, arching up into his mouth as heat engulfs my body.

"That's what I thought." He grasps the open collar of the shirt and gives it a hard yank. Buttons go flying.

"You have a bad habit of ruining shirts, handsome."

Smoothing the shirt to either side so my breasts and belly are bared to him, he gazes down at me with avid eyes. "You complaining?"

"No."

"Good. Now be quiet. I need to make you come."

My pulse surges. "We'll be late for work."

"I'll write you a note for your boss. Oh, wait." He smiles. "I am your boss. Your tardiness is excused, Ms. Sanders."

Without waiting for a reply, he cups my breasts and pushes them together, then starts to lavish my hard nipples with his tongue.

I squirm underneath him and try my best to be quiet as he chuckles, amused by my restlessness, his mouth full of my flesh.

Against my skin, he whispers, "I wonder how wet your pussy is?"

"Very."

"Already?"

"Yes. She's a shameless hussy where you're concerned."

"Show me."

I slide my hand between my legs, dip my fingers inside myself, then lift my hand to his mouth. Looking into my eyes, he sucks on my fingertips.

"Delicious. Get that hand back between your legs."

Closing his eyes, he turns his attention back to my breasts as I touch myself again. I glide my fingertips over my sensitive clit and whimper. When he tests my nipple with his teeth again, I moan.

It seems to snap some self-control he's been exercising. With a growl, he moves down my body, knocks my hand away, spreads my thighs, puts his face between my legs, and licks my exposed pussy with a flat tongue. Then he flicks the tip of it back and forth over my clit until I'm moaning loudly and pulling at his hair.

"Don't come yet. Save it for my cock."

He slides two fingers inside me and goes back to licking my clit.

Breathless, my skin burning, I rock my hips against his face and watch his tongue move. He reaches up and pinches one of my nipples, sending a pulse of pleasure spreading outward until it connects with the pleasure already pulsing between my legs.

I tip my head back against the pillow and close my eyes, abandoning any thought of trying to figure out what's going on with him because he's making me feel too good to care.

When I'm moaning loudly and bucking my hips helplessly against his face, seconds from orgasm, he withdraws his fingers from inside me.

"My sweet, greedy girl," he says, his voice rough. "Open your eyes."

As soon as I do, I get even more turned on. His mouth and chin glisten with my wetness. He licks his lips, and that simple gesture is so sexy, it makes my heart flutter.

Eyes hot, he straightens, rising to his knees. He takes his erection in his hand and strokes it as he looks me over, his heated gaze caressing my entire body.

He stares at me so long, I start to get self-conscious.

"What?"

"I just like looking at perfection. Spread your legs wider."

I do, loving how it makes the vein in his neck jump. Staring down at my pussy, he slides his finger over the slit on the head of his cock, spreading the gleaming drop of precum all around.

His shaft is stiff and veined. I can't wait for him to shove it inside me.

"That look will get you fucked hard, pretty girl."

"Hopefully soon," I whisper, my pulse flying.

"And that mouth will get you spanked."

"I can think of a better use for it." I bite my lower lip and flutter my lashes coyly.

Smiling, he crooks a finger. I sit up and scooch closer to him, taking his hard cock in my hand. He threads a hand into my hair as I close my lips around the crown of his cock and start sucking.

When I take him as far as I can until I gag, he tightens his fingers in my hair and releases a gravelly chuckle.

"I see someone's looking for a promotion."

I suck, lick, and stroke his cock until he's panting and his hands are shaking. When he moans, I know he's close.

He pulls my head back and stares down at me for a long moment, his chest rising and falling, his eyes unblinking and intense. His voice comes out in a rasp.

"What do I do with you?"

I know what he means. He's still fighting with himself, and with every second that passes, he's losing the fight.

So I gaze up into his tortured eyes and say softly, "Keep me. Love me. Make me yours."

His lids flutter closed. For a long moment, I'm not sure what he'll do. I sit watching him with my heart in my throat and my stomach in knots, wondering if I've pushed him too far.

But then he falls on me, crushing his mouth to mine and pushing me flat against the mattress, and the elation that burns through me is so bright and blistering, it's like being burned alive.

With one powerful thrust, he shoves into me.

I cry out and shudder. He lifts to his elbows and tangles his fingers in my hair.

"Be careful what you wish for, baby. And if I ever say I love you, be afraid. Because my love isn't soft. It isn't pretty. It's the monster hiding under your bed in the dark."

Then he fucks me hard and deep, staring into my eyes as I moan and beg him for more.

When I orgasm, it's with my fingernails sunk into the muscles of his back and his name on my lips, chanted over and over like a prayer.

CHAPTER 48
Cole

I drop Shay at her apartment so she can change into work clothes, giving her a lingering kiss at the door. Then I head to the office feeling lighter than I have in years.

And more conflicted.

I know I'm not a good partner. I'm moody, secretive, and unpredictable. I've been told I'm generous, I've been told I'm a good lover, but I've never been told I'm kind.

Because I'm not. Kindness is a weakness for men in my line of work.

But that's exactly what a woman like Shay needs. Along with all the other things I can't provide her: stability, openness, patience. The list is long.

And what if she wants children?

I can see it now, an adorable mini version of Shay in middle school with a mouth like her mother's when someone asks what her daddy does for work.

"Oh, he does stuff with money during the day. But at nighttime, he goes out and kills people! So don't make me mad or I'll tell him you pushed me off the monkey bars. Your body will never be found."

Leading a double life is only workable when nobody else knows what you're up to. Add a wife into that mix, add kids...

Disaster.

The only viable option is to give one or the other up. Which I've been fine with so far. I've shaped my life around solitude and secrecy, but Shay makes me want all kinds of things I've never wanted before.

She makes me want to be better.

Which is problematic, considering I already know this is the best I'll ever get.

I'm under no misconceptions that I'm salvageable. I'm rotten to the core. Nobody does what I do and finds redemption, no matter how much I believe that ridding the world of fiends like Dylan and Theresa's husband is for the greater good.

So why the fuck would I think that Shay and I could make it work?

That bastard hope is playing mind games with me, that's why.

So is that stupid goddamn book she loves so much. Nobody but an incurable romantic would think going through hell for half a century waiting for your one true love's husband to die so you can be together is anything but a horror story.

Love in the Time of Cholera my ass. It should be called *Idiots Mistaking Insanity for Romance.*

I think I'll burn my copy.

Fate decides this is a good teachable moment for me and sends me a ghost from my past in the form of a phone call.

I look at the number on the touch screen of my dashboard and tense. I hesitate before answering, because I already know this will be tough.

"Hello, Kiyoko."

"I know we said we'd only communicate through Axel from now on, but I needed to talk to you."

Her voice is soft and melodic. An image of her face flashes into my mind's eye. Black hair and pale skin, bow-shaped lips and high cheekbones.

Dark, haunted eyes.

"What's the matter?"

She exhales. "I miss you."

I hate how sad she sounds. We haven't seen each other in months, and our relationship was strained for a long time before that, but it doesn't mean I want her to be unhappy.

Quite the opposite. I want her to live her best life, which is why I broke it off with her. Having me around only reminded her every day of what she'd lost.

Sometimes people cling to reminders of their grief instead of letting go like they should. Makes them feel like they're somehow in control, when all they're doing is tormenting themselves.

"Are you all right? Other than that, I mean."

"I'm okay. Surviving. How are you?"

I think of Shay moaning my name as she dug her nails into my back this morning and smile. "I'm good."

After a pause, she says, "You sound good."

If she's hoping I'll give her an explanation, she should know better.

"Everything green with the move on your end?"

"Yes. No problems. Theresa loved the apartment. Cried when I gave her the keys. Her kid's a sweetheart. You're seeing someone new, aren't you?"

My tone gentle, I say, "You know I won't tell you that."

"You just did. Who is she?"

"Kiyoko, don't do this."

There's a long silence on her end. In the background, I hear calliope music.

She's at Granville Island again, at the park overlooking the water where she used to take her daughter on walks in her stroller.

Her tone harder than before, she says, "You know what your problem is, Coleton? You have a hero complex."

A sense of fatigue descends on me, weighing down my body. "So this is what the call is really about. You want to fight."

"I don't want to fight. I want you to tell me about your new girlfriend."

"I don't have a girlfriend."

She scoffs. "Who do you think you're talking to? I know you. I know every inflection in your voice. We've known each other for sixteen years and were together for four."

"Five."

"Yeah, but who's counting, right? None of it matters anymore. Nothing matters."

"Arguing with me isn't going to help you feel better. And you're only torturing yourself by going to that park. Go home, Ki. Go home and take care of yourself."

"I'd take that advice, but I don't have to listen to you anymore."

"What if I said please?"

"You never say please. The only thing you're good at saying is goodbye. I hope your new girlfriend enjoys disappointment."

She disconnects.

"Fuck."

I jab my finger against the display to clear it, then drive for another ten minutes before I'm calm enough to make another call. Carter doesn't pick up his cell phone, so I call the office.

"McCord Media, how may I help you?"

"Hello, Marnie. This is Cole. Is Carter in his office?"

"Yes, sir. Would you like me to put you through?"

"Yes."

"Certainly, sir. Please hold a moment."

I listen to classical music for thirty seconds while I'm on hold. Then Marnie comes back on the line.

"I'm sorry, sir, but Carter is in a meeting."

That dodgy little fuckwit. "Tell him that if he doesn't take my call, I'm getting on the phone with TriCast next."

"Yes, sir. Please hold."

Ten seconds later, Carter picks up. "Cole."

I growl, "Hello, traitor."

His sigh is heavy and melodramatic. "You see? This is why I don't tell you things. You overreact."

"I react in accordance with the situation. Which you know. You also know the reason you've avoided my calls the past few days is because you did something wrong. Now tell me what the fuck you were thinking by meeting with TriCast."

"I'm not telling you anything if you're going to continue using that rude tone of voice with me."

"It's not my tone you should be worried about, you dumb prick. It's how long the surgery to reconstruct your nose will take."

"Why does everything with you have to be a threat of violence?"

"Because that's the only thing stupid people understand."

Another melodramatic sigh. "You know I'm smarter than you are, right?"

That makes me chuckle. "In your dreams."

"You're forgetting about the aptitude tests Dad made us take when we were teenagers. My IQ is higher than yours by two points."

"Let's see how much you care about the difference between our IQs when you're missing your front teeth, genius."

"You're unbelievable."

"You're lucky I haven't told Callum about your meeting, or what would be unbelievable is how hard you'd flap your arms to try to fly after he threw you off the roof of the building."

His voice turns sour. "Yes, you two are peas in a violent little pod, aren't you?"

I know we could go back and forth like this all day, so I redirect the conversation. "TriCast. They're our enemies. You took a meeting with the board to discuss a buyout. What the fuck?"

"First tell me how you know."

"I have friends in low places. Talk. Why the hell would you meet with them?"

"Because Sophia Bianco just joined the firm as their new COO."

I wait for more explanation. When it doesn't come, I say, "Get to the point before I die of old age."

"Do you know who she is?"

"No idea."

"Never seen a picture of her?"

"What did I just fucking say? I don't know the woman!"

"I don't know her either, which is why I took the meeting."

"If you don't get to the point in five seconds, I'll smash all the windows in your Hummer."

"I don't even like that thing. I only got it to piss off Dad."

"Very mature of you. Fine, I'll smash all the windows in your Ferrari."

"Which one?"

"Jesus fucking Christ. How are we even related?"

"I don't know, but I think Mom must've had an affair with Paul Newman. It would explain my good looks. You and Callum look like Neanderthals. As I was saying, Sophia Bianco. She's the new COO at TriCast, and the most beautiful woman in the world."

It takes me a moment. When I understand what he's getting at, I groan. "You're not fucking serious."

"Oh, brother, I'm as serious as I've ever been. Wait until I show you her picture. Your eyes will fall out!"

"For God's sake, Carter. You don't take a meeting with our sworn enemies so you can hit on some broad you've never met!"

"How else was I supposed to meet her? Standing in line at Starbucks?"

"It's a miracle you've made it this far in life. I'm shocked you haven't electrocuted yourself by sticking your wet finger into a socket to see if it would tickle."

"I have, and it does."

I shake my head in disbelief.

"And who decided TriCast is our sworn enemy, anyway?

That's awfully dramatic. They're just our biggest competitor, not an invading army."

"What you don't understand about business would fill solar systems. Did you at least get this broad's number?"

"Don't call her a broad. That's disrespectful. She's a lady. An elegant, beautiful lady."

"So that's a no."

He grudgingly admits, "I'm working on it."

"If by working on it you mean you scheduled another meeting, I'll break your kneecaps."

"See? Neanderthal."

"I'm not joking, Carter. Do you have any idea how this will look if it gets out?"

He laughs, something he does far too often. "How's it gonna get out? We control the media!"

"Not all of it, fuckface."

"The most important parts anyway." His tone turns excited. "Hey, do you think I should invite her to dinner? Like send her an email and say my family wants to meet with the board privately, one on one, and give her a date and time to show up at a restaurant, but then I'll be the only one there and say there was a family emergency so nobody else could make it?"

"Sure. Brilliant. Then you'll dazzle her with your charm and utter lack of substance and we'll all be going to your wedding this time next year, is that the plan?"

Ignoring that, he muses, "But what would the family emergency be? I guess I could make up some distant relative who suddenly died."

I say darkly, "It won't be such a distant relative if you take another meeting with anyone at TriCast," and hang up on him.

There's only so much stupidity I can take in one conversation.

By the time I pull into the underground parking lot at work, I'm in a murderous mood. I lock myself in my office and force myself to focus on business for two hours, until Scotty knocks on my door with an inter-office memo.

I remove the sheet of paper and read what's written there. Then I take a black marker and write a single word in giant block letters over Shay's handwriting.

NO.

Seething with frustration from the two phone calls and what's seeming more and more like a hopeless fantasy about having any kind of workable relationship with Shay, I thrust the envelope back at Scotty and lock myself inside my office for the rest of the day.

CHAPTER 49
Shay

I'm excited to see Scotty appear in my office doorway with the brown kraft envelope in his hand. That excitement lasts until I pull the sheet of paper out, and I see Cole's response.

A big black NO scrawled across my note like a middle finger.

"Do you have anything for me to return?" asks Scotty, lingering in the doorway.

I force a smile and look at him. "No, but thanks. Have a good day."

"You too."

He leaves, taking my self-esteem with him.

In my note, I asked if we could schedule a meeting for this week. "Meeting" being code for quickie in the stairwell. I was feeling flirtatious and upbeat when I sent it, full of hope after this morning that this thing between us wasn't already over like I thought it was last night, but Cole put the kibosh on all that hope and happiness with two letters.

He didn't even bother to sign his name. Probably because he didn't have a good mindfuck closing that meant "Get lost." Not that he needed it. I got the point.

He changed his mind again.

We're not going to be together.

265

Or he decided once and for all, I don't know which because the man doesn't know how to communicate except when he's recounting how he followed me to a restaurant and ordered his buddy to spy on me over security cameras. The rest of the time, it's vague references to ominous outcomes and cryptic statements that could mean anything or nothing.

Unless we're having sex. Then he miraculously becomes a professional orator.

I shred the note, then sit at my desk until I've lost the urge to smash something. It's replaced by the urge to cry, which I refuse to give in to, so I bury myself in work.

By five o'clock, I've almost convinced myself the hurt, anger, and irrational desire to light Cole McCord on fire are all feelings created by the proximity of my period, which should be arriving any day.

I've always been good at denial.

~

The rest of that week goes by with no contact from Cole.

No inter-office memos, no emails complaining about an error in a report, nothing. Chelsea's advice is to give him space and focus on myself. We can't get together to hash it out because the hospital is short-staffed. She's working back-to-back shifts, and when she's not working, she's exhausted.

The office chatter about Dylan dies out. There are no news reports or newspaper articles about a missing accountant. Simone doesn't mention him again. Life goes on as it did before, except now, I'm obsessing over Cole the way he said he obsessed over me.

I have dinner on Friday with Jen and Angel, but as neither of them knows anything about the Cole situation, I suffer in silence.

I distract myself over the weekend by binge-watching TV, cleaning the apartment from top to bottom, taking four CrossFit classes at the gym, and teaching myself how to make pasta from scratch. The resulting linguini noodles taste like glue, so I throw them out and order takeaway from a Thai food place.

Sunday night, my mother calls.

"Hi, honey. It's me. Mom."

She has to add that last part because when I picked up the phone and heard her voice, I was so surprised, I was speechless. She never calls me. Never. I'm always the one to call and check on her, and then only rarely because it's so damn depressing.

"Hi, Mom. Is everything okay?"

Her laugh is small and nervous. "Yeah, I think so."

I'm instantly on guard. "You think so? What does that mean? Did Bob do something? Are you hurt?"

"No, no, honey, I'm fine."

"Are you sure? You sound strange."

She laughs again. I picture her standing in her tiny kitchen in her apartment in Vegas, her thin bleach-blonde hair in a messy bun, a cigarette burned down to a stub between her fingers.

As soon as one goes out, she lights another. She never started smoking until her marriage to Dad broke up, but after that, she became a chimney.

"That's probably because I haven't had a drink in a few days."

I was standing in the living room when I answered, about to dust the coffee table again, but this news is so unexpected, I sit down on the sofa. "Really? That's great."

"Yeah, I just...I don't know, it seemed like a good time to make a new start what with Bob leaving and all."

My heart leaps. "Bob left you?"

"Yeah."

"What happened? Did you have another fight?"

"No, he just up and left. Never came home from the casino one night. I figure he got himself a new woman. Only reason that man would disappear on me is for another woman. She probably has more social security coming in than I do."

Her raspy laugh is interrupted by a cough.

I'm overjoyed by the news that Bob left, but try not to get my hopes up. They've broken up before, only to get back together soon after.

But the no-drinking thing is new. The last time he left, she drank herself into a stupor. Her neighbor found her passed out on her porch, lit cigarette in hand, and called an ambulance.

"Do you need anything? Money? Food? I can Venmo you some cash if you need it."

"I'm fine, sweetie, but you're a doll for offering. As long as I've got my ciggies and Mr. Bones, I'm all set."

"What's Mr. Bones? Is that a new show or something?"

"No, it's not a show. It's a cat. A stray I found behind the dumpster here at my place. He was all skin and bones when I found him, so I named him Mr. Bones. He's sitting on my lap right now. Here, say hi to him."

I hear some fumbling noises, then the low, distinct drone of a cat's purr. Mom comes back on the line, sounding proud.

"Isn't he cute? Did you say hi? I think you'd love him. You've always loved cats. Remember that mangy orange thing we had when you were little?"

"Scooby Doo," I say, dazed.

She got a cat? She's sober? Who is this woman?

She laughs. "I told your father I was allergic, but really I just didn't like that cat. He always looked so judgmental. Mr. Bones isn't judgmental at all. He's a sweetie pie. You're my best friend, aren't you, buddy?"

She makes some kissy noises while I attempt to piece my brain back together.

"Mom, I'm so happy for you. It's really good you have a companion."

"Other than that loser, Bob, you mean," she says drily. When I don't say anything, she sighs. "I know you never liked him, honey. That's okay. I never liked him much myself." Her voice turns melancholy. "Sometimes we hold onto things we shouldn't because we're lonely."

Unless you're Cole, who uses loneliness like a shield to keep everyone away.

"I just want you to be safe, Mom. Safe and happy."

"Well, I have to tell you, honey, I've been happier these past few days being alone here with Mr. Bones than I've been in years. I think I'm gonna start going for walks around the complex. Maybe eating a few vegetables too. Do something good for myself."

I'm getting choked up. I swallow, blinking away tears, and force my voice to stay even. "That's great to hear."

"How are you doing? How's work?"

"I got a new job since we last talked."

"Oh, good for you! Do you like it?"

"It's...challenging."

She laughs again. "And a good thing too, or you'd get bored. That big brain of yours needs a challenge. You still with what's-his-name? Chad?"

"Chet. And no, we broke up."

"I'm sorry to hear that, honey."

"It's for the best. He turned out to be a cheating asshole."

She clucks her tongue. "There aren't many men like your father, that's for sure." She sighs heavily. "Biggest mistake of my life was leaving him. Have you spoken to him lately?"

"Yes. On his birthday. He sounded good."

"Good." She pauses, then says nonchalantly, "Is he still married to that Zoe?"

I smile. "It's Chloe. But you knew that. And yes, they're still married. I'll tell him you said hello next time we speak."

"Now, don't go putting words in my mouth, honey. I didn't say to tell the man hello."

She's trying to sound cross, but I know her too well. Not only does she want me to tell him she said hello, she wants me to call her immediately afterward to go over his reply, his tone of voice, and any other detail I can remember.

Like mother, like daughter.

"Okay, Mom. I won't."

"I mean..." She clears her throat. "You could tell him you talked to me. That would be fine."

"Okay."

We sit in awkward silence for a moment, until she says, "Do you have any plans for Thanksgiving?"

I always spend it with my dad and Chloe as she's always been in Vegas with Bob, and I never wanted to go near that binge-drinking rageaholic, but maybe this year will be different. If Bob stays away, maybe she and I can get together.

"Not yet. You?"

"No. Me and Mr. Bones will probably just watch the Macy's parade."

"Or you could come to LA if you want. Or I could go down there. It would be great to see you. I miss you."

Her soft intake of breath is louder than she would like because she makes up a hurried excuse about Mr. Bones scratching her arm to cover it.

"Well, think about it. You don't have to decide now."

"I will. Maybe...maybe we could talk again next week? If you want to, I mean."

The hope in her voice that leaked out before she could catch it makes my heart hurt.

Dammit. I won't cry. I won't cry. Don't cry!

I say softly, "I'd love that, Mom. How about I give you a call at the same time?"

"Sounds good. Talk to you then. Bye, honey."

"Bye, Mom."

I disconnect, then flop back onto the sofa and stare at the ceiling as tears leak from the corners of my eyes.

Hope is such an awful thing. A dangerous, awful thing. It drives people crazy.

I gave up hoping years ago that she'd change, that she'd become the mother I always needed, because it was too painful to continue holding on. But with one phone call, that old hope I thought I'd killed off has sprung back to life again like a green blade of grass can spring back after its been trampled by feet.

It's far too early to tell, but if Bob is gone for good and the sobriety sticks, I might get to meet the woman who's been missing for more than twenty years.

I scroll through my recent calls log and stare for the hundredth time at the number Cole called me from last Monday. Then I debate with myself for the hundredth time whether I should save it to contacts, delete it, or block it.

In the end, I don't do anything. I just shut off the phone and pour myself some wine.

Nothing happens Monday at work. Tuesday and Wednesday pass uneventfully too. Then on Thursday, I'm waiting for the elevator to take me down to the cafeteria ten floors below when the doors open, and I'm knocked on my ass.

Between two other people, Cole stands inside.

He looks incredible.

He's wearing a dove gray suit. His white dress shirt is open at the throat. Freshly shaven, his skin glows with health. A hint of a sunburn burnishes his cheeks. His dark hair gleams under the lights, but it's slightly messy, as if he's been running his hands through it.

The way my body reacts to seeing him, you'd think I was jabbed with a cattle prod.

Energy courses through me, setting my nerves alight and sending my pulse into overdrive. I'm sure the breath I suck in is audible. I freeze, unsure if I should turn and run or get on the elevator and die of a heart attack.

He lifts his gaze to mine.

Our eyes lock.

The floor opens up and swallows me.

No, that's just how it feels. But the sensation of falling is so acute, it leaves me dizzy. I'm so disoriented, I forget to do anything but stand there gaping at him.

The doors slide closed.

At the last moment, Cole reaches through and stops them.

They bounce slowly apart again, and he steps back.

Swallowing hard, my pulse thrumming, I step on the elevator, nod politely at the other passengers, then turn and face the closing doors.

His gaze on my body is a thousand heated needles, piercing me from behind.

One person gets off on the twenty-fifth floor. The other person gets off on the twentieth. Then Cole and I are alone on the elevator, and I'm carefully practicing deep breathing so I don't pass out from nerves.

I think he'll let me get off on my floor without saying a word to me, but the moment the doors close behind the last person and the elevator starts to move, he jabs his finger onto the Stop button.

The lift shakes a bit, then settles. I stand staring wide-eyed at the closed doors with Cole behind me and my heart pounding like mad until he says gruffly, "Excellent work this week, Ms. Sanders."

His voice makes my nipples tingle. The timbre of it, so deep and husky, so beautifully masculine...it makes me remember things I shouldn't.

Why am I such a fool for this man?

I close my eyes and take another deep breath. "Thank you, Mr. McCord."

"How's the 401(k) audit coming?"

I close my eyes and breathe, breathe, breathe. "I should have it completed by tomorrow."

"Should? Or will?"

He moves closer until I feel his body heat. He lifts a lock of my hair to his nose and inhales. Then he makes a low sound in his chest, the exact sound of pleasure I've heard him make when his face is between my legs.

Steady, girl. Steady.

"I...I will."

"Good. That's very good, Ms. Sanders. I'm pleased." He lowers his head and inhales deeply against my neck.

My nipples harden instantly. I swallow the moan of need building in the back of my throat.

His warm breath washing over my skin, he whispers, "I've missed you, baby. I've missed you so fucking much."

"Really? Hmm. I must've missed all your phone calls. And your emails. And your inter-office memos. No, wait, I *did* get one of those. It wasn't exactly filled with longing."

After a moment, he says, "You're angry."

"You're right. I am. Not only angry, but frustrated and confused too." I turn around, face him, and push him gently back a foot or two. "Why have you been ignoring me?"

"I could never ignore you."

"Yet you have been."

"No. I've been obsessing over you. I can't stop thinking about you. It's all I do. I'm fucking useless."

My pulse is jagged. I want him to pull me into his arms and hold me, but that also makes me feel pathetic, so I don't ask him to. "Have you spied on me over the security cameras?"

"No, but only because I told you I wouldn't act like a complete animal anymore. I've wanted to. I've wanted to pay someone on your floor to report all your movements back to me too, but I didn't do that either."

Falling into his eyes, I say, "You've been behaving yourself."

"I'm still a wreck."

"Baby steps."

We smile at each other.

He says, "I need to tell you something."

"What?"

"I like you."

"Is that your idea of a compliment?"

"Yes. Because I don't like anyone. But I like you very much. Aside from wanting to fuck you silly, I mean. I think you're smart, witty, and incredibly good at your job."

I narrow my eyes at him. "Have you recently had a fall? Hit your head hard on the ground maybe?"

"No. Why?"

"Just wondering why we're suddenly getting along so well."

"We always get along well."

"Yes, but usually there's a bed involved."

"About that..." He studies my mouth for a moment, then lifts his gaze to mine. "I want another sleepover."

CHAPTER 50
Cole

She stares at me for a beat of silence, then folds her arms over her chest and says acidly, "No. I'm sure you're familiar with the word, because you say it so often."

I don't know why I was expecting this to be easy.

"You're referring to the memo."

"Yes, I'm referring to the memo. You remember the one with the giant black letters scrawled right over my polite request to see you?"

"I was having a bad day."

"I've had nine of them since then."

"So have I... Wait, you've been unhappy too?"

I can tell she's annoyed with herself for admitting that, because she tosses her hair over her shoulder and adopts a bored attitude. "I've been great."

I step closer to her, dying to feel her lips under mine. "Great, huh?"

"Amazing, actually."

"Hmm."

"I'm not joking."

"I didn't say you were."

"Your face is saying it for you."

"Shay?"

"Yes, Mr. McCord?"

I keep my voice gentle and look straight into her eyes. "I'm sorry I was so abrupt on the memo. I'm sorry I haven't contacted you. I haven't been able to get you off my mind, and I don't know what the fuck to do about it. All I know is that I saw you standing there when the elevator doors opened, and I wanted to touch you so badly, I started to salivate."

She studies me for a moment, then starts to laugh.

"Why are you laughing?"

"Because it's ridiculous how easy it is for you to dazzle me."

"I dazzle you?"

She stops laughing and says crossly, "Oh, don't look so pleased with yourself. You know you do. And no, we're not having a sleepover. I told you I didn't want to be a bootie call."

I never thought having someone say no to me could be so adorable.

"Okay. I guess I'll be forced to keep doing this for the foreseeable future." I withdraw her panties from where they lie folded neatly inside the pocket of my suit jacket. Holding them to my nose, I inhale deeply, savoring the delicious scent of her cunt.

Her face turns scarlet. "You brought them to *work?*"

"I told you they'd go everywhere with me."

"I thought you were exaggerating."

"I needed to keep you with me."

"What you need is therapy."

"What I need is you."

We stare at each other until an alarm sounds. It's the elevator, complaining about being stuck between floors.

"Time's up, Mr. McCord."

"Let me come over tonight."

"No."

"We don't have to do anything. We can just talk."

"No."

Frustrated with her stubborn refusal to give me what I want, I scowl at her.

Which, naturally, makes her laugh.

She turns and presses the Stop button, setting the elevator in motion again. Turning back to me, she says, "Don't forget, Mr. McCord, there's a company policy against fraternizing between employees. I know, because you specifically told me the first day I started."

The elevator doors open. She turns and steps out onto the landing. She's about to walk away from me without another word, so I do the only thing I can think of to make her reconsider.

"How's your mother?"

She freezes in place. Then she spins around and stares at me with wide eyes and parted lips, the color draining from her face.

We're still staring at each other as the doors slide shut.

CHAPTER 51
Shay

I can't breathe. I can't think. I can't do anything but stare at the closed elevator doors as my pulse burns like wildfire under my skin.

I recall the murderous expression Cole wore the night of our dinner date when I told him my mother's boyfriend beat her up. I recall his scraped knuckles and blood-stained shirt the morning I woke with no memory at my apartment when he told me about Dylan. And I recall his eerie calm and splattered briefcase the night he wandered into his kitchen after leaving me alone to "work."

Goose bumps form all over my body.

It was *him*. He's the reason Bob left.

Disappeared, more accurately, probably into a deep hole dug in the desert sand.

Holy shit. I'm in love with Tony Soprano.

"Hello, Shay."

With a strangled scream, I jump and spin toward the voice. Simone stands there, smiling at me.

"Are you just breaking for lunch now? It's a bit late in the afternoon. I hope we haven't been working you too hard. How's the 401(k) audit coming?'

Breathless, I stare at her in her lovely cream-colored suit and triple strand of pearls and don't know whether to burst into tears or hysterical laughter. "Fine. It's coming along fine. I'll have it completed by tomorrow."

"Good." Her smile turns into a frown. "Are you all right? You look a little pale."

I swallow and nod, desperately trying to pull myself together. "Yes. Just hungry. I have, um, what's that low blood sugar thing?"

"Hypoglycemia."

"Yes, that's it."

I can tell by her expression of doubt that she doesn't believe me, but I don't care. Without another word, I stumble past her, headed blindly into the cafeteria. I don't bother trying to get any food down, I just navigate to an empty table, collapse into a chair, and stare at my hands when I flatten them on the tabletop.

They're shaking hard.

I stay in the cafeteria until my shaking has stopped, and my pulse has settled. I know I won't be able to concentrate on work, but I take the elevator back upstairs and sit at my desk looking busy for the benefit of the cubicle field visible through the glass walls of my office.

I shuffle paperwork, click around aimlessly on the computer, and smile as if I'm not having an existential crisis, and my boss/sex partner isn't a man who makes other men disappear.

All very normal, nothing to see here.

At five o'clock on the nose, I leave the office and drive home to wait.

I know it's not a question of if Cole will show up. It's only a question of when.

Like a werewolf, he arrives at midnight with the full moon.

I've been pacing for hours. I've had three glasses of wine. I've resisted the urgent need to call Chelsea for assistance with my nervous breakdown, but I know this is something I have to handle alone.

Plus, she'll probably advise me to find a new job ASA-fuck-ing-P, and I don't want to hear it.

I can't deal with logic right now. That part of my brain expired with one simple question this afternoon.

"How's your mother?"

So innocent, yet so not.

The master of mindfuckery strikes again.

I'm in the middle of pouring myself another glass of wine when I hear a floorboard creak. I look over and there he is, standing in my kitchen doorway like some sort of gorgeous, murderous ghost who appeared from thin air.

My heart starts to thud. My mouth goes dry. I slowly set the glass back down on the countertop and turn to him, trembling.

"It's after midnight."

"Yes. I apologize for the hour. I was delayed by work."

I glance at his knuckles, but they're not covered in blood. Licking my lips, I look into his eyes again.

"How did you get in? The front door is locked."

"Was locked. And I'm going to install a deadbolt. That lock isn't safe."

My laugh is small and only slightly hysterical. "You picked it. Are you a professional burglar too?"

"Amateur." From his back pocket, he pulls out a credit card and holds it up between two fingers. "Not very sophisticated, but it does the trick."

"Evidently."

He doesn't move closer, he only watches me with smoldering intensity as he slips the credit card back into his pocket, and I try to calm down by gulping air.

"You're hyperventilating."

"Seems reasonable under the circumstances, don't you think? I'm surprised I'm not bleeding from my eyes."

"How much wine have you had?"

"Not nearly enough to help me cope with the fact that you made Bob disappear. I think I'll need a few cases of wine before I can handle that."

"You're fine. It's just fresh."

"I'm going to sit at the kitchen table now. Don't make any quick moves, or I might pass out from nerves."

"No, stay where you are. I'll come to you."

He moves toward me slowly and with caution, like he's approaching a wild animal who might bite.

Tonight is the first time I've seen him wearing anything but a suit. He's in jeans, boots, and a T-shirt, all black. He looks ridiculously handsome. And normal, like he's just an average guy, and not the morally gray vigilante billionaire unaliver of bad guys he actually is.

I remember how I replied "All the most dangerous creatures do" when he remarked that Chelsea looked innocent the first night we met, and marvel that the universe so enjoys playing its little jokes on me.

"It's okay," he murmurs, reaching out and caressing my face. "You're okay, baby. Just breathe."

I close my eyes and breathe deeply as he takes me into his arms. We stand together silently for a while, our bodies pressed together, until he decides it's time to pick me up.

He carries me out of the kitchen and down the hallway into my bedroom, then kicks off his boots and lays next to me on the bed so we're facing each other, looking into each other's eyes.

"Hi, beautiful."

"Hi."

"Talk to me."

"I was hoping you'd start."

"What do you want to know?"

I study his features for a moment, admiring how fine and symmetrical they are and wondering how a rich guy who looks like a GQ model winds up doing what he does.

"How much leeway do I have? Because I know you're Mr. Secrecy, and you don't normally answer questions."

Looking contemplative, he rubs his thumb slowly back and forth over my cheek. "Can I ask you something first?"

"Yes."

"Are you mine?"

My throat closes. My chest tightens. If I cry, I'm going to beat myself up. "You know the answer to that."

"I want to hear you say it."

"I thought you didn't do relationships?"

"I don't. But you stole my heart the first night we met, and I finally realized it's hopeless to keep trying to resist you. Every time I see you, it's like the first time I'm seeing the sun."

I close my eyes and remind myself to breathe. He strokes my hair until I'm calm enough to speak again.

"I'd be lying if I said I wanted anyone else other than you. Or can think about anything else. You've taken my brain hostage."

"Hostage is good."

"No, it isn't. Hostage is bad. Hostage is when something's held against its will."

"Open your eyes."

When I do, he's gazing at me with a look of such adoration, my heart skips a beat.

Eyes shining, he says quietly, "I meant it's good because you've taken my brain hostage too. And my heart. And my soul. What's left of it anyway. It's all yours, if you'll have it."

I squeeze my eyes shut again. When I speak, my voice is choked. "Goddammit."

"What?"

"I'm in love with Tony Soprano, and everybody knows what happened to him in the end."

He pulls me against his body and hugs me tightly, sliding an arm underneath me so I'm cradled. Then he throws a leg over both of mine so I'm completely surrounded by his warmth and strength.

Inhaling against my neck, he sighs.

"I dream about your smell," he whispers. "I wish I could replicate it from eating cologne and flowers like that idiot Florentino did."

I raise my head and look at him with lifted brows. He rolls his eyes.

"Yes, I read *Love in the Time of Cholera*. Emery said it was your favorite book. But I have to tell you, baby, I've never read such depressing bullshit in my entire life. I needed a prescription for Xanax by the time I finished."

"You talked to Emery about me?"

Instead of answering, he makes a face.

"When?"

He admits grudgingly, "The day you started as my assistant."

"After I told you she was the one who referred me for the job?"

"Yes. But don't be angry with her, she wouldn't answer any of my ten thousand questions about you except what your favorite book was. She said I should have a conversation with you instead."

"That's a surprising suggestion, considering conversations are your least favorite thing."

"Not my *least* favorite."

"No? What is?"

He answers with total nonchalance. "Getting blood stains out of white carpeting."

When I stare at him in horrified silence, he chuckles. "I'm kidding."

"I can't deal with gallows humor at the moment, Cole. Have mercy."

He tucks my head into his shoulder and kisses my hair. "Mercy it is."

I close my eyes again, flatten my hand over the center of his chest, and count the beats of his heart until I get to sixty. Then I sigh and snuggle closer to him, hoping this man I'm so enamored with won't someday be the subject of a true crime documentary.

He strokes my back and hair, stopping every so often to kiss my cheek or my forehead. He's so gentle and sweet, it's almost impossible to reconcile this side of him with the other side I know exists.

The side where all his monsters live.

After a long time, he murmurs, "Are you okay?"

"Yes. Which means I should probably be incarcerated."

He knows what I mean. "You're not a danger to society because you can accept darkness more easily than other people."

"I don't know if accept is the right word. It's more like welcome it with open arms."

"You didn't have a crisis of conscience over the others."

"No, but Bob is close to home. And I'm not having a crisis of conscience over him. I'm glad he's gone." After a moment, I add, "Thank you."

"You're welcome. If you have others who need taking care of, make me a list."

"Oh my God! Or wait, was that more gallows humor?"

"No. You can literally make me a list."

I groan. "I'll pretend I didn't hear that."

"You never know. Having a man like me around can be extremely handy."

"Please stop talking now."

"Okay." There's a short pause, then he says, "How am I supposed to answer questions if I can't talk?"

"You know what? I don't care if you're bigger and stronger than me and know how to get blood out of white carpeting. If you don't shut up for a minute, I'll kick your ass."

He rolls on top of me and laughs into my neck. When he comes up for air, he kisses me deeply, pressing me into the mattress, and makes a soft sound of pleasure in his throat.

"Shay?"

"What?"

"Tell me you're mine."

Gazing up into the depths of his beautiful blue eyes, I know that whatever strange forces brought us together are the same ones that make resistance useless. The connection we shared that first night hasn't diminished with time, it's only grown stronger.

So I give up any lingering hesitations and surrender in full.

"I'm yours. I belong to you, Cole McCord, come what may."

He closes his eyes. When he opens them again, they burn with a new—darker—fire.

"Good, baby. Because you offered this monster a home, and he's taking you up on the invitation."

CHAPTER 52
Shay

He kisses me again, then rolls onto his back and arranges me on top of his body the way he likes to, cupping my head in his big hand as I rest my head on his shoulder.

He inhales deeply, exhales in a gust, then begins to talk in a low, emotionless voice.

"In Japan, people who go missing are called *jouhatsu*. Literally translated, the word means evaporated. Like people all over the world, they vanish for different reasons, but many of the *jouhatsu* in Japan do so on purpose with the help of companies called *yonige-ya*."

"What does that mean?"

"Night movers. They're specialists in helping people disappear."

Already fascinated, I wait quietly for him to continue as he absently strokes my hair.

"I was first introduced to the idea when I was in boarding school in London in my teens. I had a friend named Kiyoko there whose family was wealthy, like mine. But one of her uncles had a gambling problem and went into deep debt. He borrowed money from the yakuza to try to repay it but defaulted on the loan. And if you don't make good on your debts to the yakuza, you don't get to keep breathing."

"I take it they're organized crime like the Mafia?"

"Yes. So Kiyoko's uncle hired a night mover to help him disappear. He was never heard from again. The only reason the family knew what happened to him is because he left his mother a note. But they never spoke of him after that. Like suicide, becoming *jouhatsu* is a taboo topic in their culture. When it happens, everyone acts like it didn't. You vanish, and nobody ever mentions you again."

I lie in his arms and think about that. To permanently vanish without a trace. To start over somewhere new where no one knows you, and your past can't follow.

I can't decide if it's wonderful or depressing.

"During boarding school, Kiyoko and I became close friends. After we graduated, we went to Oxford together."

"You went to Oxford?"

"Yes. Don't sound so impressed."

"Why not? It's impressive."

"University doesn't teach you how to think. It only teaches you how to conform and take tests. I wish I'd skipped it altogether, but my father has a thing about higher education. He didn't go to college, so he made sure his three sons did. Oxford is where I met Axel, by the way. I hated him at first. Thought he was a snobbish jock. Archery, boxing, cricket, fencing, he did it all. Turns out, he only went so hard in athletics to annoy his father, a member of the British peerage, who wanted him to have a law practice like he did. Once I found that out, we became best friends."

He chuckles. "There's nothing like shared fucked-up family dynamics to bring people closer. Anyway, After Oxford, Kiyoko moved to Vancouver, and I came back to LA. Axel decided he'd had enough of England, so he applied for US citizenship and moved to Virginia to attend the FBI Academy."

Cole pauses. He exhales again. Then he says, "Kiyoko and I lost touch for a while. Until her daughter was murdered."

My heartbeat ticks up. I whisper, "Oh no."

"Yes. Which is bad enough. What makes it worse is that the killer was her own father."

"Oh God. How awful. What happened?"

His voice drops, but it gains an edge of hatred. "Kiyoko was raped. She got pregnant. But she wanted to be a mother, and she knew the circumstances weren't the child's fault. So she decided to have the baby and never tell her how she was conceived. Fast forward two years, and Kiyoko's rapist is released from prison."

I'm aghast. "Two years? That's all?"

"It's more than most rapists get. Canada doesn't have a minimum sentence for sexual assault crimes. So this sicko somehow discovers Kiyoko had his baby. And he decided that baby belonged to him. He tracked down Kiyoko's home address."

Cole is silent for a long time. I don't dare speak. I can feel how much he's struggling.

Finally, he says in a rough voice, "He assaulted her again. Beat her near to death. Then he took the baby." He inhales a ragged breath. "I won't tell you what he did to her, but her little body was found wrapped in plastic bags and stuffed into the trash bin in a men's restroom at Stanley Park."

I'm so horrified, I can't breathe. I lie stiffly with my heart pounding and my mouth open, tears welling in my eyes.

Beneath my palm, Cole's heart beats as hard as mine does.

"When I heard what happened, I flew up to see her. The condition she was in...no one should ever have to go through what Kiyoko went through. She almost didn't recover. She healed physically, but mentally it was tougher. We grew very close. I moved there and stayed with her until she could function again. And in that time, I fell in love with her. And I decided the man who hurt her and took her baby away would never be able to hurt anyone else again."

I'm outright crying now. I can't stop it. Tears stream down my cheeks. I don't bother trying to wipe them away because I know more will be coming.

"I found him. I killed him. I made sure it took a long time. And when it was all over and I told Kiyoko, she didn't say a word. She just kissed my bruised hands and hugged me. We never spoke of it again. But that night, I vowed I'd do what I could to prevent any other woman going through what she went through. I vowed I'd use my money and power in service of something bigger than my own selfish needs. I'd use it to help the helpless. Women like Kiyoko and her daughter who the system failed."

I sob and burst into fresh tears.

Cole hugs me hard and silently holds me while I cry on his shoulder.

After a while, when I'm more calm, he wipes my tears away with his fingertips and kisses me gently. "I'm sorry."

"Don't be! I'm sorry for *you*! Cole, what you and she went through together...I can't even imagine."

When he speaks again, he sounds exhausted. "The way we started, what I did...it wasn't the basis for a good relationship. I wasn't her knight in shining armor. I was this constant reminder of what she'd lost. I came back to LA to work in the firm, but we saw each other as often as we could. Weekends, holidays, whatever. But every once in a while, I'd catch her looking at me as if she hated the sight of me. Like I made her sick. She denied it, but I knew what she saw when she looked at my face. I was a tether to the ugliness in her past. I wasn't good for her. I was only hurting her more. So I ended it."

I think of him sitting alone in that booth the night we met at the hotel bar in Beverly Hills. I think of his grim expression, his air of misery, and hate myself for being so cavalier when I sat down.

"You look like a lot of women's biggest regret," I told him.

How could he ever forgive me?

I start to apologize, but he gently shushes me.

"You never have to say you're sorry for anything, Shay. I know where your heart is. I know it's all good. You're the only person in the world I knew I could tell that story to who wouldn't condemn me for what I did. So thank you for being my safe space. You've been giving me more grace than I deserve since the day we met."

My heart aches. It hurts so much, it feels as if it's going to burst and kill me.

"Where is Kiyoko now?"

"Still in Vancouver."

"And Axel's here."

"He graduated from the academy and worked for the FBI for a while, but he's not a guy who enjoys taking orders from others. So he called me up, and we decided to work together. We formed our own night moves outfit. With my money, and his training and contacts, we can get a lot done."

"You said he was your personal shopper."

He chuckles. "And if he knew that, he'd kill me."

I'm trying to piece it all together in my head, but I'm missing details. "So these night moves you do. How do you find the people who need to disappear?"

"Mostly from women's shelters. I have contacts who report to me. I can't help everyone who's abused, but the women with children are a priority. They get a new identity and a new place to live."

"So you take care of their abusers. The way you did with Dylan."

"Most of them. Sometimes, the women don't want their abuser dead. If she prefers, I'll let her watch me beat him to a pulp, then make him transfer all his money and real estate holdings into accounts we've already set up in her name. Usually that only happens if he's wealthy."

"But what if he retaliates? What if he decides not to let her go and finds her?"

His voice turns dark. "I make sure he understands that isn't an option."

I think about everything he's told me, trying to imagine what he's been through and what his life's been like.

But I can't imagine it.

The loneliness. The heartache. The danger...

Especially the danger.

Alarmed, I sit up and look at him. "You'll get caught."

"No, I won't."

"Yes, you will," I insist, starting to panic. "If this is a regular thing you do, there's no way you can't!"

"The chief of police is a close family friend."

I stare at him blankly until I understand what he's saying. "You mean he *knows*?"

He nods. "His fifteen year old daughter was killed by her boyfriend. Used to like to get rough with her. Smack her around. One night he took it too far and snapped her neck. But because he was a minor with no priors and had a very good attorney, he didn't serve time. Got probation and community service. Didn't matter who her daddy was, the boy still walked."

I gape at him, horrified all over again.

Gazing into my eyes, he murmurs, "There's no justice in this world for good people. Only evil gets what it wants."

"That's incredibly depressing."

"That's why religion was created. Without an afterlife to hope for, most of us would give up and slit our wrists."

I sigh. "I need another glass of wine."

He studies me, his face somber. "Do you understand now why I said I don't have relationships? Why I don't let people get close?"

When I nod, he says, "If we do this, Shay, if we commit to each other, you have to promise me something."

"What is it?"

"That if you ever start to hate me, you'll walk away. Because I already know I won't be able to walk away from you. I already know I'm not strong enough. This thing with us, this connection...it's everything I ever wanted, and everything I know I don't deserve. So I'm gonna hold onto it as if my life depends on it. I'm gonna hold on even if I should let go. You'll have to be the one to end it, if it comes to that. Promise me you will."

Tears well in my eyes again. I'm surprised I have any left. "I promise."

He peers at me very intently, as if to make sure I'm telling the truth. Whatever he sees satisfies him, because he nods and holds out his arms.

I lie on his chest and snuggle closer to him, as close as I can get. "So what do we do about the no-relationship policy at the company?"

"We work around it."

"Meaning?"

"Meaning we're discreet. Very discreet. We continue on as we have been, except no more liaisons in the stairwell. We only see each other outside the office and preferably not in public."

"So basically only at my apartment or your house."

"I know it's inconvenient, but if my father gets wind that we're together, he'll go ballistic. My brothers won't care, except that it will make us all look bad, like we think the rules don't apply to us. But the worst thing would be how you'd be treated by the other employees. Everyone would think you only got the job because we were sleeping together. It wouldn't be pleasant for you."

In his pause, I can tell he wants me to imagine all of it. Being snickered at, being ostracized, being hated by his father. Maybe even being fired by his father.

So much for making a good impression on the parents.

"You're right. It wouldn't be pleasant. Let's avoid that."

He hesitates. "If you don't work for me, however, none of this applies."

"If you're asking me to quit, the answer's no. It's the best job I've ever had. And the best paying."

"I had a feeling you'd say that." He plays with my hair while he thinks. "What if I gave you enough money that you'd never have to work again?"

"And what if I sewed your lips shut while you sleep so you wouldn't say anything so silly again?"

He allows me to simmer in annoyance until I'm calm, then I sigh. "I'll reconsider in a year."

"About taking the money?"

"No, about finding a new job."

"Oh." He's quiet for a moment. "But you do realize I'm a billionaire."

"Stop talking. Just stop. I'm not interested in your money."

His silent laughter shakes his chest. "Okay, sweetheart. No more talking. We'll just lie here instead."

He strokes my hair and back. He holds me like I'm fragile, and he's worried I might break, every once in a while giving me a squeeze and a kiss on the forehead. I'm spent emotionally and physically, stifling a yawn as I think about everything he's told me and what the future will bring.

And I promise myself that no matter what happens, we'll stick it out. We can make it, even though there are all sorts of obstacles. We'll make it because we both want it to work.

It's like I completely forgot how life loves to fuck me over.

CHAPTER 53
Shay

The next day at work, I'm floating.

I feel as if all the clouds have been swept away from the horizon, and everything will be sunshine and rainbows from now on. Cole's secrets have been revealed, we've agreed how to move forward, and if I'm worried about all the ways this could go sideways, I tell myself I'm not.

Scotty brings me an inter-office memo at ten o'clock.

> Ms. Sanders,
> Please bring me the audit report when you've completed it. I'd like to go over it with you.
> Yours,
> Mr. McCord

I type up that damn report so fast, the keys on my keyboard melt. Then I hustle upstairs with the report in hand, grinning like a lunatic.

When I see Marion at her desk, however, I try to act composed. "Good morning, Marion."

She smiles and waves. "Good morning!"

294

Surprised she's so cheerful, I stop at her desk. "How are you?"

"I'm doing great, thanks!" She glances toward Cole's office and lowers her voice. "You're in luck. He's in a good mood today. Dare I say he's acting almost human?"

I try not to show how happy that makes me, but if she looks close enough, she'll see my heart beating through my blouse. "Really? That's interesting."

"He actually smiled at me. Can you believe it? Anyway, go right ahead." She gestures toward his office.

"You don't need to announce me?"

"He told me to send you in as soon as you arrived."

"Okay, thanks."

I head to his door, pressing the smile from my lips. When I knock, I hear an instant, "Come in," from inside.

When I open the door, he's already on his feet, headed toward me. I barely get the door closed behind me before he takes me in his arms and kisses me hard.

"Mr. McCord," I say breathlessly. "You're very eager this morning."

He growls, "I should've fucked you before I left your apartment."

Stifling a laugh because we're standing near the door and I don't want Marion to hear me, I grin at him. "But then I would've been late again."

"And I would've written you another note. How did you get more beautiful since I last saw you?"

He peppers kisses along my jaw and down my neck, making me shiver. "I didn't. You're just biased. I brought the report."

He takes the folder from my hand and tosses it to the floor. Papers go flying, scattering over the carpet. Then he picks me up and carries me over to the leather sofa by the windows.

He lays me down on it and pushes my skirt up my thighs.

I glance nervously at the door. "What are you doing? I thought we were supposed to be discreet!"

"I need to discreetly bury my dick in your perfect pussy, Ms. Sanders."

Kneeling beside the sofa, he pulls my panties down my legs and removes them, balls them in his fist, puts them to his nose and inhales deeply, then shoves them into his pocket. Then he puts his face between my legs and eats me until I'm rocking my hips against his face, desperate to orgasm.

Before I can, he rises, unclasps his belt and unzips his slacks, takes his hard cock in his hand, and shoves it inside me.

"Mr. McCord," I whisper, gazing up at him with my pulse flying. "This is highly irregular. I might have to report you to human resources."

He takes my mouth and fucks me hard and fast, driving into me with powerful thrusts. We're both quiet except for the sound of our ragged breathing. When I come, I'm looking into his eyes. I say his name in a broken whisper, and it sends him over the edge.

Jerking, he empties himself inside me silently, his face pressed to my neck and both hands under my ass. He digs his fingers into my flesh and shudders, then releases the faintest, most erotic moan.

We lie there holding each other and panting until Marion's voice comes over his desk phone intercom.

"Mr. McCord, your father's on his way to see you."

He lifts his head and stares at me. "Fuck."

We scramble to our feet and fix our clothing. I smooth my hands over my hair as Cole strides across the office to pick up the papers strewn all over the floor. When he's got them all together, he shoves the folder at me and takes his chair behind his desk just as his father raps his knuckles sharply on the door.

Panicking, I throw myself into the chair across from Cole's desk and clutch the folder in my shaking hands.

Cole looks at me. "Ready?"

"Oh God."

"You'll be fine. Just smile." He calls out, "Come in."

The elder McCord walks through the door.

Wearing a double-breasted pinstripe suit and a chunky gold watch, his bearing regal and his dark hair graying at the temples, Cole's father looks exactly like what he is: rich and powerful.

"Hello, son."

"Dad. This is unexpected."

"We need to talk about your brother."

When he glances at me, I try to look like I'm not sitting here with his son's semen leaking out of me.

"Good morning."

I stand, smiling nervously. "Good morning, Mr. McCord. I'm Shay Sanders, Cole's assistant."

He approaches with his hand out, smiling. "Call me Konrad. Welcome to the firm."

We shake hands, then my heart nearly stops when he looks at my mouth and frowns.

"Your lipstick is smeared, dear."

Kill me. Just kill me right fucking now.

Wiping my mouth, I say, "Oh, gosh, really? How embarrassing. I ate a croissant at my desk this morning. Those things are so messy."

Konrad says, "That's why I never eat them. Crumbs all over the front of my suit. Makes me look like a derelict. Try a bagel instead. The ones in the cafeteria are surprisingly decent."

"Oh, uh...I will. That's a great idea. I do love a good bagel!"

Konrad beams at me while Cole sits at his desk, smirking.

"Well, I'll just leave this here for you to go over later, Mr. McCord." I set the folder on the edge of Cole's desk, then back away toward the door, wringing my hands and smiling like a contestant on a game show. "It was lovely to meet you, Mr. McCord," I say to Konrad. "Have a wonderful day."

I turn and walk stiffly to the door, hoping there isn't a wet spot on the back of my skirt.

Half an hour later, I'm at my desk when my phone rings. "Shay Sanders speaking."

Cole's warm voice comes over the line. "Good morning, Ms. Sanders."

I clear my throat and attempt a professional tone, though my heart started pounding with the first syllable he spoke. "Hello, Mr. McCord."

"I was just calling to let you know what a good job you did on the audit. The report you gave me this morning was exceptional."

His voice is a warm, sexy drawl, laced with humor. I know he's not talking about the report.

"Thank you. I take it your meeting with your father went well?"

He chuckles. "Yes. After you left, he remarked what a lovely girl you are. I told him I wasn't entirely satisfied with your performance so far, but I had hopes you'd improve."

"Gee, how generous of you."

"If I told him how I really felt about you, he'd be taken from the building on a stretcher."

Warmth spreads through my body. I smile at my computer screen. "So he didn't notice anything."

"You mean how incredible you look after you come? All flushed and glowing? No, he didn't notice. Nice save on the lipstick, by the way."

I groan and cover my face with my hand. "I thought I'd die."

His voice drops. "I thought I'd die when you came for me. Your pussy was so wet, baby. I can't get enough of it. I can't get enough of *you*."

Blushing furiously, I glance out my office windows at the cubicle field. No one is looking in my direction, but I feel so conspicuous, I might as well have a scarlet letter A embroidered on my chest.

"Me too," I whisper. "This being discreet thing might be harder than we anticipated."

"We'll figure it out. What time should I pick you up tonight?"

"Pick me up?"

"You're spending the weekend at my place."

"I don't recall being invited."

"Don't play coy with me. You want to wake up next to me just as much as I want to wake up next to you."

Smiling from ear to ear, I shake my head. "You're a handful, Mr. McCord."

"See you at seven, Ms. Sanders."

He disconnects, leaving me incandescent with happiness.

He's early again, ringing the bell just as I'm rushing to finish packing. When I open the door, he looks me up and down, then steps inside and hugs me, lifting me right off the ground.

I hug him back and laugh. "Oh hi."

"Oh hi yourself."

"You're very tall. My feet are dangling."

"Maybe you're just short."

"I'm not short. You smell incredible. Is that something new you're wearing?"

He sets me down, kisses me softly, and smiles. "Nope. Just love pheromones. You ready to go?"

A thrill runs through me at his mention of the word "love," but I don't make a big deal of it. "Almost. I have to finish packing."

"You say that like you're going on a two week vacation to Europe."

"Oh, that's right. You don't know I'm an over packer. Well, better you find out now what you're in for."

I lead him into my bedroom. On the bed are the two suitcases I've already packed, along with the open weekend bag on the floor by the dresser that I'm still working on filling.

He looks at them and lifts his brows.

"I know. It's a problem. I'll wear the same yoga pants five days in a row at home, but put a suitcase in front of me, and I'll pack every piece of formal wear I own, plus a dozen pairs of shoes and twenty handbags."

"Do you really think the ballgown is necessary?"

"That's not a ballgown. That's a bathrobe."

He eyes the puffy pink silk robe spilling out of one of the cases. "It's voluminous."

"It's pretty!"

"You won't need it. If you packed any panties, bras, or nightgowns, you can take those out too."

"Ugh. Fine."

As I pull the robe from the case, he slaps me playfully on the bottom. Then we're grinning at each other.

"Why do I feel like I'm nine years old, headed to Disneyland for the first time?"

"Because you're adorable. But watch out. At my Disneyland, Mickey Mouse fucks Minnie on the jungle cruise."

He kisses me again, I finish packing, and then we're off, headed to his mansion in the hills with the radio blaring, holding hands and singing along to our favorite songs.

We're still holding hands when I glance out the driver's side window and see a cargo truck barreling through the intersection against the red light.

I don't even have time to scream Cole's name before it crashes into us at full speed.

CHAPTER 54
Cole

It's a funny thing, karma.

Just when you think life is going your way, karma shows up to remind you that there's a price to be paid for everything.

The bigger your sins, the bigger the price.

And the longer you'll pay for them.

CHAPTER 55
Shay

I t's the beeping that gets me. The incessant beeping, like one of those annoying back-up sensor alarms on a car. Except it never stops, not even for a second.

Irritated by the noise, I open my eyes. My lids weigh a thousand pounds, so they slam shut almost immediately. But it's enough for me to catch a glimpse of an unfamiliar room, bright with florescent light.

"She's awake! She opened her eyes! Call the doctor. Get him in here quick."

I recognize that voice. It's my mother's.

Why is my mother here?

Where am I?

The irritating beeping continues.

A confusion of scents hangs in the air. Flowers and perfume, hairspray and mouthwash, body odor and bleach. There's something else beneath it all, an underlying stench I've never encountered before. Like the smell of something rotting, it's deeply disturbing.

I open my eyes again, this time focusing on the person looming over me, bending down over the bed. It's Chelsea.

Her eyes are red and swollen. Her face is blotchy, and her

blonde hair's a mess. I've never seen her look like this. And why is she in her work scrubs?

When I speak, I'm surprised by how weak and scratchy my voice sounds and by how much my throat hurts. "Hey, girlfriend. You look like shit."

She grabs my hand and bursts into tears. "Shay. Oh God. Thank God."

I look around the room. My parents stand together at the end of my bed. My father is gripping the metal guard rails that surround the mattress with both hands as if he's hanging on to it for life.

"Hi, honey," he says, his voice choked. His clothing is rumpled and his eyes are red, and I realize that, like Chelsea, he's been crying too.

The beeping grows louder and faster as cold fear seizes me.

I'm in the hospital.

This is a hospital room, and my parents and Chelsea are here because I've been hurt.

Suddenly, I can't catch my breath. It feels like a thousand pound weight is crushing my chest. I swallow, blinking against the harsh light of the room, and try to sit up.

I can't move.

Panicking now, I look down at myself.

I'm covered by a thin blue blanket, but my arms and legs are where they should be. Slender plastic tubes are stuck in both arms and the back of my right hand. The tubes lead up to bags of clear liquid hanging from a silver pole beside the bed. Next to the pole is the heart rate monitor causing all the beeping.

A young doctor in a white jacket sweeps into the room, followed by a big male nurse in blue scrubs. He must've been who my mother ordered to call the doctor. Chelsea moves aside to make room for the doctor at the edge of the bed but doesn't let go of my hand.

"Hello, Shay. I'm Dr. Dayan. How are you feeling?"

He has a gentle voice and a gentle smile, and now I'm even

more afraid than I was before. My tongue doesn't want to work, so I stare at him in terrified silence, waiting for him to speak again.

My expression must be pretty dire, because he starts to explain things to me slowly, as if I might not understand his words.

"You were in a car accident. You're in the ICU. We gave you drugs to reduce the swelling in your brain, so you might feel disoriented and confused for a while. That's normal."

I'm in the ICU?

As if summoned by that thought, the pain in my body makes itself known.

It's everywhere but worse in certain places. My head aches and my right hip throbs. My spine doesn't feel right, as if it's out of alignment, and all the nerves between the discs are pinched. And my throat is so raw and tender. Even my vocal cords are sore.

Everyone in the room is holding their breath. I can sense it without looking at them. The feeling of collective dread hangs in the air like an evil mist.

And I understand that I've been hurt very badly. That these people I love weren't sure if I would live or die.

Cole.

My heartbeat goes haywire. My mouth, already dry, turns to dust and ashes. Cold descends over my entire body, making it feel as if I've been wrapped in sheets of ice.

I whisper, "Is Cole okay?"

Leaning over to shine a penlight in both my eyes, Dr. Dayan says, "You'll be weak for a while. That's normal too. Muscles atrophy quickly when they're not used. Your throat will hurt as well. Your breathing tube was removed this morning when we stopped the paralytics."

I don't care about a stupid breathing tube right now. What I care about is the man who was in the car with me.

"Where's Cole? Chelsea? Is he all right?"

Chelsea and the doctor share a glance. Then she squeezes my hand.

"Let him examine you, okay? Then we'll talk."

Her voice is soft. Too soft and tinged with sorrow. And I know what it means.

Cole isn't okay.

Whatever's wrong with me, it's worse with him.

The sound of screeching tires and shattering glass fills my ears. The sensation of tumbling through empty space grips me. I suck in a breath that feels like fire and smells like smoke and burning fuel.

While the doctor taps my leg to see if I can feel it, I close my eyes and start to cry.

～

I wake to darkness.

It's not total. Light from the hallway spills through the open door of the room. The curtain that surrounds the bed has been drawn to one side so I can see into the hallway to the nurses station beyond. Three people sit at the desk, an older woman in pink scrubs who's typing on a computer keyboard and two younger women doing paperwork.

The only light inside my room comes from the hallway and the moonlight spilling through the window.

It must be very late, but I don't know the time. If there's a clock in this room, it's not within sight.

I turn my head on the pillow and see my mother sleeping on the small sofa under the window, her legs drawn up and her arms wrapped around herself. She's pale and too thin. Dark smudges under her eyes belie her exhaustion.

In the moonlight, she doesn't look like she's sleeping.

She looks like she's dead.

But then she inhales and mumbles something incoherently, and the band of pain around my chest eases.

It tightens again when I think of Cole.

I have to know how he is. I have to know what happened to him. I barely remember anything about the accident that put me here, only that quick glimpse of the oncoming truck and a few snatches of the collision, but I know it must've been devastating. Lifting my head feels like being hit with a sledgehammer. Sitting upright leaves me gasping in pain.

Dizzy and nauseated, I squeeze my eyes shut and stay still for a while, gathering the strength to swing my legs over the side of the bed. At some point, someone lowered the guard rails, so I'm not trapped anymore.

When I feel more steady, I slide one leg at a time around, then gingerly scoot to the edge of the mattress until I can set my feet on the floor. It's icy cold, even through the ugly blue hospital socks I'm wearing.

I try not to think of how I got into those socks or this pale blue gown either. I don't wonder who had to take me out of my other clothes, or about how they must've been cut off my body. I push all thoughts out of my head and concentrate on standing up.

The effort it takes leaves me panting and covered in sweat.

I grab onto the metal pole that holds the bag of liquid I'm hooked up to. It's got wheels, thank God. As carefully and quietly as I can, I shuffle around the end of the bed toward the open door, praying my mother doesn't wake up and stop me.

She doesn't.

When I reach the door, the nurses are still occupied with their work.

Weak, shaking, and in pain, I slink past the nurses station, slowly making my way down the hallway. The doors to the patient rooms don't have windows, so I can't see inside, but as I'm passing a room with a door painted bright yellow and numbered nine, the door opens suddenly and a doctor stands there.

He's startled to see me, but I don't pay attention to him.

I'm looking at the person lying on the bed in the room beyond.

It's Cole.

I only recognize him because of his hands, lying still on the bed, and his father, who's seated in a chair beside him.

Cole's head has been shaved. A ragged black line of stitches snakes down the left side of his face, temple to jaw. A tube is stuck down his throat and held in place by wide strips of white tape that stand out vividly against the mottled purple-and-blue bruising on his skin.

A machine is breathing for him.

I must make a cry of distress, because Konrad glances up and sees me standing out in the hallway staring in.

Our eyes meet.

His are hopeless and shining with tears.

My legs give out, but the doctor catches me before I fall. The last thing I see as the door swings closed behind him is Cole's father as he drops his head into his hands and starts to cry.

CHAPTER 56
Shay

The next morning, after my doctor has a quiet conversation with my parents outside in the hall, I'm moved out of critical care to a regular room on a different floor. I hold my mother's hand as a nurse wheels my bed down the hallway and onto the elevator.

No one will tell me anything about Cole.

Not the doctor who came out of his room last night, not Dr. Dayan or the nurses, and not my parents, who take turns sitting with me while the other goes on a break.

My father's wife, Chloe, stayed in Oregon to look after their two dogs. He seems lost without her. My mother, on the other hand, is doing remarkably well.

"Don't you think that nurse is cute?" she says to me once I'm settled in the new room and the nurse in question is gone. "I've never seen such big muscles on a man. I suppose his job takes a lot of strength, though, lifting unconscious people and whatnot."

She sits on the ugly plastic chair next to the nightstand, removes knitting needles and yarn from her big lumpy purse, and starts to knit, chatting brightly as she works on something that could be a pot holder when it grows up. Right now, it's the size of a coaster.

"That ICU doctor was cute too. Dayan. Very handsome. Do you think he's Armenian? I had an Armenian boyfriend once, though not nearly as handsome as this one. Nice head of hair, though."

"Mom."

"Your father looks well, doesn't he? Needs a haircut. I suppose that Zoe of his likes it long, her being a hippie and all. Can you imagine being raised in a commune? So strange. I have no idea what he sees in her. Maybe she sneaks pot gummies into his breakfast cereal."

"Mom."

"You'll be happy to hear that I'm still not drinking, honey. And not a peep from Bob. Good riddance to that crabby bastard, right? I can't believe how long I stayed with him."

"Mom!"

Startled by my volume, she finally looks up at me. "Yes, honey?"

"You talked to Dr. Dayan about me this morning, right? Before they moved me?"

"Yes."

"What did he say?"

She lays the knitting on her lap and considers me. "That I shouldn't tell you too much until you're stronger because we don't want to upset you."

I close my eyes and count to ten, resisting the urge to scream. "That's stupid."

"Which is what I told him. Your father agreed with the doctor, but he's on pot gummies, so we're not listening to him either. What do you want to know?"

"What were the results of the brain scan?"

"The swelling has resolved. There's no hemorrhaging. You might have some short-term memory problems because of the drugs they gave you, but that should resolve too."

Should not will. I'll worry about that later.

"What else?"

"Your bruising will last a few weeks most likely. You might be sore for a while longer than that. But overall, you're extremely lucky." Her voice drops. "That crash could've easily killed you."

"When can I go home?"

"Tomorrow or the next day."

"Good. And what's happening with Cole?"

She glances down at her hands. She runs her tongue over her teeth. Then she looks up at me again and exhales heavily.

"He'll make it. But they don't think he'll walk again."

I turn my head and look at the ceiling.

It's not until my mother jumps from her chair and hugs me tightly that I realize I'm sobbing.

"It's okay, honey. Oh, honey, I'm so sorry."

But she misunderstands. She thinks I'm crying because my boss won't walk again.

I'm not.

I'm crying because the man I'm in love with is going to live.

Later that day, Cole's father visits me.

He introduces himself to my father, who's reading the newspaper. Dad stands and they shake hands, then Konrad asks if it's all right if he has a word alone with me.

When Dad looks at me, I nod.

"Okay. I'll be back in a while." He leaves, quietly closing the door behind him, and Konrad stands at the edge of my bed looking down at me.

I know I look awful. My hair is greasy, my face is bruised, and I reek of sweat and disinfectant. None of that matters, however. I could be missing all my teeth, and I'd still be desperate to talk to him.

"Mr. McCord. How are you?"

He runs a hand over his hair, a gesture that reminds me of Cole. In the same business suit I saw him in yesterday, he looks worse for wear. He needs a shave, his eyes are bloodshot, and the lines in his face seem to have grown deeper since the day we met in Cole's office.

"I'm awful. Thank you for asking. How are you, dear?"

"The same. How's Cole?"

He gazes at me silently for a moment, then moistens his lips and shakes his head. "I should've guessed sooner. He was in such a better mood than usual. But it wasn't until I saw you two in his office that I knew."

Oh God. He knows.

My heart palpitating, I say, "It's my fault. Cole kept telling me we couldn't have a relationship, but I kept pushing for one. Please don't be angry with him. If anything, you should be mad at me."

He furrows his brows. "I'm not angry with anyone. You made my son happy. And nothing makes that boy happy. So thank you for that."

I bite my lower lip to keep it from trembling, but it does anyway. My eyes fill with tears.

Konrad exhales heavily again, then stretches his neck and closes his eyes. "I've made so many mistakes with those boys. Especially Cole. He's the hard-headed one, like his father."

He's lost in thought for a moment, then seems to shake it off, opening his eyes to stare at me with new energy.

"Do you care for him?"

My voice sounds very small in the stillness of the room. Small but full of conviction. "I love him."

"He's not an easy man to love."

"I know."

"He's impatient and demanding."

"I know."

"He's secretive too."

"I know."

"And he's incredibly stubborn. I've never known another person as stubborn as him."

Smiling through my tears, I say, "You do now."

After a moment, a small smile lifts his lips. It fades quickly, and his demeanor turns brusque. "Good. You'll need to be. Because if you're serious about him, you're in for a hell of a time."

"I heard the doctors don't think he'll walk again. Is that true?"

He waves a hand dismissively. "Doctors think they know everything. They don't. They don't know Cole either. If you tell that boy something can't be done, he'll make sure he does it. What I meant was that *he'll* give you a hell of a time. But don't let him discourage you, Shay. You hang in there. If you really do care for him, hang in there, no matter how hard he tries to push you away."

I'm getting all emotional, and I hate myself for it. My face is screwed up, and my voice comes out strangled. "Why would he push me away?"

"Because he thinks he doesn't deserve love. I don't know why, but he's been looking for proof his whole life that he's not worthy of good things."

He stops for a moment, gazing down at his feet. His voice lower, he says, "Maybe I was too hard on him."

I reach out and take his hand. He startles at the contact, but squeezes back when I tighten my fingers around his.

"He speaks very highly of you. Your wife too. He loves you both very much."

I might as well have shot him through the heart for how his face crumbles hearing those words. He turns away, swallowing hard, and clears his throat.

When he's composed himself, he says gruffly, "Thank you. Now I'll let you rest. Get better soon, young lady."

He pats my hand, then stiffly walks from the room.

I suspect he only held it together until he was around the corner.

∽

I'm discharged the next morning. They send me home with pain medication and instructions to go to the ER immediately if I experience sudden headaches or balance problems. Everyone keeps telling me what a miracle it is that I survived such a catastrophic accident with only a few days in a medically-induced coma and some nasty bruising.

The driver of the other car didn't fare so well. He broke both collar bones and six ribs, suffered a punctured lung and a ruptured spleen, and has lacerations all over his body. The nurse told me he'll be there for a while.

When I asked him how long Cole would be there, a shake of his head was the only answer.

My mother stays with me at my apartment for a week. Dad stays at a hotel for a few nights, then returns home to Oregon and Chloe. Chelsea visits as often as possible, bringing food for me and cigarettes for my mother, who doesn't drive because she lost her license years ago. Jen and Angel visit too, but the entire time I'm with anyone else, I'm thinking of Cole.

When I call the hospital and ask to be transferred to his room, the operator informs me she doesn't show anyone admitted under that name.

There's nothing on the news about the accident. There's nothing in the papers. There's nothing on the web.

The only place I find a mention of it is in the LAPD's online traffic collision report, but when I return to look at it a day later, it has mysteriously disappeared.

Such is the power of owning the media and being besties with the chief of police.

As soon as the taxi taking my mother to the airport pulls away from the curb outside my apartment, I drive to the hospital and take the elevator to the ICU floor I was on with Cole. Not knowing what name he's checked in under, I tell the nurse on duty that I'm here to see the patient in room nine.

"You can wait in the room down the hall," she says, pointing. "He's only allowed two visitors at a time."

I thank her and walk down the hall, shaking and sick to my stomach. When I enter the waiting room, Axel is there, standing in the corner by a vending machine.

He's talking to the most beautiful woman I've ever seen.

She's Asian. Everything about her is lovely. Face, hair, figure. Wearing a simple black sheath, she's got her arms wrapped around her body as if for protection from something.

She glances over and catches me looking at her, and I know. I just know who she is.

Kiyoko.

Cole's ex.

Axel follows her gaze and sees me. He murmurs something to her, squeezes her arm, then walks over to me.

"Hullo, luv."

My eyes fill with tears. "What happened to miss?"

His smile is faint. "Miss went out the window when Cole decided to lose his mind over you. How are you?"

My lower lip quivers. I swallow, choking back tears. "Not good. How is he?"

He exhales heavily, shoves his hands into his pockets, and shakes his head. "Awake, but not able to speak."

My entire body goes cold. My heart starts to pound painfully hard. "Oh God. That's not good."

"No, it isn't. But he's strong. And he's being well taken care of."

I glance over at Kiyoko.

"That's an old friend of Cole's and mine. We all went to university together. Let me introduce you."

He takes my elbow and gently leads me over to where she stands.

"Kiyoko, this is Shay. Cole's girl."

I say, "Hi. It's nice to meet you."

She gives me a sad smile. "Hello, Shay. It's nice to meet you too. I'm sorry it had to be under these circumstances."

"Me too. Axel says he isn't able to talk."

"It could be damage from the breathing tubes. But I don't think so. I think he just doesn't want to. And depending on how bad his spinal cord injury turns out to be, he may never want to speak again."

The three of us stare at each other while I breathe around the sobs building in my chest. "Can I see him?"

Axel says, "His brothers are in with him now, but when they come out, I'm sure he'll want to see you. Why don't you have a seat, and I'll let them know you're here."

Kiyoko and I sit in the uncomfortable chairs and look at everything but each other as Axel leaves the room.

After a while, she sighs. "He sounded happy last time I spoke to him. That's how I knew he was seeing someone."

This feels like a minefield I don't want to start trampling around in. I try to think of something diplomatic to say that won't be upsetting. "I'm glad you're still on good terms."

She looks at me. "We still love each other, if that's what you mean."

When I blanch, she shakes her head. "I didn't mean it like that. He's got flaws, but disloyalty isn't one of them. I don't know if he told you, but he's the one who broke it off with me."

I think I should retreat to safer territory. Two women who've been with the same man should never talk about him unless they both hate him. Otherwise, someone's getting her feelings hurt.

"How did you find out about the accident?"

"Axel called me. I came as soon as I could." She nods at the bruising on the right side of my face, which was black but now has faded to a sickly yellow. "How do you feel?"

"Lucky. Awful. Worried."

She studies me for a moment. I sense there's something she wants to say, but then Axel returns. His expression is pained.

I leap to my feet, heart palpitating. "What is it? What's wrong?"

He looks at Kiyoko, then at me, then stands there looking uncomfortable.

"Well, he's talking."

"Oh thank God!"

Kiyoko stands. "Is he in pain? Does he need anything? What did he say?"

When Axel looks at me, I already know what he's about to tell me. I know, but it still hurts like he drove a knife right into my heart.

"He said to tell Shay to leave and not come back. And he said..."

He pauses to shake his head and sigh. "I'm sorry, luv, but he said to tell you it's over."

CHAPTER 57

Cole

When Axel returns ten minutes later, he's smirking.

Sitting in the chair beside my bed, Callum looks at him and says, "How'd she take it?"

"Oh, I'd say she took it rather well. Took it like a champ, in fact. Nary a tear in sight. She did give a nice little speech though. Quite rousing."

Carter looks interested. "Really? What did she say?"

Axel looks at me and smiles.

"She said, and I quote, 'Tell that stubborn SOB that I'm not going anywhere, and he doesn't get to break up with me. Not like this. If he wants me to go away, he'll have to say it to my face. And he'll have to be convincing. Which he won't be, so tell him to forget about even trying.' Then she sat down, crossed her arms over her chest, and glared at the vending machine."

My brothers look at me, then Callum starts to laugh.

"Well, well. Looks like the Grinch has met his match."

I want to tell him to fuck off, but I don't have the energy.

So I just lie there in bed and let the tears leak from the corners of my eyes.

317

CHAPTER 58
Shay

H e's in the hospital for another two weeks. He undergoes surgery on his spine and has countless diagnostic tests and imaging. And still, he refuses to see me.

I come every day straight from work and sit in the waiting area. His father brings me sandwiches and sneaks in wine that we drink from paper cups. His mother, a slender redhead named Catherine, teaches me how to play bridge. His brothers come and go, and so do Kiyoko and Axel, but he never allows me into his room.

I could barge in, but I get more and more angry with him with each day that passes.

He's trying to freeze me out, but all he's doing is pissing me off.

On a Tuesday, his older brother Callum comes into my office at work to tell me Cole has been transferred to a private rehabilitation facility where he'll receive physical therapy and ongoing care.

Then he drops a bomb on me.

"He won't be going back to work. He resigned as CFO of the company."

Shocked by the news, I stare at him until I find the power of speech. "Why? Are you saying he'll never be well enough to work again?"

He gazes at me silently for a long moment, then shakes his head. "I don't know what it means, but that's what he decided. And he asked us not to tell you where he is now, so I'm sorry, but...I won't."

When he leaves, I throw up into the trashcan.

~

A month passes. Every moment apart from him is a doctor's waiting room hell where my name is never called and there aren't any exits.

~

One Friday night, after I've made my way through two-thirds of a bottle of wine and worked myself up into a lather of hurt and indignation, I take out my cell phone, find the number he called me from what feels like years ago, and send him a text.

> The night we met, you told me that any man who'd let me go has a personality disorder.

I follow it up with six exclamation points, because I'm feeling dramatic. Expecting nothing, I shut off the phone and go to bed.

In the morning when I turn it on, there's a message from Cole.

> And I was right. But I have more than one.

I'm so thrilled that he responded, I almost drop the phone. Pulse throbbing and hands shaking, I stare at the screen and try to decide what to send back. Because I'm nothing if not direct, I go straight for the jugular.

> I miss you. I love you. I won't stop just
> because you're ignoring me.

> Forget me. It's over.

That makes me so mad, I scream. Standing in the middle of my bedroom, I look up at the ceiling and scream at it until I feel better. Then I let my thumbs fly.

> It's not over. Don't be such a wuss. Let me
> come and see you.

> IT'S OVER.

> Bullshit. I know you. I know what this is. You
> won't scare me off so easily.

Shaking with anxiety, I wait for a response. When it doesn't come, I dial his number. When he picks up, I almost pass out from relief.

"Hello? Cole?"

No response, but I hear him breathing.

"Okay, I'll talk, you listen. Please don't hang up. God, where do I start? I feel like I'm having a heart attack."

Pacing the floor, I chew my thumbnail until I can pull myself together enough to form a coherent sentence. "I know you're hurt. Nobody will tell me how badly, but all I care about is that you're alive. It doesn't matter to me if you have a disability. It doesn't matter to me if you can't walk. All I want is you. Please let me come see you. Please."

After a minute of silence where I die a thousand deaths, he finally speaks.

"I'm not a man anymore."

His voice is raw, aching with anger and pain. Hearing it makes my heart clench and tears spring into my eyes.

I whisper, "Don't say that. You're still a man. Your masculinity doesn't depend on—"

"*I'm not a man!* Do you understand what I'm saying? I can't be with you anymore, Shay! I can't be with anyone! I'm not fucking functional!"

I start to bawl. Tears stream down my cheeks. My whole body is racked with uncontrollable sobs. I sink to my knees on the carpet and cry so hard, my sides hurt.

"I d-don't care."

"You should fucking care!"

"I don't. Let me see you. Please."

"Goddammit. Why don't you ever listen to me? Why do you have to make everything so difficult? Why can't you just let it go?"

He's angry and frustrated, breathing hard. And I'm desperate to keep him talking. This feels dangerous and out of control, as if everything hinges on this conversation. Our past, our future, our whole lives.

It feels like we're holding hands at the edge of a high, windswept cliff, deciding whether to step back or jump.

"I can't let it go because I love you."

His voice turns bitter. "You loved Chet too. Look what that got you."

My heart is breaking. It's splitting in half. It's tearing itself into pieces.

"I won't answer if you call again, Shay. I won't see you. Forget about me. Go live your life. It's over."

A white hot ball of rage explodes inside me. I'm still crying, but I'm furious now too. At him for being so unreasonable, and at myself for being so reckless with my heart.

At the top of my lungs, I shout into the phone, "Fuck you, Cole McCord! You don't get to tell me how to live my life! You don't get to tell me who to love! And I don't care if you don't want me anymore, I still want you, and I always will! You dumb, stubborn man, your worth doesn't depend on your legs or your dick or any of your other body parts. And I'm sorry this happened, God fucking knows I am, but sometimes life is shitty, and the only choice we have is to make the best of it! *We don't give up.* Not on life, and not on each other. And I swear to God, if you give up on us, I'll never forgive you. So get your head straight. When I said I belonged to you, that meant forever. Like it or not, I'm yours!"

I disconnect and throw the phone against the wall. It shatters into pieces.

Then I fall facedown on the carpet, curl into a ball, and sob until I fall asleep.

CHAPTER 59
Cole

I should've known she wouldn't make it easy for me. That woman has defied me at every turn since the day we met.

Kiyoko takes the phone when I hand it to her. We sit in silence for a while, then she says, "I really like that girl."

I close my eyes, swallow around the lump in my throat, and let the tears slide down my face. "Me too."

"So what's next?"

"We keep waiting."

"It's already been more than a month since you resigned."

"She'll come around."

"I feel like we could all be dead by then."

"Yes, there is that possibility. But if there's one thing I know for sure, it's that you can't tell her what to do. She has to think it's her own idea."

"Gee, who does that sound like?" When I don't respond, she says, "I don't know, Cole. She might just quit."

I'd laugh if I had the energy. Instead, I wipe my cheeks with my hands and dry them on my sweatpants. "Believe me, the word quit is not in that woman's vocabulary. When are you going home?"

"As soon as I know you're okay." She pauses, peering at me. "Oh. That wasn't really a question."

"I won't let you put your life on hold for me either."

"Don't be an idiot."

"Too late. Already am."

"You need friends around you right now."

What I need is Shay, but I'm not that selfish. I'll never be a burden to her. I'll never take advantage of her love.

I'll never be like that fuckwit Chet.

No matter how much it's killing me, I have to let her go. I don't think I could ever forgive myself if I didn't.

"Go home, Ki. You've done enough for me. Thank you for everything, but it's time for you to go back to Vancouver."

"Pardon the interruption. Are you ready to start again, sir?"

We look over at the smiling woman standing near us. Her name tag reads Willa. She's the third physical therapist I've had since I checked into this rehab facility, and by far the best.

She doesn't let me give her any shit. The others were far too intimidated by me.

I wheel around to face her. "I'm ready. And don't take it easy on me. No excuses, Willa."

"In that case, I'll go get my whip," she teases.

"Perfect."

Kiyoko stands from her chair, leans over to kiss me on the head, then straightens and gazes down at me with soft eyes. "For the record, I think you're making a mistake."

"It's not fair to expect you to look after me."

"I wasn't talking about me. I was talking about Shay."

I close my eyes and exhale heavily. "Not this again."

"Not everybody gets a chance at real happiness, Cole. Most of us aren't that lucky."

I open my eyes and stare at her in disbelief. "Lucky? I'm not lucky."

"Yes, you are. But nobody else can convince you of that. You have to realize it for yourself." She smiles sadly. "Maybe you'll get a sign from the universe."

She turns and walks away.

CHAPTER 60
Shay

I get through the weekend by the skin of my teeth. On Monday at work, I'm barely coherent. I walk around like a zombie, going through the motions and avoiding everyone's eyes.

It's starting to sink in that it's really over. Cole doesn't want me. And no matter how much I want him, relationships take two.

It occurs to me more than once that I should quit and find a new job, but I can't bring myself to do it. This place is the only concrete reminder I have of him. Leaving it would feel like a betrayal. Like a denial that what I told him he meant to me was real.

Knowing he'll probably never read it, I write him an inter-office memo and give it to Scotty to put on Cole's desk. After he leaves, I call Chelsea's cell. She picks up on the first ring.

"Hey. You okay?"

"I'm surviving. You?"

"Slightly better than that."

We're quiet for a moment, then she says, "Do you want to get together for drinks?"

"I thought you'd never ask."

"Great, I'm off tomorrow. How's six o'clock?"

"Perfect."

"Where to?"

"I know where I want to go, but I'm afraid you'll say no."

She laughs. "When the hell have I ever said no to you?"

That makes me smile, the first time I've done that in a long time. When I tell her where I want to meet, she doesn't miss a beat.

"Okay. See you then."

"See you then. I love you, Chelsea."

She pauses. When she speaks again, her voice is soft and has a slight wobble in it. "I love you too, you nonsensical twat."

We hang up, and I'm trying not to cry.

The next night, we're sitting at a table in the middle of the hotel bar in Beverly Hills where I first met Cole.

The term "glutton for punishment" was invented for people like me.

We ordered straight from the bar instead of having the waitress bring us our drinks, a new paranoia I doubt either of us will ever rid ourselves of. I've got whiskey, she's got a skinny margarita, and it feels like old times.

Or at least it mostly does. Except for the hole in my chest where my heart used to be.

"So catch me up," she says, sipping her drink. "What's the latest?"

I give her a shortened version of my last phone call with Cole. It makes her eyes bug. Then she frowns. "I heard his spinal injury was sacral."

"If I spoke ER nurse, I'd know what you mean."

"Him being who he is, everything was super hush-hush at the hospital, but a nurse from the critical care unit told one of the nurses in pediatrics I know that the patient they code named Mr. Big had a sacral injury. Every spine injury is serious to varying degrees, but of the different types, that one's considered the least serious. Many patients are able to walk."

I almost choke on my whiskey. "*What?*"

"It all depends on the person and the level of damage to the nerves, but yeah."

My heart is hammering so hard, I have to press my hand on my chest to try to slow it. "I don't think that's it, then. He made it sound like nothing below the waist was working."

"I'd go in and look at his file for you, but everything's tracked in the system. I'd be fired if I got caught. We're not allowed to access information on patients we're not directly caring for."

"I'd never ask you to do that."

She smiles. "You totally would, and you know it."

"Yeah. I would. But don't. If you got fired, it would just be the cherry on top of my clusterfuck sundae." I sigh and take another sip of whiskey. "So if him being there was so hush-hush, how'd they know to call him Mr. Big?"

"Oh, he didn't get that nickname because he's a McCord. He got it because he's so girthy. The nursing assistant who changed his bedding started calling him Mr. Big the first night he was admitted."

I stare at her in horror.

After a moment, she says, "At least they didn't call him Mr. Shrimpy. Or Boomawang if it was curved. I've heard those too."

"Dear God. Remind me never to set foot in a hospital again."

She raps her knuckles on the table. "Knock wood."

We sit in silence for a while, nursing our drinks. Then she says, "So your mom. How's that going?"

"We're talking every Sunday now. She's still not drinking. I keep waiting for the other shoe to drop, but so far, so good. I'm going to see her for Thanksgiving."

Chelsea reaches out and squeezes my hand. "Okay. Silver linings, right? We take 'em where we can."

I exhale and shrug. "Yep. Have you talked to Jen or Angel

lately? I've been so wrapped up in my own little bubble, I haven't reached out."

"They're good. Angel's got a new boyfriend so she's been preoccupied. Sounds serious about him. And Jen's thinking about changing jobs."

"Again?"

"She hates her boss. Says he's a real asshole. The whole company can't stand him."

I smile at that, then suddenly I'm fighting back tears. I whisper, "I don't know what do to."

"Oh, honey." She squeezes my hand again. "There's nothing you can do but wait. See if he comes around."

"But am I being stupid? Am I just refusing to acknowledge reality?"

"You're in love. We're all morons when we're in love. It's the oxytocin. It messes with your brain function. Just give him some space. He's in survival mode."

I shake my head. "You didn't hear him. He was so angry. Oh, I forgot to tell you."

"What?"

"He resigned as CFO."

Her mouth drops open. "Wow."

"That was pretty much my reaction too."

"Who told you that?"

"His brother."

She sits back in her chair and stares at me. "So that means the position's open."

I shrug. "I guess so."

"Why don't you apply for it?"

"You're funny."

"I'm not being funny. I'm dead serious. You're his assistant. You know exactly what his position entails. Who better than you to step into his shoes?"

I take a sip of my whiskey. "That was an unfortunate choice of words."

"Oh God. I'm so sorry. I didn't mean it like that."

"I know you didn't." I sigh and drink more whiskey. "But I'm not qualified for that job."

"Bullshit. You've got the education and the experience."

"Even if my resume says I might be a good match, it's a family-owned corporation. I'm not family."

"Maybe that's exactly what they need. An outsider with fresh perspective." She's getting more excited as she speaks, drumming her fingers on the table. "Plus, you're a woman. Every corporation is worried now about how bad having an all-male board looks."

"They're not public. They don't care."

"Trust me, they care. They're a global business. Even if the dad doesn't because he's old school, his two brothers must be aware that it's not good for their image to have a bunch of dudes running the place."

I make a face at her. "The last thing I want is to be hired for a job because I own a vagina."

She scoffs. "Why the hell not? Half the men who are in the jobs they're in were hired because they're men. Our CFO at the hospital has the IQ of a banana, but he got the job over a more qualified female candidate. It happens all the time."

She's making a lot of sense, but I'm not comfortable with the idea of applying for Cole's job. It seems too mercenary. Too cutthroat.

Too much like I don't care about him and never really did.

"I know what you're thinking, but if you're going to stay working there anyway, why not climb the corporate ladder?"

"I don't know, Chelsea. I don't think I'm ready for that."

"Then you better get ready to have a new boss."

When I make a face, she says, "Somebody has to do that job. It might as well be you."

"The last thing that family needs right now is me trying to insert myself into their business in a leadership role. What would they think of me?"

She gazes at me for a moment, then shrugs. "Maybe they'd be

grateful that someone who cares for their son and brother is such a good match for the job he doesn't want or can't handle anymore. Maybe they'd be happy to give the position to someone they can trust instead of a total stranger."

I remember what Cole said to me the day I started work when he found out Emery recommended me for the job.

"We're very private. We have to be. You can't imagine the targets we are for every kind of scumbag out there."

My thoughts start to spin with the possibility. I say slowly, "They are pretty weird about strangers."

"And you've already passed all their nutty background checks. Plus, think how hard it will be for them to find a new person to fill that job. Not to mention expensive. Every business would rather promote someone from within who's already familiar with the company culture and has an established work record. It makes sense on every level. If you were a guy in this position, you'd already have submitted your resume."

"There's only one problem with this picture."

She waves a hand in the air. "So you two were playing hide-the-sausage. Big deal."

"It is a big deal! It complicates everything!"

"Not if he never comes back, it doesn't." She hesitates, then sighs. "And I'm sorry to pour salt on fresh wounds, but from what you've told me, it doesn't sound like he has any intention of being with you again."

"Forget about me. Go live your life. It's over."

Though it hurts like hell to admit, she's right. He definitely wasn't equivocating. He made his feelings perfectly clear.

"I don't know, Chelsea. I'll have to think about it."

"I hear you. But don't wait too long. Opportunities like this don't last forever. You might not get the job, but you'll probably be kicking yourself a year down the line if you didn't at least try."

～

I can't sleep that night. I stare at the ceiling, going over everything, having every argument and counter-argument in my head.

I finally decide she's right. I've got nothing to lose by submitting my resume.

So the next day, I do just that.

CHAPTER 61

Cole

"Fuck. *Fuck!*"

"I know it hurts, but concentrate. You're doing great. Just stay focused on putting one foot in front of the other. Go slowly."

"All I can do is go slowly!"

"You don't have to shout. I'm right in front of you. Right foot. Good. Left foot. Good. Keep coming."

My legs are on fire, but my feet feel like lead. I'm gripping the rubber rail covers of the walker so hard, my knuckles are white. My arms shake. Sweat pours down my face. I could be having a heart attack.

But I'm standing. On my own two feet, I'm standing up.

It's exhilarating.

It also hurts like a motherfucker.

When I stumble and curse, Willa moves quickly to my side to support my weight. I lean on her, panting.

"Do you want to keep going or take a rest?"

"Keep going." An electric jolt of pain shoots down my left leg. I grit my teeth against it. "Or maybe rest for a few minutes."

"Hands on the rails. Let me get the chair."

I grab the walker again, using my arm strength to hold myself up. My arms were big before, but in the past few weeks, my biceps have grown noticeably bigger.

Pretty soon, I'll give Emiliano a run for his money.

Willa positions the chair behind me and holds onto my upper arm as I lower myself into it. Then she stands there beaming at me.

I chuckle. "I'm your star pupil, aren't I?"

"No. You're actually pretty average."

"I know you're only saying that so I'll keep trying hard." Over on the weight bench, my cell phone starts to ring. "Let's take five. Then I expect you to start shouting obscenities at me like a drill sergeant."

She says drily, "That's your thing, not mine. I'll bring you back a water."

As she heads to the front, I wheel over to the phone. The number on the screen shows that it's my brother.

"Callum. How are you?"

"Good. Am I interrupting?"

"No. What's up?"

His tone warms. "Just thought you'd like to know someone threw her hat in the ring for CFO today."

Finally. I smile, shaking my head. "Oh yeah?"

"Yeah. And she included a cover letter as well, listing all her qualifications and a twenty-seven-point bulleted list of why she's the best person for the job."

"Of course she did. What did Dad say?"

"He said he had to talk to Mom."

"So that's a yes. Carter?"

"He said we've needed a female on the board since the eighties."

"Another yes. What about you?"

There's a pause. When he speaks again, his voice is softer than I've ever heard it.

"You know what I think. If she can handle you, she can handle anything. Being CFO of McCord Media will be a cinch."

"I think there's a compliment in there somewhere."

"There is. For her. You coming to dinner on Sunday? Mom's making a roast."

"You mean Elise is making a roast, and Mom's going to sit there and accept all the praise as if she actually knew how to operate an oven."

"Exactly. See you at six. Oh, and Cole?"

"Yeah?"

His voice turns gruff. "I'm proud of you, brother. And I know we never say it, but...I love you. I'm sorry it took almost losing you to realize how much."

He disconnects.

When Willa returns with my bottle of water, she finds me hunched over with my hands covering my face so she can't see me cry.

CHAPTER 62
Shay

When the phone rings at seven o'clock Friday morning the next week, I'm at my desk reconciling the general ledger, a monthly task I approach with the same dread I have about getting a root canal.

I know it will hurt, but I'll feel better when it's over.

"Shay Sanders speaking."

"Hullo, lass. Working early again, I see. How are you?"

The voice is deep, male, and has a lilting Irish accent. I'm sure I've never heard it before.

"I'm well, thank you. Who is this?"

"A friend of the family."

"My family?"

Mystery man chuckles. "Aye, if all works out as it should."

Intrigued, I sit back in my chair and change my focus from the computer to the call. "I'm sorry, I don't know what you mean. Is there something I can help you with?"

"Aye. When they offer you the CFO position, ask for more money."

I blink in surprise. "Excuse me?"

"Ask for more money, lass. Equal pay's important, wouldn't you agree?"

I glance through the glass walls of my office out to the cubicle field. It's empty. As usual, I'm the first one here, but for some reason, I half expected to see a prankster grinning at me through the fronds of a potted palm.

"Who is this?"

"Already asked and answered, but if it's a name you're looking for, mine's Killian Black."

I decide to play along, though this Killian Black character is more than a little irritating. "Pleased to meet you, Killian. How do you know anything about the CFO position?"

"You'll soon discover that I know everything about everything, lass."

"Ah. You're an Irish Magic 8 Ball, is that it?"

"You sound doubtful."

"Don't take this personally, but if we're going to be family, you should know that overly cocky prank callers are pretty high up on my ick list."

He chuckles again. I get the sense that the more irritated I become, the more amusing he'll find me.

"Just remember what I said about the salary. After you get started, I'll be in touch again. In the meantime, you should pick up *One Hundred Years of Solitude*. I know Márquez is your favorite writer, so it's surprising you haven't read that one yet. He won the Nobel Prize for it, you know. Emery has three copies of it at her shop. By the way, your mother wants to move closer to you, but she doesn't know how to bring it up. You can hash it out when you have your weekly call on Sunday."

I sit staring at the wall with my mouth open and my brain full of static.

"Lovely chatting with you, lass. And congratulations. You'll make a fine CFO."

He disconnects, leaving me listening to air.

Half an hour later, I'm still sitting at my desk in a cloud of confusion when Ruth from human resources calls to tell me that the elder Mr. McCord would like to see me in his office immediately.

CHAPTER 63
Cole

When Callum calls me, he's laughing.

"Brother, that girl of yours is something else."

"What do you mean? What happened? Don't tell me she turned down the position!"

"No, she didn't turn it down. She accepted the offer. On the condition that Dad double the salary."

Good for you, baby. Good for you.

I'm happy because it's what I wanted, but my heart also hurts. I miss her every day. Sometimes so fucking much, I can't breathe.

He pauses for a moment, then says gently, "She asked about you again."

"What did you tell her?"

"Same thing as always. What you told us to say. That you're fine, and that's it. You know you're an idiot, right?"

"So I've heard."

"How long are you going to keep this up?"

"She deserves better than me."

"I know it's wrong, but I think about punching you a lot."

"Thanks. That's very helpful."

"All right, you stubborn bastard. I know you won't listen to me. Maybe the universe will send you a sign. God knows nothing else has been able to convince you. Oh, by the way, I've got a courier coming to you with something I found on your desk. He should be there any time."

"What is it?"

"An inter-office memo envelope. No idea how long it's been sitting there, but I figured you might want it."

An inter-office memo. My heart starts to pound, but I try to keep my voice casual. "Great, thanks."

"You got it. Talk to you soon."

I wheel to the front of the rehab center and wait impatiently until the courier arrives. As soon as I've signed off for the package, I rip open the brown kraft envelope, withdraw the sheet of paper, and start to read.

Dear Mr. McCord,

Our last contact was two days ago. It's amazing how many tears I've shed in forty-eight hours. Though I suppose I shouldn't be surprised. When you lose such a big a part of yourself, it feels like you'll never recover.

If I was too harsh on you, I'm sorry. I'm sorry for hurting you, but even more than that, I'm sorry for my part in all of this. I should have listened when you told me to walk away that first night. I should have been more responsible. More careful. Less reckless with both our hearts.

I miss you terribly.

The only thing that makes it bearable is knowing you're still out there somewhere. Well, more bearable, anyway. Right now, it feels as if I'm walking alone in the dark, not even bothering to search for a light at the end of the tunnel because I know there isn't one.

*I hope you won't forget me. Because you carved your name
into my heart, and it will stay there forever.*

Yours in perpetuity,
Ms. Sanders

"Willa! *Willa!*"

Breathless, my heart pounding like mad, I wheel around the
corner of the main reception area and down the hallway to the
large, glassed-in physical therapy room, then make a beeline to
where she stands talking with one of the center's doctors.

"Willa! I need you! Right now!"

She looks at me with lifted brows and an amused expression.
"Good morning, Cole. Where's the fire?"

In my veins, but I don't say that. I don't want to sound like a
lunatic. "Let's try the quad crutches again."

"You sure? I recall a large amount of F-bombs were dropped
last time we tried the quad crutches."

She's teasing, but I know she's pleased. "Yes, I'm sure."

"All right, let's get started. Just woke up this morning feeling
ambitious, did you?"

Shaking with adrenaline, I grin at her. "No. I got a sign from
the universe."

CHAPTER 64
Shay

A week after I start my new position at McCord Media, Jen, Angel, and Chelsea take me out to dinner to celebrate.

Chelsea made no comment when I said I wanted to go to the hotel bar in Beverly Hills again, but I could tell she was wishing I'd get over it.

Get over *him*.

Because that's about as likely as my apartment building taking a direct hit from a meteor, I'll keep coming to this damn bar until one day I see Cole here again. Fate didn't bring us together and put us through so much only to leave us strangers.

If there's one thing that *Love in the Time of Cholera* taught me, it's that true love always wins in the end, even if it takes fifty fucking years and enough heartache and tragedy that it can be accurately compared to a plague.

Life would probably be a lot easier for me if I wasn't such a diehard romantic.

"So how's the new job, Ms. Big Shot CFO?"

Angel grins at me from across the table. She's got that newly-in-love glow, and I'm trying not to be bitter about it.

"It's unbelievably hard, and the workload is ridiculous, and pretty much all day every day, I feel like I'm in way over my head. Other than that, I'm loving it. How's it going with your new boyfriend? Chelsea seems to think it's pretty serious."

She nods. "It's serious all right. I let him bang me in the butt."

Jen bursts out laughing. Chelsea rolls her eyes. And I fight off the vivid memory of Cole and me on the lounge bed beside his pool the night he decided to use melted butter as something other than a condiment.

I'll never be able to look at lobster the same way again.

Sighing, I take a sip of my whiskey, then listen absently as Jen and Angel debate the merits of butt sex versus condoms in preventing pregnancy. The trio of businessmen sitting at the table next to ours is riveted.

Chelsea lightly kicks my foot under the table to get my attention.

"You okay?"

I think about it for a moment. "Define okay?"

"That's a no. Anything I can do?"

I smile at her and shake my head. "You're already doing it."

She chews on the straw in her skinny margarita in silent contemplation for a moment. "Any word from you-know-who?"

"No."

"I had an idea. With all this money you're making now, you could hire a private detective to find out where he is."

I sigh, shaking my head. "Wouldn't do any good if he refuses to see me. Takes two to tango, right?"

"I suppose. Though I've had several relationships where the guy didn't even know we were dating."

"You always did like the aloof ones."

"What fun is it if they fall at your feet? There's no challenge to that."

I say sadly, "I don't want a challenge. I want someone so obsessed with me, he can't think of anything else."

I want Cole.

Chelsea reaches over and squeezes my hand. "It'll work out how it's supposed to."

"I know. But as we all know, patience isn't my thing. Anyway, let's talk about something else. How's it going at the hospital? Are you still short staffed?"

Chelsea doesn't answer. I glance up at her. She's staring over my shoulder with big, unblinking eyes, as if she can't believe what she's seeing.

"What's wrong?"

She says faintly, "Um. You might want to turn around."

Frowning, I look over my shoulder. Then I see what she's looking at, and my stomach drops, my lungs seize, and my pulse skyrockets.

The dark-haired man in the booth is gorgeous, but I can tell with one glance that he's also trouble. A wolf dressed in sheep's clothing. In a conservative black suit and white dress shirt, he could be any other businessman enjoying a drink with friends after work.

Except he's alone.

And he's not enjoying himself.

He looks how I feel: miserable.

Tears well in my eyes. My chest constricts. With the ragged pink scar snaking down the side of his face and his hair buzzed short like Axel's, he looks so much the same as the last time I saw him but also very different.

But dear God, how those blue eyes still burn.

To the right of his booth sits an empty wheelchair.

I'm on my feet without making a conscious decision. I run across the bar, dodging tables and almost knocking a waiter off his feet, then throw myself into Cole's outstretched arms and burst into tears.

I cry as he holds me tightly, rocking me and murmuring my name over and over like a prayer.

Still sobbing I say, "It's you. You're here."

He answers in a voice impossibly warm and soft. "Callum sent me your memo with a courier. I figured since I'd carved my name on your heart, I should probably claim it." His voice drops to a whisper. "Forgive me. Please forgive me for being such a fucking idiot. I don't know what made me think I could live without you because I can't."

I want to pound a fist on his shoulder, but only cling to him instead, relief and euphoria burning through me. "But how are you *here*?"

"Just lucky timing, I guess."

Wet faced and hiccuping, I pull away and look at him.

His smile is small and breathtakingly beautiful. "Okay, fine, I called the chief and had him put one of his guys on you."

"His guys? You mean a police officer?"

"Yes."

"You had me tailed by the *police*?"

"It sounds bad when you say it."

"Because it is bad."

"It was only the one time. I just needed to know where you'd be today so I could come see you."

I decide it doesn't matter how he found me. Right now, I'm too overwhelmed to do anything but cup his face in my hands and kiss him.

Against my mouth, he murmurs, "I'm fucked up, baby. I'm really fucked up."

"Don't care. Stop talking and kiss me."

"It's not gonna be easy. I've got a long road ahead. I won't ever be the same as I was."

"You're alive, Cole. You're alive, and I love you. Everything else is details."

I kiss him all over his face, not caring that people are probably staring or that our lives will be complicated or that I might never get to feel him inside me again.

The only thing I care about is him.

After a moment, I stop kissing him and frown. "Cole?"

"Yes, baby?"

"Did you by any chance forget to take anything out of your pockets?"

"No. Why?"

"It's just that something hard is poking me in the butt."

When he smiles a knowing smile, I lose my breath.

"But I thought..."

"It's happened a few times. The first was when this nurse was giving me a sponge bath in the hospital. It was pretty embarrassing, but he told me not to worry about it." His smile grows wider. "I mean, he was pretty cute, though. Way cuter than a hairless Chihuahua."

I'm crying again. Crying and laughing at the same time. Then he's crying too, and kissing me, and telling me over and over that he loves me.

And that I don't look like a hairless Chihuahua, not even a little bit.

Epilogue

COLE

Two months later

I t's the little things that get me. The intimate little things nobody else sees but me.

How she looks when she wakes up first thing in the morning. The way she combs her hair, puts on her makeup, yawns late at night when she's sleepy, closes her eyes when she takes the first sip of coffee in the morning.

How she smiles when I touch her.

How she sighs when I kiss her.

How she cries after she comes.

Most of the time it's with my fingers or tongue, but those little blue pills sure do come in handy. God bless big pharma.

Now if only they could manufacture a drug that would make me walk like I used to, I'd be all set.

"Honey, be careful."

"I'm fine."

"I know you're fine, but the doctor said to take it slow now that you're home."

"Turtles move faster than I am."

"But you're not using your walker!"

347

J.T. GEISSINGER

Leaning heavily on my cane, I look up at her. "Love."

"Yes?"

"Please be quiet and let me do this."

She takes a deep breath, then nods. Then, practically vibrating with anxiety, she bites her lower lip and watches me creep slowly across the living room carpet toward my wheelchair.

By the time I reach it, I'm panting. I drop the cane, grip both arms of the chair, and catch my breath.

"Okay, I'm not saying anything, but if you need help sitting down, I'm right here."

I close my eyes and chuckle, shaking my head. "Good to know you're not saying anything." I manage to get myself turned around and into the wheelchair with only a few grunts and curses, then I look up at Shay and beam.

"See? Nothing to worry about. Now come sit on my lap."

That's one command she always obeys without a fight. Smiling and obviously relieved I didn't break anything in my six-foot walk, she comes over to me and carefully sits on my lap. Then she drapes her arms around my shoulders and kisses me.

"Hi."

"Hi yourself."

"Do you need some water?"

"Aren't you going to tell me how amazing that was?"

"Oh yes. Pardon me. That's was very amazing. Now do you need some water?"

"No, baby. My hydration level is adequate."

She furrows her brow. "Only adequate?"

"Stop worrying about me."

She snorts. "Sure. Tell me to stop eating too, that's about as likely."

"Speaking of eating, that reminds me. Let's not sit Axel next to Chelsea tonight."

"Why not?"

"He's got a weakness for mouthy blondes, and I need him

348

focused on the business. Until we find someone to take my place doing moves, he's too busy for a relationship."

"Is he too busy to get his soul crushed? Because that's more her speed."

"Just put her at the opposite end of the table. Next to your mother maybe."

"Trust me, that won't help. If she decides she likes him, Chelsea will have him eating out of her hand in ten minutes."

I sigh. "Wonderful. Our first time hosting Thanksgiving dinner together, and I'll have to spend it watching your best friend wrap mine around her pinky finger."

"Have you spoken to Kiyoko lately?"

"Last week."

"How's she doing? I'm bummed she couldn't come."

"She sounded good. She moved to a new place in Vancouver, some high-rise apartment building with a view of the water. She's glad I've got you to look after me."

"Me and all your medical personnel. You know, I think that big guy who comes on Thursdays with the anchor tattoo on his forearm has a thing for you."

"I never should've told you about that male nurse in the hospital. Besides, anchor tattoos don't do it for me. It would have to be a dragon or something cool like that for me to be interested."

We smile at each other. For the millionth time, I think how lucky I am to have her.

I still don't think I deserve her, but I'm selfish enough that I no longer let it get in the way.

She looks down at the collar of my shirt and starts to fiddle with it. "So...is it strange having me here all the time?"

I put a knuckle under her chin and tilt her head up so I can look into her eyes. "No. I love having you living with me."

"You know I kept my apartment in case you want to kick me out."

"Say something like that again, and I'll run over your foot with this chair."

Her head still lowered, she peeks up at me. "You could tell me, you know. I promise I'll only cry for a minute."

"Am I going to have to spank you?"

"I'm serious, Cole. I love being with you, but I know this is a big change for—"

"I have an idea," I interrupt loudly. "Why don't you put your hand in my pocket?"

She crinkles her nose, and I sigh.

"Not for that. God, your mind is dirtier than mine."

"Why else would I want to put my hand in your pocket?"

"Could you do me a favor and do what I ask you one time without questioning it?"

Her smile is brilliant. "What fun would that be?"

When I glower at her, she relents.

"Fine. This is me sticking my hand in your pocket."

"Not that one. The other one."

She gives me a sour look, then leans to my other side and pats around my hip until she finds the pocket of my sweatpants. Then she shoves her hand inside.

I can tell when she finds the ring by the way her eyes widen.

"You said you were a size six. I didn't forget."

Her hand shaking, she withdraws the platinum-and-diamond ring and stares at it. Her eyes fill with tears.

"I love you, Shay. I fell in love with you the first day we met when you sat down at my table and smiled at me. And I'll love you until I take my last breath. Nobody else has ever been as good to me or for me as you've been, and I want to spend the rest of my life trying to be that good for you. So please do me the honor of marrying me, because without you, I'm nothing."

Her face crumples. Tears slide down her cheeks. She throws her arms around my shoulders and starts sobbing.

Holding her, I start to laugh. "I take it that's a yes?"

"It's a yes, you impossible man! It's a yes!"

"You didn't even really look at the ring."

She wails, "I don't care about the ring!"

"You should probably look at it, though. Owls aren't known for their great taste in jewelry."

She buries her face in my chest and sobs. "When I stop crying, I'm going to kill you."

I kiss her on the top of her head and blink away the water from my eyes. Grinning, I whisper, "I know, baby. I know."

Acknowledgments

I read an article in TIME magazine in 2017 that stuck with me. It was about the companies in Japan that help people vanish, and the people called *jouhatsu* who disappeared without a trace, and I found the whole premise fascinating. So thank you, TIME, for that inspiration.

If you haven't yet met Killian Black and his twin brother Liam, I encourage you to start with the Dangerous Beauty series where Killian first appears. He and Liam are then featured in the Beautifully Cruel series, and also in the Queens and Monsters series. His group of morally gray cohorts, the Thirteen, will be featured in some future series, but Killian will continue to pop up before then, because he insists.

Thank you as always to my editor, Linda Ingmanson, for your invaluable expertise.

Thank you to my agent, Jenny Bent, for being awesome.

Big thanks to my reader group, Geissinger's Gang, for always being there and supporting me.

Mitchell Wick, thank you for what you do, and thank you, Michelle Lancaster, for photographing him doing it.

Thank you to Lori Jackson for your wonderful cover designs and quick turnaround times.

To Nina, Kim, Sarah, and the entire team at Valentine PR, thank you so much for all your support!

Thank you, Jay, for so many years of laughter.

About the Author

J.T. Geissinger is a #1 international and Amazon Charts bestselling author of thirty-two novels. Ranging from funny, feisty romcoms to intense erotic thrillers, her books have sold over fifteen million copies worldwide and been translated into more than twenty languages.

She is a three-time finalist in both contemporary and paranormal romance for the RITA® Award, the highest distinction in romance fiction from the Romance Writers of America®. She is also a recipient of the Prism Award for Best First Book, the Golden Quill Award for Best Paranormal/Urban Fantasy, and the HOLT Medallion for Best Erotic Romance.

Connect with her online in her Facebook reader group, Geissinger's Gang, or sign up for her VIP newsletter at www.jt-geissinger.com.

Also by J.T. Geissinger

Morally Gray Series

Liars Like Us

Fall Into You

Queens & Monsters Series

Ruthless Creatures

Carnal Urges

Savage Hearts

Brutal Vows

Beautifully Cruel Series

Beautifully Cruel

Cruel Paradise

Dangerous Beauty Series

Dangerous Beauty

Dangerous Desires

Dangerous Games

Slow Burn Series

Burn for You

Melt for You

Ache for You

Wicked Games Series

Wicked Beautiful

Wicked Sexy

Wicked Intentions

Bad Habit Series

Sweet As Sin

Make Me Sin

Sin With Me

Hot As Sin

STANDALONE NOVELS

PenPal

Perfect Strangers

Midnight Valentine

Rules of Engagement

.

ί

Printed in Great Britain
by Amazon

41228602R00209